The HIDDEN HARVEST
BOOK ONE

# BREAD UPON the WATERS

A Novel
by
Anne de Graaf

Published by Bethany House Publishers
A Ministry of Bethany Fellowship, Inc.
11300 Hampshire Avenue South
Minneapolis, Minnesota 55438

Printed in the United States of America.

**Library of Congress Cataloging-in-Publication Data**

De Graaf, Anne.
Bread upon the waters / Anne de Graaf.
p. cm. — (The hidden harvest ; bk. 1)

1. World War, 1939–1945—Poland—Fiction. 2. Man-woman relationships—Poland—Fiction. I. Title. II. Series: De Graaf, Anne. Hidden harvest ; bk.1.
PS3554.E11155B73 1995
813'.54—dc20 95–484
ISBN 1–55661–618–X CIP

To Erik

ANNE DE GRAAF is the author of eighteen children's books, translated into more than 25 languages. This is her first novel. She has also worked as a journalist and economics translator for the Dutch government. She lives in The Netherlands with her husband and their two children.

# Acknowledgments

I owe a special debt of gratitude to Elżbieta Gajowska, who translated countless books and documents, accompanied me on fact-finding missions in Poland, interpreted while I struggled with the language, and helped check the text for historical accuracy. More than anything else, though, I am thankful for her friendship and those of the special circle of friends in which she has included me.

I was truly honored to meet several people in Poland whose personal stories provided the basis for this novel. They know who they are, and I will always be extremely grateful for their trust.

I have many dear friends in the United States, The Netherlands, England, Poland, Denmark, Hungary, and Kenya who have encouraged me through the years to finish this project. They have my deepest gratitude.

I am indebted to Anne Christian Buchanan, the editor I have been waiting years for.

I also want to thank my parents, my first and most enthusiastic fans.

Erik was with me every step of the journey. Julia and Daniël made me smile and let me work.

In many ways this book belongs to all of you.

NORWAY
SWEDEN
FINLAND
Oslo
Helsinki
Stockholm
(EST.)
(LAT.)
(LITH.)
(RUS.)
Baltic Sea
DEN.
Copenhagen
Gdańsk
(Danzig)
POLAND
(BYELORUSSIA
Bug R.
Berlin
Warszawa
Brest (Brześć)
G.D.R.
(EAST
GERMANY)
Łódź
(Littmannstadt)
Wisła R.
Dresden
Wrocław
(Breslau)
Bonn
Jelenia Góra (Hirschberg)
Praga
Kraków
B.R.D.
(WEST
GERMANY)
CZECHOSLOVAKIA
(U K R
Vienna
(MOLD)
Budapest
AUSTRIA
HUNGARY
ROMANIA
YUGOSLAVIA
Belgrade
Bucharest
Adriatic Sea
ITALY
BULGARIA
Sofia
Rome
GREECE

EUROPE AT THE END OF WORLD WAR II
Moscow
(RUSSIA)
S. S. R.
U.
(KAZAKHSTAN)
Stalingrad
Artemovsk
INE)
Caspian Sea
Black Sea
(GEORGIA)
(AZER-BAIJAN)
(ARMENIA)
Ankara
TURKEY

# Preface

## Of Fact, Fiction, and Truth

Although this is a work of fiction, it tells a true story. It is based on personal interviews with real individuals, including a family whose dramatic experiences touched me deeply, inspiring me to write this series of books in the first place. At their request, the real events have been fictionally woven together with stories of other people, some more real than others, and the places and names have been altered. And yet the important events in this book really did happen—even a few I hesitate to write as fiction because they are so incredible. What is miraculous and deeply mysterious in reality can seem merely implausible as fiction.

This series also tells the moving true saga of the Polish people, whose endurance and faith have won my heart. As far as research can make it so, historical accuracy has been maintained—no easy task when British, American, Soviet, and Polish versions all tended to conflict. Since 1989, when I began this project, more materials have become available for public scrutiny in Poland, and again the "facts" have changed.

Most important, people have become less afraid to talk about the past, sometimes for the first time since the war ended. Theirs is the version I have chosen to portray. After all, it is their true story.

Hoek van Holland, June 1995

Cast your bread upon the waters,
for after many days
you will find it again.

—Ecclesiastes 11:1

# 1

## MID-JANUARY 1945

She tried to stop herself from crying.

Hanna stared at her husband, willing away the tears that blurred the sight of him. She memorized the curve of his jaw, his shoulders, the soft hair at the back of his neck, his eyes, blue and clear, staring back at her now. "Tadeusz," she whispered.

His arms closed around her. Hanna wondered when she would feel him so close to her again. A train pulled into the station. The crowd pushed against the couple. Hanna's mother, Helena, stood by.

For one crystallized moment the rest of the world did not matter. The war, which was grinding to a bloody end, the panic that polluted the air around them with fear, the shouts of women and children and soldiers and conductors—none of it was there. Hanna drank in the sight of her husband's eyes on her.

Tadeusz gazed down at his twenty-year-old bride. She had pulled back her black hair and pinned it into a knot at the base of her neck. But the cold wind had pulled wisps of it loose, so that now her dark eyes and lashes were framed by even darker curls. When Tadeusz hugged her, he could feel her smallness. She wore a brown wool suit, not new but sturdy and warm. Tadeusz was thankful she hadn't suffered much because of the war. Just as he was thankful for her German passport.

He kissed her. "We will see each other again."

She kissed him back, wishing they knew it was true.

Helena tugged at her sleeve, and the spell was broken. "Now, Hanna, we must go. Look, our train is already filling up."

"Yes, go, you must." Tadeusz gathered both women into his arms. "It's a long way from here to there," he said with a determined smile.

Just that morning they had prayed together, hand tightly in hand. But they did not pray now. Instead, Tadeusz put his hand on Hanna's stomach, still flat despite the baby growing inside her. "You take good care of her for me."

Hanna had to smile. "How can you be so sure it's a girl?"

Tadeusz laughed. "Oh, I know my girls." Then he looked up suddenly and the smile faded.

He saw what she now heard, a woman screaming. The sound ripped through the hall. Hanna gripped Tadeusz's arm out of instinct.

Across the next set of tracks they saw a space clear in the crowd. Two SS officers threw a man onto the ground as one of them stepped back and kicked him. Again and again the boot thudded against the man's back. He lay rolled into a ball, his arms protecting his head. Hanna could not tear her eyes away from the boot moving back and forth, back and forth.

A young woman was being held back by others in the crowd. She screamed again, "Paul!" She struggled against the arms holding her, then broke free. Throwing herself at the boot, she clung to it as if it had a life of its own, trying to stop its movement.

The Nazi soldier roared when the woman tackled his leg. In an instant his comrade drew a pistol and shot, three times. The woman's hands slipped from the boot as she crumpled into a pool of her own blood. The soldier she had clung to stepped back, breathing hard.

The man named Paul moaned. The second soldier rolled him over and nodded. The officer who had kicked him drew his own gun with a businesslike motion and shot Paul in the head.

Then both soldiers looked up at the watching crowd. An engine hissed steam. For one second people on both sides of the tracks met the eyes of the two officers. Dull sunlight fell through the windows.

In a moment the crowd resumed its shuffle from one set of tracks to another. One by one those who had watched turned away and pushed through the crowd. Slowly the whispers turned into murmuring.

Hanna had seen it happen before, on the streets, outside restaurants. Brutal beatings had become too common at this strange place in time. She could tell by the faces around her that she was not the only one who had grown strangely accustomed to the brutality of the past six years. But it had gone on and would go on, at least until the war ended.

Soon the two corpses were hidden by the crowd. Hanna had almost forgotten them when Tadeusz squeezed her hand one last time. He touched her chin, lifting her face to his. "I can't wait," he whispered. Then he kissed her and left. Gone in the crowd, so fast.

Hanna caught her breath. She didn't want it to end like this, not so quickly. She watched him rush away, his head bent down, his collar turned up around his neck. Then, out of instinct, she looked behind her and saw that someone else was following Tadeusz's progress through the crowd. She had never seen the man before. When he realized Hanna was looking at him, the man turned.

But the stranger was not the reason Tadeusz had left so suddenly. Now Hanna caught sight of the SS officers pouring into the station hall, sweeping through the crowd in their long black coats.

Hanna whispered to her mother, "We were lucky, look. He was right to leave now."

The officers were conducting a random check of people's papers. If Tadeusz had been caught at the train station, he might have been killed like the couple whose deaths they had just witnessed. For unlike Hanna and her parents, Tadeusz was not a German citizen. His was the crime of being a Pole living in Poland.

Technically, Tadeusz was a Polish prisoner of war. The fact that he had worked as an engineer in her father's firm since two years after the war began did not change his prisoner's status. Neither did his marrying into a German family three months ago. In fact, the marriage could have gotten them both shot, because Poles and Jews were strictly forbidden to marry Germans. They had managed to marry in secret, despite the war and despite their different backgrounds. Even after he had become part of the family, however, officially Tadeusz had remained under Johann's custody.

Just two days earlier, the Nazis had ordered all men to remain in the city and at their jobs, even though Russian troops were predicted to enter Kraków any day. The penalty for anyone who disobeyed was death. And if a Pole like Tadeusz were to be caught in a place like the train station, the Germans would have assumed he was trying to escape.

Hanna shuddered. Even her father would not have dared to leave Kraków, even if he had been well enough to do so. Too weak to go to the station, he had hugged his wife and daughter goodbye at home.

But women had not been included in the Nazi order. And one look around the train station was enough to see how any woman, Polish or German, felt about staying long enough to let a Russian soldier lay his hands on her. Most of the throng was female, mothers and wives and daughters fleeing westward. They all carried something, bundles or children of different ages. Many wore layers of dresses, one on top of another.

Helena tugged on her daughter's sleeve again. "Hanna," she said in German, "we must go."

Helena and Johann had only started speaking German with Hanna since the war. They were both natives of Śląsk (Silesia), an area that, through the years, had been alternately German and Polish. They were legally German because of the way the map had been drawn when they were born, but they thought of themselves as Polish. They spoke Polish fluently and had raised their daughter to do the same. Johann even had a sister whose nationality was Polish, having been born in a year when their home region was part of Poland.

Helena and Johann had grown up as German-Poles, in families that had once sworn allegiance to Polish kings and rejoiced when Poland finally became independent after the First World War. At that time, Johann had come to Kraków with his bride to study and later had set up his structural engineering business. When their daughter was born, she too grew up German by birth, Polish by allegiance. When war broke out, there never had been any question that the family's allegiance would lie with Poland. Johann could never have guessed, though, that his being born in a place and time which happened to leave him with German nationality would attract to his young engineering firm the heavy industry projects needed by the German war machine. And that circumstance had given the family their own way of fighting back. Their German citizenship had provided them with a protective cover, enabling them to help their Polish neighbors more effectively. Now they were counting on it to get Helena and Hanna out of the threatened city.

It was a plan Johann had devised several months earlier. Helena and Hanna had stayed in Kraków as long as they dared. Now they would travel to Dresden, ahead of the front. Their German papers would enable them to travel freely as long as they did not enter any Russian-held territory.

"Yes, you're right." Hanna shook herself. She thought of the six-week-old baby she carried. And she thought of her mother. Safety was what mattered. And only in Germany would they be safe from the advancing Russians.

The two women joined the crush of people headed toward the train. Before they could even reach its side, more Nazi soldiers shoved past them. The men spoke to the conductor, motioning with their hands.

Hanna heard a cry go up from the women in front of her and strained to see what was happening.

"What is it?" she called out.

A woman turned around and said, "The doors are locked. They say the places are already reserved for German wounded coming in from the front."

Hanna joined the other women shouting, "We must leave tonight, do you hear?" One of the soldiers turned to look down at the crowd. He undoubtedly knew better than they how close the Russians were. As his eyes raked over their faces, the women fell silent. Many looked down at the ground. No one wanted to be singled out. Those on the edge of the crowd moved away.

Hanna took her mother's arm and turned around. "I don't know what we're going to do," she told her. "We have to get out of here."

Helena called out to a conductor, "Excuse me! *Bitte!* The next train to Dresden? When can my daughter and I . . ."

As she listened to her mother, Hanna felt a hand on her shoulder, a man's hand. She turned and gasped. The face so near to her own was that of the man who had watched her say goodbye to Tadeusz. She had forgotten about him when she saw the SS officers arrive.

"Tell your mother you should not go to Dresden," he said. "Not for a few weeks at least."

Hanna stepped away from the hand and looked at him more closely. He was dark—black eyes, olive skin, straight blue-black hair. His breath smelled stale. Hanna shivered. "Dresden?" she mumbled, realizing he was one of the few men in the crowd not in some sort of uniform.

His eyes held no warmth as he continued, "That's right. Even if you could find a train with room to take you." Then he nodded and walked away.

Hanna watched him turn up his collar just as Tadeusz had a few moments earlier. He walked with a slight limp, favoring his left leg. Hanna turned to her mother. "Did you hear that?" she asked, trying to place the man's accent. His German had been good—perfect *hochdeutsch*—but he had not spoken with a Berlin accent. Nor had he spoken with any accent she had ever heard before.

"I heard," her mother said. "But pay him no mind. At this point we'll just have to catch whichever train we can."

Hanna nodded, lost in thought. She searched for the man in the crowd, but he had disappeared.

---

They never found places on the train to Dresden. Later that night they managed to climb into a freight car on a train heading for Breslau. At least it was across the border, they told themselves. From there, they could move even deeper into Germany as Johann had planned for them.

The heavy metal door rolled shut on the group of women. Hanna and Helena found a spot on the rough wooden floor and soon settled down like the other passengers, hugging their possessions and trying to rest. Fading light fell on them from air vents in the roof. With a screech of train on tracks, they moved away from Kraków Central Station.

In the windowless twilight, Hanna imagined the yellow-brick homes they must be passing on both sides of the track, the tall towers and the walls of the Wawel Castle rising out of the mist, indifferent to the forces assailing the city. Proud Kraków, her father always called his adopted city, seat of Polish kings, home to a hundred churches.

During the long period when Poland had been nothing but carved-up pieces belonging to Russia, Prussia, and Austria, Kraków had been the city the people of Poland had cherished. Even after the court had been transferred to Warszawa at the end of the sixteenth century, Poles had come here to gaze at the stone buildings and listen to the church bells and to feel Polish. Then as now, whenever Poland was not free, the eagle of Poland's national emblem had flown without its crown. Yet Kraków's churches and university and culture had long endured and provided the country with a city the Poles could call their own.

"And it's mine, too," she whispered, squinting at the dark figures around her but still seeing the city outside the rumbling car. Hanna's parents' German papers had decided who she was in only one superficial way. At certain periods in history, families must choose. Johann and Helena had taught their daughter to love Poland, and to love Kraków. And the war had only served to intensify that love.

Watching what the Germans had done during this war, knowing what her father and others had suffered for their opposition to them, learning to love Tadeusz—all this had granted Hanna a unique perspective on Poland, her homeland, but not her country. She could not have felt less German than she did at that moment.

Hanna thought back to the days when all the hurt and blackness and fear had first started. More than five years ago she had heard the whine of air raid sirens for the first time over Kraków. Unlike Warszawa, the city had surrendered without a fight, so its buildings had been spared. Then the Nazis had proclaimed Kraków the seat of its so-called General-Gouvernement, now under the direction of Hitler's one-time lawyer, a man named Hans Frank. But Kraków citizens like Johann and Helena and Hanna found no pride in this arrangement. The Poles knew only too well that making Kraków the capital was the Nazis' way of saying that Poland was nothing but a region of Germany . . . where Poles happened to reside.

Hanna had led an extremely protected life during the war. As Germans in what Germany called its reclaimed area, and as owners of an engineering firm the Nazis used, her family had been granted privileged status. But they had heard the stories, believed the rumors, and viewed what was going on around them as wrong—very, very wrong. They had done what they could to help their fellow Poles, and her father had paid the price. Hanna winced to remember him as she had left him, face haggard, shoulders sagging, barely able to walk. *Will we ever see him again?* she wondered.

Now it would only be a matter of weeks before the Soviet forces drove the Germans out of Poland. And Hanna knew the arrival of the Russian troops would merely be trading one enemy for another. It had been happening all over Poland, the tales flying in from already occupied areas. As the one army retreated, the other advanced, both making sure they destroyed as much of her homeland as they could.

By eavesdropping on her father and his friends, she had heard of what was happening to Warszawa even as the Russians were supposedly liberating it. As far as she knew, the Germans were still dismantling the city while the Russians did nothing but look on from the other side of the Wisła (Vistula) River. Hitler had given the order that not even one building should be left standing in the city. So his troops were bombing and torching one neighborhood after another. And instead of moving in and driving the Germans out of Warszawa, the Russians were waiting until there was hardly anything left to liberate. Hanna had heard her father say the words they all dreaded believing, "A weaker Polish capital serves the Russian purposes just fine."

Hanna shuddered. She prayed her city would not suffer as Warszawa had. But there were rumors that the Nazis had already laid explosives under all the major buildings in Kraków and would level the city as they left, even the Wawel. She had heard that elsewhere in Poland, thousands of civilians were being killed, then written off by the Soviets as war casualties.

The train ran on into the unseen darkness. The endless rhythm of the train, the swaying of the people around her, and the image of the unlit forests they must be passing through haunted Hanna. "Where am I? What has happened that the world has become so strange, that the strangeness is so normal?"

Now Hanna made the deliberate decision to allow herself to think about Tadeusz. She hugged herself, chilled despite the warmth of the bodies around her. She could no longer keep from wondering what would happen to her husband and her father once the Soviets took Kraków. Her thoughts raced faster. For the first time now she had nothing but the darkness to distract her from the thoughts she had kept at bay during these last, final hectic days.

She wondered if Tadeusz might find a way to save himself and her father from being arrested. Hanna was not sure, had never directly asked, but she thought Tadeusz knew someone in the Resistance. Just the week before, he had disappeared for an entire day without any explanation. She had been frantic, terrified he was being held and tortured. But then he had come home and told her he could not explain his absence. She knew enough not to ask more than once. After he shook his head she had buried the information.

But now she kept on wondering if his disappearance meant he was arranging for the Underground's protection.

Hanna frowned. No, what was she thinking? She had nothing to go on. And why should Tadeusz and her father be kept safe when so many others would suffer? It was impossible, they were trapped.

"We're Germans," she mumbled to herself. "They'll say we are the enemy, and we are."

# 2

## MID-JANUARY 1945

Now that the Germans were finally leaving, Jacek Duch knew that he too must flee Kraków. To be captured by the Russians and held for questioning or worse would prevent him from fulfilling his mission. The early days of the new government would be crucial. Those who were in the right place at the right time would be the ones running the country in a few months' time. And the right place to be was Warszawa.

Jacek had been up all night. He had the information his friends needed, and there was no more Polish Home Army for him to piece together. It was time to get a few hours sleep before he met his contact, then left the city.

Jacek ran his hand through his hair and turned left down an alley. The barks and growls of two dogs fighting startled him. He did not often allow his thoughts to wander while in the open. Out of habit, he checked to see who was walking behind him. When he saw no one, Jacek slowly walked up the steps to the cheap hotel. He looked down on the street one more time as he closed the door behind him. Again no one.

"Wake me up in five hours," he told the old man who gave him his key. Jacek checked to see if the keys of the rooms next to his still hung on their hooks. Good. He could sleep without some drunken fool waking him up. And he wouldn't have to worry about someone watching him through that gap in the plaster.

He climbed the stairs carefully, his left leg much improved, but still stiff. Jacek checked the strand of black hair, his own, still wedged between the door and the wall. Once inside, he locked the door behind him and fell on his bed, utterly exhausted.

Several hours later, the sound of loud clapping woke him. Jacek sat up. He squinted into the winter sunshine streaming through the broken blinds. He glanced at his watch. He had another half hour before the old man would call him.

Jacek stretched, then heard the clapping sound again. He crossed the room to the window and pulled two slats apart with his thumb and forefinger. Below was a small courtyard, shared by the back sides of the four houses bordering it. Two women stood there now, beating carpets they had thrown over wooden stands.

As Jacek watched, they finished one carpet, took it down, rolled it up, bound it with rope, then flung another over the rack. "They're taking the rugs with them." He stroked his chin, allowing the beating sound to mesmerize him.

The women struck the carpets with flat, round-ended woven clubs. The rhythm reminded Jacek of his own mother who, even in America, had pounded her carpets on Tuesdays and Thursdays. The habit was a holdover from the days when Jacek was a baby and they had still lived in Gdańsk.

"My hometown," Jacek murmured, then grimaced. This was one of the first times he had lowered his guard enough to think back on his childhood. He could not often afford to do so. For several years now, he had disciplined himself to talk only in Polish, to think Polish thoughts and to remember Polish memories, even if they were only part of his cover.

Jacek's real memories did not include his time in Gdańsk. He had been only three when his parents left Poland a few years before the First World War.

Somehow they had managed to emigrate to New York. The first home Jacek could remember was the tenant housing of a dirty neighborhood where everyone spoke Polish anyway. He remembered the bedbugs nibbling at his legs while he slept. His mother had worked nights at a factory, sewing soles onto shoes. During the day, she had cleaned the house of a wealthy family on the other side of the city.

His father drank vodka.

Jacek could still see his mother standing on the balcony of their apartment, a rug draped over the banister. A cloud of dust rose around her as she beat it as hard as she could.

That was what she had been doing the day she argued with Jacek's father. Jacek did not even know what they had been fighting about. He remembered his mother's voice saying, "But this is our home now. America has been good to us." Maybe Jacek's father had lost his job again. Anyway, he stumbled toward Jacek's mother, tripped as he reached the balcony, and fell on her.

Jacek could still see the two of them entangled in some ghostly waltz. He had looked up from his blocks to watch them struggle in slow motion. She was trying to shift her balance to get out from under his weight. He was grabbing for something to break his fall.

Instead he pushed her. And suddenly everything happened very fast. "Mama! Mama!" Jacek heard his own voice call after the woman who no longer stood beating carpets on the balcony. Then the living room had filled with people, neighbors, men in blue suits speaking English. And Jacek had ended up going to the first of a long series of orphanages and homes.

He shook himself. The beating sound had ceased. The women were dragging the carpets and tapestries back inside their homes.

Someone knocked at the door. "I'm awake!" Jacek snapped. He heard the old man shuffle back down the hall.

Jacek quickly splashed water onto his face from the bowl by his bed. Three fleas floated on the surface. He changed and packed the clothes he had washed and draped around the room the previous day. Then he straightened up and checked his appearance. His hair slicked back, his face clean shaven, trim body encased in a silk suit, he would certainly stand out. The dark wool of his overcoat matched the color of his hair.

Jacek lifted his right foot and felt the weight under his heel. He had hidden the notebook in a hollow space of his shoe. In all the times he had been searched, no one had ever managed to find the switch that caused the heel to swivel open. He looked around the room one more time. Satisfied that he had everything, he left his room and the building.

As he wove his way down the streets toward the train station, Jacek privately said farewell to Kraków, hoping the Russians might be kinder to the city than they had been to him. Jacek did not expect to be back again for quite some time.

Jacek ran across the busy road opposite the train station and passed through the front entrance. Once inside he scanned the crowds, impatient to find his contact and be rid of the notebook.

A crowd had gathered at the other side of the tracks. They all seemed to be staring at something on the ground.

He caught sight of a group of SS officers and scuffed his right foot nervously, shifting his weight, checking, looking, watching, not sure. He sensed that something had just gone wrong. When the crowd at the other end of the hall started to disperse, Jacek decided to get a closer look. His eyes flitted back and forth across the faces passing him, then came to rest on a couple embracing.

The man was tall and blond. It took Jacek a moment to recognize the man who had saved his life a week before. "Ah, Tadeusz, old friend," he muttered under his breath. He did not move toward the couple, but leaned up against a kiosk and pulled a half-empty pack of cigarettes out of his breast pocket. Hidden behind a swirl of smoke, Jacek watched the blond man kiss the young woman.

She had to stand on her tiptoes to reach the man's lips.

"She looks young," Jacek mumbled. "He hasn't done badly at all."

Just then the man looked up past Jacek, touched the girl's chin, and walked away.

Jacek checked behind him to see what could have caused Tadeusz to leave like that. He smiled wryly when he saw the SS guards coming through the double doors. Then he turned back to watch Tadeusz's bent head move away through the crowd.

Suddenly Jacek found himself staring into the blackest eyes he had ever seen. So the girl had caught him watching them. He quickly turned and stepped behind the kiosk thinking that at least now he knew who to hurt if Tadeusz ever became a threat. When he had counted to ten and checked again, the girl was gone.

Jacek spent the next few moments scanning faces. People had started shouting along the adjacent track. Jacek came out from behind the pillar and watched as hundreds of women began yelling at a conductor standing next to a Nazi officer.

Then he saw the girl again, standing with an older woman who was calling out something. Jacek moved closer. She wanted to go to Dresden. He frowned, checked the date on the newspaper in his hands, and resolved to do Tadeusz a favor, to make them even. Jacek Duch did not like to stay in any man's debt. Besides, he had half regretted not getting to touch the girl before she disappeared the first time. Now that he had a second chance, Jacek moved toward her, reached out and felt the good wool of her jacket.

"Tell your mother you should not go to Dresden. Not for a few weeks at least."

She swirled. Her eyes flashed at him, surprised, as she stepped away. "Dresden?"

He said, "That's right. Even if you could find a train with room to take you." Jacek could not afford to say any more, so he turned and left the girl.

He moved through the crowd, trying to forget her eyes, aware of a growing annoyance. Where was his contact? The drop was supposed to have taken place by the main entrance the minute he had walked in the door.

He thought over the events of the previous night and day. He had just barely escaped from the *Wehrmacht Waffenanstalten* without being caught. Now that he knew better just how little the Germans still had at these two munitions dumps on the streets they liked to call Warschauer Straße and Montelupistraße, he needed to get rid of the information as quickly as possible. Should he try and deliver the notebook himself to the Russian troop command and then head back to Warszawa? He didn't like the idea of contacting the Russians before he was ready to.

Jacek looked at his watch, then glanced behind him. He noticed a man with a moustache sitting on a bench near the door. Hadn't he seen him earlier?

A few minutes later he let his newspaper fall so he could glance behind him, and then he saw the man look quickly away. Had he been targeted? To make sure, Jacek headed for the main entrance. When the man did indeed follow, he knew for certain that it was time to leave. Once outside, Jacek zigzagged his way through the streets, ending up at the busy St. Florian Gate at the old city walls.

This was on the street the Germans had renamed the Wehrmachtstraße, but what everyone else in the city stubbornly continued to call Ulica Basztowa. The biggest joke when the Nazis had occupied Kraków and insisted on renaming all the Polish streets had been when they attempted to transform Rynek Główny, or the main market square, into Adolf-Hitler-Platz.

Jacek glanced backward and saw his man just turning the corner. Although Jacek headed east, he knew enough to stay well away from the new tracks the Germans had laid along the eastern edge of the city. Those were the secret tracks, used since their construction almost two years earlier to bring in extra troops and munitions as well as ship out the rest of the Jews and any other undesirables they found in Kraków. Jacek knew from personal experience just how well guarded that section of the city was. He circled back, reentering the main station hall from the side entrance, then leaned up against the wall and waited. When the man with the moustache came in after him, Jacek was ready. He stepped backward and hid behind a pile of bags. The man looked right, and left, then walked hesitatingly forward.

Jacek now knew he was dealing with an amateur, often

the most dangerous type. He deliberately passed in front of the man as he walked very fast toward one of the trains. Steam enveloped the engine as the pistons started to pound. He hoped he was moving obviously enough for the man to follow. If he did, Jacek could get rid of him once and for all.

Jacek swung onto a car and walked quickly down its length, stepping over the people in the aisles. He entered a compartment that already had six people sitting in it and crossed to the window. Looking back, he saw his man climb onto the train just as it started moving.

He left the compartment before anyone could ask him what he wanted, then moved from one car to the next, working his way down the train. He could feel the sweat gathering on his forehead. The hollow heel under his right foot seemed to make a louder clicking noise than its mate.

The train jerked and Jacek stumbled, nearly dropping his bag. He moved to the door, waited until the train had gathered more speed, then threw his bag out and leaped off the car just behind the engine. He managed to land well and roll only once in the snow. His leg was holding up well. Thanks to the clean wound, it had healed better than he could have hoped for.

As he picked up his bag, Jacek turned to look up at the windows full of faces rolling past him. He did not see the moustache. Even if the man had seen him, Jacek would be long gone by the time he managed to get back to Kraków.

Jacek waited until the train was out of sight to make sure no one repeated his stunt. Then he slapped the snow off his legs and thighs and walked back toward the platform.

One more look around the crowded station, and Jacek knew his contact was just not showing up. The time had come for a decision. Jacek left the station and headed back across the street, up to the center of the city and the market square. At number 35 he entered the Café Europejska, where he had first met the man who had not shown up at the station. He was counting on the chance that the café was some sort of contact point.

Jacek saw as soon as he entered that he and the waiter were the only ones in the café. He ordered in German and started waiting. As time went by he tried to read the paper, but he could not concentrate.

Dusk fell, then darkness, and Jacek was still waiting, his fourth cup of coffee grown cold at his elbow. Staring out the window, Jacek watched the moon rise over a church and thought about Barbara for the first time in many months. So very long ago, he and Barbara had promised to think of each other whenever they saw the moon. It had been their way of trying to feel close, no matter how much distance separated them.

"Barbara." Jacek whispered her name. "Even they didn't know about you until later—much later. . . ."

A long time ago, Jacek had realized the only way out of the orphanages was to study hard and do well at school. If he did that, he was told, he might be taken into a home. When this finally did happen, though, the ten-year-old's hopes were dashed within a week of the move. The people he moved in with did not want a son, just a form of cheap labor. Jacek was made to shovel coal and scrub floors until one of his teachers reported his absences from school. Then Jacek had gone into another home, and another.

All that time, a certain teacher had shown an interest in Jacek, even after he had left the district. This same teacher was finally able to convince what would become Jacek's last family that the boy should be allowed to study for a scholarship. And so Jacek managed to survive until his eighteenth birthday. Then he left his last set of foster parents, never to see them again, and went to college in Boston.

There he had trouble settling down. He took German and impressed his professors by his quick mastery of the language. But he didn't want to major in German. In fact, Jacek seemed unable to make up his mind what his major would be. Finally, he finished the requirements for a degree in art, then obtained a grant to pursue master's work in mathematics. And that was when he met Barbara.

She was not Jacek's first lover, but she was the first he had ever really cared for. A dark Cajun beauty who spoke in a coaxing Louisiana accent, Barbara worked as a waitress in one of the student restaurants. She was five years older than Jacek, and she gave him the mothering he had always missed.

She made sure Jacek ate well, passed his exams, and seriously worked toward his degree. She provided him with a stability he had never known. Her little room in the boardinghouse became his home as well; the landlady looked the other way whenever he sneaked down the stairs early in the morning to head back to his own student quarters.

Jacek was finishing up his thesis by the time the stock market crashed. He and Barbara were not rich enough to be affected, but they noticed many a son of wealthy parents dropping out of school. Since Jacek still had his grant, he just carried on. But it was during this period at school that he and Barbara finally decided to get married, among other reasons since it saved on the rent. They didn't tell anyone but the landlady, who stood as their witness.

Not much changed because of the marriage. He still

spent the nights making love to Barbara and the days playing with mathematical formulas. He never ceased to be fascinated by the ease of knowing right from wrong in the equations filling his mind. It had been a simple way to live, with none of the difficult choices the rest of the world seemed to be struggling with.

And then one day a man with a hint of a Brooklyn accent approached Jacek and asked if he could buy him a cup of coffee. The man seemed to know all about Jacek. He knew he had spoken Polish as a child, and that he spoke near-fluent German. He knew Jacek had an art degree and said, "You're working on a degree in math now, right?"

As far as Jacek was concerned, the man knew too much.

"I bet you'd like to go back to the country you were born in, wouldn't you?"

Jacek was surprised at this. He knew that there had often been times when he had wondered what Poland was like. But those were the sort of questions any son of immigrants asks.

"Secret yearnings?" Jacek asked. "Not me."

"I happen to know your parents told you many stories about Poland. And didn't the stories often end with, 'But this is our home now. America has been good to us'?" The man's eyes sparkled.

"What the. . . ?" Jacek had looked up quickly. He masked his shock as best he could at hearing the familiar words, then realized the man must have gained access to Jacek's orphanage file or the police file on the accident. Jacek dimly remembered telling someone a very long time ago what his mother had said during her last argument with his father.

He thought fast and figured if the man sitting opposite him had already done that much research, he would know he had just quoted Jacek's mother out of context. Jacek decided to play along until he could find out just what was going on.

He swallowed. "Yes, I have to admit, I have been curious. But Poland is on the other side of the world right now, and I'm having a hard enough time making ends meet here. Besides, school seems a pretty safe place to be these days."

"Well," the man said slowly, "I won't argue with you about that. But I'm not really here to talk about playing it safe. I'm here to talk about serving your country. And making money. You interested?"

Jacek shrugged his shoulders.

"Okay. Let's talk about the first one." Jacek would rather have talked about the second.

"There are things happening over in Europe that we want to know more about. We've been looking for people like yourself who come from these countries and can speak the languages. The President needs you to send us information about what's really happening there."

Jacek wondered if the President knew about these needs.

The man's voice droned on, "We need young men who can blend in with the locals. Then when war breaks out, we . . ."

"When?" Jacek interrupted him. "I thought the Great War was supposed to be the last."

The man scowled at Jacek. "Don't be naïve. Of course there's going to be another war. But before it happens, we want to find a few things out. You can help gather that info for us."

Jacek's eyebrows lifted. "Us?"

"Military intelligence. Your reports will go to the War Department."

Jacek had never heard of such a thing, but before he could comment, the man continued, "So we want you to pack and leave after graduation in June."

"But that's in four weeks. I just . . ." Jacek stopped. Something kept him from saying Barbara's name. After all, they had only been married a month.

"Of course you can be ready in four weeks. Now, look, we're offering you money, a lot of it, the opportunity to really make a difference when it comes to keeping America safe, plus adventure and free travel. We already know you got no ties, nobody to keep you here. Your mother is dead. Your father's a lifer. You don't have any close friends except for that Southern belle." The man's eyes narrowed.

Jacek looked him straight on and heard himself saying, "She means nothing."

"Exactly my point. Her type are a dime a dozen. So there's nothing keeping you from taking a little trip for orientation in June, then off to Poland for six months."

Jacek looked up. "Six months?" He was still thinking about Barbara.

"Sure, six months isn't much. When the time's up, we fly you home. Pretty simple. Short and sweet."

Jacek's thoughts raced. "Well, what if I were to say no? I mean, you seem so certain I would accept."

"We haven't talked money yet. Half a grand a month."

"Oh."

"Now don't get me wrong. This is no mercenary job. You'll be working for this country, which has done a lot for you. Now's your turn to return the favor. You're in an enviable position, young man."

"All right." Jacek needed to get away from the man's

moving mouth. "Let me think about it."

"I need to know by day after tomorrow. Here's the phone number of my hotel. Think it over, but not too much. This is the sort of thing you've got to decide in your gut."

"Right." Jacek shook his hand, relieved when the man finally left. Then he sat down again and whistled low and deep.

That night Jacek had told Barbara everything. "It's only for six months, honey. 'Chance of a lifetime,' the man said."

"The money is good," she purred. "Lord knows we could use it. I'm sick and tired of waitin' tables. This mean I could stop working?"

"Yeah. But wouldn't you miss me for six months?"

"As long as it's only six months. A half year. What? Miss you? Come here, I'll show you how much I'll miss you."

The next morning Jacek had called his recruiter at the hotel and asked if they could meet. In the coffee shop the man grinned when Jacek stood up to meet him and stretched out his hand. "Does this mean what I think it does?"

Jacek returned the plastic smile. "Yes, I'm your man. But don't get the wrong idea. I'm not doing this out of love of country. Since you know my history so well, you'll know the social services here haven't done so much for me. No, let me finish." As the man started to object, Jacek held up a hand.

"You know that. Granted, I wasn't left to rot on the streets like a lot of poor beggars are these days, but I survived in spite of your precious system, not because of it."

"Okay, you've made your point." The man's smile had dimmed considerably, but he seemed unwilling to rock any boat of his making. "Whatever the reason, welcome aboard. By the way, my compliments for not telling me the news over the phone. That's lesson number one. Now, you'll be hearing from us before June. We'll arrange the train trip down south."

The man continued, "You may or may not see me there. I'm mostly out recruiting. But don't worry. You're a natural. When I threw that curve ball and quoted your mother's words before she died, you didn't blink an eye. Well done, kid. You'll do just fine."

Jacek said nothing.

"No offense, kid."

---

And so it had begun. Even now, years later, Jacek could not define what had made him do it. The money, the intrigue, the sense of purpose, some primeval tug back to his homeland? Or had it been the man's scornful grin, daring him to say no?

A lot had happened since then. So much, in fact, that Jacek now had no doubt whatsoever about his motivation. He looked down at his feet and saw that he had unconsciously been tapping the hollow heel against the floor tiles of the café. He shook himself irritably.

Now that no one had shown up, Jacek felt gripped by uncertainty. He did not know how else he should unload the notebook and wondered if he wouldn't be better off throwing it away somewhere. One thing was certain. He had to get out of Kraków as fast as possible. Then the waiter approached him.

"Are you looking for Paul again?"

Jacek instinctively tensed his muscles. He had learned a long time ago not to trust go-betweens, but now, he was desperate enough to take a chance. He nodded, "I was supposed to meet him somewhere else and he didn't show up. Has he been in today?"

"Haven't seen him. Do you want to pay?"

Jacek relaxed. "Yes, then I'd better be on my way." He gave the waiter his money and stood, only too glad to leave the café. He did not like staying in any one place for too long. Especially now.

Jacek returned once again to the train station and took one more look around. Satisfied, he read the signs posted at the beginning of each track. A train heading north had just pulled in and was starting to take on coal. He walked slowly toward the engine, pushing his way through the women crowding around the train, and got on, slipping a large bill to the conductor, who looked the other way as his hand opened and closed around the money. Depending on how damaged the railway line was, he might even make it to Warszawa within the week.

Not for the first time Jacek realized he had a lot of time to make up for. If the postwar confusion and panic worked in his favor, he might just be able to pull his mission off, even if it was in a slightly revised version.

His bosses wanted a man in key leadership position for the crucial postwar period, especially now that it appeared the Bolsheviks would be running the show without the benefit of their wartime allies. Jacek was hoping he could hide his Polish Home Army involvement and stress his conversion to communism. The notebook could have played a key part in the process. Perhaps it would still serve as a means of wiggling his way into communist circles.

Jacek knew that all he had been working for would come to a head during the next few weeks. In a neighborhood of demolished Warszawa called Praga, the Russians would soon be setting up a provisional government. Everything he had survived was hanging in the balance. He did not mind meeting the Russians again, as long as it was on his terms, not theirs.

After so long, it would all happen very soon now. Jacek sighed. For the second time that day he thought of his recruiter. They had dueled a double-faced masquerade. Again the wry smile flitted across Jacek's face.

Jacek's employers may not have known that Jacek was married to Barbara. But Jacek knew. What he hadn't known when he accepted the government job and said goodbye to his wife was that Barbara was already pregnant.

Now the six months had become six years.

# 3

## Mid-January 1945

Hanna sat on the train heading out of Kraków, her despair at parting with Tadeusz tossing her aimlessly like a storm at sea. Her thoughts continued to fling themselves back and forth between hope and despair, until finally the rhythm of the tracks brought her out of the future and into the past. There she finally settled, remembering the safe haven of love discovered, love learned.

When does love enter a heart? At what point do all other emotions focus on the attraction, then grow into love? Is it, as fairy tales claim, during the first kiss? When is a heart changed by love, into love?

Hanna already knew there was no single second she could hold up as the one in which she had fallen in love with Tadeusz. Rather, a series of events rose from her memory. Theirs was a love made brilliant by the fires of doubt and fear around them, a love shaped by the crushing weight of war. It was alive and dazzlingly different, depending on how the light of memory hit its facets.

Yet in her thoughts, on that train plummeting into dark forests, away from war, through the war, into war, the gem Hanna scrutinized shone no less brightly than that of fairy-tale fame. Slowly, tenderly, she turned over memories already made precious by the loss of her husband at her side. "Every day I will think on these things," she determined.

"With God's help we will stay close. I swear we will."

---

Tadeusz had come to work for her father in the autumn of 1941, when Hanna was seventeen. While several of her girlfriends were going out with dashing young members of the Nazi officers' corps, Hanna had stayed at home. There was never really any question of her doing otherwise. She and her parents viewed the Nazis in Kraków as the occupying enemy.

Of course, this was not something they talked about openly. Tadeusz had not found out what the family's true sentiments were until more than a year after he arrived in Kraków—and long after he and Hanna had met for the first time.

One night, several weeks after he came to work for Johann, Tadeusz stood alone in the basement office, surrounded by a small forest of drafting tables and stools. Leaning against one of the tables, he pored over a chart. Tadeusz did not even notice when Hanna entered the room. She had come looking for a book her father had left there during the afternoon.

Now she saw a pool of light and a dark figure bent and scribbling with one hand while the other twirled a compass over the table. The lamp lit his bright hair from the side, leaving half his face in shadow.

Even then, something had tugged at her. Perhaps it was the way his shoulders hunched forward, or the wide stance of his legs as he leaned against the table. She remembered thinking, *Why doesn't he use a stool?*

Or perhaps it was simply the high cheekbones, still gaunt, the pinched face belying the strength she could see in his arms and shoulders. In any case, Hanna chose to watch him for a few moments before she finally knocked.

"*Proszę.*" He looked up and squinted at the darkness.

Hanna walked over to Tadeusz. She held out her hand, palm down, and answered in Polish. "We haven't met yet. I'm Hanna Müller. Please excuse me if I startled you."

Tadeusz stepped forward and brought her hand to his lips. "Tadeusz Piekarz." He did not meet her eyes.

Hanna thought he must be at least thirty. She said, "I've come here looking for a book my father left behind earlier today." She paused and added softly, "My father speaks highly of you, *Panie* Piekarz. He's glad you have joined us."

Tadeusz looked up suspiciously, as if wondering whether she might be taunting one of her father's prisoners, then quickly looked down again.

Hanna coughed. "Yes, well, I won't keep you from your work. Good evening, Panie Piekarz." When Hanna found the book weighing down the heap of papers on her father's desk, she turned and left the room.

And that was the beginning. A book on a pile of papers. A pool of light in a dark cellar room. A man catching himself listening to a girl's heels clicking long after she was out of sight. She feeling his lips on her hand. If these things make up the beginning of love, Hanna could not know. That they were the start of her change of heart, there was no doubt.

Hanna and Tadeusz began to discover not so much each other—for the one quickly grew aware of the other's presence as soon as the other entered a room—as themselves. They experienced feelings previously only pretended, heard themselves saying words misused in the past, but now so fitting. And in responding to each other differently than they ever had to anyone else, both Hanna and Tadeusz learned to see themselves truly, and this altered vision changed their perceptions of each other, and the world around them.

---

Hanna knew that Tadeusz watched her, especially when she was in the garden. She was often there when the weather was warm, working on the vegetable plot, or tending the few chickens they kept, or talking with her friends among the flowers. And she was aware that he would eavesdrop on their conversations. She could see his blond head poking out the window of the attic room where he slept with the other engineers. Once she met his eyes, and he quickly ducked back from the window.

And then one day she had sat alone in the garden next to the big lilac bush, reading. And she had to swallow twice when she saw Tadeusz walking toward her along the path. When he stopped in front of her, she did not know what to say, so she read the title of the book he carried. "History?" she asked.

He nodded. Then he leaned toward her and half closed her book, which lay open on the table, to get a better look at the cover. "Also history?"

Hanna could smell his musky scent, that and cigarettes. They looked at each other, both very close, then looked down at their similar books. She had wanted to seem grown up for him. He had wanted to prove he was too old for her. Now, as they realized the irony of what had brought them together, they both started laughing.

His deep laughter brought tears to her eyes as her laughter touched his heart, changing him forever. In laughter, then, their souls were first knit together.

On that day tall yellow rose bushes, tended so faithfully each day by Hanna's mother, mixed their scent with that of the lilacs. Surrounded then by the scent of summer, Hanna and Tadeusz talked about books. It was the first of many times that they would share their love of the past. Often they discovered from each other histories that were entirely different from what they had learned at school.

It was not that the German history books were full of lies or that Polish books were full of boasts. Rather, as in all history, the versions differed as a result of their omissions. Down through the years the shape of history owes more to those events not mentioned, not included, not recorded, than to those that are described on pages of books. Together Hanna and Tadeusz learned that somewhere in between it all lay the truth.

During these talks, as Hanna grew to know Tadeusz, she discovered an intensity of purpose about him. It was as if he had the ability of focusing all his attention on one thing. He spared nothing. If it happened to be her, she felt overwhelmingly flattered. If it was his work, not even she could interrupt his concentration.

Tadeusz and Hanna tried to talk of little else but the past, which at least was safe. In this way they shared many late afternoons, talking in the closed garden as if they had both been shut away there by some wicked witch called war.

And in those weeks trust had its own battle against doubt and suspicion in Tadeusz's heart. Not surprisingly, he hated Germans. Now he was struggling with feelings that flew in the face of all he thought he knew. Hanna hurt with him. It was no easy feat to set aside a lifetime of prejudice, then learn love.

Of course, both Helena and Johann had noticed the attention Tadeusz paid their daughter. Hanna had come to them about it, and they had warned her to be careful, which was less than they had done when a friend of hers had suggested she go out with a Nazi soldier two years earlier. Johann had, however, given Tadeusz increasingly difficult projects, and nodded with satisfaction when the young man lived up to his expectations. Johann had noticed from the outset that Tadeusz was brighter than the other engineers in the group. He liked him instinctively and was attracted by the same focused intensity Hanna had noticed from the start.

More and more often, Johann entrusted Tadeusz with documents that had to be delivered downtown. So far Tadeusz had not betrayed Johann's trust in him. The older man could see the way his daughter's eyes riveted onto Tadeusz's back every time she entered the drafting room. It was not likely that any man who had won such attention from a girl like Hanna would run away. Johann could sense what was beginning to take shape between his daughter and Tadeusz.

There came a day, however, when all this changed. It happened when Tadeusz received a letter from a childhood friend telling him that both his parents had been shot by the Nazis.

Hanna heard it from her father, who had heard it from another engineer named Marek. For days afterward Tadeusz did nothing but work long hours, then throw himself into bed and sleep a few hours. He was the first up and the last to go to bed. A deep fury had settled over his grief, overshadowing all he saw and felt. She felt it like a wall between them.

On a sunny afternoon on the fifth of September, 1942, Hanna went downstairs to where the men were working. Under her arm she held a basket and an envelope. She approached Tadeusz from behind and touched his elbow. He whirled on her as if she had struck him. She breathed a silent prayer, knowing it was exactly a week since he had heard about his parents, and took a deep breath.

"Father has some plans he wants you to bring away. I was heading toward the market to see if I can trade these eggs for meat. The new regulations prohibit the private sales of meat and dairy products, so the farmer we had an agreement with won't be coming to the house anymore. But I might find him or someone else at the market who will have something to trade for these eggs and—"

She was running on out of nervousness and she knew it. Tadeusz interrupted her. "Even though you know they've promised the death penalty to anyone hiding agricultural products."

At least she had his attention. Hanna took him by the elbow before he could turn away and said, "Come on. No one's going to shoot me for a few eggs." She caught her breath, hoping he wouldn't notice the reference to what had plunged him into his depression in the first place. "You need some fresh air. Father's ordered me to get you out of this basement. You haven't been outside for a week. And we need some meat," she rushed on. Without a word he took the envelope of papers from her and followed obediently.

Once outside, Hanna slipped her hand inside his. Again he said nothing. "This is good for me, too. I've been nothing but a *Hausfrau* lately. Father says we have to hurry before the ministry building closes, though."

She looked up at Tadeusz's face. It was not often that they had a chance to be alone together. Until a week ago they had been carefully growing closer, although they had not yet reached the point in the relationship that either could describe as serious. Tadeusz's doubt was proving too strong a barrier, and now the news about his parents seemed to have built that barrier into a wall.

A tram rattled past them, ringing its bell at a horse and cart that stood in the way. The man slouched in the cart just waved at the conductor. Both Tadeusz and Hanna noticed, but did not comment on, the large sign in the window of the first car: *"Nur für Deutsche."* For Germans only. The Nazis had stepped up segregation in the city to the point that certain hospitals, restaurants, trams, parks, and even benches in the city parks were now strictly forbidden to Poles.

Tadeusz and Hanna hurried down the twisted streets and reached what used to be the royal kitchen building in Wawel Castle, now remodeled as the offices for the General-Gouvernement.

Finally breaking his silence, Tadeusz told her, "I'll just be a moment."

"It's all right, the market is only a few streets away," Hanna said. "It might take some time, so I'll meet you there. I want to see what I can find."

"Well, wait for me before going home, all right?"

Hanna smiled to thank him for his concern, but Tadeusz was already running up the stairs two at a time. He stopped at the door as two men with SS patches on their left collars came out of the building. Then he waved at Hanna and disappeared inside.

She turned and headed toward the Kazimierz neighborhood just south of the Wawel. Before the war the eastern streets of the area had made up the Jewish quarter. Just a year earlier, however, the Nazis had taken all fifty-five thousand Jews and relocated them to the district of Podgórze. Then they had moved Polish residents from the western part of the city into the now-empty Kazimierz and nearby Stradom, appropriating for themselves the houses left behind. In addition to relocating the city's population, however, the Germans had also removed most of the men, and as in the rest of the country, deported them to Germany for forced labor.

The neighborhood Hanna entered as she walked down Ulica Krakowska had changed with its inhabitants. Instead of the almost Middle Eastern market atmosphere that had typified the area before the war, an extensive black market wove its way between the tiny back streets. There on any given day, anything from Hungarian cigarettes to silver candlesticks could be bartered for.

The black market was also the only area within the city in which the Resistance had nearly won back control from the Germans. Outside the city the Polish Home Army had almost entirely secured the nearby hills and forest, clearing it of German troops. It was rumored that it probably would take only one more attack on Nazi patrols inside the Kazimierz quarter for the German command to issue orders forbidding its soldiers from entering it altogether.

At that very moment, in fact, a group of German soldiers were marching toward the area, only a few streets behind Hanna. They had just turned down the street that the Germans had renamed the Essenweigasse, but the Polish residents, including Hanna, still called Ulica Józefa. They knew, as did most of the city, that farmers sometimes came here to sell their produce, and they had been sent to enforce the autumn orders Hanna and Tadeusz had spoken of.

Hanna walked down a back street that ducked under an archway. An alley cut behind a church, leading to a square. As she started to cross the cobblestones, she stopped and looked behind her, expecting to see Tadeusz.

Even as she wondered why he hadn't caught up with her yet, she realized something had changed. Only a few moments earlier the streets had been full of men wearing flat caps, women in scarves and long coats split in the back, people pulling carts. Now the crowds had disappeared.

Hanna listened, then heard the stamp of boots goose stepping. "A patrol," she gasped. Too late, she knew that sound and the empty market could only mean there would soon be a Resistance attack. The Resistance must have gotten word out to the people who lived in the neighborhood that they should get off the streets at this time. Now the Resistance was going to try to clear these streets from German patrols once and for all.

And then she heard the whining sound of planes coming closer. Hanna's heart froze.

A quick look around revealed she was not the only one to be caught unawares. Two old women sitting on a bench had bent their necks upward. Wrinkled hands shaded their eyes from the sun.

Hanna felt the low rumble before she heard it. Now the very ground shook and moaned like some giant snake trying to roll over. The old women stood, clutching each other, then ran for cover.

Hanna wanted to follow them, but panic had risen up inside her. She swallowed. Her feet seemed anchored to the stones. A plane flew low, close enough for her to see the flag painted on its belly. "English!" she said out loud.

Hanna heard a huge crash somewhere behind her. The heaving ground shook her out of her trance. She looked around the square. She stood alone, the only one still in the open. Then surprisingly, she found she could move. She ran back to the church and crouched in its shadow as another plane flew past, this time higher.

Hanna felt the blast, not knowing if the attack was coming from the Resistance bombs on the ground or the British bombers in the sky. Had the attack been coordinated somehow? One thing she did know instantly—this was no Molotov cocktail.

"Tadeusz!" she screamed. From the church she could see the archway she had just passed under. Tadeusz might have been behind her, or behind the soldiers. Now, as the archway came crashing down she heard a man cry out. "Not Tadeusz," Hanna cried, hugging herself as another bomb rocked the ground around her.

Tadeusz had finished his business and was just stepping outside when he heard the shelling. From where he stood at the top of the building steps, Tadeusz could see pockets of smoke rise from the direction of the black market. He dashed toward the sounds, down one street and into a back alley, but the archway facing him had just collapsed. Dust still rose from the rubble heap.

And now, forged by fear, the love in both their hearts took its true shape. They both focused on opposite sides of the broken bricks blocking the street where the archway had stood.

Tadeusz took a deep breath and quickly retraced his steps, running toward the square along a different street. Gasping, he reached it and stood alone, turning, turning. Tadeusz cupped his hands around his mouth and shouted, "Hanna! Hanna!"

She looked up from where she crouched. How was it possible? she wondered. She must be hearing his voice because she wanted to so badly. So intently was Hanna watching the archway that it took her several seconds to realize the voice she heard was real and coming from the square itself. Hanna looked in the direction of the sound and saw a man turning around and around. Again it took a few seconds before she could focus and recognize him as Tadeusz. Hanna stood up then. "Over here!" Tadeusz caught sight of her and came stumbling toward her, drunk with relief.

"I didn't know, I thought you might have . . ." The whine of another round of bombs drowned out Tadeusz's words. He dove toward Hanna and tackled her, covering her body with his own. Dust and bricks fell around them. Powdered with plaster, the couple lay still, their bodies hugging the wall of the church. Hanna could feel his weight, his breathing in her ear. Tadeusz smelled her hair even as he raised his arms to cover his head from yet another blast that rained bits of glass and stone down upon them.

For long moments they lay without moving. Even after the bombs stopped falling, after the ravens started calling to each other again in the branches overhead, even after other people began coming out of the buildings, Tadeusz covered Hanna. They felt each other's heartbeats. Their blood pumped in time.

Then Tadeusz rolled to one side and Hanna sat up, clinging to him. He held her close and stroked the black hair turned gray by dust. His eyes had taken on a steely light. They knew. They both knew what the fear had helped form inside them. Hanna opened her mouth to try somehow and put it into words, but Tadeusz covered her lips with his finger.

"Shh, don't. Just let me hold you, keep you safe. Let me feel our being alive."

They sat like that, shaking from shock, until they heard the bells ringing in the church tower at their backs. Only then did they stand and start walking home, Hanna still hugging the basket of precious eggs under one arm.

As Hanna linked her other arm into Tadeusz's, she felt as if it belonged to a different man than the one she had walked with less than an hour before. She knew they had both been changed. With the bombs, his wall had weakened. And she had stepped over it.

But it was strange to realize the truth of their love. They still had so much traveling to do before they could acknowledge this destination already reached.

Tadeusz was struggling with a new perspective. "Hanna, I know this is a hard time for us, but I need to know something from you. I need to know so much, everything about you. Help me . . ." He spoke the words even as he thought them. "Help me know . . ."

Hanna knew instinctively what he was trying to say. ". . . yourself, so you can know me and we can know us . . . and this. Yes. Oh yes." She flung her arms around Tadeusz and kissed him full on the lips. He held her like that, tasting her sweet breath, licking the gritty dust from her lips. Then Tadeusz stepped back and laughed at Hanna's young impulsiveness.

She watched him stare at her as the blue in his eyes changed from steel to soft sky.

"All right," he said. "Hanna, I need to know something before we can go on from here. Do you trust me?"

They stopped. Hanna looked away from Tadeusz. Her relief that they could grow even closer was tinged by disappointment. Still she had hoped they could move directly from the past of their books into the future of her dreams. She had gone on hoping the war might pass their garden by. But now they no longer sat between the flowers. Around them piles of plaster and bricks rose like mirror images of the changes going on inside them both. Tadeusz waited for a response. Hanna nodded.

"I'll be honest, it's about your father. Marek told me the first week I came here that things are not what they seem. I've been here more than a year and I still don't know what he meant. I have an idea though, and I hope I'm right. I'm sorry, Hanna, but we both knew we would someday have to talk about our differences." He had taken her hands in his, but she still would not look up.

"I don't want to hurt your family, because they're yours. But mine . . ." He swallowed.

"I know. I'm so sorry."

Tadeusz stuck his chin out. His grief was still too fresh. "I need to know something," he repeated.

"Yes," she whispered.

"All right then. Tell me where your father is when he's not home. He's sometimes gone for whole days and nights." Involuntarily, Tadeusz squeezed Hanna's hands harder and harder.

She caught her breath as he crushed her fingers but willed herself not to pull away. "It has nothing to do with his work." Her voice shook. Now she would tell him what no one else could. She would tell him what only her mother knew in detail. "I know what you're hoping, that he's a member of the Underground." She dropped her voice. "Well, he's not, or he wouldn't have let me come down here today."

This made sense to Tadeusz. He nodded, "Your father probably doesn't want you to say anything, Hanna, for our sakes, I have to . . ."

She stopped him by finally looking up into his face. "No, Tadeusz." Hanna hesitated. "Father told me I could tell you when you asked. You see, he knew you would."

Tadeusz said nothing, so she went on. "Father has been

taking his money down to one of the Nazi offices. It's something he's been doing for three years, since the beginning of the war. He's not a member of the Underground. But he didn't have to be to notice so many people disappearing. Especially the Jews, Tadeusz, from here." She motioned at the crowded houses on both sides of the street.

"We've heard what happened to the families who used to live here. When they were moved to Podgórze they ended up at the so-called 'Liban' labor camp." She lowered her voice. "Many are already dead. And Father knows about other places, camps for the Jews and other types of prisoners. And . . ." Hanna swallowed and rushed on. "And we've heard other things now that some of these camps have been finished, but they might not be true. Anyway, Father has been trying to buy the release of certain families. In the early years of the war, it was easier. The Nazis have always been easy to bribe. But lately they ask him questions, sometimes keeping him all day. I . . ."

Hanna looked down at her white knuckles. Tadeusz had stopped squeezing her hands, but now she could not let his go. "He's been warned that he's endangering himself and us by continuing to speak out against whatever it is Germany is doing with these people. They told him if he doesn't stop, they might send him to one of these camps. Or us. The last time he tried to help a family, the SS kept him overnight. He didn't tell me what happened, but I know he left again this morning with more money. You see, Tadeusz, I am telling you the truth; I just don't think Father wants me to know too much. But he believes that as long as he keeps turning out reliable work and helping their engineering corps, we'll be safe. The Nazis need Father's plans."

Tadeusz nodded, his eyes far away. He had thought

Herr Müller was supporting the war effort with his engineering projects. Instead, the man was using his company to make money off the Nazis and buy back some of their prisoners. And there was no doubt that by hiring Tadeusz, Marek, and the other engineers, Hanna's father had kept them all out of work camps in Germany, so his company could also be viewed as a means of ensuring protection for those under his roof. It began to make sense.

Hanna looked around and continued, "The Nazis just think he is throwing his money away, and they don't care as long as it's in their direction. But if they ever thought he was helping the Resistance, or that one of you were working for the Home Army, all the people we're helping and can still save would be doomed. So please, Tadeusz, don't do anything foolish. You believe what I've told you, don't you? Does it help some?"

Hanna knew she had talked too much. She felt out of breath, yet her eyes pleaded with Tadeusz. She had prayed so often that his heart might soften and believe.

Finally he nodded. "Yes, sweet Hanna, I trust you. Your father is a good man. I'd already discovered that your family is not typically German. Your secrets are safe with me."

In the end, this was what had slain Tadeusz's dragons of doubt and prejudice. He had told her this later. Hanna and her parents lived what they believed. The words Tadeusz had just heard from Hanna fit the acts of compassion and courage he had seen over the past year, and this was why he could believe her.

Even at that moment, Hanna sensed the peace her words had brought him. Now, finally, they could both dare to look at the present. On that day, Hanna and Tadeusz first glimpsed the prism of colors seen through love learned, one band of which is called trust.

Autumn then had faded into winter, and with the cold, conditions had worsened for everyone in Kraków. The market had long ago dried up as a source of fresh produce. The huge Müller household lived off of the preserved bounty from the Müller's garden and from the precious chickens. And word had gone out that anyone coming to the Müller home would not be turned away. So in addition to the twenty men lodging under the Müller roof, there now came a stream of beggars asking for food.

Hanna and her mother always managed to have a pot of soup on the stove for those who came asking. "There are so many much worse off than us," Helena told her daughter countless times.

But people didn't just come looking for food. Sometimes acquaintances would come by asking for help, saying that family members had been arrested. Hanna remembered that one of her schoolteachers had come, and their old housekeeper, Mrs. Fisiak, had visited. Johann and Helena had talked with these people in his study on the second floor, and they had always emerged with somber faces. Hanna rarely knew the outcome of these interviews, but she did know her father had tried to help.

As it turned out, in the weeks and months to come, the demands on Herr Müller's team of engineers also grew. No sooner would one project be completed than another two would be assigned. Yet not one of the projects was ever of strategic importance. Only state-owned companies were allowed to do such things as designing bridges. But the Müller firm supplied much of the background and research used later by the military's own corps.

Because they were kept so busy, Hanna and Tadeusz saw less and less of each other. There were the weekly prayer meetings led by her father, which Tadeusz had finally begun to attend, and he went to church with them on Sundays, but the only times they could be alone anymore came when Hanna could manage to get downstairs while Tadeusz was working at night. Some nights, just sharing a room was enough. Other times they both needed more.

On one particular evening, Tadeusz was working while Hanna sat in the corner, mending socks. He turned around from his table to watch her. He had felt nervous for most of the day, knowing what he would ask her that night should she be able to get away. He had to give the deepening of their relationship a name. As Tadeusz walked toward her, Hanna looked up and was startled yet again by the intensity of his gaze.

"My Hanna," he began. He sat on the floor at her feet, gently taking the mending out of her hands. He hugged her knees. "My Hanna, we've both known I would ask you this. But now I need to hear the words. Hania, will you be my wife?" He called her by her Polish nickname for the first time, and she would never think of herself as anything else.

Hanna caught her breath. Although she had known this was coming, she had been sure he would wait until after the war. She shook her head to clear her mind, to focus on the face before her. She cupped his chin in her small hands. "Yes . . ." Her voice cracked. "Yes."

Then Tadeusz crumpled into her arms. She held his head in her lap as if he were a small boy, rocking him back and forth. Their joy could just as well have been pain, it cut so deep.

So they had become secretly engaged. But no date was set. And after they announced the news to Hanna's parents, Johann and Helena had embraced the young couple, congratulating them, then growing more serious.

Johann sighed and scratched his bald head. "I think I speak for Helena in saying we couldn't be more pleased at your news. There is, however, an additional issue at stake here. Before this relationship can become any more serious, you must come to terms with the fact that you are of different faiths. As you know, Tadeusz, we are not Catholic. Differences like this have brought pain in many marriages, so you must think about it carefully. This is a private decision, though, and, Hanna, your mother and I will be praying for God to show you and Tadeusz clearly what needs to happen." Then the older man took the younger into his arms once more. It was the only time that Johann and Helena brought up the subject of Hanna's being Protestant, a member of the Brethren church, and Tadeusz's being Catholic.

Weeks became months, then one year went by and half of another. Hanna and Tadeusz had set their wedding date for late October 1944, but still, the war would not come to an end. It had become increasingly difficult to free any prisoners taken by the Nazis, no matter how high the bribe, so Hanna's father had made fewer treks downtown on behalf of people who came to him for help. And then, a month before the wedding, after one such visit Johann did not come home at all.

They waited and prayed until a full week had passed. Then Hanna and Tadeusz met with Helena to decide what must be done. Hanna said, "He's never been gone this long."

Helena reached up to her daughter's hair and absently brushed it between her fingers as she spoke. "I'm going down to Ulica Pomorska." It was the address of Gestapo headquarters. "I have some money, enough to make even the Germans sit up and take notice."

Hanna knew there was only one way her mother could have come up with that much cash. "Your ring, Mother?" she asked softly. "Did you sell the ring Father gave you when I was born?"

"Never mind, child." Helena turned away to cover the fear in her eyes. Hanna started to say something, then couldn't, and found herself crying as Tadeusz folded her and her mother into his arms.

"Shh, he'll be all right. But listen, I can't let you go down to that place," he said to Helena. "Not alone, anyway."

Helena placed a hand on his shoulder. "Bless you, Tadeusz. But if you go with me you'll just end up as bad off as Johann, or worse. No, I must go in there alone." She paused. "But you could wait for me outside."

Hanna and Tadeusz felt relieved that they could finally do something. The threesome headed west across Kraków, staring around them at familiar city streets that had been transformed into a German officers' camp.

Tadeusz and Hanna waited at the wrought-iron gates of the complex the Germans called Schlesienstraße 2 while Helena crossed the courtyard to the Gestapo offices. A half hour later they saw her being escorted to another corner of the yard and down a flight of stone steps. Tadeusz and Hanna could read nothing from her expression. When she reemerged from the basement a few moments later, though, there was no mistaking the grief wracking her face. This time she ran across the courtyard without an escort and stumbled out of the gate.

"What is it? Mother, tell me!" Hanna had never seen her mother so upset. She and Tadeusz supported her from both sides.

"We have to get her out of here, get her home," Tadeusz said, glancing at the glaring guards nearby.

"Your father," Helena gasped. "They let me see him, but he was crumpled on the ground, in the corner of this cell. He didn't even look up when I called to him through the window in the door. Oh, God in heaven, what have they done to him?"

"And the money?" Tadeusz asked.

"Gone, of course. What else could I do?" Helena said. "And now I'm supposed to wait. The SS man said he would intervene personally on my behalf."

Tadeusz snorted. Hanna looked at him sharply, but she understood. It was hard to trust someone who wore a skull and crossbones on his collar. For Helena's sake, though, they both kept quiet.

Late that night Hanna, whose room was at the front of the house, heard a knock on the door. She wrapped herself in her dressing gown and went to peer through the small window. When she saw no one, she opened the door.

"Father!" she cried. He lay slumped against the doorpost.

"My legs, my legs," he mumbled. "Get help."

Hanna ran upstairs and woke her mother. "God in heaven, stand by us," Helena whispered. "Run, child, run up to the attic and wake your boy Tadeusz, and Marek. At least those two can be trusted. Run!"

Hanna flew up the small stairs but stopped when she entered the attic room. It smelled heavy with the sweat of men. She started to cross the room toward Tadeusz, but he woke before she could reach his side.

"What is it, Hania?"

"They've brought Father home, but he can't walk. We have to get him off the street before the patrol comes by.

The new curfew started at eight this week. Bring Marek, and hurry!"

Together, Marek and Tadeusz were able to drag the older man's body inside the house. Since Hanna's bed was the closest, they gently brought him into her room. Tadeusz returned to the hall and checked to make sure the front door was locked and all curtains drawn. Then he went back to the bedroom to help Marek and Helena undress Johann. Hanna was sent to fetch pots of hot water and strips of old sheets for dressing the wounds.

To the horror of the four people tending him, Johann's body was covered with welts and open sores. Both his kneecaps had been broken, and he was missing several teeth. The damage done to Johann was more than physical, though.

Over the next few days he drifted in and out of consciousness, and his conscious moments were spent in a kind of feverish delirium.

"Writing on the walls!" he called out once. And then he recited a litany of the inscriptions that had stared indifferently back at him during his torture sessions, carved in stone by those who had passed through that same cell. During one such outburst he spoke softly, in a daze, "Words . . . So many words . . . in Polish and Russian and German and Czech. Words in Latin . . . so many words. Couldn't understand them all . . . but I remember . . . remember how they looked. Remember . . . 'For Warszawa and a woman's name,' 'God knows why I'm here,' 'Innocent.' "

One night he seemed driven to talk about what had happened, as if putting it into words might finally purge the memory. He mentioned a man named Jurek who had shared the cell with him the first night. "He was with the

Home Army and was part of the assassination attempt on Krüger, one of the Gestapo heads. He had been wanted by the Nazis for over a year. After they finally caught him, they kept him in my cell."

"Did you say Jurek?" Tadeusz asked.

When Johann described him, Tadeusz whistled softly.

"Do you think you knew him, Tadeusz? Short man, black hair? I hope not, since he was sent to Płaszów on the morning Helena came to see me. I'll never forget the sight of that Krüger coming in personally and snapping shut his cigarette case as he told Jurek where he would be dying.'This case is made of Polish hide like yours, pig.' That was the last thing he said."

Helena gave a little gasp, remembering that the Gestapo officer she had given the money to had also had a leather-looking cigarette case.

Johann continued, "I saw the marks on the inside of the door. The cell had a pipe running through the middle. Thousands must have been killed in that place, thousands, and they kept track of time on that very wood and stone. Oh!" he gasped, feebly extending his arms toward his wife and daughter, "Thank God I am home with you."

But Tadeusz turned away from the scene and privately mourned a childhood friend.

So it was that after three long weeks of Johann's recovery, and after almost two years of engagement, Tadeusz and Hanna had finally been married. Hanna had dried bunches of flowers from the garden woven through her hair. She wore her good tweed outfit. Tadeusz wore a borrowed suit. They gave no rings to each other. They had no rings to give.

They were married in the tiny Brethren church Hanna and her parents attended. Tadeusz had struggled with the decision to marry outside the Catholic church, knowing his parents would never have approved. But his parents had been dead for two years, and during that time he had undergone so many changes. The church had meant little to him as a boy. Here his faith had grown. He assured Hanna he felt at peace about the decision to join her church as well as her family.

On that first night together, spent in Hanna's girlhood bedroom, she and Tadeusz had managed to shut out the war more effectively than their garden wall ever had done. For one long, golden night, they were able to forget the bombs, forget the torture and the fear, forget all they had lost and all they stood to lose. They were together, and they loved each other, and that was enough.

And yet even as they awoke the next morning they knew that even their love might not be enough to keep them safe. With every passing day, the war was growing more dangerous for them. The rumble and roar of bombs could be heard all up and down the Polish countryside. The Germans were losing ground, and the Russians were sweeping over the land in a rush of revenge. Down every main road, Soviet soldiers guided horse-drawn wagons filled with candlesticks, tapestries, and other booty past crowds of refugees carrying what was left of their homes on their backs.

Both Tadeusz and Hanna knew it was only a matter of weeks before that tide of panic finally reached out and swept over them. So on that first morning together they prayed for a word of comfort and assurance, something they could both hold on to in the months to come.

They found it in the little Bible Hanna had given Tadeusz, in the Book of Isaiah. They read the verses together in her room, Hanna sitting on the edge of the bed with her black curls pressed against his bright blond head:

> When you pass through the waters,
>     I will be with you;
> and when you pass through the rivers,
>     they will not sweep over you.
> When you walk through the fire,
>     you will not be burned;
> the flames will not set you ablaze.

---

Sitting in the train that night, Hanna felt the comfort of those words and the strength of what she and Tadeusz shared. The intensity of their love had become something tangible, a part of her. She was not about to give it up just because a war had pushed them apart.

In the end, the difference in their nationalities and the years of hate and prejudice had made little difference to the love in their hearts. She held on to that. A diamond cannot lose its brilliance in the dark.

# 4

## JUNE 1938–DECEMBER 1941

Jacek had no idea why he had been so set on keeping Barbara a secret from his handlers in army intelligence. It had something to do with fear and a sense of identity, a need to have something that was his alone. The people who had hired him already knew so much about him. He needed to have something in his life they didn't know about. And she had remained his secret for some time after he arrived in Poland.

He still couldn't believe that Barbara trusted him so much from the beginning. When they said goodbye in 1938 she had let his face slide out from between her hands. She had touched her painted fingertip to her lips and to his. Then Jacek was gone. And in leaving her, he had left behind all that was tender and vulnerable in himself.

This process began immediately, during his training with army intelligence, which challenged him for the first time in his life, both emotionally and physically. Then came the day when Jacek finally learned the nature of his assignment. "You'll have to play on whatever team is winning over there, no matter how long it takes. Your only contact with us will be sporadic, possibly once a year. You're part of a pilot project, an investment in the future, so to speak.

"We may bring you home to check on how the field

agrees with you. And we may not. But remember, the more time you put in, the higher the pay. Any questions?"

"It looks like a long six months."

"Well, you showed more promise than we expected. Besides, would you have said yes if you knew this was an extended assignment? You don't have any reason to stay behind, do you?"

Again Jacek lied about Barbara, "No."

"Then welcome to the army." The instructor shook Jacek's hand. Two weeks later he was on a boat crossing the Atlantic.

The year 1938 was coming to a close by the time Jacek actually arrived in Warszawa. He settled in well behind his cover. It was not difficult. All he had to do was pretend to be a student, something he'd already been most of his adult life. He mingled with men and women his own age, listening to most of them convincing each other that Hitler could not be trusted. By early 1939 the relationship between the Germans and Poles, especially in border areas, had already gone from strained to nonexistent.

Jacek found a place to live, a room above a small restaurant that served as a home base. From here he often strayed for weeks at a time to travel along the western border. His instructions were simply to observe and report back any significant troop movements he noticed in his wanderings.

Before leaving the States, Jacek had been told, "Your primary value will be long-term. So learn to blend into any Polish crowd and brace yourself for war. That's when we'll need you most. And afterward, of course."

"Afterward," Jacek had repeated to himself, and the sinking feeling had returned. He wondered why he had not told them no right then and there. It was a question he would ask himself many times over in the years to come.

So during the early months of 1939 Jacek attended lectures, refined his Polish, and learned where the back streets of Warszawa led. At night he made a few friends, earning himself a reputation as someone who knew how to listen.

When the university closed for spring break, Jacek headed south. He familiarized himself with the railway routes. Then he focused on the part of Poland bordering Śląsk, bought a motorcycle and roamed the back roads. When he returned to Warszawa, he checked out a few leads and was able to report back through his contact that several Polish companies along the border were acting as fronts for bringing in weapons from Germany. Many of the German-speaking Poles in the southwest were getting ready to welcome Hitler when—not if—he came.

Jacek filed the information, not for the first time, by leaving it in a locker at the Warszawa train station. Whoever his contact was picked up the papers sometime later and relayed the information back to his superiors. Jacek was suspicious that the man who picked up his reports might also be spying on him. After all, they had told him he was on a sort of probation for the first year. So once Jacek had settled in Warszawa and finally felt at liberty to write Barbara, he made sure he gave her the address of his landlady's sister. That way, he hoped, the watchers would still not find out about his marriage. During that first year this secret balanced out all the changes he had experienced since graduation, providing at times the only stable factor in his life.

When Jacek finally received Barbara's first letter, two times the six months promised her had passed. As he turned the envelope over in his hands, he knew the game had gone on for far too long. He sat down heavily on the edge of his bed and gazed at the handwriting. The letter felt fat. Carefully he tore it open and tipped the contents onto his lap.

Two photos fell out. The first looked like one she must have taken herself while standing in front of a mirror. Her lingerie had grown tight around the middle. Jacek pursed his lips and blew air between them as he reached for the second photo, which showed a bald baby wrapped in a pink blanket.

Jacek could hear his heart racing. He quickly read through Barbara's schoolgirl script. He could see her bent over the pages, her left hand turned under as she slowly wrote out the words of her first communication with him in a year:

> . . . Thanks for the money. Your bank finally started transferring it every first of the month. Your letter was so short! I decided to keep on waiting tables until I heard from you. But when so much time passed, I got worried. And now that Amy's here, I've had to take some time off. Me and a friend of mine who has a little boy trade off baby-sitting.
>
> I won't have to do that no more now with your money. It's too bad it took so long to get here. I just wish I could have let you know earlier about me being pregnant. You know, honey, this hasn't really been very easy. I think you should quit that government job and come home now that you've got a family and everything. You've given them their half year and then some.
>
> I've been feeling real lonely lately, and there's a nice man who's the brother of this friend of mine, and he keeps making jokes about you never coming back, that there's going to be trouble or something. But I don't

have to worry about that too, do I? Besides, I know you better than that.

Send me a postcard if you can. What does Poland look like? All my love, Barb.

Jacek whispered, "Amy." He liked the way his daughter's name rolled between his lips. Then, for the first time in many months, he spoke English out loud, "Poor Barbara, I've really put you through it. I don't blame you for playing the martyr this time around."

Jacek stood and paced back and forth across his room. He leaned over the basin of water on a table next to his bed and splashed water onto his face. When he stood up, he watched his cheeks dripping in the cracked mirror.

Jacek was surprised at himself. The thought of pulling out of the job had caused a sense of loyalty to his army intelligence bosses to well up inside him. He reached blindly for a towel, wiped his face, then sat down at the small desk by the window and wrote,

> I can't write much on paper, but I have to stay here for now. When Hitler invades Poland, he'll finally have given our boys an excuse to nip him in the bud. Please trust me. I'm so proud of you, doing all this alone. Keep sending me photos of our little girl. She's beautiful, and so are you. Give little Amy a kiss from her daddy. Please write soon. This silence I've put us through is driving me crazy. All my love, Jacek.

Jacek waited for six weeks, expecting to hear from Barbara, even though he knew there was a good chance the letter might get lost on the way. At first he worried when he heard nothing. Then gradually, as his movements became increasingly affected by the fever of pending war, Jacek thought of Barbara less often.

Throughout that period Jacek stole back and forth across the border, filing reports that listed evidence of Hitler's plans to invade. By the end of July, Jacek could actually document an increase in German troops massing just outside Poland. In the report describing those movements, Jacek pressed for a meeting with his liaison officer. After more than a year away from home, Jacek was curious about who was reading his reports.

In the train locker where he found the note acknowledging his request, there was also a train ticket to Berlin and one from there to Gdańsk, along with authentic German identification papers. Oh yes, and he would be traveling as a farm equipment salesman. He snorted and thought that someone certainly had a sense of humor.

---

Jacek had wondered why the meeting was set in Hitler's Berlin. Once there, however, he discovered that the lion's own den was a safer haven than the forest where he roamed.

Two nondescript men of average height confronted Jacek when he knocked on the door of a small apartment in the Berlin suburbs. A quick look around showed they, like him, had just arrived. Two suitcases stood unopened in the corner of the room. Faded floral wallpaper hung in strips along the top of the far wall. Jacek smelled cigar smoke, heard a toilet flush. Then a third man entered the room.

"Jacek Duch."

"Yes, sir." He looked the man up and down, automatically memorizing his broad shape, balding scalp, and flat nose.

"Duch, there have been a few changes in the last year. Mr. President has put army intelligence in charge of foreign espionage here in Europe. That means I'm your G–2 liaison officer. Our Chief of Staff, General Marshall, thought I should see you in person. You can call me Mr. Jones. Original, heh?" The man shook Jacek's hand, then reached up to clean his teeth with a toothpick.

"George, get this boy some coffee." One of the two men who had opened the door disappeared into another part of the apartment. "Now, we don't have all that much time, so why don't you elaborate on what's in here." Jones flung a folder onto the coffee table between him and Jacek.

Jacek picked it up and ruffled through the papers. Inside were all the reports he had written since arriving in Warszawa. So they had arrived in one piece, after all.

As if reading his mind, Jones added, "By the way, it wasn't your request which made this meeting happen. True to our word, it's time for you to get the reevaluation we promised. This isn't stateside, so it's been a bit more than six months, hasn't it?" Jones winked. "You've been turning in some good work, Mr. Duch. But there are two points I've been brought out here to discuss with you."

George reentered the room rattling a tray of coffee and cups. As he set it down on the table, Jones asked, "How do you like your coffee?" He motioned to a chair across from him, and Jacek sat down.

He had heard very little of the rambling speech except for the words, "two points." He had also noticed that the man called George had taken out a notebook and was scribbling furiously. Jacek wondered what other jobs this George did. He resolved that if they didn't like his work, it was tough. All the same, Jacek surprised himself by breaking out in a sweat.

The Jones man wore a plain gray suit, but he held himself as if he were in uniform. He droned on as if speaking at a lecture, "The first point. We don't like you predicting what's going to happen all the time. What did you learn during training that your primary function is?"

"To observe," Jacek answered automatically.

"Righto. But you've been playing fortune-teller, and that's not nice. You stop writing in these reports"—Jones shoved the folder with a pudgy finger—"that war's going to break out any minute, okay? We don't like that. There are some big boys upstairs who are betting on there not being any war."

Jacek could barely keep himself from interrupting. He thought Jones must be playing with him, but the man's next words confirmed Jacek's worst fears. "And it's not just Washington that thinks it, either. The Brits and Frenchies know it too. So just stick to the facts, all right? Any questions?"

Jacek's mind reeled. What this man was describing was nothing short of a conscious decision to ignore the facts.

"Excuse me, Mr., eh, Jones, but I seem to remember a certain someone back in Boston, and another someone at training, telling me your same people in Washington were counting on war breaking out. That's one of the reasons I'm over here. What's that place called again, the War Department? All these reports do is confirm that's exactly what's going to happen. As you can see, there is no room for doubt that Germany intends to invade Poland . . ."

Jones raised his left hand and said softly, "I don't *care* what your reports confirm, do you understand? Your job is to keep writing them. Let us be the ones to decide their interpretation."

Jacek tried a different tack. "All right. But tell me this. Am I right in thinking you have a fair idea how many troops Hitler has at his disposal? I mean, I assume there are others like myself doing similar recon work for the army, right?"

Jones nodded.

"Now, let's do some simple subtraction. Take your figures for total troops and Panzer divisions. Subtract my figures for what's been moved in the direction of Poland. What are you left with?"

Jones's eyes narrowed.

"Exactly," Jacek continued. "I don't know what the balance is, but I'd wager it's not much. Use my reports for this purpose, if for no other. I'm certain Hitler is throwing his full weight into the oncoming, alleged"—he cocked his head at Jones—"offensive against Poland. He'll be leaving his western flank wide open. When war breaks out, we could end it within a week. If we hit him hard and fast in the very beginning from the west, it could all be over."

Jones raised his hand, "All right, all right. Duch, you've had your say. Don't think you're the first one to suggest this. You need to know, though, that there are a lot of others who are just as convinced there won't be a war. Hitler wouldn't dare. And if he does, a worm like him's not going to last longer than a month. Luckily, none of this is for you or me to decide. So let's move on to point number two. Now I want to tell you something. You've not been playing straight with us."

Jacek was only half listening. He was still thinking about the consequences of what Jones had just told him when Jones leaned forward and hissed, "About your Barbara."

Jacek dragged his eyes up to meet the other man's. At the very mention of his wife's name, Jacek found he could no longer swallow.

Jones shifted his weight and reached into a coat pocket.

Then he threw four letters onto the table. Jacek couldn't help himself as he shoved the folder aside and picked them up, one by one. The handwriting on the envelopes was Barbara's.

"The broad's your wife. Didn't you think we'd notice the bank transfers? Your money's not piling up as fast as the accounts of others in your program. That's because they don't have anyone to spend it on, and neither should you." Only now did Jacek take in how enormously fat Jones was. His thighs ran over the sides of the chair.

Since there were no more secrets, Jacek stood as Jones continued, "You lied to our recruiter."

Jacek hesitated, then said softly, "He lied to me."

"You've put us, and yourselves, in a very tight corner, let me tell you. Hadn't you noticed that you're in a single man's sleeper post? Whether or not Hitler makes his move, we're going to need you right where you are. And you'll need to have been there a while to be of any use. Don't you see? It's already too late to pull you out."

"You didn't hear what I said." Jacek walked over to George, saw it was shorthand he wrote, then spun around to face Jones's back. "Your man told me this would be a six-month stint. No more. With training, it's already been more than a year."

"You could have pulled out at training. You were informed before you left stateside."

"Exactly. I was informed. You tell me how much of a choice I had."

Jones reached into the same coat pocket that had contained the letters and pulled out a cigar. As he lit it, he said, "That's weak, and you know it. I don't know why you've played this game with yourself"—he paused—"and her. But I'll only ask you once. Will you divorce her?"

"Of course not!" Jacek could hardly believe what he was being asked. If he were to make a break with anyone, it would be with G–2. Besides, despite all the weeks he may not have thought much about Barbara, she was still his wife, and now they had Amy. "What would I plead, for love of country?"

"Well, then you've got to choose, my boy." Jacek still could not see Jones's face. "You think I haven't been listening to you. You're wrong. George here has put it all down in black and white code. You said it and you know yourself that the work you're doing here is invaluable, absolutely invaluable in terms of world peace. Weigh it up. The army wants you. But if you stay on and don't divorce that woman—and forget about that baby, how do you even know it's yours?—you'll be putting yourselves through an indefinite separation. Let me know your answer within the next five minutes.

"We need you. We figured once you got out in the field you'd be smart enough to see that and you wouldn't think twice about staying longer. We tell everyone six months to start with. But when they tell us they're single, they aren't lying. Now you've gotten yourself into trouble."

Jacek didn't need to hear Jones tell him what he had been doing was worthwhile. It was the root of a conflict he had been trying to ignore for months. Now there was no way he could continue turning his back on it.

"Five minutes." Jones stood and motioned to George to follow him out of the room.

After the two men left, Jacek returned to the table and opened one envelope after another, quickly thumbing through their contents until he found what he was looking for. On the back of this latest photo Barbara had printed, "Your Girls." Jacek had no doubt that Amy was his. That crack of Jones's had been a cheap shot. He ran his finger over the faces.

"How will I ever make you understand?" he whispered. "These guys have got me in a corner." Jacek put the photo and letters into his coat pocket.

When Jones returned, Jacek was ready for him. "Well?"

"You know the answer. I stay married."

"Could be a while before you see her again." Jones started to point at the table, then noticed the letters had disappeared.

"Yeah, so you said, a few times already," Jacek said. "Maybe it won't be so long if you follow the advice in my report."

"I'll give you that round." The two men locked gazes. "All right. I'll make sure somebody important hears what you've told me today. If Hitler makes his move, we'll be ready for him. Who knows, if this thing blows over quickly, we might be able to bring you home soon, after all."

"If you don't, I might quit and come home on my own."

"So you might, so you might."

Jacek did not for a moment believe Jones, but he took the hand Jones stretched out to him anyway. He held it a few moments longer, just to make his point before releasing it. He'd been lied to once; he wouldn't let it happen again. Now at least he knew what was what.

When Jacek left the room Jones watched him walk down the hall, then turned to George. "If he won't divorce her, let's hope she divorces him. A woman's not a good enough reason to lose any agent, especially one as good as he promises to become."

---

Before leaving Berlin, Jacek's orders had been clear: "If

war does break out, be where it happens." It turned out that he was already there when the first shots were fired in the city of Gdańsk, which the Germans called Danzig.

During the previous week, Jacek had confirmed much of what he had already heard rumored. The Baltic port city of Gdańsk was as good as German. Although the city had technically belonged to both Poland and Germany since the end of the Great War, the Nazi Party had been running the city government since 1933, and since then most of the formerly Prussian residents of Gdańsk had been wholeheartedly converted to National Socialism. On that fateful morning Jacek was close enough to the military depot to hear explosions coming from that side of the city. A German battleship moored in the port on a "friendly" visit opened fire on the northern port of Westerplatte, marking the start of the Second World War.

As soon as he realized what was happening, Jacek hastily tried to slip in and out of the different sections of Gdańsk, compiling information about the strength of the German Fourth Army's offensive. Then, in all the confusion, Jacek managed to slip out of Gdańsk.

He spent the next two weeks working his way back down to Warszawa, trying to gauge in as exact terms as possible the extent of the Nazi war machine. It was not difficult, as both the Sixteenth and Nineteenth Panzer Corps were bulldozing their way far into the Polish countryside.

When Jacek finally did manage to get back to Warszawa, he stayed up two nights in a row, writing down in the code he had learned all he had heard and seen concerning the invasion. Even as he wrote, German bombers continued to strafe the city. The Germans could take it any day. If Jacek were picked up for questioning, he would be shipped off to Germany to work in the factories there. He could not let that happen to him, not this early in the game.

Jacek had a second reason for wanting to get the results of his reconnaissance out of Poland as quickly as possible. Deeply troubled, he could not understand why there had not been any Allied retaliation against the German aggression. He hoped that once they read this latest report, there could finally be no more doubt that Hitler was concentrating virtually all his strength on the invasion of Poland. Surely the British and French military intelligence networks would confirm his own findings. Only a few short months earlier, their governments had been the ones to promise their protection should Hitler move against Poland.

As soon as Jacek finished, he packed his few belongings into a bag and told his landlady he was leaving the city. "Just tell them I checked out a few months ago, and you don't know where I've gone."

As he turned to go, she stopped him with a hand on his arm. "Haven't you heard yet?" she said.

"What?"

"The Soviets. This morning they crossed the eastern border. I heard the news on the radio." She squinted up at him.

Jacek swore out loud, which satisfied her. Then he handed her the keys and the rent he owed and thanked her.

After the door slammed shut behind him, Jacek closed his eyes and leaned against it. "It's over now. It's all over. We waited too long. They didn't listen to me. Germany alone we could have stopped, if we'd moved in right away like we promised. Now that the Russians have joined the Germans, Poland doesn't have a prayer."

He tied his bag onto the back of the motorcycle and took off for the station, zigzagging his way through the piles of rubble. At the station, Jacek went straight to the baggage lockers. When he opened his to deposit the report, a small packet of papers lay there waiting for him. He quickly slipped it into his pocket, replaced it with his own file, shut the door, and turned the key. Then he headed for the nearest men's room. Once inside a booth, Jacek sat down to read.

His orders were written on a single sheet of paper. He was to join up with the Polesie Reserve Army Grouping. His new identification papers looked as though they had been issued by the Polish Army headquarters itself. He was a mathematics professor from the university being mobilized as a reserve officer.

His mission for the war was, very simply, to entrench himself in the Polish leadership, first as an officer in the reserve, proving himself in battle, and later in the Underground.

As far as Washington was concerned, Jacek should lie very low. The drop point would be the post office box numbered 77 at the main office in Brześć. Any new orders would be waiting for him there after the first of every year.

Jacek sat there longer than he expected, pondering what the new developments meant. The fact that he was being asked to provide background information for decisions that belonged in a more orderly war than the one he found around him was beside the point. He was one tree who could barely see the proverbial forest. Now that the war had actually started, he could no longer justify his staying in Poland.

Unless, very simply, it was what he wanted to do.

And this was the bare truth. Jacek had come into himself. He knew this even as he stood up and threw the paper into the toilet. As he pulled the chain, he had no doubt that the men above him knew the war would last a long time, had known all along. There had never been any question of his returning to Barbara. The time for proving his love by protest had slipped through his fingers back when he was still fooling himself. As he fled the city, Jacek wondered how long it would be before he ever saw another American.

---

Once at the front, it had not taken long for Jacek to discover that he had been plunged into that very specific hell on earth called a two-front war. The Polesie Grouping Jacek had been sent to join was located slightly south of Warszawa, just across the Bug River to the east. He assumed his cover easily; no one had the time to check his references. The panic blazing through him when he first came under fire was as real as that of the other reserve officers. Few if any of the teachers, businessmen, and doctors around him had any military experience. Jacek joined their ranks as they led peasants and farmers, trying to organize a ramshackle defense with plow horses and outdated rifles.

The sense of betrayal Jacek had felt back in Berlin, when Jones admitted Jacek was being spied on, had only deepened in Warszawa when Jacek realized his reports and warnings had been summarily ignored. Now, living the consequence of some Allied decision made on a telephone cable running between London and Washington, Jacek began to experience a shift in identity.

The first step in that shift had been his realization that he would stay in Poland, despite Barbara.

Now, in the heat of battle, the shift deepened. "I am Polish," he caught himself saying as he jabbed a bayonet into a German boy over and over again. Jacek's military training, brief though it might have been, his college days, even his childhood—they all started belonging to another man.

Yet the man who told his troops, "We fight for Poland," still believed help could come. "We must fight on. The rest of the world will have no choice but to notice." The private knowledge that the carnage could have been avoided, that the rest of the world was, in fact, turning its back on Poland, only fanned a bitter wind on the flames of Jacek's fighting spirit.

During the first two days and nights, Jacek hardly slept at all. He and his men dug and fought in trenches. On the third day, the Soviet troops that had crossed the border while he was still in Warszawa swooped down, joining the German tanks.

"Bury your weapons! Hide in the woods!" Jacek heard the orders being yelled down the trench, but even then he could not believe the swiftness of their defeat. It had only been a matter of days, all melted together by the heat of battle.

Jacek peered over the pit and saw fields around him heaped with corpses. Tanks plowed over the barbed wire, coming straight toward his ditch. He ducked and ran along it, calling to the men still in position, "Go, go, go! Everyone out! Get to the woods behind us. Move!"

Jacek stopped when he felt a hand grab hold of his ankle. A man lay half-submerged in the filth oozing between Jacek's boots. The hand squeezed Jacek's leg again. Jacek knelt down and placed two fingers under the man's chin.

"You are alive. All right, come on, then." Jacek rolled the body over his shoulder and threw it onto the opposite bank. He scrambled up, heaving the dying man over his back. Then Jacek ran. As he watched the last of his men disappear into the trees, he measured the distance to go, thirteen steps.

"Don't look behind. Twelve. Eleven." He exhaled and inhaled, concentrating on his balance, the clods of earth between his feet. "First turned by a plow centuries ago. Go. Go."

Jacek could feel the man's arms slapping against the back of his legs. Then the ground started shaking. Without looking back, Jacek knew a tank was roaring up behind him. Still he ran on.

"Seven. Six." Pebbles flew up from the ground. Only afterward did Jacek hear the shots.

A voice shouted at him in Russian. Pain seared through Jacek's left leg. His knees gave way as he crumpled to the ground. He grabbed his breast pocket and ripped the photos of Amy and Barbara away from his shirt with the cloth. These he shoved into the sleeve dangling beside him. The last thing he saw before passing out were the whites of the rolled-up eyes of the man he had carried, his body now riddled with bullets.

A few days later Warszawa capitulated. The day after that, Germany and the USSR partitioned Poland down the middle, so that the entire country lay under the brutal hands of both its enemies.

During the first weeks of October, the Soviets systematically screened the Polish population on their side of the demarcation line. The security branch of the Soviet Special Forces, the NKVD, interrogated Jacek and tens of thousands like him, men with degrees who had volunteered to be officers in the reserve units and now were sentenced to an indefinite period of hard labor in Soviet prison camps. The NKVD then tracked down the families of these men and shipped them off to work camps, often in the Russian wilderness. By mid-June 1941, more than 1.5 million Poles had been deported to the camps in Russia. One particular group of fifteen thousand men was sent to three camps in western Russia. Jacek was among them.

It was inside the first camp that Jacek started discovering the extent to which he could control the movements of his mind. He first noticed this when the bullet wound in his left thigh was allowed to fester. At the labor camp a prison doctor cut into the layers of flesh before gouging out the bullet. Jacek's only anesthetic was a rag the guard had stuffed into his mouth.

After the initial interrogations, Jacek learned about endurance. For weeks on end he dug ditches for pipes, driven on by the guards' whips despite his aching leg. At night he collapsed onto a wooden bunk inside the windowless dugouts. For toilets they used a huge, open hole in the ground. Every morning a guard sloshed three hundred grams of wet bread into every prisoner's bowl.

Then there came a day when the guards told them they each must write two lines to their families back home. Jacek addressed a letter to a fictional brother at the drop box he had been assigned in Brześć.

> The tribunal sentenced me to ten years. The weather here is quite warm for March. Give my love to Mother. Jacek.

The next day he was not allowed to join the other prisoners. Without any explanation, two guards ordered him to strip, then marched Jacek to the camp commandant's office. There the guards proceeded to beat him with clubs until he lay rolled up in a corner, his hands covering his face.

Only then did the commandant speak, "What is at this post office box 77?"

"My brother," Jacek answered in Russian. He had already picked up some of the language during the last weeks.

"Why don't you send your letters to his house? Where does your brother live in Brześć?"

The questions fell on Jacek like hammer blows, one after the other. He knew he had no choice but to lie. And these lies would have to be made up as he went along, the most dangerous kind.

He spoke slowly. "My brother travels a great deal."

"Why?"

"For his business."

"What kind of business?"

"He buys fish on the coast and sells it to restaurants and hotels."

"Why didn't you send the letter to your mother?"

"She's senile and lives in a home for the elderly."

"What is it called?"

"Our Lady of the Forest."

"What is your brother's name?"

"Bartek."

And so the interrogation went, hour after hour, the questions pounding like nails into Jacek's already aching head.

Finally, the guards ordered Jacek to stand outside, still naked, for the rest of that day and the next night. To keep from fainting, Jacek recited mathematical equations, theorems and laws, all in Polish.

And it was at this point that Jacek learned yet something else about himself. Jacek invented a life for himself, something he now realized he should have done as soon as he was captured. He filled in the details of the cover he had received on his last day in Warszawa. He retraced in his mind the back streets of that city in what he fantasized as being his neighborhood. He was a bachelor. Jacek furnished a room. And he tried to review the bits of his story he had already revealed to the commandant. During the next interrogations he vowed he would be more prepared.

He could not help but wonder why he had been singled out. What did they already know about him? Somewhere far away inside, Jacek knew he possessed knowledge that would condemn him to certain death, or worse. What that knowledge was and who he had been, everything except Barbara and Amy, he now forced out beyond the edges of his memory.

The next day the commandant had Jacek brought before him again. Immediately he began to fire questions at Jacek, some the same as the previous day, some new. Once Jacek realized he would not be beaten again first, he could not help but lower his guard slightly. An hour into the new line of questioning the commandant repeated, "The name of your mother's home for the elderly?"

"Our Lady of the Woods."

There was a pause as the secretary who had recorded the previous day's interview stopped scribbling, flipped back to the front of the notepad, looked up, and shook his head at the commandant. He, in turn, nodded at the two guards. Without another word, he turned and smiled at Jacek.

Despite the chill that smile sent through Jacek, relief flooded through him now that he knew the questioning was finally over. Jacek allowed the two men to half carry, half drag his exhausted, naked body to a hole behind the dugouts. The guards threw him into a shallow pit and covered the opening with a piece of sheet metal.

Jacek sat in the dark and waited. "They still know nothing," he told himself over and over, not wanting to remember what it was they did not know.

In the hole, there was no room for Jacek to lie down. The cramped space allowed him only to sit with his knees shoved under his chin. Even so, Jacek fell asleep, exhausted from the previous night's ordeal. He awoke a few hours later with a roaring headache and coughed, surprised to discover he could hardly breathe.

He reached up and ran his hands along the perimeter of the metal above him. There were no air holes. His leg wound throbbed, as did all the fresh sores and bruises from the beating. Jacek tried to slow his breathing, quenching the panic. He waited some more, counting the heartbeats between each breath. When he finally heard voices above him, his head was throbbing from lack of oxygen.

"You!" The commandant shouted down at Jacek as three guards slid back the covering. "You!"

The rush of fresh air weakened Jacek even further, making him feel giddy. He smelled his summer uniform as it was tossed down to him before he felt the cloth hit his face. From very far away he heard the voice say, "There's something about you I don't like. We're sending your letter, and you can be sure we'll watch who picks it up. In the meantime, I'm sending you to somewhere special for further questioning." Jacek closed his eyes and knew he should be alarmed, but couldn't summon the energy.

A week later, while the rest of the camp was being transported to a place near Smolensk, Jacek was jammed into a cattle car already full of men, women, and children. The weight of the people behind and around Jacek forced him to stand upright. He caught a last glimpse of his camp just before they slid the heavy door shut and bolted it.

Jacek soon discovered the only opening in the car was a small vent near the roof. The crowd inside was constantly jostling for positions beneath this opening. As the day became night, then day, with no one noticing the difference, this hole became all-important. For many, during the long days to come, the air from this vent would not be enough.

Jacek focused on survival and nothing else. He shoved his way closer to the vent, then surprised himself in refusing to give ground when others pleaded for their turn near the fresh air. When the guards passed moldy crusts through the hole, Jacek divided the bread among those still able to eat, but he kept the lion's share for himself.

He said nothing as one by one the people inside the car with him lost their minds, cried out, or cut themselves and beat their heads against the wall until they fainted. As the train traveled steadily eastward, Jacek convinced himself he would survive this train trip, no matter what.

When soldiers finally slid open the doors, Jacek and the nineteen other survivors fell forward onto the platform. Their destination was a prison in a place called Artemovsk. There he and twenty-five other people were kept for a year and a half in a cell ten feet square. Jacek was called out so often for questioning that he came to actually believe, without any reservation, the story he repeated again and again.

And then, on October 12, 1941, Jacek and two thousand other prisoners, men and women, were gathered in a group outside, given a kilo of bread and one fish each, then told to begin what would become a death march. Although the prisoners did not know it at the time, their destination was Stalingrad, nearly five hundred miles away. Only 550 of the two thousand survived that journey in the snow, and many more succumbed in the barracks where they were kept at Stalingrad.

By this time Jacek had grown used to the dirt and smells, the stench of unwashed wounds and frostbite. His youth and strength stood by him, as those who ate slowest often had their bread stolen. Some prisoners even took the clothing from those who lay dying, then gave it to the guards in exchange for additional bread or water. Every morning the guards ordered prisoners to throw that night's harvest of naked corpses outside, into the snow.

After three weeks in Stalingrad, Jacek's transformation had become all but complete. The process that began on the battlefield south of Warszawa had reached its conclusion. On the day when the camp commandant announced that because of Germany's invasion of the Soviet Union, Poland had allied itself with the Soviet Union for what would doubtless be a glorious victory, Jacek was given two kilos of bread, one kilo of fish and forty-five rubles, then set free.

As guards herded the prisoners outside the barbed-wire perimeter fence, Jacek noticed a group of old women, locals, gawking at them with scarves tied under their chins. Jacek stared back, thinking he recognized at least one set of eyes.

"My Barbara." The thought pierced the cloud of confusion he had plunged himself into for so very long. Seeing those eyes reminded Jacek of the decision he had taken somewhere back when the pain first started, a decision to cling to the memory of his wife. It had been dangerous, a link with a past that could have betrayed him. But in the two years of prison camp that he had just endured, this thought had been his only source of comfort.

In the end, it was this curious combination of Jacek's

almost total change and his memories of Barbara that had saved him. During those years, during the interrogations at Artemovsk, the beatings, the near starvation, Jacek had shut down his mind to everything but this secret world. He became a Polish professor fantasizing about a Cajun waitress. The sheer absurdity of it all had granted him the necessary balance to convince himself and his various interrogators that he was very, very good at keeping his mouth shut.

For even there, Jacek had refused to say goodbye to Barbara. Again he felt her body. Again he heard her voice. Again she had become his secret. And in the years just over, he had hugged that knowledge to himself as an asylum inmate hugs a pillow.

# 5

## LATE JANUARY 1945

Tadeusz cringed as the scream tore up his spine. "Johann, will it never end?" He hurried to one side of the window and ripped off a corner of the newsprint.

Johann doused the candle he held. "Careful, don't let them see you. We're not finished here yet."

Tadeusz did not reply. He was trying to focus on the street below.

When he saw the woman who had screamed, Tadeusz swore under his breath. Two soldiers stood watching as a third was raping her. Before Tadeusz could move, the third man stood, took back the tommy gun his comrade was holding for him, and shot the woman. The sound of the three men's laughter filtered up to Tadeusz from the street below, followed by the tinkle of glass as they shot out the streetlight.

"I think it will end soon. Probably very soon." Johann put a hand on his son-in-law's trembling shoulder. He pulled the drapes over the hole, then limped across the room to the fireplace, leaning heavily on his cane. "Tadeusz, sit down."

Tadeusz obeyed, but he could not stop thinking of the scene he had just witnessed. His helplessness was almost too much to bear. The knowledge that he had not been able to rescue that woman, just as he could no longer help

Hanna, if such a thing should threaten her, tormented Tadeusz. Not for the first time, he thanked God she was gone from Kraków, and yet . . .

"Tadeusz, did you hear me?"

Johann's voice dragged him back from the nightmare he had already imagined too often, back to the present reality of Johann's dark study, the bright fire in the hearth, the disarray of papers stacked around the room.

"I'm sorry, Father," he said. "I'm sorry, it's just . . . Hania."

"Yes, of course. She and Helena weigh heavily on my heart, too. All we can do at this point is pray that the Lord will keep them safe. But it is good that your wife is on your mind. Actually, this is why I must talk with you. Don't you see? If you go now and the Russians find you on the streets, you're just another Pole they've liberated. In my study, though, helping me burn Nazi documents which only further incriminate us both, you become their enemy.

"You've seen for yourself what sort of chaos there is outside. They'll be doing house-to-house searches soon. Go, Tadeusz, I beg you."

Johann held his hands out, palms turned upward. He looked around the room as if he hoped someone could supply him with the words to persuade his son-in-law. But no one else was there. It had been days since Marek and the other engineers finally decided to leave.

"What must I say?" the old man persisted when Tadeusz didn't answer. "Please go. This is for Hanna."

At the mention of his wife's name, Tadeusz looked up into eyes that were so like hers. "I can't, Father. Don't you see? I could never face her if I left you."

"You may never face her at all if they find you here with me."

Tadeusz smiled gently, thinking of all the other man had sacrificed over the past six years. "I'll have to take that chance," he said. "You were the first one to teach me about counting the cost, remember?" The timbre of his voice grew deeper. "Now come, we still have a lot to burn if we're going to convince the Russians you are just an average citizen who put up with the German occupation."

Johann sighed. "How can I persuade you?"

"You cannot." Tadeusz had already gathered another armful of papers and tossed them into the hearth.

"The other men listened to reason."

"The other men were not invited to call you *Ojciec* on their wedding days, Father."

"Trust my daughter to marry a stubborn man," Johann mumbled, even as a smile lit his face. He, too, was reaching for a stack of papers.

The two men worked steadily, trying to shut out the sounds of the Russian tanks rumbling down the street in front of the house. Over and over again they heard shouts and crashing glass, but they continued to feed paper into the fire.

An hour later, Tadeusz headed for the door. "I'm going to make one more trip down to the basement." Johann did not answer. Tadeusz glanced back and saw the older man stooping carefully to gather an armload of paper. He was in his own world, humming quietly to himself, his bald head reflecting the firelight.

Johann had changed, and not just because of his beating three months earlier. When Tadeusz first met Johann, he had stood tall, stiff, "a little too German," Tadeusz had thought at the time. Now he was stooped, his shoulders slumped. Tadeusz watched Johann straighten up, slowly and stiffly, his knees obviously bothering him.

Then a sense of urgency seized Tadeusz. He knew as well as Johann what would happen if the Russians found out that the Müller family had worked for the Germans. The two of them would almost certainly be shot and counted as casualties of war. A shiver ran up Tadeusz's spine as he slipped down the stairs.

In the basement Tadeusz broke down the last of the stools and tables, piling the wood in a corner. Then he made sure Johann's desk was empty and scattered a bag of coal over the floor. He thought it might even pass for an ordinary basement.

As he emerged with a last armful of rolled-up plans, he stopped for a moment, listening. Then he charged up the stairs two at a time.

When he burst into the study, Johann whirled, fear written on his face. "What is it?"

"Listen. It sounds like they're next door." Tadeusz let a few scrolls tumble onto the carpet. The rest he stuffed into the fireplace. The flaring flames lit both men's faces and cast shadows on the far wall.

"I might be wrong. Besides, our lights are out; they may pass us by." His hope sounded hollow.

Both men looked at each other. "Ah, my boy." Johann held out his arms, then disappeared into Tadeusz's own. The two held each other for a moment. Then, without speaking, they picked up the final papers and plans and threw them into the fire, watching as six years of hard work went up in smoke.

"It's strange, you know," murmured Johann.

"What's strange?"

"I've worked so hard for so long, put so many years of my life into building this firm. But now it's gone, and somehow I feel relieved."

Tadeusz didn't answer, didn't know how to answer. So he stood and stared into the fire and wondered how so much had changed so quickly. Had it really been less than a week since he said goodbye to Hanna at the train station? Since then, whole dimensions had shifted. The General-Gouvernement had left Kraków on the night of January fifteenth. All the prisoners in the concentration camp at Płaszów, a suburb in southern Kraków, had been taken to Oświęcim (Auschwitz), and all traces of the camp at Płaszów had been erased. The Gestapo had destroyed all records of the prisoners tortured and killed at their headquarters on Ulica Pomorska. Then, on the seventeenth, even Hans Frank had left the city, and that same afternoon Tadeusz had heard the Soviet air raids bombing German troops as they fled. On the eighteenth he and Johann had both witnessed explosions coming from the direction of the munitions dumps. They had watched from Tadeusz's attic window as the dynamite planted by the Germans destroyed the bridges crossing the Wisła River. Then yesterday at dawn, from the same window, they had witnessed the Russians crossing toward them on the ice. And all the while, until the last German soldiers left the city in hurried disarray, the Nazis had brutally enforced the law forbidding all attempts to surrender or abandon the city, even when they knew full well that time had run out.

The reason the Germans had been caught by surprise was that the Soviet Second Ukrainian Front units under Marshal Ivan Koniev had encircled Kraków. He attacked from the west instead of the east, cutting the Germans off so they barely had enough time to burn their endlessly meticulous records, let alone carry through with their plans to dynamite Wawel Castle and Kraków's other major buildings.

"We need to pray." Johann interrupted Tadeusz's thoughts for the second time that evening.

"Pray?" Tadeusz echoed.

"Yes. We've finished here, haven't we?"

Tadeusz nodded and knelt, while Johann eased himself onto a chair. As they bowed their heads in the dark, their shadows danced on the far wall. Outside they heard the pang of pistol shots.

Johann sighed, then nodded. "We pray for Poland, for her poor people. May we learn to forgive."

*Forgive.* The word ricocheted in Tadeusz's head. So much had changed in the last few years that he could even consider that word. That he could even begin to accept what had happened in his young life and believe that God could have a plan for it. By the side of the man who had taught him this, Tadeusz knelt and thought back to the days before Johann. Before Hanna. Before he had lost so much, and found so much more.

---

Tadeusz had been an only child, but not a lonely one. With his three best friends, Henryk, Tomasz, and Jurek, he had spent many hours playing at heroics in the narrow cobblestone streets of Łódź, near the small café his parents owned in the city center. Surrounded by monuments to Poland's past, he and his friends had invented adventure after adventure, sparring with Crusaders, driving back the Mongols, defending the Polish crown against the Swedes. As Polish boys, they had many enemies to choose from. In those days, they always won.

As Tadeusz grew older, he had begun helping his parents in the café for a few hours every afternoon. At first that meant sweeping and emptying the trash. Later he had helped his mother bake the poppy-seed cakes customers came from miles around to sample. He had helped his father keep the books and wait on customers.

But both his parents and the Jesuit priests who were his teachers were determined that Tadeusz would do more than continue the family business. While still a teenager, Tadeusz had started studying for an engineering degree at Lwów Technical University. He managed to finish a year ahead of schedule, and with honors, and he had no problem finding a company in Łódź that would take him on.

Tadeusz had been pleased to start his adult life in his own hometown, near his family and his three childhood friends, who remained close despite their diverging paths. Henryk by then was an apprentice carpenter. Jurek, more focused and passionate, was determined to be a writer. He supported himself with odd jobs while preparing articles and editorials for a small local newspaper. Tomasz, an aspiring actor, worked in his family's shop and made the rounds of auditions for local productions.

Whenever they had time, however, all three of them gravitated to the Piekarz café. They and their girlfriends and their other friends brought Tadeusz's family plenty of business. Tadeusz still helped out on an occasional evening. This only served to attract more of his friends, eager for good company and a free slice of cake.

Conversations in the café were always lively in those heady years of independence following the Great War. Then all of young Poland was debating the mistakes of previous generations and pointing to their own achievements. In 1939, however, when the Germans crossed the border and invaded, the boasts of what Poland could become faded away. Many young people left the city and hid in the woods. Others disappeared into the Underground ranks of the Polish Home Army. Tadeusz chose to stay with his parents, at least for a while. He was all they had.

Tomasz was the first of Tadeusz's circle of friends to receive a letter ordering him to report to a work camp deep inside Germany. Jurek, always small and fast, had already disappeared. No one knew for sure where, but many suspected he had joined one of the Home Army groups in Łódź or Kraków.

"That's what I'll do, too!" Tomasz had boasted on the last night before he was due to leave for Germany. There in the café, Tomasz gave a performance that had reminded Tadeusz of the battles they had played at as boys. But Tomasz was not acting, and this time, it was no game.

"Germany!" Tomasz jumped on a table, his dark eyes flashing. "Just watch them take me there. I'll run away." He spat. "Like Jurek, I'll fight in the Underground for as long as it takes!" Everyone in the crowded room cheered.

"I would rather die than go to Germany. Never!"

That night, after closing, Tadeusz had echoed his friend's words to his parents. They were sitting at a back table, huddled over a candle, the shades pulled. His mother and father held tight to each other's hands, fearing to look into their son's future.

"I haven't got my letter yet," he reminded them. "I could still disappear like Jurek did. Go underground like Tomasz was talking about."

"Perhaps he's right," his mother said. She glanced at her husband, but he shook his head.

"Tomasz was foolish tonight," he said. "He should know better than to make such announcements publicly."

"It wasn't public," Tadeusz objected. "It was here. We're all family here."

"Not all. Not anymore, now that there's war. And don't you forget it."

Then, as if to prove his father right, a little puddle of blood greeted Tadeusz the next morning when he unlocked the front door to leave the trash on the curb.

"Someone's killed a dog," he muttered to himself, but the trail of red spots led him on, into the alley. He followed it until, in a dark corner, he saw the body.

He dropped to his knees and turned over the stiffening form. Two bloody lines joined at the nose. A swastika carved Tomasz's face into four.

Tadeusz's stomach heaved; he turned and threw up. Then, panting hard, he gently rolled the body into his arms and stood. Staggering under the dead weight, he brought Tomasz to the kitchen entrance behind the café.

When his mother opened the door, she covered her mouth and cried out, "It's begun already." Then, "Oh, his poor mother!" Tears streaked her face as she helped Tadeusz lay down his burden.

But Tadeusz had no tears for his friend. Instead, he felt the first glint of a hard rage, a sharp-edged bitterness honed by fear and helplessness. Before, he had resented the Germans and worried about his future. Now, his hatred was deep and personal.

Tomasz's death effectively ended any discussion in the Piekarz family about Tadeusz's running away. His mother grew nearly hysterical whenever he raised the possibility; his father's face became grim. Besides, Tadeusz realized, it was already too late for running away. His name had to be on the city list of young, eligible males, ready and able to be put to work for Germany. He expected to receive a summons any day.

But although Tadeusz lost his engineering job when the

Germans took over the company he had worked for, confiscating the building and materials and arresting his employer, Tadeusz ended up staying in Łódź—or Litmannstadt, as the Germans rechristened it—for much longer than he expected. Once his job was gone, he started working with Henryk, who had become a carpenter. The Germans needed skilled laborers to work on their various building projects, so Henryk had been ordered to stay in the city. In this way Tadeusz started learning the carpentry trade from his friend. However, as long as Tadeusz did not actually have a letter in his possession ordering him to stay and work in Łódź, he was still in danger of being captured in one of the roundups conducted randomly by the SS in various parts of the city. Often the men and women taken in this way were used as slave labor.

A year passed, and then another, while Tadeusz learned construction alongside Henryk, until the day when the dreaded letter arrived. Even as Tadeusz stood in the bright sunshine, tearing it open and letting the envelope blow away, Henryk came running up to him. He stopped short when he saw his friend's stricken expression and gave him a questioning look. Tadeusz nodded.

"I'll be gone by tonight. They want me to work as a farm laborer in Hanover," Tadeusz swallowed.

"Then it looks like this arrived just in time," Henryk said softly. "Look, this is why I hurried over here." Henryk handed another letter to Tadeusz, who skimmed the contents, then went back to read it more closely. Henryk explained, "It's from a friend of my father. He says there's a small engineering office in Kraków looking for Polish engineers. Since all the German engineers have been conscripted into the army, this Müller has been given the right to employ Poles."

"So I wouldn't be cutting wood or cleaning toilets. That's it!" Tadeusz clapped his friend on the back. "I've got to tell my parents." He turned and ran up the street.

"But we have to move fast on this!" Henryk called after him. Tadeusz waved in acknowledgment as he disappeared around the corner.

Within five minutes a grinning Tadeusz was back at Henryk's side. "Come on! We've got to get to the post office so I can phone and ask whether a reversal of the order is possible."

They wound their way through the streets and arrived panting at the post office. They had to wait until a group of German soldiers had finished their business. Then Tadeusz stepped forward and showed the two letters to the officer in charge of work assignments.

"Would it be possible to change the orders?"

The officer read both letters, then looked Tadeusz up and down. He asked to see his school credentials. Tadeusz fished them out of his pocket.

The soldier flipped through the papers until he came to the hundred złoty note, then nodded.

"You will have to telegraph *Herr* Müller first and arrange an invitation. Make sure he has room for one more prisoner."

Tadeusz caught his breath at the last word. As he walked with Henryk over to the telegraph window, he muttered through tight lips, "That's what we are, you know. Even if I do get to stay in Poland like you, we're still just prisoners. The Germans and the Russians own us and tell us where to work and what to do. Prisoners in our own country . . ."

Henryk jabbed Tadeusz in the ribs. "Shut up. Be thankful you might get a break. C'mon, don't make the same mistake Tomasz did."

At the sound of his friend's name, Tadeusz broke into a cold sweat. "I'll never forget that face," he whispered. "Never."

He sent the telegram, then waited a few hours for a reply. He did not want to take the chance of having it arrive after he had been put on the evening train to Hanover. When his name was called, he grabbed the yellow slip and hurriedly read its contents.

"Yes! It's all right." He threw an arm around Henryk. "But I still have to leave tonight." He looked up at the clock. "In two hours! It's a good thing Mother is packing my bag now. Let's hurry back." As they returned to Tadeusz's home, he said, "I don't know why we're so happy about me going to Kraków. I should be staying here and taking care of my family. Like you are."

Henryk was silent for a moment. Then he told his friend, "Look, just think of it as better than Hanover. Your family will be here waiting for you when you get back."

"If only I could be sure of that."

Tadeusz's last hour in Łódź flew by. His initial relief soon turned bittersweet, especially when his parents went with him to the train station. They had to watch as a Nazi soldier shoved Tadeusz spread-eagled against a wall.

"Hands apart."

Henryk pulled Tadeusz's parents away from the scene. "Don't say a word, or it might get worse."

The soldier was about Tadeusz's own age, with eyes the color of Tomasz's. He finished his body search, then snatched away the papers Tadeusz held. "Krakau," he snorted, using the German pronunciation for the city. "You won't get off before then, I'll make sure of that. Just remember, you're a Polish dog. Maybe in Krakau you might be some good to us. Now get going!" He kicked Tadeusz in the shins.

Tadeusz's face burned with the shame that his friend and parents would have to see him treated that way. But when Tadeusz glanced toward them, he saw only their concern that he would not lose his temper. He took a deep breath and spoke to them. "*Żegnajcie.*"

"Not goodbye!" his mother called after him. "We will see you again!"

"Soon!" his father echoed.

Tadeusz looked back to see them waving with Henryk's two protective arms around their shoulders. Tadeusz had never seen his parents looking so old or so alone.

For most of the trip the German soldier assigned to escort Tadeusz abused him with taunts and the occasional blow. Tadeusz said nothing, could do nothing, although inside he seethed. Through the compartment window, even in the dark, he caught glimpses of a devastated country, destroyed and plundered, villages burned to the ground and homeless villagers wandering the roads. By the time he arrived in Kraków, he had resolved to escape the engineering job at the first opportunity and seek out the Underground.

After arriving at the Müller home, however, Tadeusz was surprised by the relative freedom they allowed him. It did not take him long to strike up friendships with the nineteen other engineers. Once he realized the nature of the projects they were working on, he decided to postpone any escape plans and concentrate on sabotage instead.

Before long, Tadeusz discovered some other things about the firm that surprised him. The first thing he noticed was that all the engineers seemed to be doing their best work. The second thing was that they even worked hard when Herr Müller was not around. The third thing he noticed was that Herr Müller was rarely around.

One day he asked one of his colleagues, "Marek, what's keeping us here anyway? The old man is hardly ever here, and no one is guarding the door. We could walk out anytime we wanted."

Marek set his glass of corn coffee down next to the chart he had been studying. "And be picked up on the streets and shot because we don't have papers? Come on, you know better."

"All right." Tadeusz smiled. "But seriously, tell me why we stay here and work so hard for this German pig? You even worked here before the war, when the other engineers were German, right?"

"Which is why you're here."

"All right. But do you mean to tell me you haven't even tried to sabotage his work? Have you blinded yourself to where these plans go? Don't you know who we're helping here?"

Marek sighed. "You're right. And yes, I do know where these plans go, to the Nazis. Things aren't what they seem here, though. Just keep that in mind."

And it had been at that point of indecision that Tadeusz had met Hanna. He had heard from one of the other engineers that the boss had a daughter. "A cold frog," the man had told him. "You won't get anywhere with her, and even if you did, it probably wouldn't be worth your while."

He still did not know what had happened. Hanna was not anything like his other girlfriends. They had all been full of loud fun and talented in artistic sorts of ways. Against his nature, against his wishes, against his very will, he fell in love with the quiet girl during that spring and summer. She turned his hatred upside down, and his heart inside out.

Her hair had fascinated him. The black curls struggling to get free begged for his hand to smooth them back. Touching those curls had made him kiss her. Feeling her soft lips, then seeing her upraised face had made him want to take care of her.

And all the while he knew he would have to exorcise the hatred in his heart. Long after their first kiss he told her about Tomasz and was shocked when she wept.

"Your tears are more than I could give him," he said bitterly.

"What you're feeling will only hurt you, not the ones who killed him," she answered.

He merely grunted and changed the subject. He was not ready to let go of his hatred.

Gradually Tadeusz became aware that loving might have other implications. Faith, for example, was an important part of Hanna's life, and he soon realized that faith meant something different to the Müllers than it did to him. Before coming to the Müller household, Tadeusz had never met anyone who was not Catholic—except for the Jews in the quarter of Łódź where he grew up, a different matter. Certainly he had never met anyone who took their faith quite so seriously and quite so personally. In addition to attending services at the little Brethren church three blocks away, they held prayer meetings in the living room every week. The engineers were invited to attend, and some did. Tadeusz had always refused, but now he found himself growing curious about those gatherings.

The way Hanna and her family spoke about God, as if He were in the room with them, seemed odd to Tadeusz, though strangely appealing. And he had never even thought of reading the Bible for himself, as Hanna urged him to. Still, he was surprised at how clear the language was in the little Polish-language Bible Hanna gave him. He made a point of reading it every day.

This was, in fact, what he had been doing on the day in late August when Marek brought him the letter from Henryk. "*Frau* Müller said this arrived today."

Tadeusz looked up from reading and rubbed his eyes. He stared at the letter for a few minutes and actually caught himself praying that it would not be bad news. He only needed to skim the first lines, however, to know that particular prayer would not be answered. His deep gasp caused Marek to turn and watch him. But when Tadeusz said nothing and turned to look out the window, Marek left the attic.

The fury that burned through Tadeusz at that moment felt all the more intense because it stirred up the old anger, first kindled when he had found Tomasz's body, then later fed by the treatment he had received on the train heading south to Kraków.

He read through the letter one more time, forcing himself to shut out the images summoned by the words. But he could imagine too clearly the events Henryk described. The late-night raid on the street outside their home, his father's objections to the restaurant's being taken over, one shot, his mother's screams, then another shot—all details witnessed by a neighbor shivering behind a curtain across the street and later told to Henryk.

Tadeusz carefully folded the letter along the same lines Henryk had, then placed it in an ashtray and threw a lit match on top of it. Then he went down the three flights to the basement, fully intending to work until he dropped, if that's what it took to numb the pain.

A week later Tadeusz found himself listening to Hanna's voice, remembering it as if he had not heard it for a very long time, as she asked him to go to the market with her. And then they were caught in the British air raid, and something important changed. The whine of the alarms that rang through the city, the crash of rubble falling, the panic he felt when he realized Hanna was out there in the midst of it—all served to crystallize his love for Hanna and his determination to seek revenge.

There was only the one question still needing to be resolved, however, before he could execute his plan. And as Hanna answered it for him following the raid, even as the streetlights flickered, dimmed, and went out, Tadeusz knew finally that the grief which fed his hatred would have to find some other release.

He walked her home through dark streets and handed her over to a vastly relieved Johann and Helena. The air raid had caused the gas, water, and electricity to be turned off.

The very next day Johann once again invited Tadeusz to the prayer meeting, and this time he accepted. Even before he knew the secret behind Johann's strange disappearances, Tadeusz had noticed the family's willingness to give, to help others, and also their serenity of spirit. Whatever they had, he wanted as well.

Now he, too, bowed his head and prayed as the others had, in expectation. He lay his anger and sense of betrayal before God, and did not realize his cheeks were wet until he felt Johann's hand rest gently on his shoulder. That day had marked the beginning of a new way of enduring the war.

It was in this place, then, that Tadeusz had chosen for

himself to follow the teachings of Jesus. His father-in-law taught him that the cost was high, but Tadeusz was willing to pay the price. Slowly, very slowly, he noticed himself changing. His love for Hanna became more intense, and the hatred for the Germans took on a new form, easing somehow.

Tadeusz was deeply touched by the sincerity of the people who met regularly for those prayer meetings. Week after week he watched as grown men bowed their heads, murmuring "amen" to the prayers Johann offered up. There seemed to be a real, comforting presence in the room. He did not understand the difference between the religion he had grown up with and the vital faith these men and women seemed to live on.

When Tadeusz asked Hanna to marry him and Johann confronted him, for the first and only time, with the fact of their religious differences, Tadeusz did as Hanna was teaching him. He prayed for guidance, clear guidance. He felt he had only the memories of parents to tie him to the church of his upbringing. Living with the Müllers, he had learned to share their faith, so that by the time he and Hanna married, he was attending the small Brethren church every Sunday. Somehow he felt his parents would not have disapproved, since he was himself at peace with the decision.

Once he and Hanna were married, that peace expanded, touching all aspects of Tadeusz's life. The three short months he shared with Hanna as her husband were steeped in peace, despite the war, and despite the threat of separation that hung over them.

But then he had met the dark stranger, whose secret posed a great enough danger to his and Hanna's fragile joy to shatter his peace. Tadeusz had not dared to tell Hanna about the encounter, though he knew she suspected. The less she knew, the better he could protect her. He hoped.

A few weeks later, as if the meeting had been a precursor of evil, Tadeusz found himself bringing Hanna and her mother to the Kraków train station. And now his heart cried out, when, when will I see her?

Tadeusz shook himself back to the present.

"And, Lord," his father-in-law's voice droned on, "we pray for our enemies, as You taught us to."

Tadeusz was startled by the silence around him. He opened his eyes. Johann sat quietly, his eyes remained closed. It was Tadeusz's turn. With time and Hanna's love, Tadeusz had learned to pray out loud, although he did not like doing it with anyone but her. Now, he started to speak, "For Hanna, for her mother, for their safety, for the baby Hanna carries, please protect them from harm. Please. God, I beg You," Tadeusz's voice cracked on the last word.

Then he stopped. The sound of crashing wood had burst in upon them. Downstairs someone was breaking down the front door. Angry voices charged up the stairs. Tadeusz and his father-in-law stood.

# 6

## JANUARY 1942–JULY 1944

Jacek had spent most of the trip back from Stalingrad forcing himself to emerge from the cocoon of beliefs he had woven around himself during his two years in Soviet camps. Somewhere under the layers of assumed identity he had discovered the significance of a post office box numbered 77. With that memory had come others, a flood, until by the time he was approaching Brześć, Jacek thought he knew who he was.

But although he did go straight to the main post office when he arrived in Brześć, he did not immediately approach post office box 77. Since it was already after the first of a new year, there should have been new orders waiting for him. But the Soviet commandant had told him the box would be watched. He hoped the drop point had not somehow become a trap.

So Jacek staked out the post office, pretending to sleep on a bench near the boxes, watching the area to see if anyone else might be doing the same. He did not have much trouble, since he certainly looked the part of the many transients sleeping in doorways along that street. He had no key, but he pulled out a thin wire he had found attached to an appliance in a pile of garbage. This he twisted and inserted into the box's lock, all the while keeping an eye on both entrances to the area. Should anyone actually enter, he already knew he would slouch to the floor and feign a drunken stupor.

Jacek turned the wire twice to the right and let out his breath when he felt the lock give. After one more check over his shoulder he slowly opened the door, half expecting it to be booby-trapped. Then he put his hand inside and pulled out a letter with a Russian stamp on the envelope and one small slip of paper. The paper was dated January, but not 1941 or even 1942, but 1940. On it were the words in Polish: "Welcome back. Knew you'd make it. Proceed to Kraków same number and follow original plan."

The original plan would be the orders he had received in Warszawa. The letter he was not so sure about. Jacek moved the hand holding it up and down. As he did so, a strange tingling sensation ran up his spine. He whirled, half expecting to see someone watching him, ready to grab him, but there was no one. Then he looked down at his hand. No, the strange feeling came from the letter.

He quickly shoved it into his shirt and walked out of the building. On the way he passed one of the local police with his dog. As the dog brushed past him he held his breath, waiting for the bark and rough hands, which never came. Once he was outside, the cold hit Jacek in the face and he turned into it, the letter burning hotly against his chest.

A few streets farther, when he was certain no one had followed him, Jacek entered a deserted schoolyard and sat down on one of the benches. The hand taking out the letter trembled, then ripped into the thin envelope. The cheap newsprint paper that came out between his thumb and forefinger confirmed every one of the fears Jacek had just spent the walk from the post office facing.

He saw the words without reading them, words he

could no longer remember writing, but which he knew by heart, and knew could just as well have cost him his life:

> The tribunal sentenced me to ten years. The weather here is quite warm for March. Give my love to Mother. Jacek.

He began to smell the hole in that first camp again, to feel the headache from lack of oxygen. Then he summoned the strength of will to thrust all such memories back into the dark spaces he had assigned them. To function again, Jacek concentrated on the significance of his note having survived, having never been claimed.

Above all else, it meant he was alone. Jacek had never known how many American or even Allied military intelligence gatherers there were in Poland. He had not even known anything about the means by which his information was channeled out of the country, or who his contact had been in Warszawa. But it was clear that he had lost his original contact in Brześć. And whoever that had been, he had not been replaced, since the paper with his orders was put in the box just after the outbreak of war.

A tremendous sense of abandonment washed over Jacek, not at all what he thought he should be feeling at the moment. He would have expected anger or disbelief, not the haunting thought that in all the war, in all the world, he stood alone and cut off. The only person who could have connected him with all the other people in his life had disappeared. Now even Barbara could become nothing more than the fantasy he had lived with for so long.

Jacek's eyes fell on the slip of paper with his orders. So G–2 had known he was captured. *How had they known he would make it?* he wondered. And he was supposed to go to Kraków. The thought that someone might be waiting for him there offered itself as consolation.

The strange emotion Jacek had just experienced fell away as he started to consider his possibilities. Where else could he go, really, except Kraków? How could he get out of the country? The only identification papers he had were the Soviet naturalization papers they had issued him when he left Stalingrad. He had no money and knew no one.

Jacek resolved to follow his orders. It was his only chance of finding someone who could get him out of this quagmire.

---

It had not been difficult for Jacek to leave Brześć and head south toward Kraków. Those returning from camps in Russia made up an entire segment of the population moving across the country, branching out from the east into all the corners from which they had been taken. They sought home as they remembered it and were lucky to find even one person from their displaced past. Jacek fit in well with the rest as he walked through the countryside and rode on top of freight cars. Between cities he ate by scrounging from the fields and stealing from farms; in the towns he stole from shops and went through the rubbish piled on the streets.

Once he arrived in Kraków, Jacek quickly repeated his routine from the Brześć post office. To his dismay, he found post office box 77 empty. But then he realized the note in Brześć might have meant this was his drop point. Jacek left a few words scribbled on the back of an old newspaper: "March 1942—am doing as ordered. Anyone home?"

Then Jacek began to roam the streets of Kraków, listening to gossip and asking few questions. He wandered around the narrow alleys, retraining himself to watch and eavesdrop, doing what was necessary to get himself established in the new city.

He had long since stolen a pair of trousers and shirt from a wash line and discarded the old prison-issue rags, so he now no longer looked the part of a refugee. Then he found a place to stay, with an old woman who had not been picked up with the rest of her family when the Germans broke into her home. She had happened to be gone when the Gestapo staged their raid. Now, finding herself alone in a huge house, she was only too glad to take in the young man who knocked at her door and said he had noticed she had no family and would she like a lodger? She had not even asked how he knew she lived alone. Some days Jacek managed to earn money by helping farmers unload their goods at the market. When they gave him produce instead of złotys, he gave this to his landlady.

Once Jacek had taken care of his food, shelter, and clothing, nothing else stood in the way of his pursuing the same mission he had begun on a battlefield just east of the River Bug—becoming involved with the Polish Underground.

In the end it was the Germans who helped him meet the partisans. On the night of April 7, 1942, the Nazis ordered a blackout from 8:45 in the evening until 4:55 the next morning. Jacek figured darkness would provide the ideal cover for finding out what was really happening in the Kazimierz quarter, where he suspected the Resistance was based. He set out around nine in the evening to see what he could find.

To Jacek's surprise, he found a school, hidden and secret and very Polish. When the war began, the Nazis had stamped out all forms of Polish political and cultural organizations. They had disbanded Polish societies and closed secondary and postsecondary schools. As early as November 6, 1939, the Gestapo had closed and sealed libraries, reserving the Jagiellonian for Germans only. A month later the Germans had ordered all Polish history and geography books to be taken from Polish children at Kraków schools, then a month later they had gathered and destroyed all remaining schoolbooks.

On this particular night more than two years later, Jacek discovered the Polish way of meeting that challenge. As he walked down streets where no lights shone, he suddenly knew he was not alone. By now he no longer had to consciously check if someone was following him; he did it instinctively. Now the "click, click-click" behind him of someone's broken heel refused to fade. The more he wound in and out of the small streets, the surer he became that it was no coincidence he walked in this neighborhood and was not alone that night, despite the curfew.

Finally he ducked into a doorway, and instantly the clicking sound ceased. When he poked his head out to squint into the darkness, a rough hand grabbed him from behind the neck.

"So you're not as good as you thought," a guttural voice muttered in Polish. "Don't even think about fighting me." And before Jacek could challenge the stranger, he felt something hard, round, and narrow poke into his side.

"Tell me what you're doing out here."

Jacek took a deep breath and then an even greater gamble. For weeks he had waited for just this sort of encounter, and now he knew he had to play his hand boldly. "In this part of the city, or on this particular night?"

The man's next word confirmed he had been found by the right side. "We've seen you nosing around."

"I'm out here to find another way to fight this war. I

thought you might find some use for me."

He felt the grip around his neck ease slightly. "Why would we do that? What can you do?"

With nothing else to fall back on, Jacek used the same cover he had used when he first joined up with the Polesie Reserve Army Grouping. "I'm a mathematics teacher."

Silence. Then, a guffaw and hard clap on the back. "Well, I don't know how this happened, but you're just what I was in the market for. Literally. Meet me back at the big church." The hand released Jacek, and he waited just a second before turning, but whoever it was had already slipped into the shadows.

Jacek felt suspicious that it had been so easy to make contact, but he knew he still would be watched. He wasn't in yet.

Jacek headed for Corpus Christi, the huge brick and stone church with one tower. When he reached it, Jacek walked along the stone wall, then stopped at the door with expanding diamonds carved into its front. Within seconds a man with a moustache appeared from the opposite direction. He spoke with the same guttural tones as the man who had caught up with him in the doorway, "Follow me back to the monastery." He unlocked the gate, and the two men walked through the covered gallery linking the church with the monastery. Once inside, Jacek found a network of meeting rooms, all full of young people, all very quiet. It had never occurred to him that the church would house a school.

The man with the moustache introduced himself as Karol. "I am one of the professors here, and if you check out we would be more than glad to welcome you on board."

"Isn't this a little—"

"Dangerous?" Karol finished for him. "Showing you

this, or meeting in one place? Yes to both questions. I'll know if you can betray us soon enough, but that doesn't worry me. Now you're here, and what you see around you is the result of trying out different ideas." He paused and waved at the room. "This has not been a good one. So many students under one roof is just too risky. After tonight our university meets in small groups, and in different locations every night."

"University?" Jacek asked. The other man nodded.

"At this point we can only offer a degree in the Polish language. Soon we hope to offer degrees in mathematics, law, philosophy, and medicine. So you see why we can use you."

Within a few weeks Jacek was busy almost every day and most evenings, giving classes at both the secondary school and university levels. He was kept running from one corner of the city to the other, always meeting with small groups of students, often in their living rooms, sometimes in the back rooms of shops or the cellars of restaurants.

Teaching mathematics was not really what Jacek had had in mind when he imagined himself fighting with Polish partisans. But for the rest of that year, at least, that seemed to be where they wanted him. He suspected they spent some of that time checking out his story, as much as they were able to, and watching to see if he was indeed trustworthy. He concentrated on proving himself so.

During the first week of 1943 Jacek revisited his post office box and found his note gone. In its place was a package with various identification papers for both German and Polish nationalities. The latter accredited him as the mathematics teacher he had been before he disappeared into the Soviet Union. Karol would be glad to see he had "found" his degrees.

With the package was a typewritten note explaining in code that G–2 had handed him over to something called the Office of Strategic Services. He had begun his career working for the army. Now he was working in an organization devoted primarily to sabotage, espionage, counterespionage, covert action, and subversion. Yet all the change from G–2 to OSS meant for Jacek in real terms was that he now had support, that someone knew where he was and what he was doing. The note stated simply, in English,

> Same orders as before. Leave reports in old code every 31st, as needed. You're not alone. Karl."

Jacek felt immensely relieved to receive the message and know he was connected again. This time he found it reassuring to know that someone might be watching him. He did not dare ask himself why there had been no letters from Barbara in the package.

---

Ever since beginning his work at the underground university, Jacek had let it be known that he was willing to do more for the Resistance than teach. "We'll be needing fresh faces soon enough," one of the men had answered. This was Felek, tall with red hair and a very broad chest. True to his word, he enlisted Jacek's help early in 1943.

The Germans had started off that year by holding frequent roundups in the black market and on trains. They arrested more people than ever before, packing them off to factories in Germany or, worse, to the concentration camps.

By the first of March the situation had come to a head, with one curious twist. Whole streets full of people were reported missing, but no one had seen them go anywhere. The Kraków Home Army had lookouts posted at the main train station, but for the last week or so, no one had seen any large transports. Nonetheless the arrests had continued and even intensified. Where were these people disappearing to?

Felek gave Jacek the job of finding out how the Nazis were managing to get such vast numbers of people out of the city without anyone noticing. After almost a year with the Home Army, Jacek was glad for the chance finally to prove himself. He had discovered it was not easy to find out who was who in the Underground. In fact, Felek was the only officer Jacek had met. When he asked why, Felek said they tried to minimize the number of people each person might betray if captured. One thing was certain. The only ones to hold leadership positions were those who could lead, *and* take the greatest risks. Jacek hoped Felek's mission would give him a chance to impress his superiors, whoever they might be.

For months already, there had been an area in the eastern part of the city where the Germans seemed intent on building something behind long rows of high fence. So on the particular night Felek gave him the assignment, Jacek headed east.

He had to wait several hours and follow the fence nearly halfway around the city center before he could see what was on the other side. There were guard dogs growling and barking at him whenever he came too close, so for the most part he kept his distance.

By a small tributary of the Wisła River called the Białucha, however, Jacek managed to find a way under the fence and through the water, and he could hear no dogs nearby. Crossing at that point meant getting wet, but it was worth it. For once Jacek reached the other side and climbed past the thorny bushes there, he noticed a set of railway tracks. At first he thought these were simply the tracks heading westward out of the city. Then he took a closer look and saw an extra set of tracks swinging to the north. And alongside it was a partially built track, almost completed.

Jacek followed the tracks a short way until he was sure of what he had found. This was a new railway route, heading east to west, almost certainly built for the purpose of shipping prisoners out of the city unnoticed.

Jacek looked around and found himself in an open field. Just as he was thinking it was probably time to get out of the rail yard, a shift in the breeze brought him the sound of a crying child. He stopped and turned full circle to locate the direction of the sound. Then he followed it until he reached a small copse of trees.

He was now standing somewhere near the railway tracks again. On the other side of the trees, a few hundred yards farther on, Jacek saw lights and a small crowd of people. When he heard dogs barking, he was almost ready to turn back, but then he saw they did not face his way. Jacek edged closer, counting on the trees to give him the cover he needed.

Jacek saw the boy whose cries had caught the night wind. He wore round, black glasses and shin-length trousers and was still sobbing. Around him stood women with scarves, bundles tied with four strands of rope, and other children with shawls around their shoulders. About seven German soldiers stood around them in a semicircle; two held dogs. The soldiers were yelling something, and the women were shaking their heads. Jacek could just barely make out the letters on the train behind them all: *Deutsche Reichsbahn, Karlsruhe, 34234.*

Then, as he watched, the soldiers let their dogs go. Growling, both Dobermans lunged at the boy. They knocked the child flat just as one of the women screamed and threw herself into the struggle. The rest of the small group edged past the scene and boarded the train. The woman thrashed at the dog with her feet, kicking him in the stomach until he let the boy go and turned on her instead. In the struggle the boy's glasses flew off his face. Jacek breathed hard, transfixed by what he saw. Somehow the woman managed to haul the boy to his feet and throw him at the waiting hands stretched out through the train door. Limping and crying, the woman heaved herself into the car after him. One of the Nazis slid the door closed and padlocked it shut, laughing over his shoulder at his comrades. Then he hit his palm against the door twice and yelled up at the engine.

Too late, Jacek now saw why the dogs had let the woman go. Their attention turned elsewhere, they stood sniffing the air, and now they were facing his direction. Jacek eased himself backward, into the trees, cursing under his breath as he tripped over a log. Then he scrambled to his feet. As he heard the train pull away, Jacek shot one last glance behind him. What he saw only confirmed his fears. The dogs had picked up his scent and were headed his way.

Jacek started to run. Blindly he dashed through the trees, back in the direction he had just come. His first impulse was to take the shortest route to the fence, but he knew, and had to tell himself now, that it would only trap him. Besides, it was precisely where they wanted him to go. No, his only hope was to reach the river and get out under the fencing there, the same way he had entered the complex.

Just before Jacek reached the meadow, he heard men's voices shouting in German. They were gaining on him. He crashed through the undergrowth, each breath tearing into his chest. Already the dogs' barks seemed too close. Jacek faced the meadow, desperate to be across the open area. Despite the lack of moonlight, he knew that once he hit the grass he would be an easy target for his pursuers, and the dogs would be able to run much faster.

Jacek gasped; he had no choice. He could not afford the time to circumvent the meadow. So he took off, forcing his muscles to throw his legs forward. Midway across the field he knew he would not make it. He did not dare waste the energy to look back, but he could tell by their higher pitched barking that the Dobermans had also reached the edge of the trees and were even at that moment lunging toward him. He fully expected them to be snapping at his heels any second.

Still, Jacek kept running. Then a gunshot ripped into the night air, steaming past him. Jacek lunged to the right, then to the left, frustrating the dogs even further as he managed to put some distance between them. He thought he saw a movement in the bushes that marked the end of the meadow. Was he really that close?

Another shot flew by him. But this time, Jacek had seen the flare of the shot coming from directly in front of him.

He heard one of the dogs yelp. He ran on, barely able to breathe, then dove into the berry bushes. On all fours, the thorns ripping his face, Jacek crawled down the embankment toward the water. Behind him he could hear more gunshots, more shouts, but no dogs. He stumbled into the small river and slid down in the mud. Panting hard, he gulped one huge breath and let himself down into the water, then wiggled under the fencing as he had less than a half hour earlier.

On the other side he clawed his way up the other bank, only to have his hand met by another. Too weak to be surprised, Jacek grabbed hold of the outstretched wrist and heaved himself up the bank. Only then did Jacek look up as the other man's strength rolled him onto his back so he could catch his breath.

He squinted into the darkness and recognized Felek's voice, "Close call, friend. Let's go."

Jacek dragged himself upright and felt Felek's arm go around him. One part of him concentrated on not tripping, while another part realized that Felek must have been following him. He wondered if Felek was there to check on him, to back him up, or both.

With Felek's help, Jacek managed to work his way through the streets, heading south. Once or twice they stopped to listen and to let Jacek regain his wind. Although the two men met no one along the way and heard nothing, they still did not speak until they saw Corpus Christi looming ahead of them.

They both relaxed somewhat, believing it was just a matter of minutes before they reached the safety of the cellar rooms in the monastery. When they came to the crossing with Ulica Szeroka, however, a high-pitched scream caused them both to flatten their backs against the brick wall.

"To the right, at the end of the street," Felek whispered.

Jacek nodded. He had recovered and could move on his own now. He was just about to suggest they go look when another scream, followed by a single shot, split what was fast becoming the end of the night. Felek grabbed his arm and charged down the street.

As Jacek followed him, he was impressed that such a large man could run so noiselessly. Felek's head wagged back and forth, and the big boots he wore must have been hitting the cobblestones hard, but Jacek heard nothing.

Jacek knew that the old Remuh cemetery was situated at the end of this street. He did not like the fact that the sounds they had been hearing came from a place full of centuries-old Jewish tombs.

Without a word Jacek and Felek crossed to the left side of the street and crouched down, edging their way closer to the cemetery gate. They could hear voices, men and women pleading. They crept forward and crouched behind a row of sarcophagi, and only then could they hear the actual words.

A man's voice, "You have no right!"

A woman, "God save us!"

Both were answered with coarse laughter from the SS officer who stood with his back to Felek and Jacek. Behind him they could see about sixty people milling around.

At the sound of the man's voice, however, Jacek's breath had caught in his throat. The man was speaking English.

"I tell you our government will hear of this!"

"And who will them tell?" The SS officer spoke thickly.

Jacek searched Felek's face and saw him struggling to understand the foreign words. Then Felek turned and cupped his hands around Jacek's ear, *"Po angielsku?"*

Jacek nodded. The language was English all right, but Felek could not have known that the accent was American. Jacek felt a chill run up his spine as he heard his own mother tongue for the first time in almost four years. He felt confused by a purer loyalty to these people than he had known earlier that night, when the guard dogs had attacked that boy.

Questions battered him. *Were these more of his people? Did his contact stand there somewhere? Who were they actually? Tourists, students, U.S. embassy personnel?*

"We should do something." He squeezed Felek's shoulder.

The other man looked at Jacek curiously. His red eyebrows shot up as he shook his head. "Of course we should, but look around you. Are you crazy?" He nodded toward the ground in front of the man who seemed to be speaking for the rest of the group.

Jacek noticed for the first time that a body lay there. The body of a man. He looked around and counted nearly forty Nazi soldiers, noting they were all heavily armed. He should have known. Felek was still looking at Jacek when the shooting began.

Both men backed away instinctively, but could not help watching spellbound as the soldiers moved forward in a line, advancing on the crowd, shooting with every step they took. They backed the Americans up against a wall and kept shooting round after round after round until the bodies lay piled on top of each other, still twitching after death.

Throughout the entire six minutes it took to kill all those people, Jacek's ears burned with the familiar sounds of his own language, "George!"

"Oh, God, no!"

"Help us someone. Stop! We're Americans!"

Jacek shook with emotion, his face flushed. He covered his ears and wondered how had he possibly landed here, of all places and times? What on earth had happened?

Silence finally brought him back to himself. He had

closed his eyes without even knowing it. When he finally opened them, he saw the SS officer standing with one shiny black boot on the head of a dead woman while several soldiers went through the corpses' pockets.

Jacek still felt unsteady. Even as the question *why?* rang through his thoughts, the SS officer answered it for him. As his men handed over the watches and rings and cash they had found on the bodies, the officer turned in Jacek and Felek's direction and snorted, *"Juden!"*

Jacek felt sick to his stomach. So they had been American Jews. When the German soldiers had finally left the cemetery, Jacek swallowed hard. "Do we bury them?" he asked.

"No, they'll see to that." Felek looked up at the windows of the homes bordering the cemetery. "There are enough of them left where they can still take care of their own." Jacek could already see the curtains moving. Only then did he realize the long night was over. As dawn broke he had no trouble seeing the wreckage before him or the Hebrew letters on the stone he was leaning against.

"We must go, my friend." For the second time that night, Felek helped Jacek to his feet and guided him toward the monastery. This time they arrived without incident, and since the curfew was over and they did not seem in any danger, Jacek left Felek there and went on to the old woman's house where he rented a room. He was only too glad to sink into the bed that awaited him.

---

Whatever the test had been on the night of March first, Jacek seemed to have passed it. Soon he was doing regular reconnaissance jobs around the city. There was plenty to report as the occupying Germans continued the process of emptying the city of Jews and others deemed undesirable, and the Resistance workers continued their steady work of sabotaging the Germans.

In one night, the Germans wiped out the entire Jewish ghetto in Podgórze. About two thousand men, women, and children were killed. Many of the sick were murdered in bed. The Germans arrested the remaining three thousand and put them on the same train line Jacek had seen. By the next morning no traces were even left of the ghetto. It was as if it had never existed.

This event only strengthened the resolve of the men and women working in the Kraków Underground. Several operations were set into motion. One involved the shooting, in mid-April, of a Gestapo head named Friedrich Wilhelm Krüger. The plan backfired, however, and according to Felek, the worst part was that the Germans had positively identified all four of the men involved, including himself. When Jacek asked for details, Felek first warned him that that had been half the problem—too much had been said about the plan in the first place. Felek swore they would never make the same mistake again.

During all these events, and over the months to come, Jacek settled into an easy schedule of moving from meeting place to meeting place, teaching, going out on his reconnaissance missions, then eating and sleeping in the old woman's house. Sometimes whole days passed when the daily routine lulled him into a feeling of security. It granted him a measure of comfort, in contrast to the pain of his prison years. And Jacek discovered, to his surprise, that teaching gave him a great deal of pleasure.

In January 1944 this period of experiencing the war as a backdrop for his own healing came to an abrupt end. Jacek had allowed himself to become a teacher and a low-key Resistance fighter. At the same time, he was aware that he needed to seek the Underground leadership more aggressively. So it was that by the time he approached the post office box after New Year's, he was just regaining himself to the point that he could acknowledge it was time to go back to being a full-time spy.

What he found radically shook the frame of mind he had managed to erect for himself since arriving in Kraków. While the rest of the world around him seemed caught up in events beyond their control, it only took one piece of paper to send Jacek's world spinning back from reality. The life he had come to think he controlled, just as he could the outcomes of the formulas he taught, now once again was threatening to retreat.

What he found was a notice of divorce.

If he had been thinking clearly, anticipating as he had before the war, his cynical side would have seen this coming. Instead, the weakness exposed in Artemovsk had blinded Jacek to the probable, while goading him into believing what had, after all, only been a dream.

No letters accompanied the carbon copy. Scribbled on top was a message in ink:

> 1944—carry on same deep-sleep mission. Should wake up soon. Sorry about the enclosed. Richard

Karl, then Richard. *So the war should end soon,* was Jacek's first thought. There was nothing new in that prediction. He folded up the paper and slipped it numbly into his pocket, telling himself he would read it in his room back at the house. At that moment he did not care if somebody stopped him and wanted to know why he happened to be carrying a divorce decree issued in Boston, Massachusetts.

Once Jacek was alone and had perused the few paragraphs several times, he lit a match and held it to the corner of the decree. The grounds stated for the divorce were absenteeism. Five years after the fact, he was still asking himself why he had not resisted this manipulation of his life and hers. He could have left, said no, stopped. The words *what if?* resounded through his thoughts like a death knell. What if he had remained in Boston, become a professor? What if he had said no to Jones, or come home when war broke out? Now there was no going back.

Not to Barbara, anyway.

Once his divorce from Barbara was a known factor, Jacek had little trouble accepting it. That in itself surprised him. Was the reason he did not resist this latest seemingly arranged event the same as in the past? Or was he relieved finally to have nothing that might hold him back from doing what he wanted?

---

When weeks went by during which Jacek forgot about the divorce, forgot about Barbara even, he finally had to accept that for the last five years she had been nothing but a fixation, a focal point when the rest of the world had spun in pain. And he reminded himself that he had also forgotten her for months at a time during his first year in Poland. If he had been honest he would have left her behind then, when he was still somewhat in control, during that period which had ended on the day he roared out of Warszawa on his motorcycle.

Now, finally, he regained some of that same control. And with time he learned to view Barbara's divorce as a final push in the direction he had been heading ever since he returned to Poland. Jacek knew who he was, now more so than ever. He became more assertive around Felek, almost demanding to be included in the action. He said he wanted to take more risks.

Felek did not question Jacek's change in attitude. Too many of the young people who came to the Resistance were hot-headed with hate. Felek already knew Jacek had far greater control, and thereby, the potential to be much more effective. He had just been waiting for Jacek to reach the same conclusion.

"I wondered how long it would take for you to get over the camps. I think it's time you met Ina. She's in charge of special operations."

"She?"

"She."

Jacek's introduction to Ina brought him face-to-face with an issue he had not been willing to face when he was still married to Barbara. He had not been with a woman for five years. The intangible bond with Barbara was only partially the reason. It had also been a matter of logistics. In the camps it had been impossible. Before and after that he hadn't met anyone he liked, and he could not bring himself to pay a woman, although enough had offered.

When Felek showed Jacek into a room where a small woman sat behind a table full of maps, Jacek found himself reflecting that circumstances no longer prevented another involvement. In other words, he liked Ina.

He began to work with her, planning, using the training that military intelligence had taught him and passing it on to her. Together they set up a plan to assassinate a Gestapo officer named Koppe. The operation was set to take place in July.

Months before that time, Jacek and Ina had already become lovers.

Ina kept her brown hair bobbed short. Jacek liked her

smallness. She fit well into his arms, into the life he had shaped for himself. She was the only one he ever told about the experiences in Artemovsk and Stalingrad. She had some stories of her own to tell, which explained her cold decisiveness whenever she was plotting yet another attack on the Germans. Jacek had never met anyone who could stay as calculatingly cool as Ina.

Even on the night before the Koppe attack was due to take place, Ina fell asleep within five minutes of curling herself up against Jacek's side. He had put his arm around her, and when he heard Ina's steady breathing, he thought how he had never felt more awake. Their plan tomorrow was as risky as anything the Underground had tried since he joined their ranks, and Jacek's heart pounded with the idea that they might pull it off.

Jacek looked down at Ina and smelled her hair. His arm was going numb, but as he gently pulled it out from under her, she opened her eyes.

"Do you love me?" she asked in her child's voice.

Jacek raised an eyebrow. Neither he nor Ina had ever brought up the subject of commitment in their relationship. All such concepts belonged to that impalpable time entitled "after the war."

"Of course I love you," he said. "I'm here, right?"

She put her head on his chest so he couldn't see her face. "We're both here," she said.

Jacek was quiet for a moment, wondering what she wanted from him.

"Tomorrow . . ." she began, but her voice trailed off.

"Tomorrow we both have a big day, so we both should get some sleep." Jacek wasn't sure he liked where the conversation might go. To his surprise Ina laughed, something he seldom heard her do.

She raised herself up on one elbow and smiled down at him. "We are so alike, you and I. Both afraid of the same things, both running from similar ghosts. Don't worry, my love, I won't push. But I do wonder sometimes . . ."

"Wonder what?" Jacek could not help himself. The faraway look in her eyes would not let him go.

"I wonder what we, as in you and I together, would have been like if we had met when there was no war." She paused, then laughed again."Shopping and wallpaper, babies maybe."

"Working nine to five in a school, meals and summer walks together." They both laughed, then stopped. The picture hurt. And neither could voice the thought that followed—that they had both been in the war so long that they could no longer picture themselves living normal lives.

Ina whispered reluctantly, "We've sunk so far, I don't even know your real name."

Jacek felt her confusion, but it did not fit within the parameters of their relationship. Neither of them had ever asked the other for the truth, and Jacek wasn't about to start now. He brought a finger up to Ina's lips and said, "Shh," then took her into his arms. "Not now. We don't need that, not you and I."

So, instead, Jacek and Ina clung to the comfort they could give each other. On this night, as on so many others, they both resolved to feel nothing but grateful for the touching, the talk, the other's presence. It was miracle enough.

---

The Koppe plan involved five other people besides Jacek and Ina. And these five only found out about their roles three days before it was scheduled to happen.

On July 11, 1944, the partisans took up their various positions around the Wawel Castle, or Krakauer Bung, as the Germans had renamed it. Ina posted herself between Ulica Grodzka and Ulica Bernardyńska. The attack was due to take place on the road running parallel to Bernardyńska street.

They had studied Koppe's movements and knew he always took this route at that time of day. Three of the seven served as lookouts. The others, including Jacek and Ina, concealed arms under their coats and stationed themselves across from each other, so that when Koppe's car drove by, they could catch him in a cross fire.

A man with the code name Rayski was the first to notice the black Mercedes as it turned down Ulica Stradam. He began to signal to Jacek, who was the closest. Jacek saw him wave a red handkerchief, but then Jacek swore out loud. Shots were being fired from somewhere nearby. The handkerchief fluttered upward with the wind and the man Rayski crumpled down to the ground.

Even as he turned to warn the others, Jacek saw the SS vans pulling into the street. How was it possible? The Gestapo had known just when and where to strike. They must have been tipped off.

Jacek caught sight of Ina's face as she poked it out of a doorway to see what had happened. She was too far away for him to call to; shouting would have just drawn attention to them both.

Jacek stared at his lover, willing her to look his way. When she did, their eyes locked. And Jacek knew, knew by the cold air that settled between them, that he could not save her.

A heartbeat later he was racing down the alleyways,

back to the relative safety of the Kazimierz quarter. He knew these streets so well now that it did not take long for him to become certain that no one was following. He had escaped and perhaps even escaped unnoticed. He wondered if he should have remained behind and helped the others. No, they had all agreed that if something went wrong, they should separate and follow different escape routes.

So Jacek did not know, until Felek visited him late that night, whether any of the others had made it back. As soon as he opened the back door of the house, though, the answer was clear in the grim set of Felek's mouth.

"Come in," he said to Felek.

"The old lady?"

"Asleep in the back."

Felek bowed his head to fit through the doorway. Once inside, Jacek closed the door behind him and the two men stood in the kitchen darkness. Jacek made no move to light the candle on the table.

"You know then," Felek said softly.

"That no one else made it, no, I didn't know. But I guessed as much when I saw the number of vans they brought to pick us up with." He paused, then asked, "Ina?"

"Not dead, at least not yet." Felek took a deep breath in stages. "She and two others were arrested. Three are dead. She was the best."

"I know."

More silence, until Jacek thought he could read the other man's thoughts. "Do you know who tipped them off?"

"Could have been anyone. Who is there to trust anymore?"

Jacek knew he had to be careful. "But not anyone knew.

Just a few knew. I . . . Ina . . ." His voice trailed off. At that very moment her horror stories, the few she had related, came back to him. Now she had one more, probably right now, God knew what they were doing to her.

Jacek shook his head and was surprised to find that Felek had moved very close to him. He could feel the other man's breath against his cheek as Felek watched him carefully. "What is it?" Jacek asked.

"I have something for you."

Wildly, Jacek thought Felek was going to accuse him of being the traitor. Why not? After all, he was the only one to escape safely. He put up his hands in a defensive motion and nearly struck Felek when the man grabbed one of his hands with his own, holding on with an ironclad grip.

Felek's other hand shoved something cold over Jacek's little finger. "Easy, we're on the same side, remember? This was hers; now it's yours. It goes with the job, head of special operations. Congratulations," he said grimly.

Before Jacek could react, Felek had already opened the door and walked outside. Then, as if he had just remembered something, he turned and said to Jacek, "I found it in the gutter where it must have rolled when they grabbed her. She knew what she was doing."

"You were watching?"

"No, I came afterward. After they had left I walked over to look at the spot where she should have been standing. And I found this. The problem is I still don't know who gave us away." Felek sighed. *"Dobranoc."*

Jacek closed the door behind him and locked it. As he climbed up the stairs to his room, his right hand rubbed against the ring on his left. There was some sort of emblem or seal on the front. Behind the closed and shuttered windows of his room he finally dared to light a lamp. When he held his hand near the flame he could make out a small Polish eagle with a crown and flowers on both sides.

It was a ring for an officer in the Polish Home Army. So he had made it. He was in.

Now its metal caught the light as it bounced off his wedding ring, a piece of gold not even the Russians had managed to steal, too thin and too tightly clamped around his finger. The two rings lay lifelessly beside each other, like two loves, lost and undiscovered.

# 7

## Early January 1945

Hanna rolled over on her side. It was still very early. She lit the candle by her bed and watched Tadeusz sleeping. Despite his blond hair, the stubble covering his chin and neck was dark. She adored watching his face, the long nose and high cheekbones, the fine hair at his eyebrows. They had been man and wife for just over two months, and Hanna still felt intense joy every morning she woke up and found him snoring softly next to her. Now the thought that they might soon be separated made the moment even more dear.

The big house was quiet. Hanna doubted if even her parents were up yet. Tadeusz sighed and rolled onto his back, both arms bent at the elbows and his hands under his head. Hanna thought he looked so vulnerable, like a child. And yet he was the one who gave her the confidence to be that way, and to trust him. She ran one finger very softly over his chest, tracing the patterns of light hair growing there.

Tadeusz sighed louder, "Poor me." He smiled and opened one eye. "How is it that you always wake up before I do?"

In answer, Hanna lifted her face and kissed his chin and cheeks, finally his lips. "Would you rather wake up some other way?"

"It could be worse," Tadeusz grinned and scratched his chin. Then he groaned and rolled over to look at the clock ticking on the table by their bed.

The bed itself was actually a sofa that folded out. Since the room had been Hanna's bedroom before she married, it was cluttered with signs from her childhood: a small white desk in the corner, a mirror with hair ribbons hanging from the corners, one wall lined with bookshelves, white and yellow curtains, posters of ballerinas on the opposite wall.

Tadeusz liked the room. He felt it helped him get to know Hanna better. On the small table next to the clock lay an open Bible. In the evenings Hanna read to Tadeusz from it before they fell asleep.

But that wasn't what Tadeusz was looking at now. He picked up the clock and brought it closer to his face. "Do you know what time it is? I thought you were going to let your poor husband get his sleep this morning?" He rolled back toward Hanna and pulled her into his arms. Tadeusz grinned again and winked at her. "What are you up to?"

Hanna struggled one hand free and hit him playfully on the head. She loved the feel of his arms. She often ran her own hands up and down them, just to feel the muscles. "Don't you wish." Her serious tone belied the words.

Tadeusz kissed the top of her head, then pushed her away slightly so he could see her face. "What is it, my beautiful Hania?"

Hanna shook her head shyly. The same hand that had just hit Tadeusz now took one of his hands and moved it around from the small of her back to her front. She deliberately moved his hand down to her belly. "Here." She paused and looked up at his face, then waited.

Tadeusz looked puzzled for a moment. He wondered, feeling her narrow waist. He could easily hold her there with both hands touching. Then he caught his breath. "No?"

"Yes," Hanna said. With all her heart she hoped what happened next would be right. Everything depended on how he reacted.

"A baby? Already? I mean, so soon?"

"Well, why not?" she asked hesitantly.

"Are you sure?"

"It's still early, but yes, I'm sure, especially now that I've been sick a few times."

"Sick? I mean, a baby?" Tadeusz could barely whisper the word.

Hanna nodded again.

"A baby! Our baby!" Tadeusz folded Hanna back into his arms and breathed the words into her hair over and over.

When she finally pulled away from him, there were tears on Hanna's cheeks. She rubbed them against his skin and smiled up at him. "It's all right then?"

"It's all right. Oh, Hania, you know that if the war were over I'd jump out this window and run around the house telling the whole world what has happened."

"Then it's a good thing the war isn't over." Hanna laughed. She paused for a moment. "It is foolish though, now, to have a baby, isn't it?" Her eyes pleaded with him.

"Well, the timing might have been better, but when do babies ever come at a convenient time? No, Hania, don't worry about this baby. He or she—no, she—will be fine. She's got the best mother in the world, and I'll make sure she feels my love for her from the moment she is born. This baby will be cared for and prayed for." He paused. "Hania, I promise we'll be back together by the time she is born. This baby will make it, and so will you and so will I. It's in God's hands. Let's trust. You can do that. You've taught me how."

Now it was Hanna's turn to sigh. As long as Tadeusz had no regrets, neither would she. "Oh, Tadeusz, if only you knew how much you've taught me, too." She fell back into his arms. A few moments later she said, "How do you know it's a she?"

"I just do."

"Should we tell my parents?"

"Let's keep it a secret just a little longer. Our secret, and hers."

Hanna nodded. She and Tadeusz stayed that way in the candlelight, with his hands on her stomach and her back against his front, until Tadeusz said, "I can't stay here. I'm sorry, Hania, I have to go outside and walk this news off. I have too much energy in me."

Hanna knew what Tadeusz did not say, that he needed to think about the baby and where he might be when it was born. He had just made a nearly impossible promise. Just the night before, they had discussed Johann's plans for her and her mother to leave Kraków. How could either of them know where they would be in a month, let alone when the baby was born?

"Go ahead then. But promise me something else."

"What's that?"

"Don't run around the house yelling to the whole world that I'm pregnant."

"I wouldn't dream of it," Tadeusz laughed and ran his hand through her curls. "Now back to sleep. You need to rest for two now." Tadeusz leaned over and kissed Hanna gently.

"Poor me," she sighed, and they both laughed.

Tadeusz reached for his clothes. Once he was dressed he blew out the candle on the table by Hanna's side of the bed and was amazed to see she had already fallen back asleep. Tadeusz slipped out of their bedroom and walked the few steps down the dark hall to the front door. He unlatched it, then slipped outside.

The cold air was like water splashing over his face. Tadeusz had put on his coat before leaving the bedroom, and now he made sure all the buttons were closed. He blew on his hands, then jammed them into his pockets. Then he breathed in deep, put his head down, faced the wind, and started walking.

Up and down the narrow streets Tadeusz paced, crossing the city. He hardly noticed where he went in the dim darkness, he was so busy working through the idea that he would soon become a father. The more he thought about it, the more Tadeusz felt a sinking feeling inside. He knew only too well that this was probably the worst time and the worst possible place to bring a child into the world. Tadeusz walked faster.

It was all so unfair. The war had lasted too long. Tadeusz slammed his fist into his other hand. He knew there was nothing he could do about Hanna's being pregnant, nothing now, and so his thoughts jumped back and forth.

The baby would come despite his goodbyes to Hanna. The baby could be born without him. The baby could die in the womb, might not make it through the next eight months . . .

And yet, surely this was a miracle from God, a new life at a time when there was so much death around them. Tadeusz found himself thinking of his mother, of how she had loved babies and mourned that she could not have another. He found himself imagining the expression on her face when he told her she was going to be a grandmother. And then he was hit again with the realization that she would never know.

He stalked another several blocks in frustrated introspection. When would he ever be in control of his life again? *But when had he ever been?* he reminded himself. *And whoever is?* was his next thought. Yes, he had meant what he said to Hanna. He would trust. *Not that he had much choice,* he then thought cynically. Tadeusz stopped short. Wasn't that the point? He did have a choice. He could choose not to doubt.

Tadeusz wandered on like this until he found himself at the bottom of Wawel hill. The castle and cathedral loomed tall in the dawn light. Tadeusz listened to the blackbirds in the trees until they stopped.

The deadly silence hanging in the air brought Tadeusz out of his daze. He stood and waited, not knowing what for. Then an explosion from behind the gates shattered the silence. Tadeusz looked up the hill and heard gunshots, the sound of running boots, shouts. Out of instinct he crouched, looked around and saw a space behind a bush, an alcove where a statue must have stood once. He stepped into it.

---

Just before dawn, when the city was quietest, when there was the least amount of troop movement, Jacek slipped into a corner of the Wawel courtyard. The wide pillars supported all four sides of the palace, the ground floor of which was a covered courtyard. Windows from the apartments on the next floor looked down on the courtyard.

It was a place where a hundred eyes might be watching. Jacek knew this, because for days on end two of the eyes noting all the daily activities had been his.

Jacek knew this assignment would be his last for the Home Army. Already the Resistance forces in Kraków were down to a skeleton force, and it was becoming clearer every day that the days of German rule in the city were drawing to a close.

Most of Jacek's comrades had left for Warszawa many months before to reinforce the summer uprising. And more had been taken in the huge roundup the Germans had staged in the streets of Kraków on the sixth of August. About eight thousand people, mainly young men, had been arrested then. A few days later these prisoners could be seen sandbagging defensive posts all around the city while German soldiers battered them with clubs to keep them working.

Jacek's professor friend Karol had also been arrested at that time. When Jacek went looking for him, he found himself standing with rows of women lined up along the roads where their men were working. They had been calling out to the prisoners, asking about others who were missing, sometimes promising to hand over a package of food as soon as they could get close enough. When Jacek could not find Karol, he had just turned and walked away from it all.

Autumn in Kraków had been marked by increasing disorder in the city and the rising threat of the Soviets, along with intense efforts on the part of the Germans to pretend all was well. October had marked the fifth anniversary of the General-Gouvernement in Kraków, and

Hans Frank, Hitler's man in Poland, had celebrated in style. Then, as if he had wanted the world to know that the Third Reich had nothing but good news, Frank had gone on to stage a harvest festival in the city in November.

But once the new year began, the time for parties, even farcical ones, had finally come to an end. It was Jacek's job now to make sure there would be no more gala affairs at the Wawel Castle. Jacek's orders were to assassinate Hans Frank.

All the terror, all the camps for the Jews and gypsies and Catholics and political prisoners from the rest of Europe, all that had reduced Poland to rubble had originated on the orders of this man. Now in the final days of the Nazi occupation the Home Army wanted revenge. Fear of retribution was minimal. This time the Germans would be too busy running from the Russians to punish the Poles. At least that's what the Underground was hoping.

Jacek was a logical choice for the operation. He had performed his duties well as head of special operations in Kraków. During the last half year he had staged several small operations, not one of which had ended as disastrously as the Koppe attempt. For the Home Army, that in itself was a victory. Before the Warszawa uprising Jacek had been in contact with the different groups operating in the wooded hills around Kraków and had built up a modest reputation for himself as someone ruthless, cunning, and above all, effective.

As far as Jacek's American bosses were concerned, he was doing superlative work. His orders had altered only slightly. He was to do whatever it took to work his way into the postwar government in Poland.

Jacek had acknowledged the orders he had picked up on the second day of 1945 by leaving a note a week later. To his surprise there was already another communique waiting for him. This had stated his next drop point would be in another twelve months, this time in Warszawa. He also received papers identifying him as a German official and a warning that, whatever else happened, he must remain in Poland over the next few months. "Surprises" were in store for all major German cities. Dresden was mentioned by name as having been targeted for the first week in February.

By this time, of course, the Germans in Kraków were frantically trying to strengthen fortifications all around the city, as well as eradicate the proof of their crimes over the last five years. Everyone knew it was just a matter of weeks, perhaps only days, before the Soviets reached the city.

Because the situation was becoming so chaotic, and because of what Jacek had learned from both the Krüger and Koppe missions, he had decided to tackle this last assignment alone. And that's why he had spent the last week staking out the hill to Wawel Castle. This castle, where Polish kings had once been crowned, had been Hans Frank's residence for the last five years.

Jacek knew too well what Frank looked like. He had spent enough nights lately sleeping under a nearby bridge. Disguised as a refugee he had crouched in the shadows, watching trucks rumble up and down the cobblestone hill from Ulica Kanonicza. Jacek had already had several clear views of his target. He had black hair like Jacek, a square jaw, a pointed nose, and a small mouth.

For days Jacek had watched Frank being driven to and from the castle in his car. At night he had learned the layout of Wawel hill, the castle, the nearby cathedral, the gaps in the wall, the shortest routes down into the center of the city, all the hiding places. He even knew the location of all the manholes so he could hide in the sewers if needed. During the days he watched the number of troops and noted that more were going than coming. By the time Jacek could trace his different escape routes in his sleep, he had known it was time to act. Now, in just a few minutes, his assignment should be complete.

Right on time, somewhere upstairs on the balcony stretching down the long side of the courtyard, Jacek heard a door slam. He heard boots on stairs as Frank emerged from the far archway. Jacek waited. He had watched Frank do this morning after morning, crossing the courtyard in the predawn darkness to begin his working day. Jacek already knew the route Frank would take, straight across the courtyard, then turning left just before he reached the corner where Jacek crouched.

Frank did this, heading toward Jacek as his hands tried to close the top button of his uniform. Just before he took the turn, Jacek looked into the face of the man he was about to blow to bits, a small man who would not have looked important out of uniform. Jacek held his breath, took out the homemade bomb already warm from his hand, lit it, and threw.

But a guard behind Jacek had already tackled him in the split second before Jacek let go of the bomb, throwing off his aim. Before Jacek hit the ground, he could already tell the bomb would miss Frank. With a deep grunt he fell, his elbows slamming onto the gravel. He flipped over and turned his full attention to the guard. Quickly and expertly, he threw his weight into the man instead of trying to pull away.

Jacek yanked his knife out of his boot and twisted it in the guard's stomach before the man could even groan. Then he looked up and his eyes locked onto Frank's, who had not moved from the spot Jacek's bomb had missed. For a shadow of a second the two men stared at each other. Jacek was close enough to see Frank's chest rise and fall once when the realization, too late, that Frank was afraid of him struck Jacek like a slap. As he wrenched his knife out of the corpse beside him and brought it up to throw, Frank began shouting. More guards clattered into the courtyard.

With one motion Jacek lowered his arm and heaved himself to a standing position. Then he dashed between the pillars and into the main entrance tunnel that connected the courtyard with the square at the front of the palace. On the way Jacek brushed so close to a Nazi guard coming from the opposite direction that he could smell the man's hair cream.

As he emerged, Jacek heard the soldier he had just passed swearing behind him. The square exposed him totally. There was only one place other than the palace he had just left where he could hide. Jacek sprinted across the open area and dove through the doors of the nearby cathedral.

Jacek was all too aware that if it had not been for the Germans' greed, he would have no hiding place. Frank had ordered the great Cathedral of St. Wacław and St. Stanisław to be shut at the same time he declared the establishment of the General-Gouvernement. The great church contained too many reminders of past Polish pride and glory, nearly a thousand years' worth. In these final days before the war ended, however, the Nazis had reopened it and busied themselves emptying the cathedral of its treasures.

Jacek knew from his observations that the cathedral was open; he had spent part of his reconnaissance exploring its myriad recesses. Jacek did not even pause to see if he was alone. He knew where he was going, the only place where he might possibly escape from the men pounding after him.

Jacek veered left, toward a set of stone steps that led down to the royal tombs. Here, several corridors linked the crypts of medieval families. He plastered himself against the wall, making a conscious effort to control his breathing as he listened to the shouts and shots above him. Jacek moved quickly away from the stairs and down the first hall.

The catacombs were completely dark. Jacek felt his way along the arcade in front of a small room. No one had lit any votive candles here since the war had started. Polish kings, their wives and children all lay in their sarcophagi in a place where homage was no longer paid to them. The air was heavy with dust. Jacek shuddered involuntarily when a web thick with dirt caught his face. Slowly Jacek moved forward, his hands outstretched. To his own ears his breathing seemed to echo from the very walls.

Just as Jacek reached the first crypt, he heard footsteps clattering down the stairs. He edged into a niche behind the tombs to his right. A light bounced against the far wall, then was doused.

Jacek could smell someone else's sweat. He thought he had heard two, perhaps three people following him. He traced in his mind the route he would follow. Jacek kept himself low and moved forward. He would have to reach the narrow steps near the southern entrance to the church before his pursuers did. Everything depended on that, but now they were too close. He waited, hearing his heartbeat. Then he allowed himself to relax slightly as the footsteps moved away from him down the narrow passage to the left, which led to the coffins of the last Jagiellons. This was the break he had been hoping for.

Jacek knew which passages were dead ends and which ones led to the other entrance. For some reason he thought of Barbara's eyes. Then he was off, feeling his way around dusty statues and unrecognizable shapes until he reached the steps leading to the next corridor. He stayed in a straight line, running his hand along the wall to the right until his foot bumped against another set of stairs. These led up, curving past the broad steps to the right for the crypt under the Tower of the Silver Bells. One, two more sets of stairs, and he would be at the south doors.

But this was not where Jacek went. Instead, he deliberately kicked his boot against the steps, making a loud, scuffing sound, and doubled back quickly the way he had just come. He knew he was taking a chance, but he was certain it was the only chance he had. He had no doubt that guards had already been posted up those stairs at the south entrance.

As soon as the guards heard him moving, they had lit the lamps and were after him. But Jacek knew these corridors better than they. He had visited them many times at night since the Nazis had started clearing out the cathedral. He crossed the corridor before the soldiers reached it and headed back toward the original stairs while the soldiers went the other way. So far, the gamble had paid off.

Slowly Jacek climbed up the marble stairs he had descended just moments before. He expected at any moment to see boots standing beside his head. When there were none he chanced a peek over the edge of the stairway into the cathedral. On the other side he saw what he had expected, a group of guards waiting at the south stairs.

Jacek crawled up the last stair and flattened himself onto the floor. Then he started wiggling his way toward the front entrance. The pews hid him until he was within a few yards. As he stood there was a shout, but he had already made it outside by the time a shot was fired. More shots rang out of the cathedral, then a familiar pain tore into his left leg. He did not stop.

Somehow Jacek managed to drag himself along, across the square, down the hill, taking a path he knew was not often used. The guards had seen him, were running behind him, shooting several rounds. The warm blood ran into his shoe. He could feel it caking around his toes.

As Jacek reached the wall encircling the bottom of the hill, he looked desperately from right to left. Then someone reached out from a clump of trees by the wall. Jacek was too weak to react as he let himself be dragged behind the shrubbery; he just barely had the strength to look up. He saw a tall blond man holding a finger in front of his mouth.

---

Tadeusz almost stopped breathing as guards rushed past them. "Don't let them bring the dogs," he prayed. A few moments later he heard German shouts recalling the men. Again the guards hurried past the place where the two men hid, this time back up the hill.

Tadeusz did not dare to speak. He chanced a glance at the dark man beside him. He looked pale, and he was breathing heavily, obviously in pain. Tadeusz looked down and saw blood gathering at his feet.

Then they heard the rumble of trucks pouring down the hill. The dark-haired man peered through the leaves and saw Frank's car leading a line of trucks loaded with crates. "Poland's," he rasped.

Tadeusz looked at him in surprise. How could this man know what was in those trucks? Then, as if to confirm the stranger's words, a tarpaulin blew off the back of one of them. Before the vehicle could stop and one of the soldiers could manage to catch and refasten the tarpaulin, Tadeusz had recognized Raphael's well-known "Portrait of a Young Man" staring back at them.

"You were right," he said. The man smiled, then fainted right into Tadeusz's arms. The dead weight caught Tadeusz by surprise. He took a step backward to catch the man, bending at the knees to absorb the weight.

"Ah, I was afraid of this," Tadeusz grunted as he heaved the limp body over his shoulder. One hand held the body in place while the other moved the branches slightly. Tadeusz saw no one on the road. It was still quite early, even though dawn had long since arrived. Tadeusz stepped out of his hiding place and strolled purposefully down the street. He knew it would be just a matter of moments before someone spotted him. And he knew of only one place nearby where he could take the wounded man.

Tadeusz had walked down this same street often enough. While delivering plans to the ministry building for Johann, he had happened to notice an old house along the same road. He had never seen lights on inside, and most of the windows were broken. So he had assumed, and was hoping now, that it still stood empty.

One thing was sure; he was not taking this stranger back to the Müller house. Although he was perfectly willing to help someone who had obviously done something to anger the Germans, Tadeusz was not about to put Hanna and her family at risk.

Tadeusz reached the building within minutes. Even as he turned into the doorway, he heard a vehicle coming up behind him. He held his breath and held himself against the wall as a Gestapo car drove right past him, headed in the same direction. Tadeusz lost no time in trying the door. It swung open on broken hinges with an ominous creak. He told himself that this was the only option. He had to hide this man, and he could not afford to be seen carrying him in the open. Tadeusz would soon know if he had chosen the wrong hiding place.

Inside, he found the floor littered with broken vodka bottles and rodent droppings. He paused to listen. When he heard nothing he cleared a space on the floor with his foot and eased the unconscious man downward. Then Tadeusz left him to go and explore the house.

It had been thoroughly ransacked. Anything of any use had been cleared away long ago. There was no furniture, no draperies, no fabric of any kind that Tadeusz could use to bind the man's leg with. When he tried to see if there was any running water, the pipes clanged so loudly that he was afraid they might give them away. It was clear this house would offer them nothing but shelter. Tadeusz hoped that would be enough. At least there was no one else in the house. He was sure of that now.

When Tadeusz returned to the front room, he was shocked by how much blood lay in the puddle under the stranger's left leg. He took off his coat and placed it over the man's chest, pulled off his sweater and cotton shirt, then tore the shirt into strips. Quickly pulling the thin sweater back over his head, Tadeusz swore at himself for not having bound the wound in the first place. It was a bad mistake.

He rolled up the man's trousers and breathed a sigh of relief when he saw that the bullet had not completely buried itself in the leg. He could see a dark circle of metal still sticking out of the calf. But Tadeusz knew he had to do more than just cut off the circulation. He would have to remove the bullet, a prospect that did not thrill him.

Tadeusz reached down and rummaged around inside his coat pocket and was surprised to find his drawing compass. He must have placed it there the night before. He turned it over in his palm, realizing at the same time that it was exactly what he needed to pull the bullet out with. He would not have to cut into the flesh, after all. He knew he should sterilize it, but he had no means to do so. Tadeusz did not understand why the bullet had not gone in any farther. The man had been lucky.

He wrapped strips of his shirt around the leg above the wound to serve as a tourniquet. Then Tadeusz adjusted the compass so the two points could serve as pincers. He leaned over, placing his own knee on that of the man's in order to steady him, then reached down and tried to get a good enough grip on the bullet to start working it out of the blood-caked flesh.

The man's body jerked. "Barbara! Honey, I can't find you!"

The movement and shouts caught Tadeusz by surprise. What had the man shouted? A name? But not in Polish, and not in German. He waited. The man tossed his head from side to side, now obviously in pain.

"I can't! No, don't make me! God!"

It was English, Tadeusz was sure of it. Well, perhaps this was someone who had emigrated and come back to Poland. Enough had left after the First World War. Somehow Tadeusz doubted this was the case, though. *Why would anyone return to Poland from an English-speaking country? And what reason could they have to do so during wartime?* Tadeusz shook his head and bent over the wound again.

He managed to get the ends of his compass around the bullet and pull it slightly, but then he had to twist it back and forth to work it out all the way. So much blood gushed out in its place that Tadeusz knew the bullet must have pierced a vein. He glanced up at the man he was working on. The blood seemed to be draining directly from his face. The dark eyebrows stood out starkly against the white skin.

Tadeusz quickly wrapped chunks of cotton fabric from his shirt around the wound, praying for the bleeding to stop. It did not. Within moments the rags were soaked clear through. Tadeusz tightened the tourniquet, then looked around desperately. How had he become responsible for this man's life? Hanna would be worried about him, he should get back. But he could not leave.

Tadeusz shivered from the cold. Half the windows in the house were broken, and the chill January wind cut right through the thin wool of his sweater.

The stranger kicked his right leg. "No, Jones!" he cried out. His face had suddenly become flush. His fists clenched instinctively. And then in Russian, "I'm not a spy, I'm not a spy. I want to go home."

Tadeusz sucked in his breath. He had understood only a little of the English, but he did know Russian. Then to his amazement, the man almost sat up, his eyes clenched tightly, but said nothing. Into the silence, the man crumpled back onto the floor.

"Who are you?" Tadeusz hissed. He almost did not dare to touch the man again. He hugged himself tighter as the man began to breathe more regularly. He looked down at the wound and was only slightly relieved to see the bleeding had slowed.

Tadeusz was realizing that one risk had led to another. *What should I do?* he prayed. *What would You do?*

He closed his eyes and took two breaths. There was really no doubt what was right. He would stay with the man, whoever he was, at least until he regained consciousness. He did not know if he would confront him with what he had heard, but he would see this through and make sure he at least was able to get himself somewhere safe—well, safer. Tadeusz thought of Hanna. It would be all right. It had to be.

The fugitive lay still now, too still. He would be going into shock, probably already was. The only thing Tadeusz could do was to transfer his warmth to the man. First he gently lifted him into his arms and brought him to another room at the back of the house. He wanted to get them out of the wind, and he did not want to risk the man's strange shouts attracting any attention from the street.

Once the unconscious man was settled in a corner of the room, Tadeusz lay down beside him. He stayed like that for the rest of the day, dozing off a few times, but never dreaming. When it started to get dark, he left the house to get some snow for drinking water. Rummaging for food was out of the question. It would take too long to find too little, and he did not like the idea of leaving the man alone.

Besides, more than half the population checked the garbage dumps for food every day. Anything that might be left over would not be worth eating.

When Tadeusz returned to the room, he noticed right away that the man had changed his position. He crossed over to him, bent down, then tried to force some of the snow between the man's dry lips. In the fading light he was surprised to see the eyes fluttering open. Tadeusz waited.

The expression there was at first anxious, then relaxed. The man looked around at the bare room, his eyes taking in the details, including Tadeusz's jacket on his stomach. Then Jacek cleared his throat and asked, "Why did you do that? You've brought me somewhere safe."

Tadeusz realized the man's Polish really was perfect. He spoke in one of those accents that could not be pinned down as coming from any one region, but which could still be considered native. Tadeusz thought about the question that had just been put to him. "You would have done the same," he answered. Both men nodded.

"The bullet?" Jacek asked.

"It's out. It wasn't deep. I can't get you any water; in fact, I can't get you much of anything except this snow. I think the best thing is for you to tell me where you live and I'll . . ."

"No." Jacek spoke decisively. "I mean thank you, but no." Jacek pushed himself onto his elbows. Tadeusz let him test his strength. "I owe you my life, and I am very grateful. But as you might have guessed, this was"—he glanced at his rings, which Tadeusz only now noticed—"Home Army business, and I don't want to involve you any further."

Jacek waited. It was an answer that gave the other party

a way out. Since Tadeusz did not respond, Jacek continued, "I don't live very far away. It's already getting dark, so I can make my own way home."

Tadeusz was thinking about Hanna again. If he were single, he would have joined up with this man, whoever he was, in a moment. Tadeusz swallowed. He had known what Jacek's waiting between sentences had meant, and he had deliberately not responded. Now he told himself no, what he had found with Hanna was too precious and already too fragile to jeopardize.

In any case, Jacek had his answer. He could trust this man not to betray him, but that was all. Fine. Jacek was lucky he had even risked bringing him to this place. Jacek took a few deep breaths. He chanced sitting up and scooting himself so he could lean against the wall, but the effort left him panting.

"You've lost a lot of blood," Tadeusz told him. "You can't leave here tonight."

"I'm stronger than I look," Jacek smiled wryly. As if to prove his words, he heaved himself onto his right knee, then leaned against the wall and stood on his one good leg.

"Well, I'm still not going to let you go home alone," Tadeusz said. "I'll go with you. Actually, if you're feeling so strong, I think now might be a good time to go. The streets are crowded enough for us to find some cover. It's getting dark, but not yet curfew."

Jacek decided not to waste his energy arguing. Now was no time to worry about security. After all, he would probably be leaving the city in a few weeks, so what did it matter if this man found out where he lived? Besides, now that he was standing and sweat was already beading on his forehead, Jacek knew he could not afford to refuse the help being offered. He nodded.

"Good." Tadeusz glanced down, relieved to see no blood on the floor under Jacek's leg. "Let's go." Tadeusz was anxious to get away. He did not know what to do with the fact that this man had babbled in English and Russian about being a spy. It was certainly dangerous information, and there was no doubt his patient was a dangerous man. The sooner they parted, the better.

Tadeusz put his coat on Jacek, then helped the man stand. He slid an arm around Jacek's waist, concealing it under the coat. He was surprised at how little the man leaned on him. If only they could make it to wherever he lived before the bleeding started again.

The two men headed for the front of the house, Jacek hopping slightly to keep as much of his weight as possible off the bad side. The only noticeable characteristic of the pair was the fact that Tadeusz wore no coat. Otherwise, when they bent their heads together, they looked like two limping men deep in conversation as they headed down the street.

In fact, Tadeusz was wondering how much he should ask Jacek about the reason he had been shot in the first place. He knew it would be expected, but after what he had heard Jacek say when delirious, Tadeusz was reluctant to appear too curious. He would have to be careful. He took a deep breath. "I wonder, can you tell me about the painting we saw? Was that the reason you were on the hill?"

Jacek had expected something like this. He owed the man an explanation and now figured that volunteering some harmless information was as good a way as any to repay his rescuer. "Partly," Jacek answered in a whisper, causing Tadeusz to lean even closer toward him. "The Germans are stealing, have been stealing, massive amounts of Polish art and treasures. I was trying to save something." The lie sounded unconvincing even to Jacek's ears. He tried to strengthen it with the truth.

"A small group of us has been getting art treasures out of other cities to safe places. We're hoping to save something. If we can't keep the Germans from taking it, at least we can hide what they leave behind so the Soviets won't steal it."

Tadeusz said nothing. Salvaging art was a strange thing to attempt alone, at dawn, and on foot. And the man had spoken Russian. He changed the subject. "You're not from here?" he asked.

"No."

"I could tell by your accent." When Jacek raised his eyes to look at Tadeusz's, he quickly added, "Neither am I. I come from Łódź."

"I was born in Gdańsk," Jacek said. Again, a little bit of truth helped.

A sudden impulse to find out who this man really was seized Tadeusz. He would risk one more question. Perhaps there was a perfectly reasonable explanation for the man's calling out in English like that. Perhaps Tadeusz had misunderstood. He suddenly hoped so. "Yes, the university there has a fine foreign language department." The words were out before he could think twice. He felt the man stumble, but quickly recover himself, leaning only slightly more on Tadeusz's arm.

This time Jacek did not risk looking at Tadeusz. He was familiar enough with himself to know the suspicion in his eyes would give him away. Did this man know more than he was letting on? Now it was Jacek's turn to wonder how much he dared ask. He felt Tadeusz slow his pace and looked up to see what had caught his attention, hoping for a distraction.

Tadeusz had noticed a poster dated the first of January, ordering all men under sixty and women under fifty-five to register for fortification works around Kraków. Reading this poster just added to his worries. He had been gone since early that morning. Surely Hanna would be frantic, fearing he had been picked up by the Germans looking for workers.

Jacek said carefully, "So I've heard, but I studied mathematics. Besides, I've never been able to learn to speak anything but Polish."

*Well, there it was,* Tadeusz thought. He knew enough. The power of this knowledge, just confirmed, sent a chill up his spine.

Jacek, too, knew enough. Instinctively he knew he was in no condition to dodge such questions. He did not like the fact that he had just stumbled out of surprise. It was time to part.

He stopped suddenly and grabbed his rescuer's shoulder. With the other hand he shook his hand. "I live very close to here. My name is Jacek," he told him. "Thank you. I owe you one."

Tadeusz was not surprised that Jacek had not let him see where he lived. And any last name he had given would probably have been false. He returned the handshake and replied, "I'm honored. Tadeusz." The two men studied each other's faces, one so fair, the other dark.

Jacek could not help but think Tadeusz was hiding something. Why that business about foreign languages? Why indeed? A still fear settled on the back of Jacek's neck. He cursed his current weakness. He should be able to find out whatever it was Tadeusz knew. *Well, perhaps we'll meet again,* Jacek thought. *And then, old friend, I'll make sure I owe you no more than my life.*

Both men turned to leave, already intent on what they must do next. Tadeusz knew he must find Hanna, and soon. He felt a deep urge to rediscover the new life that might in some desperate way counterbalance the fear and intrigue he had accidentally stumbled onto that morning. The sense of trust he had found with her he could feel slipping away. He needed, more than anything he had ever needed in his life, to be by her side again.

# 8

LATE JANUARY 1945

Warszawa was a distinct shock to Jacek. Jacek could still clearly remember the lay of the streets from when he had lived there as a student-spy, but he recognized nothing in the total ruin he found. Just two days after the Russian troops had finally entered that devastated city, Warszawa had been reduced to nothing but jagged walls and vast piles of brick.

Jacek wandered around in a daze, disbelieving all that he saw. How was it possible to dismantle an entire city? Had the same thing happened to Kraków, the city he had just left?

Ever since his failed assassination attempt and his rescue by Tadeusz, Jacek had realized he had no choice but to make a drastic change in strategy. Not only was the Polish Home Army disintegrating, but by now, any partisans who had managed to fight for Poland and survive the war were being hunted down and killed by the Soviets.

Even Felek was gone. A few days after Jacek's attempt to assassinate Frank, Jacek found out that Felek had been arrested in a village to the east. From what Jacek could discover, the partisan patch with the silver-threaded eagle Felek always wore on missions had been his death warrant.

All this had quite a sinister meaning for Jacek. In Kraków already, it had become clear that his superiors in the

OSS had been gambling on the wrong side. Since his return from Russia, Jacek had been positioning himself in the Polish Underground, the assumption being that they, with Allied support, would be the ones to rebuild postwar Poland. But if Jacek was reading the signs right, in a few days there would be no more Home Army. So against his recent training, against his very nature, Jacek had done the only thing he could do and still preserve his original mission. He had set out to change sides.

His search for Paul had been part of this strategy, an attempt to send out feelers around the city and make contact with the network of Soviet spies he knew must already be in Kraków. It could only be a matter of days before the Soviets made their move and took the city. Jacek had to let them know that no one else there could assess the Germans' fortifications as well as he.

On the afternoon of January 9, a boy had come up to Jacek on the street and given him a note directing Jacek to a certain café. There he had offered his services to a man called Paul. Jacek swore he could provide the most detailed information about German defenses possible. Three days later he was crawling around the two German munitions dumps in Kraków. His leg bothered him only slightly; he was amazed that it had not become infected.

What Jacek saw at the munitions dumps he wrote into the notebook he was due to hand over to Paul the next day, when he left the city. When Paul did not show up, however, Jacek had been forced to leave Kraków as quickly as possible. After warning the girl in Kraków station about Dresden, he had made it onto a train for Warszawa on the nineteenth of January. Now he was here, and he had his work cut out for him.

The Soviet officials to whom he offered his services

were skeptical. He had built up too impressive a reputation for himself for his work with the Home Army. The Soviets had arrested too many of his former colleagues, torturing them for the names of their comrades and then shooting the ones who refused to join up with the communists. Jacek's name had come up often. If he wanted to work with the new power, he would have to prove himself first. And that is why he needed his notebook. He was counting on the information it contained to set him apart from the other turncoats.

Jacek used the name of Paul to generate special interest in his case. He was interviewed again, this time by a higher-ranking group of Russians. Throughout each of his interviews he spoke only Polish, reserving his knowledge of Russian as an ace in the hole.

Only when he felt he had the attention of the Russian official interviewing him did Jacek describe the contents of the notebook he still carried hidden in his shoe. As he had expected, this upgraded his status immediately. Jacek instantly became someone the Soviets wanted to know more about. But Jacek was cautious; he knew this same curiosity could cut two ways.

The Soviets wanted to know what he knew about Paul's disappearance. And they were not impressed by the notebook, even if it did exist. It was too little, too late. Kraków had fallen into Soviet hands the same week Jacek had arrived in Warszawa. But they did want to see the notebook, and when they asked, Jacek held out for still more. There was one particular man he wanted very much to see. And he held out for that meeting.

When, after a great deal of whispering with an aide who came in and out of the room, his latest interviewer agreed, even Jacek was surprised. It seemed that, even if he had overestimated the importance of the notebook, he had underestimated the power of Paul's name. Only at the moment when this same aide handed him an envelope was Jacek certain he had worked a deal with the Russians.

Jacek was sent to an army camp just outside the city, on the Narew River. There he was led to a tent containing nothing but a huge table covered with maps. On the other side stood a tall, well-built man. There was no need for introductions. Jacek knew he was finally dealing with Marshal Konstantin Rokossovski.

Now for the first time, Jacek was careful to speak in Russian so that the marshal would know of Jacek's background and capabilities. When Rokossovski responded similarly, Jacek could not help but recognize that the man had a Polish accent.

In fact, Rokossovski was half-Polish, born in Warszawa to a Russian mother and a Polish father who had worked as a train engineer. Rokossovski had begun his military career fighting for the Russian army in the First World War. Then, in 1937, the Soviets had arrested him for no reason, and he had remained imprisoned until March 1940. So like Jacek, Rokossovski had also seen the inside of a Soviet prison camp during the first years of the war. He had been released around the same time that Jacek had been sent to Artemovsk. At that point Rokossovski had regained all his rights, as well as membership status in the Communist Party.

During the winter of 1940–1941, Rokossovski had been put in full charge of organizing and training the Soviet army. Ever since the German attack on the Soviet Union, Rokossovski had fought on the front line. There he had proven to be a soldier and strategist of rare stature. The only break he had taken from the war was when an injury forced him to stay in a Moscow hospital for two months during 1942. After that he had gone straight back to the front.

In the autumn of 1942, Stalin had called Rokossovski back to Moscow, where he made him the commander of the Stalingrad Front. Within a few hours he had left Moscow for the front again, this time at the side of Georgi Konstantinovich Zhukov, another Russian marshal who would spearhead Poland's "liberation." Now Zhukov was bragging that his First Byelorussian Front would be the first to reach Berlin. Rokossovski was aiming for a city to the north, and Jacek thought he knew which one.

He could feel the man's eyes boring into him. His notebook and his association with Paul had taken him this far, and in the process he had learned a great deal about how the fledgling Soviet apparatus was functioning at that particular time within Poland. Earlier he had removed the notebook from his shoe. Now the moment had arrived to play all his cards, so he surrendered it into Rokossovski's outstretched hand.

"Ah, my friend, you are calculating how much I can help you in the future. Tell me what I want to hear." There was a slight edge in the marshal's voice.

"Paul was my contact," Jacek ventured.

"Yes."

Jacek knew Rokossovski would give nothing away. He already had a theory as to why Paul had warranted so much attention. "I don't know what happened to him, but he was one of Koniev's best agents, wasn't he?"

Rokossovski pursed his lips, but said nothing as he turned his attention to reading the contents of the notebook. After several minutes he nodded slightly. "You have an eye for the right details, I will grant you that. But of course Koniev already knows this. Now it is of no use to us, wasted effort."

He shook his head, then leaned forward, his eyes level and challenging. "However, I am interested in the future, not the past. There's a piece of information I need confirmed. And we don't have much time. You seem eager to prove yourself, so I want you to find out about the Germans' fortifications in Gdańsk. Do you know that city?"

"I was born there." Jacek allowed himself a nod of self-congratulation. He had been right, after all.

"How convenient. We're striking this camp now because I want to be in Elbląg by the fourth. Exactly a week after that there will be a courier waiting inside the Hotel Eden, across from the Gdańsk train station, to bring me your report. The particular name I need should not be written down in any notebook, however." He paused. "It concerns our friend *Reichsführer-SS* Himmler. Find out what General Heinrici has brought in to fortify the northern territories and whether he is there to replace Himmler."

"Yes, sir." Jacek answered as he had learned to back in the camp.

Rokossovski's gaze changed subtly. "Ah, yes. I have been meaning to ask where you learned your Russian."

"Somewhere between Smolensk and Stalingrad." Again Rokossovski nodded, his eyes narrowing. He said nothing, but Jacek sensed a turning point in their conversation. Acting out of instinct, Jacek had managed to touch on the common past he shared with this man. They both knew how it felt on the other side of a Russian camp fence.

Rokossovski coughed. He rounded the table and asked, "They gave you the papers in Warszawa?"

"Yes, sir." The envelope filled his breast pocket.

"You watch yourself on the way to Gdańsk. A losing

enemy is the most dangerous type." Jacek staggered as Rokossovski struck him on the back. "Until we meet again, heh?" Then he turned his back to Jacek and began studying the charts laid out on the table.

Jacek left the tent and did not dare to check if Rokossovski was watching him go. Instead, he took care to notice his surroundings. These Russian soldiers sharply contrasted with those Jacek had come in contact with before. The boots and warm clothing must have been taken off civilian and German bodies. All the men looked well fed, and the condition of the camp itself, the tents and what weaponry Jacek could identify, also testified that Rokossovski knew how to take care of his men during a winning offensive. Jacek did not doubt that whatever they needed, they stole.

Rokossovski's aide led Jacek to a stand of trees where he was surprised to discover a train taking on coal. It looked like he had arrived just in time. The aide explained what Jacek already knew. He was guaranteed passage on this train only through Soviet-controlled territory. After that he would be on his own.

An officer barked orders in three different directions. Soldiers lounging against the trees in the shadows snapped to attention as officers who had boarded the train jumped back into the snow along the tracks. Jacek bent his head into the February wind and headed toward the front of the train. He found an empty compartment and settled onto the seat. Once the train started moving, he pulled the curtain to the outside window a little bit open.

As the train passed by the camp, he noticed one soldier in particular quite close to the tracks. Jacek could tell by the insignia that the man was an artillery officer. There he stood, leaning up against a tree, scribbling furiously in a fat notebook. One moment he was there, the next moment dark trees had taken his place.

———— ∞ ————

As Jacek found himself heading toward Gdańsk and away from Rokossovski's camp, the irony of it all unnerved even him. For Jacek had been in Gdańsk before, spying on German troops as a different man, and working for a different country. Now he was being sent to gather the same information about German defenses, but with the crucial difference that he had to get it to the Soviets, not a G–2 operative. And all the time he was still working for the Americans.

Jacek pulled out the envelope he had received in Warszawa from his breast pocket. Inside he found an ID card printed in both Russian and Polish. The Russians had also given him fake German papers to help him into the German-held zone.

Jacek did not need any of it. He already had his own set of foolproof, German-authorized travel papers, which he much preferred to the sloppy Soviet imitations. Jacek leaned over and swiveled open the heel to his right shoe, removing papers that were no forgeries. The person who had left them in the Kraków post office more than a month earlier had made sure of that. He put the other papers inside his shoe, clicked the heel back into place, and counted on his expensive clothes to make the right impression. Then Jacek stretched out his legs, put his hands behind his head, and closed his eyes.

Not until an hour later did the Soviet soldiers board the train again. Jacek knew they must be approaching the front. He answered the knock at the compartment door, handed the card to the soldier standing there, and received the soldier's salute. Now it was just a matter of time before the train crossed into German-held territory. Less than a week earlier, the First Baltic Front and Third Byelorussian Front of the Soviet army had heaved the front line westward into the very heart of Poland. Now the German lines of defense crisscrossed the country, with the Soviets pushing them farther west every day.

Once Jacek heard shelling, he knew they must be nearing Olsztyn (Allenstein), which would surely be one of Rokossovski's objectives on his way to Elbląg. Jacek watched closely for the checkpoint where the Germans would finally stop the train. He had to be sure before it happened.

Jacek was in a dilemma. Should he take his chances with the Nazis when they searched the train? They would wonder why, with his German papers, he had been allowed to travel through the Russian-occupied zone. Despite the authenticity of his documents, there would be questions, and he could not afford any delays. Besides, chances were that damage done to tracks and bridges in the area would impede any further north-south train travel.

Jacek stood up straight. He could already feel the train slowing down. Then he opened the window and stuck his head outside. As the cold air hit his face hard, Jacek knew he could not risk waiting too long. He did not know which side of the track the Germans would be on when they stopped the train.

He stood on the seat and expertly leaned out backward through the window. Then he grabbed hold of the rim running along the roof of the compartment, lifted his legs, and pulled hard with his arms.

This was more difficult than any chin-up. The wind tore at one side of Jacek's body. He paused, catching his breath, knowing that he had to get on top before they reached the checkpoint.

He concentrated his strength into his shoulders and pulled the bottom half of his body out the window. He hung there for a second, then swung one leg over the glass. Still clinging to the rim on the roof of the car, Jacek pulled himself up to a crouching position.

"Don't let there be a tunnel now," he mumbled. With a heave he let go of the rim, pushed with his legs, and threw his body toward the center of the roof. A gust of wind threw him off balance as he grabbed for the top edge. He missed, slipped, scrambled, hardly daring to breathe, then clawed his way up until one hand firmly held the top of the roof. The second hand pushed Jacek up until he straddled the top.

His chest heaved as he settled into position. Slowly, he sat up, then stood. He looked behind him, in the direction the train was heading. There was still no one in sight. Then he started running.

One, two, three paces, then he jumped. One, two, three, then another jump. He kept up the rhythm on top of the slowing train until he reached the last car. This was not the first time Jacek had tried such a stunt, yet still it left him breathless. He turned around and lay down, facing the front again, just as he heard the brakes start to screech.

Jacek pasted himself against the roof and listened. Even before the train had completely stopped, Jacek could hear voices ahead talking in German. He eased his body over to the side of the roof away from the sounds and listened. When he could no longer hear the guards, he risked looking over the top of the train.

Up ahead he saw the guards going in and out of the cars. None seemed to be near his end of the train, which is what Jacek had been counting on. Slowly, he slipped over the side away from the doors and dropped lightly to the ground. Jacek looked left, right, left again, then was off like a shot into the nearby trees. From there he watched and waited a few more moments, getting his bearings, then moved out of sight of the train. Within the hour he was making good distance away from the checkpoint, moving northward through the woods.

# 9

## Early February 1945

For a long, long time Hanna had wished the war would end. Now it seemed there was no escaping it. And she couldn't ever remember being so tired.

With a sigh she leaned back against the rough station wall among their little pile of belongings. With half-closed eyes she watched the slight figure of her mother as she stood in conversation with a conductor. Helena had been bribing him faithfully every morning for information.

They had arrived in Breslau at the end of January only to find the same panicked conditions they had left in Kraków. The station was thronging with women seeking to flee; the westbound trains were packed with German wounded, and the only way out of the city seemed to be on foot.

Helena had said no to that option. It was the dead of winter, and she was determined that her pregnant daughter would not be caught in the countryside, between fronts, in the driving snow. So she and Hanna had camped out at the train station, waiting for space on board any train heading west.

But to wait takes time, and time was something they were fast running out of.

Only a few days after they left Kraków, the Soviets had taken the city. The Germans had left in such haste that they did not even have time to ignite the explosives they had set. That much Hanna and Helena knew from other refugees who had fled to Breslau.

They had heard nothing from Johann and Tadeusz.

For the next two weeks, the stories went, there had been fierce fighting as the Soviet Army moved westward, all the way to the Oder River. Now the Soviets were already in the outskirts of Breslau, and almost all of the city's German civilian population had fled, leaving homes and property behind. As the winter's offensive sent the Soviets sprawling all over Poland, rumors of what the Russians had done in Polish villages preceded them. No one in Breslau wanted to stay around long enough to find out what would happen when the houses the Soviets burned were German homes and the women raped were the wives of German soldiers.

Hanna shuddered, pushing away her fears of what might happen to her and her mother. She pushed them to the same place she pushed her worries about Tadeusz and her father and the baby.

"Good news," Helena was saying as she sat down carefully beside her daughter. "There's a train due to pull into Breslau late tonight, and there are actually some passenger cars attached to it. If we stay alert, we might manage to get a seat."

"It's going west?"

"Well, southwest, toward Czechoslovakia. But we can stop in Hirschberg and catch a westbound train to Dresden."

Helena paused and squinted out at the surging crowd. Anxiety hung in the air with the coal smoke and the smell of sweat. Only for a moment did her strength waver. "At least I hope we can," she murmured.

---

The train arrived only a few hours later than the conductor had told Helena. They were ready, though, and as soon as the engine pulled in, Hanna and her mother pushed their way through the crowd and squeezed in between all the other women. The compartments and aisles soon filled up, but not before Hanna and Helena found seats together in a compartment with four other women. Hanna leaned back against the wooden-slat bench she shared with her mother and one other woman, closed her eyes, and sighed a prayer of thanks.

Within an hour they felt the train pulling out of the station. Helena squeezed Hanna's hand as the train started moving and reached up to tuck a few strands of silvery hair back into the bun on her neck. Her calm gray eyes met Hanna's black ones, and mother and daughter shared the thought that they were on their way, finally.

They had barely reached the city limits, however, when suddenly a red glare filled the sky. And then it seemed as if the train had descended into a blazing pit. Fire fell from all sides. The train slowed to a stop as explosions rocked the tracks.

A conductor came pushing past the women packed into the aisle. As he stepped between the parcels and bags and bodies sitting on the floor, Helena slid open the door. "What's happening?" she called out over the noise of children crying.

"The Russians have chosen tonight to try and take this side of Breslau."

Hanna covered her ears and tried to calm her breathing. Just as she was wondering how much longer it would be before a shell hit their train, it started inching its way down the track. When she opened her eyes again, the sky they saw through the window was lit orange and red. All six women watched the fireworks recede as the train gathered speed.

After a few moments, Hanna took a good look at the others in their compartment. She was the youngest, squeezed in between her mother, who sat next to the window, and an old woman with white hair. Across from them sat three women about her mother's age. One was very well dressed; Hanna noticed she wore new shoes.

The woman sitting nearest the window appeared to be wearing at least three dresses. Hanna saw that she was trying to sleep and decided to pull the curtains closed. But just as she stood up, the train lurched, and Hanna lost her balance. When she reached out to steady herself, the woman wearing so many dresses caught her hand and squeezed it. Hanna looked down at her, surprised that she was awake, and saw the tears before the woman could brush them away.

"I'm sorry," Hanna said. "Did I hurt you? I must have stepped on your foot."

"You are so much like my daughter, do you know that?" the woman said abruptly. "She's dead now, but I've been watching you since I sat down here. And you are so much like her."

Hanna thought she should smile but couldn't. She patted the older woman's hand. "Thank you. I'm sorry for waking you, though." Then she looked up and saw that the others were watching her. Embarrassed, she sat down again quickly and thought that before the night was over, they would certainly have each other's faces memorized.

Hanna looked outside their door and noticed they had stopped at the Waldenburg station. More women were boarding the train and sitting in the aisles on their various parcels. As she closed her eyes and tried to sleep, Hanna was thankful that she and her mother had at least managed to get seats.

It seemed to Hanna that no sooner had she dozed off than she felt the train slowing yet again. Her mother slept on, so she raised an eyebrow at the woman across from her and mouthed the words, "What now?" The woman shrugged her shoulders, palms turned upward.

Within moments, Hanna noticed movement in the aisle as the crowd shifted, then a Nazi officer threw open their compartment door. "*Heraus!*" he barked, scowling at the women. "Outside! We must search all the cars. There is a spy on board!"

Hanna turned to her mother, now wide awake, and together they put on their coats and hurried to join the lineup outside. A quick look showed them that up and down the length of the train, soldiers were questioning the passengers.

Helena dropped her hat in the mud and turned so that she faced the train. As she stooped to pick the hat up, she opened the hidden seam inside the hat's lining and deftly shoved something into her hair.

When it was their turn, a small man speaking in a broad Saxony dialect asked, "And did you get off the train in Waldenburg?"

"No, sir," Helena answered.

"And the *Fräulein*?" Hanna did not feel as afraid of this man as she did of the unknown Russians they were running away from. In the last year there had been a great deal of propaganda about what animals the Russians were. She had been around German soldiers for many years, however, and Hanna could tell this man was from the country.

It was this thought that now caused her to lower her guard.

"Of course not," she said.

The train sighed steam. The man looked at her more closely. Hanna noticed he had only one eyebrow. It stretched across the bridge of his nose from one eye to the other.

"Hanna!" her mother whispered, then to the German, "Please excuse my daughter. She is tired from the journey and did not mean to sound sullen. No, we did not get off the train, nor did we speak with anyone."

"Quiet, old woman. I did not ask you." He grabbed Hanna by the arm and pulled her toward him. "You think you are so smart," he hissed in Hanna's ear, "so high and mighty."

Too late, Hanna realized her mistake. "*Entschuldigung*. Pardon. I meant no disrespect. Please, sir, forgive me. I am tired, as my mother said. And you are right to be angry. I'm sure my mother and I could . . ." Hanna shot a glance at her mother, who nodded, "reimburse you for your trouble," she finished. "We have . . ."

"Oh, yes, I have an idea of what you have," the soldier sneered. "If you're like the others, you have family jewels and cash in different currencies. So if you're smart, you'll hand it all over to me now. All of it, and quickly." The man looked behind him, then swiveled Hanna around, twisting her arm behind her back so that she cried out in pain.

The woman with three dresses stepped forward. "You cannot rob us! And there is no reason to single out that girl. She could do no harm. If you are looking for spies on this train, then continue your search. But leave us in peace. We have done nothing."

The man's face went red as he released Hanna and drew out his pistol.

The woman screamed once before the soldier shot her. Then Hanna screamed, and could not stop screaming. The woman with the three dresses had looked so surprised. Even now, as she lay in the mud, her eyes remained wide open, as if disbelieving what had happened.

The Nazi knelt by the woman and tore open the lining of her coat. Then he felt her neck and stripped the gold band off her finger. He looked up at Helena and motioned toward Hanna, "Shut her up or I will."

Helena shook her. "Hanna, stop! You must stop this noise now. It's not your fault. Get hold of yourself, do you hear me?" Finally Hanna nodded, sobbing softly.

Just then the soldier on his knees caught sight of an SS officer walking toward the group. He quickly thrust his booty into a pocket, stood up, and saluted. *"Heil Hitler!"*

The officer ignored the salute. "I heard a gunshot. What seems to be the problem?"

"Interfering old ladies, that's all. This woman and her daughter were acting suspicious. The old woman interrupted the interrogation."

The other German grunted at Helena and Hanna, "Show me your papers."

Helena handed them over without a word.

As he leafed through the documents, he said, "The spy we are looking for is carrying back information to the Russians about fortifications in Breslau. He, or she," he hesitated, "is no doubt traveling on two sets of papers. So you see why we would question anyone acting suspiciously."

"Just so," the Nazi soldier said. "Which is exactly what I was doing." He glared at Helena and Hanna, daring them to disagree.

Helena ignored the warning. "If there is any question of where our loyalty lies, this should clear it up." Helena reached for her hat and handed it to Hanna.

Hanna bit her lip and quickly looked to the left and right. None of the other passengers were watching. They had all moved away when the disturbance began.

The soldier cocked his pistol at Helena. "No tricks."

Ignoring the man, Helena searched through her hair and pulled out a minutely folded square of paper. The soldier snatched it from her and placed it on the waiting palm of the SS man.

He read it and clicked his heels. "Of course there has been a misunderstanding, Frau Müller." He handed the paper to the soldier and added, "I apologize for any inconvenience."

As the SS officer left them to inspect the rest of the lineup, the soldier handed the paper back to Helena, but would not return her gaze. Then the soldier looked away and walked down the tracks in the opposite direction of the officer who had just left.

The minute he had left them, Hanna grabbed her mother's hand. "Mother, what was it?"

"No one saw, did they?" Helena asked. "I had no choice. Your father told me this paper would get us out of any tight spot with the Germans. It identifies him as an important supplier of the engineering corps."

Hanna watched as her mother replaced the paper in her hair, her hands shaking. Then a sob welled up inside her throat and she whirled around to face the corpse. Still clutching her mother's hat in one hand, she knelt beside the woman's body, bringing the white hand to her cheek.

Helena stooped beside her daughter and felt the woman's neck. "She's gone, Hanna."

"I was so stupid. And she paid the price."

"Hush, now." Helena tipped her daughter's chin up.

"She's with her daughter, remember? God rest her soul, there's nothing you can do. There are some things you must put behind you. Now come. They've finished searching for their spy. The train will be leaving soon."

"But—but we should bury her!"

As if in answer, the conductor's whistle blew, and the noise from the engine grew louder. Helena shook her head and carefully took back the hat from Hanna and placed it on her head.

The other three women were already back in their compartment by the time Hanna and Helena made their way down the aisles. "We saved your seats," the well-dressed one sitting in the corner said. Hanna noticed that she no longer wore her rings.

"Thank you so much," Helena said. "We were, er, delayed." No one mentioned the absence of the woman left dead by the tracks. And when another woman poked her head in the door and asked if the empty seat by the window was free, Helena answered, "Yes," while Hanna looked away. As the train began moving, Hanna listened to the cadence of the tracks, finally falling into a deep sleep.

Helena cast a gentle glance toward her daughter as she felt the slender body lean more heavily against her. Hanna was her only child, born when she and Johann were already in their forties, long awaited and much loved. Now Helena was past sixty. Although she had kept her trim figure, the skin around her neck and hands showed her age.

Helena sighed and also tried to doze. Quite some time later she felt the train's speed slacken and heard the high screech of brakes. Then she fell forward slightly and bumped into Hanna. "Oh, Hanna, I'm sorry. And you were sleeping so soundly."

Hanna did not feel well. Her head was leaden with

sleep. She smiled for her mother though, who looked even sleepier than Hanna felt. She yawned. "Where are we?"

"I don't know," Helena answered slowly, looking around her.

Panic gripped Hanna as she realized she had no idea how long she had slept. She stood up and slid open the door. "Do you know where we are?" she asked a young woman standing nearby.

"It must be Hirschberg. It's the only other stop the train is supposed to make tonight."

The woman's words caused Hanna to suck in her breath. "Mother, this is where we need to get out. Hurry!" Helena jumped to her feet as Hanna pulled down their bags from the rack. Both women could feel the train slowing even more.

"Oh, Hanna, how could we both have missed it?" Helena cried as they stumbled out of their compartment. Women sat on the floor, leaning against each other and against the wall. A few had found enough room to curl up in a corner. Hanna and Helena picked their way through the bodies and the packages, mumbling apologies along the way.

Hanna said, "Mother, will we make it?"

"Of course we will. Look, there's the door."

Hanna could feel the sweat running down her back. Despite all the people between them and the door, she felt relieved. She and Helena shoved past the last pile of bags and boxes just as the halting train threw them into a little group of women also wanting to get out. Hanna stumbled, dropped her bags, and grabbed the arm of a woman in the group, who steadied her.

"The train has stopped. Why isn't someone opening the door?"

"We're trying!" the women told her. Only then did Hanna notice that the three women closest to the door were struggling with the handle. "Can't you see? It's stuck. The door won't open. It must be frozen shut."

Both Hanna and her mother joined the others, trying to help. "How is it possible?" Hanna gasped. She grabbed her mother. "We've got to reach the other door!" But several minutes had already passed since they left the compartment, and now the train was jerking forward.

"It's moving!" Hanna cried. She looked at the full aisles on both sides and knew they would never reach the next door in time.

Another woman cried, "Let us out, let us out, somebody help us!" She beat on the door.

Hanna turned back to the door. "We must get out here! The train to Dresden! We must catch the train to Dresden!" It was no use. Again, she and Helena struggled to open the train door. It refused to budge. The other women around them had already stopped trying as the train picked up speed.

"Oh, Mother." Hanna had the same terrible feeling in her stomach that she had when the old woman was shot. Her parents' carefully laid plans were now worth nothing. "What will we do?"

Helena sat down on one of her suitcases. "What can we do?" She threw her hands up. "In God's name, we go to Czechoslovakia!" Helena leaned up against the wall and closed her eyes.

Hanna stared at her mother. They really had no choice. She knew their places in the compartment would be long gone, so this was as good a place as any to settle down. She looked around and noticed that the other women who wanted to get out had just sat down on the floor right by the door. So animated a few moments earlier, they now hugged hats and bags and scarves to themselves, staring at their feet.

Hanna turned away from the people around her and rested her elbows on the window edge. Her heart was still racing from the effort of trying to get the door open. Outside the snow fell in great drifts. Trees raced past her like ghosts in the dark. A baby cried in one of the compartments. Cold winds rattled the sides of the car. Hanna could feel the train pull as it slowly crept upward into the mountains.

Hanna stayed like that for more than an hour. She would not sleep. Instead, she stood guard over her mother, her unborn child, herself. The specter of the old woman's face, specked with mud, stared back at Hanna from the window.

"I killed her," she whispered to herself. Again and again she would catch her thoughts moving in time with the train: *Mother of my twin, mother of my twin.* Then she would make an almost physical effort to pry her mind away from what had happened, to concentrate on the future and to pray for Tadeusz and her parents and for the baby she was carrying.

Wrestling with her thoughts, Hanna stared and stared at the darkness until it became dawn. And then she watched the snow-laden pines take shape in the growing light. They were in the Karkonosze, or Giant Mountains, the highest peaks of the Sudety mountain range. As the train climbed, it strained to reach the summit. Hanna felt an urge to go outside and push the train over the top. She wondered how a part of her couldn't wait to be in another country, to put everything behind her, while another part was still so afraid of what lay ahead.

Soon sunlit pine woods gave way to snowy pastures. When Hanna saw the steep-roofed timber houses painted in warm colors and silhouetted against the thickly wooded slopes, she thought it was indeed a different country. For somewhere back on the summit the train had crossed over into Czechoslovakia.

Hanna sighed and finally allowed herself to slide onto the floor next to where her mother slept. She felt the weight of worry and guilt and pain lift as exhaustion took its toll. Her leg muscles and her neck ached as she closed her eyes and slept.

In what seemed like only a few seconds the train stopped and Hanna woke with a start. Women were moving all around her. She glanced at her mother, who said, "Praga. Don't worry, though, we're staying on. I've been praying, and know this is right." So both women remained on the floor, their backs rigid against the aisle wall.

They watched women stream out of the train. Dragging trunks and shouldering bursting parcels, they looked like an army of the dispossessed. Most had nowhere to go. Praga was fast filling up with refugees from the rest of Central Europe, despite the common knowledge that it was just a matter of months before the Russians broke through Nazi defenses and took that city as well.

But time was exactly what these people were gambling on. Enough time to rest, then move on, enough time to keep west of the front line. Somewhere in that time, they hoped, the war would end. And then it would be time to go back home, to whatever was left after the retreat of one army and the onslaught of another.

Hanna felt too sore, too tired to do anything but stare at the women's feet as they got off the train. Within moments they were replaced by a new group coming onto the train, plus several Nazi officers who took the papers Helena gave them and just grunted when they handed them back.

"I wonder," Helena whispered to her daughter, "if they've stopped looking for that spy." Hanna did not reply. Within a half hour the train's engine began to beat as steam built up.

Hanna said nothing until they had started moving again. "Where are we going?" she asked her mother.

"Good question," Helena smiled weakly. "Well, I thought we'd wait until we're out of Praga, maybe stop in a little town somewhere. People are always more generous away from the cities. There will be food in the countryside. We have money, and we can help with the work. I don't know, really, I . . ." Helena's voice trailed off. She realized her daughter was looking at her expectantly. "We'll keep on praying," she said weakly.

For the next two hours the train seemed to stop every fifteen minutes at towns that grew smaller and smaller. The two women stayed on until they reached a village in the wooded hills south of Praga. There they disembarked, together with one or two other people.

The village was located alongside a finger-shaped lake. Hanna heard her mother speaking in Polish to a woman carrying a baby. She nodded and pointed, then walked on. When her mother turned to face Hanna she was smiling.

"At the other end of the street there's a large house, a sort of inn, where we might find a room to rent and a meal. You see, by avoiding the cities we've found the impossible, a place to stay. And when it seems right, we'll move on again."

"But Father said we must stay in Germany . . ."

"*Po polsku,*" Helena spoke so only Hanna could hear.

"From now on, remember to speak nothing but Polish, Hanna. It won't do us any good at all to have these people think we're Germans. We had no choice but to come here, did we?" She was in a hurry to change the subject. "Now, don't forget, no German. You'll find you can pick up enough of what they say here to understand."

Hanna nodded. If her mother did not want to discuss their return to Germany, she would respect her wishes.

Later that afternoon the two women sat together over a meal of sauerkraut and apples, feeling as if they had stumbled into heaven. Obviously the hardships inflicted by the war were not as severe everywhere as they were in some parts of Poland. Helena was already making plans. "We'll go to the local church and talk with the pastor to see how we can help. There are bound to be children who need to be cared for. Maybe we can do some work for the woman we're renting the room from. What's her name? Yes, Mrs. Slovan. Did you notice how she couldn't stop talking when we showed up? She seems like the lonely type."

Hanna knew someone else who hadn't stopped talking. She marveled at the change in her mother since they got off the train. "Why?" she asked. "Why do we have to go out and do all these things?"

Her mother scowled. "Don't be so irritable, Hanna. I shouldn't have to tell you that with the money Father gave us, we are very privileged even to be able to afford a room. Too many people are sleeping on cold streets and in ditches these days, and their numbers will only grow. We're going to do the best we can to help these people as we would our own. I don't know why, but God has brought us here instead of to Dresden."

"I'm sorry, Mother." Hanna hated it when she disappointed her mother. She looked up to see the owner of the house heading toward their table carrying a cup of coffee. She asked if she could join them.

"Yes," Hanna said, trying to make up for her unkind remarks a moment earlier. Helena smiled at her.

Mrs. Slovan nodded. She spoke in Czech, but slowly and simply, trying to make herself understood. The Czech language was so similar to Polish that Hanna could follow most of the conversation. "You talk about Dresden? You hear news?"

Hanna held her breath, wondering how much more the woman had overheard.

"What have you heard?" Helena answered hesitatingly. Hanna kept her eyes on her plate.

"Finish Germans. Ha." The woman grunted.

"What?" Hanna asked. Helena shot her a warning look.

"Won't say where heard," the woman went on. She winked at them both and lowered her voice. "Someone has radio. British and Americans do it." Then she leaned close and pantomimed an explosion.

Hanna almost gasped, thinking of their original destination. She caught herself in time.

Helena spoke fervently, "The Allies are finally keeping their promise. It's about time." Hanna was surprised to hear her mother speaking Polish with a southern accent from the mountains. Hanna had only heard it a few times earlier, when they had made trips to visit her parents' childhood home. But the woman nodded when she heard Helena speak that way. It seemed easier for her.

Hanna thought her mother was taking a terrible chance. If they said too much against the Germans and this woman was an informer, they would be in trouble. If, on the other hand, she was someone who might be able to help them later, it would be important for her to believe Hanna and Helena were Polish refugees who wanted the Germans out of Poland as much as this woman wanted them out of Czechoslovakia.

"Yes! Yes!" the woman slapped her palm on the table and belched. "Radio say bombs fall on Dresden all night. All night, mind you! Bombed it to bits." She paused as if collecting herself, then peered at Helena and Hanna. "Say nothing?"

"Of course not," Helena answered. "We won't tell anyone."

The woman rose. "I go to kitchen now. Then make beds."

As soon as the woman was out of earshot, Helena grabbed her daughter's hand and squeezed it hard. "Oh, Hanna, we were spared. This is confirmation, don't you see? There's no going to Germany now. We're safer here." She paused. "For now, anyway."

"Dresden," Hanna whispered. A shiver ran up her spine, and she remembered the warning of a dark-haired man. "I'm cold, Mother."

Helena was staring out the window. "What? Yes, of course. And you're still tired, child. Go to bed and sleep straight through until tomorrow if you want. I'll bring some food upstairs and leave it by our bed. You've got to take care of yourself during these first months."

Hanna rose and went to her mother. She leaned over the stooped shoulders and hugged them. "Bless you, Mother."

"Ah, my girl." Helena took Hanna's face in her hands and kissed her cheek. "Sleep now."

Hanna climbed the stairs and entered the room. She undressed, then slipped under the cool quilt. As she drifted off to sleep, Hanna saw the pines speeding past her until they turned into smokestacks. Bombs rained down on a city somewhere to the west. Hanna watched as buildings crumbled. The train would crash. A baby on the tracks. Hanna screamed and woke up, soaked in sweat, her mother's arms around her.

# 10

## Late January–May 1945

Tadeusz glanced quickly around Johann's study. "Thank God we finished burning everything." Johann had only nodded when Russian soldiers burst into the room. They glanced at the fire flickering behind the two men and knew they were too late. Any incriminating evidence had most likely been destroyed.

One of them spoke. Johann could not understand the language, and Tadeusz was not about to let on that he could. But it wasn't difficult to know what the rifle tip meant when it pointed at them, then motioned toward the ground. They lay face down, Johann with more difficulty than Tadeusz, and waited. The rough wool of the carpet rubbed against their cheeks. Tadeusz smelled the stale body odor of the man standing over him. He wondered how the Germans, with their warm winter coats, could have allowed themselves to be chased out of Kraków by these soldiers with unshaven and haggard faces, tattered clothing, and chilblain fingers.

Johann placed his hands behind his head, touching the hard skull under his hair. He could feel his pulse at the base of his neck, waiting for the hot pain of a bullet. As Tadeusz waited, his fear broke out like sweat. The clock ticked only a few times, then into the silence the Russian spoke again, this time to his comrade. It was a question. The other man turned and climbed upstairs to the attic. Tadeusz heard him shoving around furniture and turning over beds. A great deal of noise also came from the stairway leading downstairs to the kitchen and further, to the basement.

"They're tearing the place apart," Tadeusz whispered. Johann said nothing.

The guard, meanwhile, walked around the room, poking his rifle tip into the sofa cushions and turning up the edges of the carpets. He took a painting of a sailing ship off the wall and removed a candlestick from the desk. As soon as Tadeusz reached down to scratch his leg the man jumped back into place, riveting his rifle onto Tadeusz's head.

A few moments later Tadeusz heard several soldiers leave the house laughing. The man from upstairs came down, said something, and picked up the painting and candlestick. Then an officer entered the room. Tadeusz and Johann, still inhaling the dust of the carpet, watched as their guard saluted this man and stood to one side.

The officer read from a packet of papers he held in his hand. Tadeusz was surprised to hear him speak Polish with an accent from the south of the country. "You are Johann Müller?" Johann nodded at the feet standing by his nose.

"You are under arrest . . . and you are?" The man raised his eyebrows at Tadeusz.

"Herr Müller's son-in-law." Tadeusz spoke German. He wanted there to be no misunderstanding. Johann's only chance of surviving what would come next lay in Tadeusz's remaining at his side. "What has Herr Müller done to. . . ?"

Johann interrupted him. "He's nothing. He's Polish."

"I see. Well, that makes it quite simple, then. You, as a former resident of the German population and member of the intelligentsia, are under arrest for corroboration with the Nazis." The man paused and leafed through his papers.

"We should have found more to link you with them, Herr Müller. Perhaps we will yet. And you"—he lifted his nose at Tadeusz—"I have nothing here about you."

"You can't take him away!" Tadeusz cried.

The officer raised an eyebrow. "You are free, sir, and not in a position to object. If you insist, however, come to the office tomorrow and someone will take up your case." He mumbled an address at Tadeusz, then turned and left, quickly saying something in Russian to the guard.

This man, in turn, kicked Tadeusz, motioning toward the corner. Then he took Johann by the collar and hauled him up. "No!" Tadeusz cried. Without answering, the man dragged Johann out of the house and down the street, even as Johann snatched up both his canes.

---

As soon as it was light Tadeusz ventured out onto the streets, which were littered with broken glass. When he arrived at the address given him, he found a room full of people also trying to retrieve lost loved ones. The building was a former Nazi ministry building. Once Tadeusz had been there for an hour, though, he noticed something curious: the people who were called into the office did not come out. He hoped there was a separate entrance.

When his turn came, Tadeusz entered the inner office, which was full of Russian soldiers. One came forward and asked whose case he had come to appeal. "Johann Müller. There has been some mistake."

The officer in charge ruffled through a stack of papers, then looked up at Tadeusz and nodded. "Go on. What did you want to tell us? I take it you used to work for this man. You're Polish. Why don't you tell us about your job and the type of contracts he used to work on? Unfortunately it seems that most of the records have been destroyed. Would you know something about that?"

Too late, Tadeusz realized what he'd walked into. He was there to inform on Johann. And no matter what he said, they would arrest him. So he simply shook his head. "No," he said softly. "You should take me to him."

"Yes, I think we should." The officer nodded at two of the guards. They stepped forward and took Tadeusz by the elbows. Tadeusz felt a sinking fear well up inside him. Had he survived the war for this? He tried to focus on the hope that his imprisonment would serve some purpose, that perhaps he could help Johann to survive whatever lay ahead of them.

The guards did indeed bring Tadeusz to Johann. The old man was waiting in a large warehouse near the train station. The damage the Gestapo had done to Johann's mouth showed in the toothless grin he gave Tadeusz when the soldiers pushed him through the door. That smile filled Tadeusz with the assurance that he had done the right thing.

The two men embraced without a word. Then they joined the long lines of men, women, and children being herded toward the train station.

For the next two days they watched as row after row shuffled forward to be loaded into cattle cars. Tadeusz resolved that nothing would separate him from Johann. The older man's legs seemed to be bothering him more than ever. Tadeusz made sure Johann received most of what little food and water the Russians did give them.

Around him Tadeusz heard the other prisoners whispering, echoing his own fears.

"Where are they sending us?"

"How long of a trip will it be?"

"Don't we even get a trial?"

"Don't be a fool. Ask for a trial, and you'll be shot."

"But I helped the Underground during the war. I swear it!"

"Prove it."

"I'm thirsty."

"How much longer?"

Tadeusz concentrated on his father-in-law. He tried to sit next to him, protecting him from the icy wind that swept over the station platform. Despite Tadeusz's efforts, Johann could not seem to get warm. Once they boarded the train, however, all that changed. They were put into a closed car with twenty other men. Soon the heat and the humidity and the smells became nearly unbearable.

The long trip deep into the Soviet Union seemed to last forever. Finally, after endless weeks, the train stopped. When the doors opened, Tadeusz handed out the three men who had died on the journey. His own face had grown gaunt, and Johann's knee joints had stiffened to the point that he could barely walk. Tadeusz helped him down from the car and then stared out over a barren, icy plain to a collection of drab, weather-beaten buildings.

"Kazakhstan," a fellow prisoner whispered as the brutal wind whipped his beard. "I heard the guards talking."

Then the guards were walking briskly among them,

pointing, separating them into groups. "You! Over there!" Tadeusz could only glance at Johann as the old man was led lurching in the opposite direction. He wondered if Johann would even survive the week.

---

The Russians had divided the prisoners into groups consisting of different nationalities, hoping the language differences would prevent them from organizing themselves. Tadeusz slept that night in a wooden shack with Ukrainians, Slovaks, Russians, and even a few Hungarians. Not even the cold whistling in through the cracks, the hardness of the wooden bunk, or the sharpness of his fear was enough to keep Tadeusz from falling into an exhausted, dreamless sleep.

He woke to find the unshaven face of a dark-haired man grinning at him. "Wake up, swine!" The grin widened to reveal rotting teeth with gaps in between. It took Tadeusz only a moment to shake himself awake and realize where he was, but in that moment the guard had reached up with an iron bar and landed a series of solid blows on Tadeusz's legs and torso.

"I said move! You'll learn to listen when I give you an order!"

Nearly blind from the pain, Tadeusz hobbled after the other prisoners. He ate breakfast without noticing what it was. Then he and the rest of his barracks were marched out to a field where large pits had been dug through a thinning patch of snow. He saw men emerging from the holes. Each carried a basket of dirt strapped to his back. Not until he was deep inside did Tadeusz find out the pits were part of a gold mine.

Tadeusz's engineering mind shuddered at the primitive

construction of the mine shafts. Even the deeper ones were barely reinforced, and the few wooden beams that did shore up the walls looked rotten. Shafts at different levels ran parallel to each other with hardly any space between them. In many, the ceilings were too low for anyone but a child to walk under them upright.

After his first hour of carrying stones and dirt up the ramp to the surface, Tadeusz thought he could do no more, but somehow he kept on. *If only they don't bring Johann here,* he kept thinking over and over. The cadence of the prayer brought him a measure of comfort. He recited it with every step: "Not for Johann, not for Johann."

By the end of the first twelve-hour shift, Tadeusz could no longer straighten up. That evening he experienced a new appreciation for his shabby barracks. He longed for the slab of wood that was his bed. Once he finally could ease his body down, he sighed, breathing in air that seemed fresh and sweet compared with the stale stuff he had inhaled all day. The man below him moaned. Tadeusz's last thought before he slept was of Hanna.

The next morning Tadeusz forced himself to sit up as soon as he heard the guards entering the barracks. He jumped down onto the floor and stood at attention just as the black-haired guard turned down the aisle. The man did not grin when he saw Tadeusz, but he did raise his bar threateningly. Tadeusz held his breath, and the guard passed him by. Only then did Tadeusz notice he was trembling.

He let his breath out slowly, then followed the other prisoners outside. There he compelled himself to take notice of his surroundings. As he lined up to use the hole in the ground that served as latrine, Tadeusz promised himself that he would see every detail, to make his mind work, no matter what. Carefully he took in the white steppe, where spring had already broken the back of winter and melting snow stretched out on all sides of the camp. Just within his line of sight, Tadeusz thought he could make out some trees.

Tadeusz dreaded the place he would soon return to for another twelve hours. The previous day's beating had left him with fist-sized bruises and wincing pain. But he knew the hours of hard labor would take an even greater toll in the long run.

After the dirty water and moldy bread, which was his meager breakfast, Tadeusz and the others marched back to the mines, moving like a column of ghosts. Tadeusz could hardly bear the thought of entering those dark holes again. He wondered how many days like this one still stretched before him. Then his thoughts were interrupted by a prisoner near the head of the line, who started shouting and pointing. The guards motioned for the group to stop and wait. The men watched as two guards walked up to something on the ground and kicked it.

A partially decomposed corpse.

Like a lost ball, the words bounced back and forth in different languages among the prisoners.

"Woman who ran away."

"Frozen to death."

"A few months ago."

"Spy."

"Left her children behind, though."

Within a few minutes the guards had the men moving again, headed toward the mines. As Tadeusz passed the tumbled corpse, the man beside him, who happened to be Polish, told him that in the winter, if the guards wanted to punish prisoners, all they had to do was take them a few miles from camp and leave them on the steppe. Freezing winds did the rest. This woman must have come from another camp a few miles to the east.

Tadeusz did not want to imagine it. By sheer force of effort, he brought himself back to the present. He told himself that fear had no place here, and that he should concentrate on details. It was a pattern of thought Tadeusz would follow religiously in the days to come.

Tadeusz and the other prisoners worked seven days in the mines, then seven more. He surprised himself by finishing a month in relatively good health. His young body had adapted to the work better than most. When he wasn't working, he focused on resting.

The ritual of fear prompted by the dark-haired man on guard duty who had beaten him on his first day remained, however. Dawn after dawn it allowed terror to seep into Tadeusz's heart. During the interminable days, when his mind had nothing else to dwell on, the thought of what this guard might do should he catch Tadeusz sleeping late became even more terrifying than the beatings themselves.

Tadeusz's only moments of peace came when he rested at night, trying to relax his knotted muscles. During these quiet moments he kept the fear and worry at bay by thinking of Hanna, imagining her safe and healthy, willing it to be true. During the days he focused his energies on working, carrying safely, lifting carefully, watching his step so that he would not turn an ankle. He prayed, as Johann and Hanna had taught him, hoping for a peace that would exhaust him less than any anger.

During his first few months at the camp, as the snow melted and spring came, Tadeusz did everything in his power to locate Johann. By talking to the other prisoners, he slowly came to realize that the baskets of dirt he brought to the surface were transported to a place near a stream. There women and the weaker prisoners from another camp nearby rinsed through the clods, searching for the heavy lumps of gold. Tadeusz was desperate to find out if Johann had been sent to this riverside site. Daily he prayed for an opportunity.

Then, almost three months after arriving at the camp, a guard ordered him to ride with the wagon to the stream. The man who ordinarily unloaded it had not been in the lineup after breakfast. As simply as that, Tadeusz was told that the job was his.

After nearly three hours, he arrived at the wooded spot by the stream. Tadeusz looked around frantically, trying to locate Johann, hoping he was here. Even as he trudged back and forth, unloading the baskets, Tadeusz refused to consider the alternative.

His eyes raked over the area by the stream, too far away to see clearly who was down by the water. He squinted at the figures moving between the trees, but could see only a few women bent over large shallow pans.

Not until he had finished unloading and was riding away in the back of the empty wagon did he see someone he thought might be Johann. As the wagon rounded a corner, the group of people by the water came into clear view. When Tadeusz saw the familiar stooped figure, the bald head, he stood and waved both hands.

"Johann! Johann! Father!" he called out. Instantly Tadeusz felt the blow of the guard's rifle butt against his back. It brought Tadeusz down with a thud, but not before Tadeusz thought he heard an answering shout.

Tadeusz's impulsiveness cost him any additional chance to return to the site by the stream. It was made clear to him in no uncertain terms that he would never again be given a chance to work anywhere but in the mines.

If the guards had their way, Tadeusz would stay working there day after endless day, until he too became nothing but a rotting corpse, lost out on the steppe.

# 11

## Early February–Late March 1945

After leaping off the train that had taken him away from Rokossovski's camp, Jacek spent the next two weeks sneaking back and forth on foot behind the lines. By the time he arrived in Gdańsk, Jacek's expensive clothes were ruined, and he fit right in with the rest of the refugee population.

The first thing Jacek did was find a tailor who was still in business. The sign in the window said he sold to Germans only. Jacek thought how odd it all seemed to be doing something so common in such uncommon days. He pushed the door open to the sound of a small bell tinkling above him. The shop was dark. Dust had settled on the long wooden counter. Glass cases where bolts of cloth should have stood were now empty.

A wrinkled hand pushed aside the curtain behind the counter in front of Jacek, and a small man emerged. "I am not the owner, I don't know where he is," he began, his voice dropping as he caught sight of the stack of bills Jacek was already spreading between his hands like a full deck of cards.

"All I need are some clothes." Jacek spoke in German. "Ready-made. Whatever you have in stock."

The man smiled, yellow teeth framing the gaps. "Maybe I am the owner, but of course. Sir, I would give you my own trousers for what you hold there, but they would be too small." The man paused for a moment, still smiling, and noted the breadth of Jacek's shoulders, the length of his legs, the shabbiness of what he wore.

Jacek was used to seeing people respond to him out of fear, suspicion at the very least, but this purely professional interest caught him off guard. The man's smile left no doubt in Jacek's mind that nothing scared him. *How is it possible?* Jacek wondered. *What could possibly cause such a smile?*

The old man turned his back on Jacek and disappeared behind the faded curtain. "*Moment, bitte.*"

Two seconds later Jacek heard the bell on the door make its false sound again. He glanced in its direction as the dirty glass door swung open, the low winter sun blinding him. A shape passed between him and the light, then Jacek heard the door close again. He stepped to the left to get out of the glare and saw a woman's face.

For a moment the sound and sun all seemed suspended. Dust danced in the faded sunbeams that split the space between them.

Jacek's eyes drank in the sight of the small woman. It was as if a deer had just walked onto a smoking battleground, so out of place was her beauty. She stood startled, truly unaware of her impact on Jacek. He coughed, more to remind himself of where he was than for any other reason. He watched her catch her breath and swallow, a fine down shifting slightly on her throat with the movement.

"I'm so sorry. I thought the shop was empty. We don't have much business now that . . ." Her voice trailed off.

"We?" Jacek asked.

"Yes." The old man had reappeared from behind the

curtain like an actor for an encore. He spoke quickly. "My daughter means that not many people have your resources, and of course, we have traded much for what we needed. The war, you know." In his arms he carried trousers, suit jackets, and a wool coat. "I was saving these for the end of the war, and now I know why." Again the smile. "You can try these on in there." The man glanced toward another curtain to the left.

Jacek took the clothes and swiveled to look at the woman again. She stood looking down, one hand feeling the fingers of the other. Just before he entered the changing area he paused, hoping he could catch her eye, but she would not look up. So Jacek disappeared behind his own curtain and tried the clothes on. When he emerged again the woman was gone. He handed half the stack back to the man. "I'll take these, and the coat."

"Yes, it is of very good quality. You felt the wool?" Jacek nodded. The tailor was so eager to take Jacek's money that his hand shook as he reached toward the sum Jacek offered. "You are very generous, sir, and I had not even named an amount. This will make these last weeks bearable for my daughter and me. For of course we both know this money will be worthless in what, a few months' time, perhaps?" The man eyed Jacek curiously.

His guard suddenly up, Jacek stopped counting out the bills. He lifted his gaze to the tailor's and found only a question framed in the shrewd eyes.

"What is it?" Jacek asked.

The old man pointed a yellow fingernail at Jacek's torn sleeve. "You are not from here?"

"Ah, yes," Jacek sighed. His clothes did give a lot away, which was why he had stopped here in the first place. "But

I am," Jacek smiled thinly. "I was born in Danzig, a native son, you see."

The old man nodded very slowly, his right hand rubbing his chin, as if this explained a great deal. "So you are not feeling very proud of being German these days either?" It was more of a statement than a question. Jacek wondered at the man's openness. Didn't he have a reason to be careful? Didn't they all?

The man continued, not seeming to care who heard him. "Oh, you know, at the beginning of the war we were so proud. But then my own son was taken out of school. They made him work in one of our factories east of here. Ach, and we are Germans," he added as if it should have been a saving grace. "So, when did you say you were here last?"

Jacek smiled at the man's subtle way of asking things. "Around the beginning of the war," he admitted.

"Well, then, you will notice that most of us still left in Gdańsk have changed our minds since the beginning of the war. Now I could spit on Nazism. Bah."

Jacek raised an eyebrow as the man continued in a softer tone. "Since 1941, when Germany attacked the USSR, the situation has just gone from bad to worse. You won't hear anyone shouting in parades on these streets anymore. More likely, they whimper and moan for some reason or another."

Jacek wondered when the man would realize he had gone too far. But this was not the case. The man stared at Jacek, the awareness of what he had just admitted shining brightly in his eyes. "Now, make an old man happy and let me see that money again."

Jacek snorted, enjoying the power he felt when he handled the wad of bills. He was still thinking about the woman who had passed through the room a few moments earlier. She clouded his judgment like morning mist moving through the hills. The man's confession had created an air of intimacy in the stuffy shop.

Before he knew what he was doing, Jacek asked, "Would you happen to have a room for rent?"

"If you need a room, I have a spare one upstairs," the man answered immediately. He dropped his eyes back down to his hands as he took the clothes that were too large for Jacek away from him.

Jacek had surprised himself, but he rationalized that finding a place to sleep had been next on his list of things to do as soon as he got into the city. Besides, sometimes spontaneity was the best way to make a situation seem believable. Everything about this shop seemed irregular, but Jacek had learned that this in itself reduced the likelihood of additional unexpected events. Jacek thought of the tailor's daughter and heard himself saying, "Yes, I had planned to find somewhere to stay later today."

The old man's face lit up into another empty grin. "Who can plan?"

The man introduced himself as Herr Braun. Jacek shook his hand and handed him a few more bills. "I trust this is enough?" Then he gathered up his new clothes and followed Herr Braun past the curtain.

Halfway up the stairs, Jacek heard a door open and close. He looked up and sighed. This was what he had been hoping for. Herr Braun waited until they had reached the landing, then waved a hand at his daughter. "Monika, this gentleman will be staying with us for a short while."

Jacek reached out a hand to bring her small, cool fingers to his lips. "It is my pleasure. Please, you and your father can call me Jacek. There is no reason to be formal, is there? Not in days like these."

"No indeed," Monika answered, but still refused to meet his gaze.

Herr Braun moved down the hall and stopped in front of a door. "This was my son's room. Monika will make the bed for you. You should be comfortable here. The bath and toilet are at the other end of the hall. I imagine you have not slept in a bed for some time, am I right?"

Jacek smiled and nodded, wondering how it was possible that these people still had bed linen. During the next few moments, as Monika busied herself with the bed, Jacek could not take his eyes off her. Only after she had nodded at him and left the room did he notice the Iron Cross hanging above the bedstead. A half hour later there was a tap on the door and Monika's soft voice saying there was a kettle of hot water in the bathroom for him if he wanted to take a bath. Jacek could not believe his luck. In the bath he scrubbed himself thoroughly, reveling in the luxury. Then he returned to his room and fell into bed.

Jacek woke to find he had slept straight through the evening and the night; the midmorning sun shone bright through the threadbare curtains in his room. He rose and shaved, using the razor, mirror, and bowl he found on the dresser. But the two-week run through the woods and back roads behind German lines had exhausted him. He moved sluggishly from one task to the next.

When he was ready, Jacek left his room and headed down the stairs. Just as he reached the curtain he heard the front door open and the bell above it tinkle. He paused, remembering his impressions summoned by the sound from the day before.

There was laughter. Jacek caught his breath at the

sound of it, a young woman's laughter. He could not remember the last time he had heard such sweetness. He paused and listened, despite himself aching for more. Perhaps the sound had been around him and he had simply not noticed. Now, letting the warm waves of Monika's laughter wash over him, Jacek thought back, and back and back. No, he could not remember hearing it since, since Barbara.

Jacek shoved the memory aside. He would not allow his other selves to get in the way of what he had to do. He shoved the curtain aside. The laughter stopped.

"Ah, Herr Jacek. I trust you slept well?" Herr Braun nodded at his daughter. "Monika here has just arrived back from a visit to a village outside the city. Since early in the war, everyone here, both Poles and Germans, has known that the only way to secure enough food to live off of was to leave the city and buy food in the villages.

"I don't know how it is where you have come from"—the man sounded like a tour guide—"but here all food is only available on a coupon basis, including fish, eggs, vegetables, fruit, and even berries. Well, of course most of these coupons have become worthless lately. Although it's illegal to buy and sell food without coupons, that's become the only way to survive. Food is only available on a bartering basis. And since the summer, bread rations have been cut to only a few hundred grams per person. Now, though, now even the clothing coupons . . ."

Jacek wondered why the man was going on and on. He looked up. Monika was laughing again. Jacek swallowed hard, startled by the memories the sound of her laughter summoned. The risk was too great to even think of his past at a time like this, and in such a place.

With a physical effort he blinked, thrusting the memories aside, concentrating instead on her dark brown eyes. Now he had no trouble getting her to look at him as she spoke. "Yes, and now my coupons for underwear—can you believe it? Underwear. Well, they're no good, either."

Jacek smiled. "Your underwear? No, I can't imagine." And then he laughed. The sound bubbled out of him like rich oil hidden in dark rock depths, under pressure since before time. It was an old and unfamiliar sensation, a sound Jacek had not made for what seemed like several lifetimes. His chest heaved as the laughter rocked him.

Monika and her father exchanged glances, both smiling. "This was so funny?" Herr Braun asked Jacek.

Jacek wiped his eyes, chuckling. "Yes, Herr Braun. Here and now, it was so funny. My dear, your underwear." He turned to Monika and took her small hand. "I feel this has set the tone for our entire relationship, Fräulein Monika. May your underwear continue to be a source of joy to us both."

Monika gasped, and the blood rushed to her face. She jerked her hand out of Jacek's and covered her mouth. "I . . . I, how could you? I never meant anything . . ." She whipped around and looked at her father for help, then back at Jacek accusingly.

But Herr Braun was holding his sides, trying to keep his daughter from hearing his own laughter. "Oh, Monika," he burst out. "I'm afraid you brought this on yourself."

Jacek watched in fascination as a smile stole back onto Monika's face. In the next instant she was making that lovely sound again. He thought he caught her winking at him, then she disappeared behind the curtain and flew up the stairs. Jacek could still feel the power of her presence in the movement of the air around him.

Jacek's heart was racing as he left the shop. He needed to walk around the city and get his bearings, but the tiny bell would not stop ringing in his ears. He played the scene in his mind over and over. Laughter. Who was this woman who had taught him to laugh again, and at a time like this?

Jacek walked faster, struggling to invoke his hard-earned habit of discipline. He could not, would not become involved again. Gradually, as he settled into a rhythmic stride, he began to feel himself again. His more recent self. In the afternoon, when he returned to the shop, Monika was out of sight. Jacek responded to Herr Braun's effusive greeting with a short wave and disappeared into his room.

The next two days were spent getting a feel for the city and its movements. The first thing he noticed was that there were very few SA and SS uniforms to be seen in the streets. It looked as though the Germans were leaving the defense of Gdańsk to the regular army. And that very defense, with its strengths and weaknesses, was the reason Jacek had come to the city.

During these two days Jacek had found out most of what Rokossovski needed. He came and went from the tailor's shop at strange hours, making sure he would not accidentally run into Monika. That he would take such pains was a bad sign in itself. But he had a mission to do, and time was running out. There was still one crucial place he had to visit without delay.

Jacek managed to get inside the shipyard only three nights after his arrival in Gdańsk. He had already been waiting most of the afternoon and evening, watching the gates and waiting, waiting for some sort of activity that could provide cover. Finally, in the confusion of docking and unloading a ship that had just come in from Hamburg, Jacek walked right past the guards. He shuffled stooped, like an old man, dressed like a beggar in the clothes he had worn into the city, his right arm swinging a vodka bottle. The German troops rushed back and forth, unloading munitions for the Nazis' last defense, and no one paid any attention to Jacek as he crumpled down next to a pile of trash.

He squatted, shivering in the February cold, listening and watching. All night long he moved from one place to another, scribbling notes under the cover of darkness. By the time it grew light, he had counted enough crates, seen enough new tanks, and spent enough time assessing the submarines being built to make his report. No one had noticed him.

A truck loaded with some of the ship's military cargo rumbled to a stop within a few feet of where Jacek had ended up. Too stiff to move suddenly, Jacek shook his legs, flexing the muscles until they started to cramp. Then he counted to five and rolled over, once, and twice. Looking up, he saw the filthy underside of the truck, reached up and grabbed hold of the axle. He hooked his ankles underneath and hung on as the truck clattered through the gates.

Once he was out of the shipyard, Jacek rolled out from under the truck the first time it stopped and ducked into a back alley. There he slapped his legs and thighs, trying to get his blood circulating.

Jacek had everything he needed. This was the last place on his list of locations to visit before going to meet his contact. The information he had gleaned here and elsewhere in Gdańsk over the past days would serve his new Russian friends well. Jacek thought that the Germans would probably not manage to hold on to Gdańsk much longer than a month. Two at the most.

Jacek emerged from the alley, looked around, crossed the street, and walked the two blocks to another alley behind a boarded-up restaurant. The day before he had hidden a small travel bag in a dry gap in the wall. Now he stripped as quickly as he could in the freezing weather and put on one of Herr Braun's new suits. He rolled the clothes he had worn at the shipyard into a ball and shoved them to the bottom of his bag. The beggar disguise might prove useful again.

Now Jacek looked anything but a beggar. When he had finished combing his hair and smoothing out the wrinkles in his coat, he looked precisely the part of a distinguished businessman. Jacek looked up. The street adjoining this alley was normally not busy; that's why he had chosen it. But now he could hear German shouts coming from up the street. He moved closer to the alley entrance, but remained out of sight from the street.

As people came into view, Jacek recognized what had become a familiar sight around Gdańsk, German soldiers guarding a large crowd of Ukrainian and Russian prisoners, both men and women. They had been brought to Gdańsk during the last two years of the war and forced to do street cleaning and other manual labor jobs. They were easy to distinguish from other prisoners because of their extremely shabby clothes. Despite the early hour, this particular group was being followed by a small swarm of street children as the guards moved them to a new work site. It was strange to hear children's voices, even if they were only skipping through the snow, dogging the steps of the prisoners and jeering at them. The objects of their insults could not even understand the words.

Jacek waited until the prisoners and the children had passed, then stepped out onto the street and started walking. As he headed east he could not help but notice the changes brought on by the approaching end of the war. In this port city that had been used by both Poland and Germany before the war, both populations were now bound by a single fear. Tens of thousands of German refugees were fleeing to Gdańsk from Prussian lands in the east. The stories of what Soviet soldiers had done to the Prussian villages were even more harrowing than what was happening elsewhere in Poland. For the Soviets, Prussian meant German, and these villages had suffered the desperate fate of a losing enemy. Gdańsk, which considered itself German, was doomed to the same fate.

Jacek made his way to the meeting set up by Rokossovski. He found the contact precisely where Rokossovski had said he would be, at the Hotel Eden across from the Gdańsk train station. In the front window was posted a sign, "Dogs and Poles not allowed!" When he entered and saw the empty dining room, Jacek went to the men's room and found a man there, standing at the sink and washing his hands. The man nodded at Jacek. When Jacek came out of the booth the man was still there, this time bending over backward to see himself in the mirror as he combed his hair.

"We have a mutual friend," the man said in Russian.

Jacek masked his surprise that any contact would take such a risk. The man must have had a description of him. Not willing to play for such high odds, Jacek switched into Polish. They exchanged the passwords he had learned from the contents of his envelope from Warszawa.

Satisfied, Jacek began his report, speaking in hushed tones. "You'll already have noticed, but I can confirm from all I've seen during the last days, that the Nazis' defenses are crumbling, even with the reinforcements they've brought in. The Germans had three lines of defense. The first ran up along the coast past Gdynia, as I'm sure our friend found out earlier this month. The second line includes the surrounding suburbs of Gdynia, Sopot, and Gdańsk and is based on the lay of natural surroundings such as hills, as well as houses, streets, and large buildings.

"Now, it's important to know that the Germans have ordered the third line of defense to be held at any cost. This includes the strategic points like ports and major infrastructure. Buildings within this zone will be defended on a house-by-house basis."

Jacek paused. His contact simply stood, comb still in hand, and waited. Whoever he was, Jacek thought, he didn't say much, and his expression revealed nothing. Jacek hated working this way, face-to-face; the chances of betrayal were far too great. And his success or failure depended entirely on whether this information reached Rokossovski on time.

Jacek continued, "Tell our friend that he was right. Himmler is out, and Heinrici has taken his place. Here . . ." Jacek fished out of his pocket the notes and drawings he had made the night before.

As he handed them over he explained the simple code in which they were written and showed the man his map. "Here is the main entrance. You work your way counterclockwise around the port, and you can see how much armory there is and the various stages of the submarines they're working on. No new projects here. And look—" Jacek switched to another paper.

"This is a plan of the city's fortifications as of yesterday. It will look more formidable from the outside than it actually is. The Germans have bored shooting holes in buildings, connected houses on one street by making holes in the walls. They've propped sandbags against windows on the ground floors of buildings and built small bunkers at different strategic points of the city. The Hel Peninsula will be the most difficult point in the city to take. Here, the rest is self-explanatory."

Jacek handed over the papers, then took a step backward and watched the man refold his notes and slip them into his jacket pocket. The man smiled. Without another word to Jacek, he tucked his shirt into his trousers and walked out the door.

Jacek watched him go with an odd mixture of worry and satisfaction. He had done his little initiation stint. Now they would know his worth. God only knew, he had earned it. He could only hope there would be no doubt of his allegiance once word reached Warszawa of what Jacek had passed on to Rokossovski. But he could not shake the feeling that the situation was all wrong, that he should be in Warszawa and not in Gdańsk.

As Jacek returned to Herr Braun's shop for the first time in nearly forty-eight hours, he finally let himself feel the fatigue of the last two nights. It was strange to be walking toward the shop in the daylight. Jacek passed a churchyard on the way, its brick wall covered with German graffiti: "The People Are the Army!" and "Danzig Remains German!" and "No Victory Without Struggle!" *The Germans must be desperate,* he thought, *to have their soldiers painting the walls with propaganda*. It really was true, though, the city had already become a battleground.

*"Guten Tag!"* Jacek felt the voice rather than heard it. He looked up and read, "Victory or Bolshevik Chaos." Then he saw Monika. At the sound of her voice, the inevitability of what he had been avoiding for three days came down on him like a heavy weight.

"Ah, Monika," he sighed, his eyes narrowing.

She came to him, her arms outstretched, palms down. He took her right hand and kissed it. Monika reached up and stroked the dark stubble on his chin. "You are tired?"

"Yes, I am." Jacek felt more than tired, though. He felt beaten. The eyes of the beautiful woman in front of him shone with concern. That she asked no questions only endeared her more to him. He would not deny himself the comfort being offered.

Monika asked, "Shall I bring you home?"

Jacek put his arm around her waist and simply nodded. The touch of her sent flames of warmth up his arm. He knew it was wrong, the timing was all wrong. But everything about his being in Gdańsk was all wrong. Why should an attraction like this be any different? He was too weary to sort it all out. "Yes, bring me home, would you?"

Walking down that street, entering the shop, the bell, disappearing behind the curtain, climbing the stairs, her assurance that her father was not home—these were all events that blurred together the next morning for Jacek. He woke up to the smell of Monika's perfume on his pillow. She was not there. He remembered her undressing and his surprise at his own strength. It was morning, Jacek could see that much. Hadn't they gone to bed in the afternoon? So he *had* been tired.

He rolled over and savored the memory of Monika in his arms. They had matched in many ways. Her dark eyes and his had locked more than once, a desperate act of giving when the world around them was so bent on doing the opposite.

Jacek wanted more.

He did not know how long he would be stuck in Gdańsk waiting for the war to end. The day before, he had said it could be two months. The orders in the envelope he had been given specifically stated that he should stay in Gdańsk until the city was liberated. Had it been another test?

The premonition Jacek had first felt in the Eden only intensified. He could not stop feeling that he was caught in a trap, that he had been lured to the wrong place at the wrong time. With every precious week that passed, the provisional government in Warszawa was becoming better established. And where was he?

Jacek realized he had placed himself in a terrible dilemma. In wanting to fulfill the one mission, he was being forced to abort the other. Would his obeying orders and making contact with Rokossovski be worth his absence during the formative weeks of the new government? He could not know for certain.

And so Jacek chose to seek out Monika. He chose her as his way of getting through the next weeks. She enabled him to do nothing as the panic in Gdańsk reached a fevered pitch. For months already, evacuation ships had been sailing daily from Gdańsk and the smaller city of Gdynia up the coast. These carried German refugees and Gdańsk Germans across the Baltic to Finland. The few long-distance trains heading west were crowded with the families of German officials. Any semblance of orderly evacuation quickly disintegrated. People were hurried out of the city without any means of organization or transport. The city had become flooded with refugees, all of whom were suffering from the frigid winter conditions.

This panic puzzled Jacek. Actually, it was Monika's lack of response to it that confused him. And why hadn't Herr Braun commented on Jacek's obvious involvement with his daughter? Whenever they saw each other, the old man acted as if nothing were going on, despite the fact that the walls of Jacek's room were so thin that he could often hear Herr Braun snoring. Why didn't the panic seem to touch this family?

Jacek recognized the blind fear gripping Gdańsk as the same he had felt back in Kraków in January. The difference now was that he could not leave. Together with the rest of the city remaining behind, Jacek held his breath and waited.

But the end came sooner than Jacek had predicted. Already by the first days of March, Soviet armies had fought their way from the west and north and were heading down the Baltic coast. Most of the city's population hid in underground shelters and cellars to avoid the constant shelling of the Soviet Army in the hills around Gdańsk and the bombs from their planes. Jacek and Monika and Herr Braun set up housekeeping in the basement of the shop and continued to wait for the inevitable.

One thing Jacek had accurately predicted was the German fanaticism to defend Gdańsk, no matter what. Civilians were forced to go to work, soldiers to remain at their posts and die there if necessary. By mid-March corpses of people who had disobeyed these orders or simply been unable to make it to their jobs could be found hanging from every second tree along the Adolf-Hitler-Allee, a main street coming into the city. Around their necks hung signs stating, "I thought about surrendering."

For surrender, indeed, was uppermost in the minds of everyone, especially the Russians. By the third week in March, they had captured the seaside resort of Sopot. It would just be a matter of days before Gdynia fell into their hands. Russian pilots dropped thousands of pamphlets into the streets of Gdańsk, calling for unconditional surrender by eight in the morning, on March 26. The Germans' refusal was the equivalent of a death warrant for the city's population. The same Soviet pilots returned to bomb the city into devastation, and heavy artillery was brought into the streets as the Soviet Army set about attacking Gdańsk from three directions at once.

Jacek waited with Monika and her father in their basement, and while waiting, discovered that the fear had sucked up their air to breathe. The waiting stifled them all. They filled the time with rereading old books and playing word games and staring into space. And yet they never spoke of the obvious, never talked of why they were there together.

Finally, Jacek was the one who brought the subject up. He and Monika were sitting on their bed—actually two cots shoved together in a corner of the basement. Only the breadth of the cellar and a dwindling pile of coal separated them from Herr Braun, who lay snoring in the other corner.

Jacek dreaded asking Monika a question that could shift the depth of what they shared. But since she and Herr Braun continued to keep their silence, Jacek felt he had no choice. He knew better than most that their time of waiting, their time together was running out.

"Monika?" He raised himself up on his elbow and reached out a hand to stroke her back.

*Why didn't you try to leave like the others?* he wanted to ask. In the distance they could hear the Soviet shells raining down onto the city and the German Second Army's response. Instead he said, "Tell me what is happening here? I mean in Gdańsk." He hesitated. "And with your family."

Monika nodded, as if acknowledging the sound of words she had long expected to hear. "You want me to tell you why I'm staying, but you won't tell me why you're here. I probably don't want to know, do I?"

Jacek's hand stopped caressing her shoulder. He waited for her voice, forcing himself not to respond.

"I see. So, 'what is happening here?' All right, what can I tell you? I have a feeling you already know all you need."

Jacek caught the slightest trace of bitterness in her voice. Now he crawled up behind her and took her into his arms. "Monika, what is it?"

She would not face him. She turned away even as his grip tightened and spoke softly. "You wouldn't be here if you didn't know. Jacek, you tell me nothing about yourself, then you ask me this. Do I really have to tell you? As the Red Army gets closer, more and more people are desperately trying to find a way out of here. You've seen the evacuation ships sailing out of Gdańsk every day."

"And you, sweet Monika, why aren't you on one of those ships?" Jacek could feel Monika's body start to shiver against his own.

She said, "During the last week of January, it snowed so heavily that the train lines became inoperable. The tracks were one huge gridlock, completely jammed with cars. Many of those who had managed to bring a few possessions to Gdańsk decided to leave their things on the train and risk a trip on foot to Gdynia in an attempt to secure passage on ships sailing from that port.

"Then on the last day of January a huge explosion took place off the coast here. A Russian submarine torpedoed the *Wilhelm Gustloss*, an evacuation ship packed to overflowing with people fleeing the city. I was supposed to be on that boat . . ." A sob choked Monika as she finished, "with my mother and sister."

"Ah," said Jacek. It explained a great deal.

"I was standing next to my father while he was apologizing that he had not been able to secure passage for me, promising that I would go on the next ship out of Gdańsk, and then there was this sound. It . . . it seemed to come right out of the bottom of the sea. The ship rose up into the air, burst into flames and shattered over the water, a thousand splinters of flame. Then we watched the column of smoke curl into the sky. I knew, I know, you know there are worse things happening in other places. It felt as if the chaos of the rest of the country had just hit Gdańsk in full force. Then"—she swallowed again—"a week later you walked through that door upstairs." By the time she finished, Monika's voice had dropped to a bare whisper.

Jacek turned her around and kissed her wet cheeks as she went on, "My father and I don't talk about it. We didn't talk about my taking another boat or somehow finding a place on a train. We didn't talk about the war or the Russians. We don't even talk about you." She looked at Jacek for the first time since he had asked her the question, her eyes focusing on his.

"I know."

"I thought you might have noticed that." They both smiled weakly, and Jacek thought this was what endeared Monika most to him, that smile and the sound of her laughter. But she was not laughing now.

"So," she asked, "can you tell me what I've been spared for, why I wasn't blown up with my mother and sister?"

Jacek shook his head. And now, within the same minute, like an autumn leaf, she turned in the wind. "What do you mean?" he asked, the smile still on his face.

She squinted slightly, seeking some part of him she had never yet claimed. "You brought this up. You tell me, have I been saved for this? Tell me what you will do for me."

He just blinked as she went on, her eyes putting distance between them. "Who else enters a city which is just about to be taken by the Russians when the rest of the world is selling their souls to escape? You came here, not I. Tell me who else I can ask? I have nothing left to sell."

Very slowly the realization of what Monika was saying dawned on Jacek. It did not happen often that he was this slow, this blind in realizing he had been used. He thought back to what he had shared with this woman, the times he had spent in her arms, waiting in fear. She had made that time bearable, and he had flattered himself with the conviction that she had done it for him, that they had helped each other.

No, it was much simpler than that. He had been manipulated, and that was all. The coldness in Monika's eyes confirmed it.

Jacek let go of Monika, pushing her away from him. He swung his legs over the side of the bed and drew on his trousers. "I need to go," he murmured.

"Who are you?" she hissed. "I hear you say things in

your sleep that cannot be true. I watch you, I make love to you, but I don't know you. And that's all right, those were the rules you set up from the beginning.

"No, when I say, 'Who are you?' I mean, what are you? You must work for the Russians somehow. And I'm hoping, I'm praying you can help me when hell hits this city in a few days." She looked down and took a deep breath. When her eyes next met Jacek's, the ice in them had melted. There was even a desperate smile back on her lips. "For old times' sake, maybe?"

Jacek did not answer. Instead, he got up and headed for the stairs. He was having trouble controlling his breathing. It kept coming out in gasps. He tucked his shirt in his pants and stopped halfway up the stairs to steady himself. *This is ridiculous,* he thought. *Have I cared so much, then?*

Jacek did an about-face on the stairs. He did not return to Monika, however, did not even look her way. Instead, he crossed the basement and softly shook Herr Braun's shoulder until the old man's eyes opened and he sat up. "Yes, what has happened?"

Now that Jacek was watching for it, he could hear in the old man's voice the awareness that he had overheard the conversation. "Can I do something?" Herr Braun asked.

"I think not." Jacek was a little surprised at the anger in his own voice. "I'm sure you have something to say to me now, don't you?"

The old man groped for his wire-framed glasses on the floor next to his cot and motioned impatiently with his hand. "Yes, yes, you know." He quickly clamped onto Jacek's elbow.

"You used me," Jacek said.

"I beg you, yes, I'm begging you now to protect my daughter. If she meant anything at all to you during these last weeks, please see that no harm comes to her. Can't you see? You can be her ship of safe passage now. You have the power, don't you?"

Jacek was rapidly getting the feeling that this had all gone too far. These people had obviously blown his cover. If only he could get the man to let go of him.

Herr Braun kept talking, "You think I don't know what she can expect? I will be dead in a week. You've taken an interest in her. Please, I beg you, try to save her."

"All this time," Jacek said, "you turned a blind eye and manipulated the relationship. From the moment you gave me that coat, all you were thinking about was what I could do for you."

"Who else has that kind of money?" Herr Braun let go of Jacek's sleeve as if the fabric had burned him. "I saw your face when she walked in that day. I knew it was possible. You cannot tell me I was wrong. If you ever cared, you will help her."

Jacek turned and mounted the stairs two at a time and closed the door behind him, but could not shut out Herr Braun's voice, "I beg you, whoever you are. Have mercy on us."

Jacek climbed up the next flight to his room and quickly packed his few things, put on his coat, and descended the stairs. The small bell over the shop door still sounded like a death knell in his ears long after he had turned down the next street.

———— ∞ ————

As Jacek walked, there passed before him the image of a man crouched in a dirt pit. He stopped and looked up, half relieved not to see corrugated iron stretching above him. Jacek was sweating profusely despite the rough cold. He shifted the bag into his other hand and continued walking. The streets were deserted.

He was looking for a place to survive the next few days of shelling. It wasn't hard to find an abandoned building near the city center that had a cellar. Jacek just kept walking through the doors of dark homes until he found one where no one else was hiding. During his search he had heard the sound of fighting, hand-to-hand combat even. Nearer the outskirts of the city the Germans were already engaged in the last stages of their battle to hold on to Gdańsk. Jacek knew it was out of the question for him to try to leave by means of the train station or port, for the Nazis were still holding the local population hostage. No one was allowed to leave now that the war had come so far.

For the next three days Jacek hid, as did all the rest in the city who had not managed to escape on any of the ships or trains or roads heading west. For three days and nights, Jacek heard nothing but shelling and shooting and screams. The professional in him was surprised that the Germans held out that long. Only after two nights of fighting did the Germans finally stop trying to control the movements of the people in Gdańsk. Those who could slip past the fortifications and were willing to risk capture by the Soviets did so.

On March 28 the Russians finally wrenched Gdańsk away from the Germans. By that time the lack of water, electricity, gas, and public transport meant that the Russians had captured a dying city. Jacek, armed with his Russian ID card and his knowledge of the language, now dared to emerge from hiding and welcome the liberators.

But what he saw then shocked him in the same secret places of his conscience that had still not recovered from his camp days.

The Germans may have surrendered. The shelling may have stopped and no more bombers were flying overhead. But this did not mean the danger had passed. Instead, it had only shifted from the sky to ground level. For when Gdańsk fell into Soviet hands, a new level of cruelty rapidly crept into every quarter of the city.

The Russians wanted Gdańsk leveled. Jacek saw Soviet soldiers searching every building in every street and neighborhood, breaking into homes, looting their contents, looking for prisoners. Any German soldiers unlucky enough to still be alive were killed on the spot.

Jacek wandered from neighborhood to neighborhood, brandishing his card as a pass. Everywhere he saw signs of looting and worse. He told himself he was searching for someone who ranked high enough in the Russian army to get him in to see Rokossovski. What he was really doing was trying to comprehend the devastation.

Jacek followed bands of Soviet soldiers, ducking into doorways, crouching in alleyways, watching with an almost childlike amazement as men who looked more like boys searched for something to steal, anything at all. When they had finished with an area, they set it on fire. Street by street, the Soviets had orders to torch Gdańsk and bring the population to its knees.

Jacek sensed something much more sinister in this systematic destruction than merely a victorious army enjoying the spoils of war. It was almost as if a master were teaching his newly acquired slave how things stood.

For there was more. Jacek saw these men looking for more than treasure, more than revenge. They were looking for women. And they found them, hiding in cellars, crouched behind false cupboards, shivering in shadows. Singly and in groups the Soviets raped the women of Gdańsk. They did it systematically, using their acts as a final weapon in a war that, to Jacek, felt as though it had not ended, but merely darkened in form.

In house after house, in Polish and in German, Jacek heard the cries for mercy. And only then did he allow himself to think again of Monika. By that time he had seen enough to know what to expect. He forced himself back to her neighborhood, back to the street with the churchyard, back to her father's shop. The windows were broken. Jacek stopped and stared down at his shoes, down at the broken shards of glass beneath them.

He reached up and pushed the door open. There was no sound at all. He walked in, his feet crunching on more glass. The display cases had all been shattered.

*Why am I here?* he wanted to scream at himself. Yet his legs carried him on, a force other than his own controlling them. He reached the basement stairs. He knew where to go.

He entered the cellar and did not recognize it. The floor was littered with bits of broken furniture and masses of dark curls. He lifted his eyes as if a great weight bound them down. On the cots in their corner he saw a form under a sheet, curled in fetal position. Eyes of ice blinked back at him. Someone was crying. Jacek whirled and ran.

He jogged down the streets, holding a cloth before his face as the cityscape burned out of control. Piles of rubble covered the streets, hundreds of corpses and the decomposing remains of dead horses poisoned the air. The torched church towers pointed fingers of flame toward the cloudless night sky. Near the harbor the Żuraw (Crane Gate) blazed.

The Russians continued setting fire to Gdańsk even though there no longer was an enemy. Their tanks roared up and down empty streets, now free of barricades. Fire jumped from one building to the next. The smoke drove the lucky few the Russians had failed to find from their hiding places. These women and children and old men threw themselves into the sea in a desperate effort to find relief from the fire-devastated city.

The flames, the heat, the screams of terror and fear all leapt down onto Jacek's head. He closed his eyes to shut some of it out and saw an image of himself leaping off a train. Had it only been two months?

True to no one, not even himself. Irony rang hollow to Jacek. He heard only the tailor's daughter's ragged sobs.

# 12

EARLY FEBRUARY—MID-MAY 1945

"My baby!" Hanna sobbed. "My baby—I saw her on the tracks, dead!"

"Hush, child. It was a nightmare. Hush." Helena rocked Hanna back and forth. She held her tight, brushing her hair out of her face, rubbing her back. "Hush now, I'm here. We're safe, and so is your baby."

Slowly Hanna's breathing steadied. But she could not shake the images from her sleep. "Something terrible is happening, is going to happen. I know it."

Helena looked around at the little dark room she and Hanna had chosen to call home when they arrived a few days earlier from Kraków. Now that it was February, she wondered how long they would stay there. She sighed. "Don't say that, Hanna. This war and what it's done to all of us is terrible. But you're tired now. You're worn out from that horrendous train ride, and you need to rest. Don't imagine things that aren't there."

Hanna nodded and eased herself back down among the cushions, asking herself yet again, when would it all be over, when would she be back with Tadeusz? Only three weeks had passed since she last saw her husband. But so much had happened, so much distance had been traveled both physically and emotionally, that she felt as if years had gone by. A huge ache welled up inside Hanna. She wanted to feel Tadeusz's arms around her again.

One look at her mother, however, warned Hanna that she should be careful. Helena's face told the story of her own worry for Johann, his physical health so fragile he had been unable to take them to the train station, as well as her worry for her daughter and the grandchild.

"You're right, Mother," Hanna said hurriedly. "Of course, it's just a dream." Hanna sighed and stuck her chin out. "Mother, I'm sorry for waking you. Come back to bed, and we'll go back to sleep."

Helena looked at her daughter, not quite focusing on her. After a few moments she realized what Hanna had just said and smiled. "You are a funny one, my Hania. I bet you don't even know what time it is, or what day, or how long you've been asleep, for that matter."

Helena rose and crossed the room to the window. When she pulled back the drapes, the dull sunshine of winter streamed into the room, highlighting the bald spots on the carpet.

Helena continued, "I came to bed last night around ten and was so tired I slept straight through until eight. Then I got up and went nosing around the village. Then I came back for lunch, went to the local church, then came back to see if you would be joining us for *obiad* at four, which," she paused and laughed at Hanna's astonished expression, "is in about a half hour. So you've slept for a full night and most of the day."

Hanna laughed too, glad to see her mother relax. "You're right. I had no idea." She paused. "Where are we, by the way?"

"Kuron."

Hanna nodded, vaguely remembering a sign somewhere. "I'll be right down," she answered.

Over the meal Helena repeated some of her plans for the next weeks and months. This time Hanna was more receptive to her mother's conversation.

" . . . there's a group of nuns here. As far as I could understand, they welcome whatever help we can give them. They're trying to convert the church into a place for refugees to sleep. One corner will be a hospital. It seems there are already women in the village trying to patch together blankets."

"Did you tell them we aren't Catholic?"

"No, why should I?"

"All right." Hanna held up her hands, palms facing her mother. "I was just wondering."

"Well, it shouldn't make any difference. And just in case it would . . ." Helena paused.

" . . . you decided not to give them the chance to mind." Hanna finished the sentence for her.

Helena looked annoyed. "Well really, Hanna, it's difficult enough to make myself understood as it is."

"I know, Mother." Hanna scraped her chair back. "It's all right. Shall we go?"

On the way out of the house they passed an old woman begging, and a sadness settled over Hanna. "Mother, what will happen in the next months?" Her voice sounded like a little girl's, caught asking something she shouldn't.

"Hanna, you know as well as I do. We'll probably be inundated with people just like us, running away. It can't be pretty, what the Russians have done to Kraków or the rest of Poland, for that matter." She shook her head. "Your father knew what he was doing, sending us away. We've gone south instead of west, but I'm not all that sure Germany would have been safer than this place. I still can't believe we were spared going to Dresden."

Hanna simply nodded. She wanted to ask what would happen when all the other refugees reached Kuron, but she did not.

The next weeks proved Helena's prediction right. Hanna and her mother saw a huge increase in the number of women, children, and old men coming through the little village. All of Europe seemed to be shifting during those spring months of 1945. Between February and May the German army retreated in as ruthless a manner as the Russians advanced. And before them both moved this ragged army of refugees that Hanna and her mother were already a part of, carrying bags and dragging carts full of everything from clothes to radios to photo albums. People who had left homes in Poland, Czechoslovakia, Latvia, Lithuania, Estonia, and the Ukraine, all fleeing for safety. They brought with them the tales of atrocities that had occurred in village after village as the Russian front moved closer. Kuron was simply a point on the map that happened to be far enough south and far enough west for the armies not yet to have reached it.

Helena and Hanna spent most of their days and half their nights helping in the refugee center that the church had become. Kuron was lucky enough to have the nuns, who had decided to stay and could organize some sort of arrangements for the crowds coming through the area. Amazingly, they even had at their disposal a few medicines and supplies such as bandages, and some of the nuns had been trained as nurses. This meant a semblance of a first-aid station could indeed be set up inside the church.

When they first started working at the clinic, Helena had warned Hanna not to do much lifting. She had asked the head nurse, a woman called Sister Patrice, to make sure Hanna took care of herself. "She's pregnant," she said, holding her hand in front of her stomach.

Sister Patrice had smiled. Hanna smiled back. So far, she had only been able to pick up a few words of what was said around her. But this time she understood what the nun said to her. "Too much bad." Sister Patrice motioned around the church. "Birth of baby good."

Sister Patrice was younger than Hanna's own mother, somewhere in her forties, with clear blue eyes that reminded Hanna of Tadeusz's. She was tall and held herself straight, moving with a swishing sound that always left a scent of soap behind. From that moment when she first heard Hanna was pregnant, Sister Patrice took a personal interest in Hanna's health. Hanna felt a little foolish getting special attention when so many around her were in such greater need. Still, it was lovely to share the baby's growth in her belly with someone who seemed as excited as she and her mother about the little life.

It did not take long for the local church to fill up with the people passing through Kuron and looking for shelter. Although spring came early that year, there was still frost on most clear nights. And thanks to the soldiers and bandits roaming the roads, sometimes the refugees arrived carrying next to nothing.

Helena worked in the kitchen, where she earned a reputation for being able to stretch a potato further than anyone else. Hanna's job was to assist in the corner of the church that served as a medical ward, an area divided off from the rest. Her duties included everything from keeping it as clean as possible to helping wash the wounds. She already knew how to make beds, but bathing patients, especially under such conditions, was often a gruesome experience.

Sometimes Hanna would look up and catch the eye of

a saint's statue. The sight would startle her into realizing that all this noise and movement—the babies crying, the men and women moaning, the patients without painkillers crying out—all of this was happening inside a church. Then she would straighten up from whatever she was doing and see the arched roof, smell the musty wood, catch the shine of marble, listen to the floorboards creak, watch the light dance on gold leaf, and the sunlight color the far wall when it fell across a window.

*God's house,* she would think. And again she would see the shifting bodies, hear the babble of languages, smell the unwashed bodies and infected wounds inside this makeshift ward. A feeling of being in the right place at exactly the right time would well up inside her. Then she would sigh and go back to work.

It was obvious to both Hanna and Helena that at least this area of Czechoslovakia had not been hit as harshly by the war as most of Poland. They had heard about the burning of Gdańsk and the disasters in other places, and they were thankful to be in a place where there was enough of what was needed to share with others. They felt this way both because they were strangers on the receiving end and because this enabled them to give in turn.

During these months Hanna had never failed to think of Tadeusz. Her love for him was something she held on to tightly amidst all the pain around her. She rarely saw her mother during their working days, and when they came together at night they rarely talked of what had happened to them or what they would do next. They both seemed wrapped in their separate worlds, waiting for whatever calamity was due to catch up with them now that they had decided to run no farther.

During the nights they talked of home, or the baby. One

night, Helena told Hanna a story of when she had just been born. "You used to wake up maybe two or three times a night. Johann would fetch you from the cradle next to our bed, then fall down next to me and sleep instantly."

"Father always could sleep on his feet if he needed to," Hanna smiled.

"Yes, well this time it was worse. Because when I finished feeding you, I shook him awake like he had asked me to. And then he walked with you until you fell back asleep. I just rolled over and fell asleep. But the next morning, what do you think your father said? 'Isn't it lovely that the baby slept through the night?' He didn't even remember!"

Hanna shook her head, the black curls bouncing around her face. "What? But he woke up twice and even walked with me."

"That's the point. I think he was just sleepwalking." Both women laughed and then grew silent for a few moments.

"Did you pray for me when you were like I am now?" Hanna asked.

Helena reached across the bed and took her daughter's hand. "When I was pregnant with you I prayed every day and every night. For your health, your future, even for your husband or wife, whoever it might be."

Hanna smiled. "So really you were praying for my Tadeusz even before I was born." She looked over at Helena.

Her mother nodded. "Yes."

---

During the days, Hanna had fallen into a routine of cleaning, bathing, washing, rolling bodies over, speaking kindly and binding wounds. The weeks had become months, until a certain bright morning in early May.

Hanna began the day as usual by getting up at dawn. She ate whatever Mrs. Slovan was able to set before her, then walked over to the church. When she arrived, she washed the few sheets left and did what she could to clean the mattresses of whichever cots had been left empty from the night before. She was walking along the rows of newcomers, most still asleep, when she heard someone call out in German, *"Bitte, hilfen Sie mir!"*

Out of habit, and forgetting that she was not supposed to know German, Hanna answered similarly, "I'll be right there." Then she looked toward the voice and saw an old man slumped in the corner, his face red with effort. Both his hands caressed his right knee.

Hanna was glad she had somewhere to take him. "Sir, let me help you into this bed, and then I'll get one of the sisters to examine you."

The man looked at her and nodded his thanks. As Hanna approached him, his stench hit her full in the face. She swallowed twice before coming any closer. Then she noticed the man had fainted with pain. She took a deep breath and bent toward him.

She didn't need to be a doctor to know that the odor meant gangrene. Hanna bent at the knees and strained to get one of the man's arms over her shoulder. With a heave she managed to get him standing. Then she dragged him, step by step, over to one of the few empty cots.

As she eased the man down onto the mattress, Hanna heard Sister Patrice's voice behind her. She understood much more than she could a few months earlier. "Ah, Hanna, you too big to lift like that. I help you."

Hanna turned and sagged against the nun, almost faint from the smell of rotten flesh. Sister Patrice steadied her, then noticed it herself. "Oh! Must help now. You help, Hanna? Too few people."

Hanna nodded. She retied her apron strings around the five-month bulge in her belly. The movement gave her a few moments in which to swallow her nausea. She had seen this operation begun before, had started to watch, then turned away to do some other task.

"He's so old," she started to say, as if it were an excuse.

"Yes, but strong, or not make it so far."

"Do we have to do this? Isn't there another way?"

"Hanna," the nun looked into her eyes. "He die if leave leg." Sister Patrice was already assembling the necessary tools. "Hanna, get pot water on stove and ask your mother more."

Hanna did as she was told. When she returned, Sister Patrice dropped the instruments into the pot. They clinked when they hit the bottom. They had run out of anything that even resembled painkillers more than a month before, so Hanna would have to hold the man down. She tried to remember that the amputation would save the man's life, then straightened her shoulders and said, "I'm ready."

"Right. Put cloth into mouth and hold down." The nun started by tearing the trouser cloth of his right leg, revealing blackened and swollen flesh. When the teeth of the saw bit into the flesh, Hanna tightened her grip on the unconscious man's shoulders. He lurched involuntarily. She looked down and watched his face. Anything was better than watching the nun's arm moving back and forth.

Hanna heard when the metal hit the bone. She gritted her teeth, then nearly jumped as the man's eyes fluttered open. The next instant, inexplicably, he came to.

*"Gott, Gott, nicht mein Bein!"* Hanna threw all her strength into holding him down.

"Oh, Sister, what do I do? Why can't he faint again?" she cried.

Sister Patrice only shook her head. She raised the saw up and held it away from the thrashing body on the table. Blood dripped down her arm. "Help, over here, someone please!"

Another nun appeared, her beads clicking against her habit as she walked. She glanced once at Hanna, then at Sister Patrice. Without a word she clamped onto the man's thighs.

Hanna's arms ached. She closed her eyes with the effort, then opened them to see her own sweat drop onto the man's face. His eyes stared at her, wide open with pain.

"Please, sir, try to be still," she said to him. "I'm so sorry this is happening. It had to, though. Oh, God, this is so terrible. Try to hold on now."

The man rolled his head from one side to the other. He cried, "My Gretchen, in line with the others. Trains. All shot or sent off to camps. *Ach, Krakau.*"

Hanna's mind riveted on the word. She glanced at the two nuns. They were completely occupied with the patient. Pushing down even harder, Hanna leaned over him and whispered in German, "*Krakau*? Who was arrested? What camps?"

For a moment the cloud of pain passed from the man's eyes. He focused on her. "Fräulein, you are German? You have family there? They were all arrested or shot. All the German families in the entire city. Not just the Jews. This time . . . our turn . . ."

Hanna felt the man's muscles slacken as he passed out yet again. She relaxed her grip and shut her eyes against the spinning room.

From far away she heard Sister Patrice say, "Thank

God." Hanna opened her eyes in time to watch her bind the stump in strips of cloth. "Good, Hanna. Good he understand. Ah," Sister Patrice looked up. "Just in time."

Hanna swallowed hard as the meaning of the nun's words registered. Sister Patrice had noticed her speaking to the man in German.

She saw her mother approach, carrying the second pot of boiled water. This she set down quickly and crossed over to the table.

"Oh, this looks like it was awful. Why, Hanna, you're shaking. What's the matter, child? Sit down."

And now the wave of panic hit. Hanna saw the scene the man had described. "Tadeusz!" she cried out loud. "Father!" She saw the glance the two nuns exchanged, blood smearing their arms. She was just opening her mouth to offer an explanation. Had she betrayed her mother, betrayed herself? She wanted to tell her, tell her quickly so she could set it right. And she wanted to reach out for Tadeusz, when, all at once, she knew there was something else she should be worried about.

Time stood still for Hanna as she looked down, past the table, past the man's sweaty head, past her own hands, down her skirt, to her stockings and shoes. There between her feet lay a small pool of blood.

Then, quickly, her mother grabbed her before she fainted. The last thing Hanna heard were her words, "Dear God, Hanna, the baby!"

---

With what seemed a very great effort, Hanna opened her eyes and looked at the drawn curtains. She recognized them as the ones in the room she shared with her mother. Out of reflex her hand went to her belly. She held her breath until the familiar movements answered her touch. "Oh, thank you, Lord," she whispered tearfully.

Her gasp woke up her mother, asleep on the floor by the closet. "Hanna?" She was at the bedside within seconds.

"I was so worried . . ." Helena brought her daughter's hand to her cheek.

"The baby is fine, Mother, I just felt kicks."

"I know, darling."

"But . . ." Hanna struggled to remember something important, several things important, but her thoughts felt so heavy.

Her mother sensed her confusion. "Hanna, that amputation took too much out of you. I told you to be careful, especially now that you're showing." Helena stopped herself, then tried again. "Hanna, something's happened. I should let you rest, but something's happened."

Hanna sat up in bed, and immediately her head began to pound.

"The Soviets have taken Praga."

"When?"

"It must have been around the same day you became sick."

"Sick? But I just fainted, didn't I? How long have I been here?"

"Almost a week. You wouldn't stop bleeding. We thought you would lose the baby. But besides the blood loss, you've hardly eaten anything except the broth I was able to get down you. That's why you're so weak. I'm sorry, Hanna, I know you're not up to it, but I must move you now. We must leave."

Hanna was having a hard time taking in all her mother had said. But part of her understood that the events of the last years had finally caught up with them. And somewhere in the back of her mind was a worry, a fear that the people of Kuron would no longer help them. She frowned, trying to remember why she was afraid.

Helena was struggling with worries of her own as she gathered Hanna's few belongings. Up until now, her plan for taking care of herself and her daughter had worked beautifully. In Kuron, she and Hanna had fit in easily. They had found accommodation, had met local people, had found a way to help. She had counted on becoming a contributing, valuable member of the community, someone to be trusted, so that the women who came from the area would share with Helena and Hanna the best places to hide if and when the soldiers did arrive. But what if Hanna were still too weak to travel? What if she lost her after all of this?

Before either woman could speak her thoughts, there was a knock on the door.

Helena rose and crossed the room to open it. "Yes, Sister, she's just awakened. How kind of you. Yes, come in."

Upon seeing Sister Patrice, Hanna suddenly remembered why it was that she and her mother might no longer be welcome in Kuron.

"Ah, Hanna, you better now. I worried."

Hanna searched Sister Patrice's face but saw only concern. Not for the first time, she wondered what was going on behind the nun's deep-set eyes.

Sister Patrice continued, "I have bad news. Troops very close now. You know," she nodded at Helena, "village already empty. All hiding now."

Hanna glanced at her mother. "You had to stay with me."

"I wouldn't have left you, but you couldn't be moved

until you stopped bleeding. That didn't happen until last night."

The nun was still talking, "You go now."

All three women grew quiet for a moment. The question uppermost in Hanna's mind was whether Sister Patrice had heard her conversation with the old man on the operating table and figured out that she was German. Hanna waited, then felt compelled to blurt into the silence, "I was afraid . . . afraid I had given myself and Mother away . . . afraid." Her voice trailed off as Helena shot her a warning look.

"Please." Sister Patrice had turned from them; they could no longer see her face. She started to reach for a suitcase on top of the wardrobe, then stopped herself. "No time now. Just go."

"She's right," Helena said. "Hanna, can you get yourself dressed? Let me get your clothes."

Hanna nodded, sensing that both of the older women had chosen to ignore her outburst. Now all three busied themselves trying to get Hanna ready to travel.

Within minutes they were ready. Hanna found that if she leaned on her mother, she could stave off the dizziness. She wanted to move slowly, but once outside, Sister Patrice insisted they try to run.

Past the blue and white and yellow houses they ran, Hanna panting at the start and throwing her weight onto Helena's arm around her waist. Past the church, past the square. All the way they saw no one. The village stood deserted. Even the beggar woman on the corner had finally disappeared.

Hanna closed her eyes and poured all her energy into staying upright. She thought of her ankles and willed them not to buckle. She cupped her hand under her stomach to ease the strain as she ran. The two older women half carried, half dragged her as they hurried toward the woods on the outskirts of the town.

At first they followed a trail that wound its way upward. The full foliage of trees in May shaded them. By the time they had reached an outcropping of jagged granite, Hanna was panting so hard she felt dizzy.

"Please hurry," Sister Patrice urged. She hiked up her skirts and clambered up the face of a boulder. Helena followed. Then both women reached down to give Hanna a hand up.

She was bent over double with her hands on her knees, gulping air. Hanna could hear the strain in the nun's voice but could do nothing about the weakness that crippled her from going any farther.

"Your hand, Hanna," her mother gasped. "Give us your hands, and we'll pull you up."

Hanna straightened and stretched her arms upward, letting both women haul her up the side of the rock. Once on top, she crumpled to the ground.

"Hanna, please, look at me. We must keep going."

Hanna pushed away the sweat-soaked hair matted to her forehead and opened her eyes. She looked past her mother and down, back toward the clearing where the village stood.

"Look!" she cried, pointing.

The two older women whirled, fearing the worst. Below them they could see the square around the church swarming with men, soldiers in uniform. "Did you know they were so close?" Hanna looked up at Sister Patrice.

She nodded. "Must hurry. Hanna?"

Helena bent over her daughter. "I know you can make

it. Just look how far we've come." She squeezed Hanna's shoulder.

Hanna prayed desperately for God's own strength, then by sheer force of will she tensed the muscles in her legs and stood. Leaning heavily on her mother, she stumbled after Sister Patrice.

They followed the nun into a thicket of pines. As Sister Patrice ducked under a branch, she pointed at it. "No break." Hanna understood. They must be very near the hiding place, and it was important that the undergrowth remain untouched.

Sister Patrice stopped and reached past an elderberry bush. From a hollow space she grabbed handfuls of dead leaves and pulled out branches. What remained was a hole, a large burrow. "There," she pointed. "Go now."

Hanna felt her mother ease her down onto her knees, then shove her into the cave. She could not see in the dark, but she heard her mother come in after her, then stop.

"What about you, Sister?" Helena asked.

"I cover hole, go other. Stay left. Go!"

Hanna moved forward, the dead branches and leaves biting into her knees. Within a few moments, Hanna was shivering from the cold, damp air. Her mother's hand pushed her on from behind.

"What did she mean?" Hanna said.

"She's gone somewhere else to hide. It's all right. I'm sure she knows what she's doing. This way the entrance is well hidden."

The space Hanna found herself in was barely large enough for her to crawl through. She ran one hand along the rough surface of the rock wall and limped along on her knees as best she could. At one point her hand touched something wet and she cried out.

"Hush," her mother hissed. "It's just water."

Hanna took a deep breath and went on, slowly working her way forward. Bit by bit, down, then up, through mud, then a puddle, Hanna and her mother followed the tunnel.

At the fork, they found they could finally stand if they kept their heads bowed.

"She said to the left." Helena grabbed Hanna's hand and pulled her onward.

They rounded a corner, where suddenly a large cavern loomed before them. Candlelight flickered in one corner, casting huge shadows on the far wall.

Hanna groaned and straightened, placing one hand at the base of her back. The forms dancing to her right looked like a ring of giant witches. But when she looked back at the candle, all she saw were several women huddled together. They had turned to face her and her mother, fear scrawled across their features.

"The Russians are very close," Helena told them.

One woman nodded and stood. Hanna recognized their landlady, Mrs. Slovan. She put a finger over her lips, quickly stooped and blew out the candle. "You," she pointed at Hanna and her mother. "With me. Others go." Quietly the women shuffled off to other parts of the cave.

"We in front," Mrs. Slovan whispered over her shoulder.

Hanna did not know what she could mean. Didn't the entrance lie behind them? In a few moments she knew the answer. The place where Mrs. Slovan brought them was just below what Hanna now realized must be the main entrance. The hole they had crawled through was nothing compared to the gaping door that loomed several feet above her now.

Hanna stood in the sunlight that streamed through the

gap between two tall boulders. How on earth could anyone *not* see that opening?

"God, if only they don't come this way," Hanna whispered.

Her mother shot her a glance and then looked at Mrs. Slovan, who had put a hand on her shoulder. "We wait here. Down. Sound alarm. Maybe some get out other way."

Hanna and Helena did not look at each other, both thinking the same thing. They had not asked to play this role, but now there was nothing they could do about it. Mrs. Slovan seemed very much in charge, so they squatted against the wall and waited.

Hanna moved out of the sunlight and knelt against the rock beside her mother. It was large enough so that anyone who might peer through the hole into the cave would not see them. Hanna wondered about this main entrance. What was it? Why hadn't they come through it with Sister Patrice? Perhaps they had taken the back way so Helena and Hanna would know where to find it later. Hanna wasn't sure.

She felt too tired to follow her train of thought. Then a question suddenly dawned on her. It was something that had been nagging her since she woke up from the fever. "Mother," she leaned over to whisper the question in Helena's ear. "Mother, the man who lost his leg. I have to ask you. Did he live?"

Her mother placed a finger over her lips, then watched her daughter carefully and shook her head no.

Tears sprang into Hanna's eyes, which surprised her, but a part of her knew it was a sign of just how tired she really was. Hanna wiped them away with the back of her hand. She thought about how much she had risked to comfort that man. He had been her last contact with home, with

Father and with Tadeusz. She felt too weak to keep the worry and fear at bay. The man had mentioned trains, she remembered. Where were they now? Trains to where?

Her mother touched her shoulder and motioned that they should pray.

All Hanna could do was nod and close her eyes. Then she began to shake from shock. In the chilly, dripping, stony silence she listened to her heartbeat. She knew her mother was praying, and she wanted to do the same, but it was hard to concentrate.

Then words formed themselves and she felt herself thinking, *David hid from Saul in the caves. That was also a place full of fear. Protect us now, I beg You. Let the men outside who would hurt us pass this place by . . .*

Hanna opened her eyes and looked up at the entrance, seeing it now for the first time from a different angle.

There, shimmering in the sunlight, she noticed a spider web. It stretched from one side of the hole all the way to the other. Thousands of gossamer threads joined together to form a curtain that must have been several years old. The intertwining patterns fascinated Hanna.

Then, she heard the noise of branches breaking. She sucked in her breath as her mother's hand grasped her wrist. Something was moving in the forest above them.

Hanna tore her eyes away from the light and edged up against the rock as far into the shadows as she could. The very pines seemed to shake with the movement of men tramping through them, yet the birds remained quiet.

Then the screaming began—countless screams that echoed off the rocky hills as the soldiers discovered the hiding places of other women. Hanna knew the nightmare was upon them. All their months of worrying and preparing and praying, her father's plan, the painful separation—it had all been to save them from what was happening at that very moment to the women in the forest above.

"Blind them," her mother's voice was mumbling. "Oh, blind them."

Hanna looked back up at the sunlit opening with its delicate spider-web drapery. Then, she found herself remembering a story Tadeusz had told her about a Polish king who hid from his enemies and remained undiscovered. When his pursuers saw a web covering the opening to his cave, they thought no one had entered it for a very long time, and passed the cave by.

Hanna looked up at the web crisscrossing the opening and stifled a gasp as the light behind it faded and then disappeared. Shapes darkened the entrance—moving shapes making noise. Shapes of men, shapes laughing, a shape spitting, a shape stopping. As if in slow motion, a hand pointed at the hole. Hanna could see the dirty fingernails as they tore the web to shreds.

She held her breath and pressed her back hard against the icy stone. Her hair clung to her cheek in damp strands. She clenched the baby in her belly tightly, between two hands, willing the tiny being to be as still as she, to live and keep on living, to always be safe no matter what.

# 13

## Mid-May—August 1945

Spring on the steppe had ended, and the wildflowers that had briefly brought color to the dull landscape dried up and died. Increasingly, as Tadeusz emerged from the clammy depths of the mine, the summer's soaring temperatures pressed down with a blast to meet him.

He had settled into a dull rhythm of excruciating work and all-too-brief rest, this time fighting against heat . . . and fear. And as more time went by, he found it increasingly difficult to keep his worry for Hanna and Johann at bay. It would rise up inside him almost uncontrollably, catching him unawares.

He had fear for himself, too. It manifested itself every morning, in the form of the black-haired guard with the iron bar. He rarely overslept, but if he lingered in bed for even a minute the guard was there every time, beating him brutally. For some reason this man had singled out Tadeusz as the focus of his attention. As the days of dread took their toll, Tadeusz could not help sweating and shaking uncontrollably whenever he jumped from his bunk to the ground. It became a conditioned response.

In all that time Tadeusz still heard nothing that might lead him to believe the shout he had heard in the woods came from Johann. Then, a month after the incident, he overheard a group of prisoners talking.

"He's an old man, a Pole."

"Yes, and they say he preached first for the commandant, who said afterward that he could preach at funerals."

"Ha! Whoever he is, in a place like this, he'll never be out of work."

Tadeusz hardly dared to hope. He did not think there were many men who would even dare ask permission for such a thing. But when the man who slept below him collapsed into his bunk a few evenings later, and never stirred again, Tadeusz asked if he could help bury him. The guard shrugged his shoulders and agreed.

Before dawn the next day, Tadeusz and another prisoner carried the corpse to a barren spot outside the camp. In the shadowy darkness just before daybreak, Tadeusz could just make out the bent figure of a man waiting up ahead, his guard squatting beside him.

As the stretcher approached, the old man looked up. He stared at the corpse, then slowly turned his head and rolled his eyes upward from Tadeusz's feet to his face, as if memorizing the sight. "My son." The words formed themselves on the lips of the old man as tears formed in his eyes.

It was all Tadeusz could to do to keep from dropping his load and enfolding Johann into his arms. The incident in the wagon had taught him a lesson, though. He now knew that he would be allowed to see Johann only if he did not let on how important it was. Yet this did not stop him from grinning at Johann. And Johann understood, as he always had. He grinned back, despite his mouth with no teeth.

The funeral was nothing more than Johann praying out loud for the soul of the man they buried. As Tadeusz and the other prisoner dug the grave, the two guards shared a cigarette.

"Hurry up there!" one of the guards growled.

" . . . and, Lord, we pray for this man's family, for his wife and children. Comfort . . ."

Johann's words brought on the dawn. The sky filled with countless hues of pink and orange. Then, from one moment to the next the sun rose, inflaming the steppe with light. As it rolled over the horizon it caught the five men, diminishing them to the squatting, the stooped, and the soiled.

Moments later, as he helped heave the body into the pit, Tadeusz joined Johann in chanting, "From dust to dust . . ." Then he threw dirt back into the grave until one of the guards stood and spat. It was the sign that they should go.

Walking toward the camp, the guards took little notice of the three prisoners. After all, where could they escape to in such vastness? Tadeusz took advantage of their distraction to slow his pace and come alongside Johann, who walked with the aid of a long, thick stick he must have scrounged for himself. "At last," he whispered. "Now I know my prayers have been answered."

"And mine." Johann touched the younger man's arm. "I must tell you before we are separated again that the Lord is very much present here. When I finally received permission to preach at funerals . . ."

"Finally?" Tadeusz asked.

"Why, yes. I started asking on the day after we arrived."

Tadeusz shook his head in disbelief. Only Johann would have been so quick to realize that burying the camp's dead might provide him with the opportunity to help meet the camp's spiritual needs as well as to cross paths with his son-in-law.

Johann continued, keeping his voice low. "Mind you, it doesn't mean they'll stop using the mass grave altogether."

At Tadeusz's raised eyebrows, Johann glanced behind him and pointed his head to the left. "Over there," he said in hushed tones. "Now at least some of these poor people will get a decent burial, although it means more work for those who do the actual digging, like yourself. Ah, Tadeusz, I cannot tell you how good it does this old heart to see you looking so strong and well."

Tadeusz looked down at his torn clothes and felt the filth encrusted in the folds of his skin. "Oh, yes, I've never looked better," he chuckled.

His father-in-law was not listening. "Now, down to business. This is important. I want you to pray for me."

"I've never stopped."

"I know. But this is a specific prayer." As the little group neared the camp, Johann's voice grew more urgent. "Pray, Tadeusz, pray that I will be allowed to preach every morning."

"But . . ."

"Every morning, do you understand?"

He squeezed Tadeusz's arm in a surprisingly ironclad grasp. Tadeusz responded, "Yes, of course I understand."

"You there!" The guard who had escorted Tadeusz nodded at him. "Leave the old man alone and get back to your barracks." He laughed. "Looks like you've missed breakfast."

Tadeusz threw one last look at Johann, who nodded knowingly.

As Tadeusz joined the other prisoners already walking toward the mines, he could still feel the comfort of Johann's nod. It was as if Johann knew about the aching muscles, the empty stomach, the worry, as if he knew about Tadeusz's fears for Hanna and the baby. And then Tadeusz realized he no longer felt so alone. The fear had lessened.

---

Precisely because Tadeusz could not understand how Johann had managed to obtain permission to preach at funerals, he now made a point of praying as Johann had asked him to. During the next days Tadeusz toyed with the idea of volunteering on a permanent basis to help bury the dead. He finally decided such a request might draw undue attention. Yet he felt starved for the familiar face and voice that had so comforted him during their five minutes together.

And then came a morning when the prisoners were forced to get up a half hour earlier. This gave the black-haired guard yet another chance to torment Tadeusz and the others, and he seized the opportunity greedily.

"You!" he hissed into Tadeusz's ear. "We're waking you up at the request of one of your own." He shoved his iron bar toward Tadeusz, poking randomly. "Now get up!" And the beating began.

After the guard had finished with him, Tadeusz groaned. He could hardly roll out of the bunk. When his feet hit the ground, his knees buckled. He found himself scrambling to stand, desperate to get outside before the guard returned. But then, as he limped out of the barracks, he suddenly remembered the guard's words, "One of your own."

Before he rounded the corner, Tadeusz could already hear what he could not have believed was possible. Johann's voice rang out clear and strong, "I want to tell all of you we are not alone in this place." Then Tadeusz caught sight of Johann, his body leaning to one side, weight on his makeshift cane, holding himself tightly as those in pain do. "There is a God who has suffered and endured, not unlike each of us." Johann's voice did not reflect any of his body's weakness. It resounded into the predawn darkness.

There was silence until another voice called out, coming from the prisoners' ranks. It spoke Hungarian, translating what Johann had just said. When the voice fell silent, a third joined in, translating into Ukrainian. And so it went, until all present had understood. They were not alone.

Then Johann recited from memory:

When you pass through the waters,
 I will be with you;
and when you pass through the rivers,
 they will not sweep over you.
When you walk through the fire,
 you will not be burned;
the flames will not set you ablaze.

Tadeusz's heart skipped a beat at the sound of his and Hanna's verse. Again the voices translated, and then a silence fell over the group. Slowly each man bowed his head as Johann lifted his right hand toward them to begin a blessing.

"Enough!" The same guard who had taken such pleasure in beating Tadeusz now waved his hands frantically. "That's enough, I said! Line up for food now, or you won't get any!"

The men obeyed. Tadeusz waited until Johann joined the queue, then took him by the elbow and whispered, "You've done it!"

"Our prayers have done it. God has done it. It's amazing, Tadeusz. They're letting me preach at the stream camp in the evenings and here in the mornings. I walk here on my own time and . . ."

"You walk all the way over here? That must take . . . what about your knees?"

"It takes half the night," Johann admitted. "But it's all right. I use the time to prepare my sermon. I needed every moment for this morning's message. They let me talk for five minutes, so those have to be five minutes worth getting up for." He chuckled softly. "They give me a ride back to camp. And the sifting I do there can be done sitting on a stump. My knees are fine, Tadeusz, don't worry about me. God's being glorified here, and that's what matters."

Johann continued, "And now for the next prayer request. A prison Bible. Will you pray for that, Tadeusz?"

"A Bible? Here? The Soviets don't even believe in . . ." His voice trailed off, and he nodded. He already knew it was no use arguing with Johann. Besides, they were approaching the guard who was dishing up their gruel.

As soon as he received his portion, Tadeusz turned to pour some of his food into Johann's bowl. But another guard had already intercepted Johann and was even now escorting him toward a horse-drawn wagon. Johann held on to his bowl and did not look back.

On each of the mornings that followed, Johann never failed to be waiting for the prisoners as they stumbled out of the barracks, their minds and bodies still heavy with sleep. Johann's sermons rarely lasted more than a few minutes, but the time of prayer often went on three times that long. Tadeusz caught himself wishing that Johann could be in his own camp, but then realized the older man would never last a day in the mines.

At the end of July another shipment of prisoners arrived at the camp. Some of these prisoners had managed to hold on to a few belongings that the Russian soldiers did not think important enough to steal. Among them was a man assigned to the bunk in the space below Tadeusz. On his first night there Tadeusz greeted him, but the man did not answer. Then, before he fell asleep, Tadeusz noticed the man shove something large under his head as a pillow.

The next morning, as soon as Tadeusz heard the guard banging his bar against the beds, he hurried to wake up the new man, quickly swinging his legs over the side of the bunk and jumping down. He turned around to shake the man awake. Then he saw that under one elbow lay a Bible. It was a large, leather Bible, the kind Tadeusz had seen on church altars.

Tadeusz cried out and started shaking the man in earnest. "Is it yours? Is it really yours?"

The man started awake and shrank back as if he were sure Tadeusz was about to murder him. "Mine? What are you talking about?" Tadeusz recognized the accent as his own. The man was from Łódź.

The guards' shouts interrupted him. The new man looked around, confused. Tadeusz watched as realization dawned on the tired, unshaven face and he remembered where he was.

"Come," Tadeusz said. "Come with me. It's time to get up. Let's just put this in a safe spot first, though, shall we? There will be plenty of time to talk about it later." He shoved the Bible into a dark corner of the bunk. "By the way, my name is Tadeusz."

"I'm Roman," the man nodded in a daze. Tadeusz hauled Roman to his feet just before the black-haired guard reached them, glared, and walked on.

That morning as Johann preached, Tadeusz watched the new prisoner closely. He kept asking himself how it was possible that a Bible had found its way into the camp. Then he remembered Johann was fond of saying that angels came in strange forms.

After the prayer time, Tadeusz tried to catch Johann's eye and signal the good news, but as usual the guards whisked him away right after breakfast. It was as if they had been specifically ordered to minimize Johann's contact with the others. Tadeusz had no choice but to let his news wait.

That day the new prisoners were put to work building new barracks. Tadeusz did not see Roman again until late in the evening. When Roman finally did stagger through the door, Tadeusz sat up to welcome him. Looking at the man's face, he remembered all too well the pain and shock of his own first day at the camp.

He leaned over. "Here, are you all right?" Roman did not respond.

Concerned, Tadeusz jumped down and bent over the man. He pushed the hair back from the sticky forehead. "Come on, lie down and you'll feel better. I know it might sound crazy, but after a while you won't hurt as much as you do tonight. Your body gets used to it, numbs, if you like." As he spoke, Tadeusz was thanking God Roman had not been sent down to the mines.

Roman opened his eyes. "It's my feet," he mumbled.

Tadeusz was not sure he had heard correctly. He watched as Roman sat up and unwrapped the rags around his feet. Then he gasped. The only things that made them recognizable as feet were their long shape and two big toes. Both were nothing but a mass of bloody, festering sores.

Before Tadeusz could say anything, Roman sighed, "Frostbite, from last winter. I need shoes to walk straight. They had started to heal in the train, but this morning's work cracked the sores open again."

"You've been walking around like that for half a year?" asked Tadeusz. Then he echoed, "Shoes." Tadeusz looked down at his own shabby boots, wondering if he could give them to the man. But his feet were much too small.

Roman spoke again, "I thought maybe I could make shoes out of it, but I haven't figured out a way yet."

"Out of what?"

"I wouldn't have taken it out of the church otherwise. I know it's wrong to steal from a church, but I thought I could make shoes out of it." As he rambled on, Roman reached back into the corner of his bed and brought out the altar Bible Tadeusz had shoved there in the morning.

"Of course!" Just seeing the huge book again excited Tadeusz. "You stole it for shoes?"

Roman nodded. "The leather covers looked so nice and thick. And look, the leather is soft enough to bend. Each cover is big enough for one shoe. Hey." Roman looked up and focused on Tadeusz's face for the first time. "Hey, you want this, don't you? You were so interested in it this morning. You want it?"

"Yes." Tadeusz could hardly choke the word out of his throat.

"Well, can you help me make shoes out of the cover?"

"I don't know. Probably."

"Well, then it's settled. You can have the inside; it's of no use to me."

Tadeusz smiled at the last four words. But he was already trying to think of how he could make shoes from a Bible cover.

That night Tadeusz slept three hours, then woke up at the time he guessed Johann must be setting off for the camp. He did not know how Johann had managed it, a week of nights. From a purely physical standpoint, the long walk must have had a shattering effect on the old man's body.

Yet he never complained, and he traveled unescorted. None of the guards were willing to sacrifice their sleep to make sure an old and, in their view, worthless prisoner did not escape. They probably even hoped Johann would get lost on the steppe somewhere. They tolerated him, nothing more. It was in this apparent weakness that Johann's great strength lay. The guards would not trouble him just because he seemed so harmless.

There was, however, a small group of guards who seemed to hate Johann. They openly opposed the preaching, and during the last few mornings they had heckled him during the prayer time. Just today, when the new prisoners lined up for the first time, these same guards told them no one had to get up to hear the old man speak. Anyone who chose to miss the meetings would be allowed to sleep in during the extra half hour. Tadeusz wondered why they simply did not retract the decision to allow Johann to speak. Probably they were counting on Johann keeling over from exhaustion.

These were Tadeusz's thoughts as he listened to make sure everyone around him slept. Then Tadeusz leaned over Roman and felt around in the dark for the altar Bible. Once he had it, Tadeusz heaved it up onto his chest and ran his fingers along the embossed cover. He held the pages up to his nose and riffled through the pages, inhaling the scent of ink and old books and church.

Then carefully, so as not to wake up the other prisoners, he climbed out of the bunk. He carried the Bible and a small sewing kit he had put together for himself when his own clothes had been reduced to rags—a piece of shale he had scraped down into a point and a rusty nail he had picked up beside the barracks.

Tadeusz headed for the doorway, which the guards left open because of the heat. As he settled onto the top step, moonlight fell across his lap. Tadeusz gazed up into the openness. Beams of light streamed through the clouds. Yet again, Tadeusz felt thankful for the bareness of the steppe around them. Tonight it meant the guards did not keep as close a watch on the barracks; they assumed the moonlight would show them everything.

It took all his strength to tear the covers of the Bible apart from the pages. Luckily, the leather was already well worn along the spine and he could tear it in two. He folded each piece upward. Then, with the help of his makeshift tools, he jabbed holes through the leather with the nail. After that he took the rags Roman had used to cover his feet and tore them into strips, which he threaded through the holes. As he pulled the strips tight, the leather rectangles bent upward, slightly curving at the edges.

Before the moon disappeared behind the barracks, Tadeusz had finished his labor of love. The vigil had been as much in Johann's name as for Roman. The whole time he was working on the shoes, he did not stop praying for Johann or his long trek.

There had even been moments during that night when Tadeusz heard the wind move in such a way that he thought he heard footsteps. So he had prayed for Johann's angels, for he felt confident that was the only way Johann had managed to walk so far each night.

Tadeusz was sorry when the moonlight faded. Although he had managed to finish the shoes, he had not had time to read any of the pages. Then he thought it only fitting that the honor of doing so for the first time should go to Johann.

Tadeusz felt his way back along the aisle that ran between the beds. He placed the shoes on the floor beside Roman, who lay on his stomach, snoring fitfully. The contents of the Bible he placed by his own side. He was still running his hand along the edges when he fell asleep.

"So, I've caught you again, heh, swine?" the dark face cackled into Tadeusz's face. "I'm glad to see you took my advice." Out of reflex, Tadeusz flinched backward, rolling himself into a fetal ball, only then realizing he was about to pay a high price for his night's labors.

The guard let fall blow after blow, and Tadeusz grunted in pain. The face laughed and, after an eternity, moved on. "I want to see you out there in two minutes, do you understand?"

Tadeusz ran his hands down his leg and brushed against the pages of the coverless Bible. Then he heard the silence in the barracks and was surprised to discover he was the last one there. With a heave he sat up, shoved the thick book under his shirt, and headed outside. A backward glance showed him that Roman had found his new shoes.

Tadeusz was shocked to realize he must have missed the prayer time. Yet he was pleased to see that despite the guards' offer of extra sleep, no one, not one man, had chosen to miss Johann's preaching.

Now a sense of urgency seized Tadeusz. He must get the Bible to Johann today, it would never remain safe with him.

He rounded the corner of the building and saw the group of men already standing in line for their bread. Johann stood at the back, so for once it was easy for Tadeusz to walk up and stand beside him.

"Tadeusz, you're limping. What's happened? I worried when you . . ." Johann stopped when Tadeusz placed his finger over his lips.

Tadeusz glanced around him once, then quickly reached under his shirt and pulled out the bulky pages.

Johann's eyes grew round as tears sprang into them. He took the bundle and put it under his own shirt. "I wondered. Now I know. Where did you find it?"

"One of the new prisoners brought it in. Look, I made him a pair of shoes out of the cover." Tadeusz nodded toward Roman, who had just received his meal.

"Well done." Johann beamed at Tadeusz, cradling the book against his chest. "Ah, finally some food for the soul. We can live off this. But you . . ." His voice softened with concern. "You must be more careful."

Tadeusz looked around again and caught the black-haired guard staring at him oddly. He quickly averted his gaze and fell into line behind Johann without another word.

That evening Tadeusz tried to wait up for Roman, but he fell asleep before the prisoners building the barracks showed up. In the morning he made sure he woke up in plenty of time. When he could hear some of the other men stirring, Tadeusz leaned over to warn Roman.

A hairy hand clamped onto his own. Tadeusz peered into the space and nearly screamed in confusion when he saw the face grinning back at him. "Your friend is dead!" the black-haired guard hissed. "Caught you again, heh? I heard you bragging to the old man about the shoes you made for that new pig. Figured you two must be friends or something, so I finished him off when he couldn't run fast enough. Guess you made the wrong size shoes, huh?" The man hooted hideously.

In the next instant he was on his feet and beating Tadeusz, aiming this time for the face. "That will teach you to make deals behind my back!"

Tadeusz squirmed this way and that, trying to protect his skull from the iron bar. As the pain seared through his bent arms, clear realization dawned on him. There was no longer any doubt that he and Johann should remain separated. The fact that the guard had entered the barracks early, had lain in wait for him, had singled him out in this way meant that he would have to watch himself very, very carefully. Any attention he called to himself or anyone else could literally mean death for them both.

The guard finished with Tadeusz and slipped out of the barracks. Tadeusz listened to the frightened breathing of the men around him. No one was snoring. They all had heard.

As Tadeusz tried to staunch the blood flowing from a cut above his eye, he remembered the guard's reference to a deal. He could only hope he had meant the shoes and not the Bible. As soon as Tadeusz heard the wake-up call a few minutes later, he tumbled out of bed.

When the black-haired guard passed by, he only squinted at Tadeusz. *God, don't let it be too late,* Tadeusz prayed as he joined the others heading outside. *Don't let anything like this have happened to Johann, please.*

To Tadeusz's immense relief, Johann stood waiting. Tadeusz had long ago decided Johann's body must be made of stuff different than his own. Johann would have said it was God's own strength, and Tadeusz didn't doubt it. Yet it also did not occur to Tadeusz to question how he had managed to remain relatively healthy despite the lack of food, the beatings, and the strenuous physical demands that taxed his own body every day.

On this particular morning, when Johann saw the makeshift bandage Tadeusz had bound around his head, he took a step toward Tadeusz, but the younger man shook his head vigorously.

Johann sent a barely discernible smile toward Tadeusz, then reached into the bundle of clothes he carried and pulled out the bulky pages of the altar Bible. He raised this high above his head and said, "Our prayers have been answered, my friends. The Word of God is alive among us. This is what many of you have joined me in praying for. Now listen to what Jesus said, 'Come to me, all who are weary and heavy laden. I will give you . . .' "

Before Johann could finish, the black-haired guard let out a high-pitched screech. He was standing together with a few other guards, the ones who had tried to shout down Johann during the last few mornings. Now this group began to walk slowly toward him.

"It was a mistake letting you talk this way, old man." Tadeusz's guard slapped his bar across his palm. "We thought you would have died the death of a dog a long time ago. But now you've managed to smuggle contraband into the camp, and we're going to take it away from you if we have to kill you"—he paused and cast a threatening look at the other prisoners—"and all the rest to do it. Frankly," the man wheezed, "we'd be doing the camp a favor getting you out of the way. You should have died a long time ago."

Tadeusz moved forward instinctively, but a guard standing nearby grabbed him by the elbows.

The guard with the iron bar had raised it high. He started running toward Johann, swinging the bar around and around. "This is going to take your head off, old man. And good thing, too. Then we won't have to listen to what comes out of it anymore." The man panted and heaved, step by step, jogging closer and closer to Johann.

Tadeusz tried to struggle free, but his guard held him fast. The other prisoners had grouped together like frightened animals, huddling in a corner of the yard.

The hate on the guard's face was there for all to see. It twisted his countenance, drawing the jowls down, squinting the eyes.

Johann did not run away. If anything he stood taller, his lips moving. Suddenly, the guard stopped dead and let the bar fall from his hand. It clattered to the ground as he let out a howl, turned, and started running in the opposite direction.

The guard holding on to Tadeusz was so surprised that he let go. Tadeusz, his earlier resolve forgotten, reached Johann's side within seconds. "Are you all right?" he gasped. "What, what happened?"

Johann looked down at his shaking body. "He must have seen the protection I was praying for."

Tadeusz nodded. He could not tear his eyes away from Johann's hands. Despite the attack, he had refused to let go of the pages he now grasped so tightly. His knuckles shone white. The fear still twisted Tadeusz's stomach. "What will happen to us now? Surely that guard . . ." He looked around for his tormentor, but he was nowhere to be seen.

"It's all right, you'll see." Johann took a deep breath. "That man won't bother either of us anymore. I'm sure of it."

---

All that day, as he worked in the mines, Tadeusz hoped

Johann's words would come true. In the evening, when he climbed into his bunk, he discovered his sewing kit had been removed. He hoped that one of the other prisoners had just borrowed it. But as he tried to fall asleep, Tadeusz kept seeing his guard's face as he had seen it that morning. He woke up breathing hard, soaked in sweat, smelling himself.

Tadeusz could not go back to sleep. He tried to think of Hanna, of her touch, her hands, but he had trouble remembering her softness. When Tadeusz finally heard the guards enter the barracks, he slipped out of bed, expecting the worst. But the black-haired guard approaching Tadeusz did not even look at him. As he passed by, Tadeusz noticed that for the first time he held no iron bar. The man did not say a word.

The guard behind him did, though. "You! You're supposed to report to the office right away."

Tadeusz desperately needed to see Johann, but knew he had no choice but to obey. When he reached the other side of the camp, he saw a crowd of about twenty prisoners from other barracks already waiting there.

"You men," an officer shouted from the open doorway. "You men are released. You'll be getting on a train this morning which will take you to the border."

Tadeusz looked around him at the shock and dismay on the others' faces. A great weight lifted off him, then came slamming back down as he realized Johann was not in the crowd.

He turned and ran as well as he could back to the courtyard. There, Johann stood with one hand upraised, the other balancing the bulky pages of the altar Bible. As he read his voice rang out, "And from Psalm 4, 'I will lie down and sleep in peace, for you alone, O Lord, make me dwell in safety.' " Tadeusz waited and watched the guards, but the black-haired man was nowhere in sight.

When Johann had finished with the blessing, Tadeusz approached him.

"Father—" Before he could choke out the news of his release, Johann interrupted him.

"Tadeusz, good news. They're bringing me here, to this camp. Do you know what that means? We'll be together. And now we don't need to be so careful. The guards who were bothering us before are avoiding me now. After what happened yesterday they won't dare lay a hand on us. Tadeusz?"

Tadeusz stood still. "I know what it means," he said softly.

And so it was that almost a half-year to the day after the Russians had arrested Tadeusz and Johann, they finally managed to separate them. But the strenuous labor Tadeusz had feared would kill Johann did not. Instead, on that same morning, just before Tadeusz left the camp, Johann was called before the officers' tribunal.

It had taken until the middle of the summer, but the Russians had finally found evidence indicating that Johann had done the research for key Nazi projects. Back in Kraków they had discovered the records at the office of the Nazi engineering corps, which the Germans had failed to destroy in their rush to leave the city. For this the Soviets sentenced Johann to death. Tadeusz heard the pronouncement only minutes before he was forced to board his train.

Tadeusz was not sure why they had let him go. Perhaps after all their investigating he had emerged as no more than a Polish prisoner forced to work for a German. He was not sure of much anymore. He rubbed his cheek against the wooden slats of the cattle car carrying him home. Again he felt fear. It threatened to burst inside him, to drown him, to drag him down and never let him go again. All the worst of what could be was coming true at that very moment. He saw Hanna being tortured, he saw their dead baby, and he saw Johann being rolled into a mass grave, on the dawn-drenched steppe, with no one left to pray over his body.

# 14

## Mid-May—June 1945

Hanna waited for what seemed an eternity, listening to the strange voices rise and fall, when suddenly the shadow of the shape in the opening stood and stumbled past. Sunshine streamed back into the cave. She desperately wanted to believe it was over. But only minutes after the danger had passed, more screams and course laughter filtered down to her from the forest beyond the opening.

In the next few hours there were several times when the sounds came very close to the cave, yet no one actually entered it. All that time Hanna refused to move. Even when her mother and Mrs. Slovan grabbed her by both wrists and hauled her to her feet, she shook her head. "I'll stay and keep watch."

"You don't need to, you know," Helena whispered. "I doubt they'll be back, and it's drier inside. Besides, we need to check on the others."

"No, I'll stay. You go ahead."

"It's good," Mrs. Slovan said. "Someone stay here to sound alarm for rest." She paused. "It last long."

It was true. The crashing sounds went on until finally the light began to fade. Then Hanna's mother came to check on her, to hold her so they could share each other's warmth. But still Hanna refused to retreat.

Hanna did not herself know why she insisted on remaining at the entrance. She felt driven to stay, almost fascinated by the terror going on beyond her sight. There was something else, as well. She wanted to inflict upon herself the pain of hearing the other women suffering. In this way she shared at least some of the anguish and was not completely spared.

Hanna could not begin to explain all this to her mother; she hardly knew it herself. She did know she wanted to prove to herself and the others that she was worthy of their protection. When Hanna again refused to surrender her place to the women who came to take her place, Helena stayed with her. Mother and daughter remained like that, wrapped in each other's arms, until they both finally fell asleep.

The next morning Helena and Hanna woke to the sounds of birds singing in the forest. Hanna whispered to her mother, "Is it over?" Her mother shook her head and covered her lips with a finger. As Hanna stood and stretched, Mrs. Slovan and one of the other women emerged from inside the cave. This time they insisted that Helena and Hanna exchange places with them. Helena said, "Come, you must think of the baby."

Hanna nodded. She felt very, very tired as she followed her mother into the darkness.

The other women inside the cave merely looked up when Helena and Hanna entered the next chamber. Here, too, fear had cloaked the women into silence, even though the need for it was much less acute than by the opening.

That second day was a time of waiting. A fear of "When will it happen? When will the alarm be sounded? When will we have to run?" tramped steadily through the thoughts of each woman there. It tormented them as they waited, as the hours passed, their imaginations mixing the fear with their prayers. It was not a state they could grow used to. Instead, it kept them on edge, waiting, listening, hearing something, then not, wondering, cursing the slow passage of time while simultaneously giving thanks for every moment of continued safety.

Helena busied herself with Hanna. She brought her a bowl of cold broth from the pan that stood in a corner. They dared not light a fire to warm it, not yet, since the smoke might still give them away. Then she wrapped her own coat around Hanna and settled her onto a folded burlap sack, hoping to reduce the chilling effect of the cold stone surrounding them.

Hanna seemed oblivious to her own growing weakness. She had never had the chance to fully recover from the near miscarriage. What little resistance and strength Hanna had managed to build up during her days in bed had been erased by the mad dash through the woods the previous day. And now the damp cold of the cave had allowed a chill to settle into her bones and muscles. Hanna could not stop shaking.

She looked up and smiled at her mother as she took the broth. If she hadn't swallowed hard after the first gulp, her stomach would have heaved. "Thanks," she gasped, then noticed that her hand holding the mug trembled. Her black eyes grew rounder as she raised them up to Helena's face. "Are we going to be all right?"

It was the little girl's voice Helena hadn't heard since she and Hanna first arrived in Kuron back in February. "Of course." Helena smiled back at her. "But you need to rest, and we need to pray."

All through that day and during the second night, Hanna slept fitfully. Despite the damp cold of the cave, beads of sweat gathered on Hanna's forehead and clung there until Helena wiped them gently away. This happened several times during the night.

When Hanna finally woke up on her third morning in the cave, it was to the sound of several women arguing. Her skin felt clammy, but the fever seemed to have broken. "What is it?" she asked her mother.

Helena smoothed her daughter's hair out of her eyes. She stood, groaning from stiffness. She had not dared to change her position all night for fear of waking Hanna.

"As far as I can make out, Mrs. Slovan wants to leave the cave now. She says we've hidden long enough, and the women on the outside need our help. The others think it's too early. There might still be soldiers in the area."

Hanna stretched as well, and felt her head throb. As she struggled to her feet she cringed, expecting dizziness, then wound her palms around her forehead when it hit. She gratefully accepted the cup of cold broth her mother was offering her.

"How are you?" Helena asked.

Hanna realized that, despite the headache, she felt surprisingly rested. "I feel better." She gulped down the soup and set the cup down.

Helena was about to answer when Mrs. Slovan turned to her. The expression on the gnarled face was defiant. "You come?"

Hanna looked at her mother. The long sleep combined with the thought that there might be women outside, hurting and cold, cleared her head. This was the chance Hanna had been waiting for to help, to somehow justify her own safety.

She and Helena stepped forward together, joining Mrs. Slovan. "We can't hide forever," Helena said.

"No," Mrs. Slovan answered, already moving toward the tunnel.

Hanna looked back at the small crowd of women who mumbled as they watched. The fear around their eyes had been joined by a measure of guilt. Hanna felt it too, the guilt that they had been spared when others had not. It was what prompted her now to act.

When they reached the front entrance, Hanna saw it as she had the first time, from an angle that would not have shown the web, even if the soldier's hand had not destroyed it. Helena and Mrs. Slovan scrambled up the boulder that led to the opening, then both turned to give Hanna a hand up. When the three women crept out of the cave, they emerged into bright sunlight.

Hanna wiped her forehead. The trees rustled above her. The three women clambered down the embankment, then stood still. Birds moved in the branches above them.

"It's so quiet," her mother said. "Shall we spread out?" Each of the three women hesitated, wondering how to start, afraid of what they would find once they did.

"First other caves," Mrs. Slovan said.

She led them down a path that changed from granite to a padded blanket of pine needles that muffled their steps. Mrs. Slovan started to call out names, "Emmy! Agnes! Ludmila!" She pointed toward a cliff to their left and, as Hanna and Helena were watching, seemed to disappear into the very rock wall itself.

"Mrs. Slovan!" Hanna called softly, then realized there was no sense in whispering anymore. After all, Mrs. Slovan had shouted, so now Hanna did as well. "Mrs. Slovan, are you all right?"

"Is okay. In here." Hanna moved toward the voice and did not see the three overlapping stone slabs until they stood directly in front of her. What looked like a plain rock face from the path was actually an entrance to another cave.

"You wait." Mrs. Slovan motioned for Hanna to continue up the path. "Keep looking."

Hanna looked at her mother, who nodded. "She's right. We should spread out." Then she turned to go in the opposite direction.

Hanna could hear Mrs. Slovan's muffled voice calling the three names over and over again. When she reemerged, Hanna still had not managed to move away on her own. She looked at the older woman's face, clouded with worry. "No, nothing," she answered the unasked question. "Come, we look together, yes?"

With Mrs. Slovan leading her, Hanna found she could walk without being so afraid. They had rounded the cliff and were heading up a hill when Mrs. Slovan held up her hand as a sign to stop moving. "Shh," she hissed. They listened as a squirrel chattered.

Then Hanna heard the sound, or thought she did—a woman moaning. It was off to the right, and Hanna was the closest. She turned and followed the noise through the forest, with Mrs. Slovan walking behind her. When the sound stopped, they searched the nearby undergrowth together.

Hanna called out, "Yes? Who is there?"

She stopped and listened again. Was it the wind, or had she really heard a voice? Hanna's eyes roamed over the grass, following a line of wildflowers winding between the trees, all seeming somehow familiar. Then she recognized the path she had followed a few days earlier to the smaller entrance of the cave. Hanna traced the path back toward the rocks she had needed so much help to climb. She saw a patch of wild violets, then something bright, reflecting the sun. "Over here!"

Hanna lunged toward the spot where a woman's bare hand emerged from a clump of berry bushes. The work-callused palm turned upward, a gold band shone on the third finger. Hanna tore at the thorny bushes until she saw a face covered with scratches. The hair that framed the face was dark and cropped quite short.

"Sister!"

"No!" Mrs. Slovan cried out, lunging toward Hanna's side.

"Ah, Sister Patrice," Hanna muttered as she held out a trembling hand and placed two fingers on the white throat. The cold skin forewarned her that she would feel no pulse. She looked up at Mrs. Slovan and shook her head. Only then did Hanna notice that caked blood striped both legs of the nun.

Hanna felt the cold broth rise up inside her. She quickly stood and ran a few steps away, gripping her stomach as she heaved again and again until nothing more came up. When she had finished, she found her mother's arms holding her from behind. She looked up to see Mrs. Slovan dragging the body into a nearby clearing.

"Oh, Hanna, I feel the same way. Oh, this is so terrible."

"Not her," Hanna swallowed again. She could not tear her eyes away from the bare arms and legs Mrs. Slovan lay gently onto the grass. Hanna knew Sister Patrice could have betrayed them, had had the power to turn them out of the village, could have saved herself. Instead, she had waited and brought Hanna and her mother to safety.

"Mother, she knew we came from a German family. She found out when that man lost his leg. I spoke to him in German, then didn't deny it when he asked if I came from a German family in Kraków. I was afraid she might . . ." Hanna's voice trailed off as Mrs. Slovan approached them.

The large woman hung her head, shaking it back and forth like an angry bull. "I go for more."

Hanna did not know if she meant more bodies or more help. She stared after her dismally.

As soon as Mrs. Slovan was out of sight, her mother took Hanna by the shoulders. "Now, you listen to me, Hanna. At one time it was very important not to let anyone know about our being German, and that is why we kept it a secret when we arrived. But now, looking around you and having heard what's been happening here over the past days, do you really think it matters? We're all victims here. You shouldn't think so much about your own safety. There's more at stake here than just surviving."

Hanna's eyes widened. She could feel the dizziness, see her mother's face going in and out of focus. Had she really been so selfish?

"I know you've been very sick. You need to go to bed and rest. But you understand, don't you? If there's anyone left alive we must help them. They hid us; now it's our turn to help. Summon up the strength to see this through. Try to put aside your weakness and pain."

Hanna nodded, breathing deeply. "I'll be all right, Mother. Really. Don't worry about me."

"Well, I do. But remember, although we may not be in control of these events, we are in control of how we react. We do have a choice. Will we react out of fear and selfishness? Or will we take the good Lord's way and react out of compassion, as He would have us?"

"Yes, Mother, but . . ." Hanna hesitated, then blurted out, "but why did we survive, and not her?" She glanced toward the clearing.

Helena was quiet for a moment. "I can't know that. If nothing else, she'll be spared any more suffering. Hanna, I want you to think of Tadeusz, think of your baby, look forward to a better future. Think on these things as you do what you must. This isn't your fault. And Hanna . . ."

Hanna's mother gripped her fast. "Hanna, it's too late for us to be betrayed."

Hanna let her mother's words sink in. She closed her eyes for a few moments, listening to the wind in the trees, smelling the musty dampness of the forest floor, becoming acutely aware of where she stood.

When she opened her eyes again, she saw Mrs. Slovan returning with most of the other women from the cave. They looked as if they knew the task ahead of them would grow grimmer as the morning wore on.

In groups of two they combed the woods, Hanna remaining with Mrs. Slovan, Helena pairing up with another woman. At first they only found a few corpses, their bodies twisted under tree trunks like so many limbs of driftwood washed ashore. And then the first hurt and moaning woman was found, alive.

Mrs. Slovan, still very much in charge, ordered her to be brought back to the large cave. She had already asked one of the women to return and heat up what little food remained and make beds of pine branches for the sick they might find in the woods.

Of all the caves in the area, only the cave where Hanna and her mother had hidden had effectively protected its occupants. It seemed that Sister Patrice and Mrs. Slovan had been the only ones who knew the exact whereabouts of all these hiding places. As Hanna followed Mrs. Slovan in and out of each cave, she became aware of just how lucky they had been. Apparently a plan had been agreed to ahead of time, a network of hiding places. Hanna would always wonder how close she and her mother had come to not being included.

After it became clear that the other caves were empty, Hanna spread out with the rest, but that morning she found no other bodies. She did find a small child, cold and shivering, hugging his knees, inside a hollow tree. "Come here, it's all right," Hanna held out her hands. She waited until the large eyes spilled tears before she reached for the little boy and held him to her.

When she brought him down to the cave, all the women there looked up and peered hopefully at his face, then one woman called out and claimed him. Hanna set the boy down and tucked a blanket around him, then went in search of food. As she did so, she heard the others talking in hushed tones. Because Hanna could not understand the language, again and again she had to push out the thought that they were talking about her. Hanna felt none of the comfort or compassion now spreading among the women in the cave. Whether they intended it or not, she felt cut off.

Helena happened to reenter the cave at that point and she saw the look on Hanna's face. As Hanna passed by Helena on her way to the passageway, Helena squeezed her arm. Hanna stopped and smiled weakly, then moved on.

Helena sighed. She fully expected that whatever had given Hanna the strength to join the search would wear off soon. And though she would never say it out loud, she knew that it would be a miracle if Hanna's baby were born alive. She had lost weight instead of gaining it, and had enjoyed none of the care or protection Tadeusz would have provided had he been near. Helena felt helpless. She wished she had spoken more kindly to her daughter that morning, even though she realized the stern words may have been just what Hanna needed to endure the day.

The afternoon seemed suspended in time. Helena had the bad luck of finding several women's corpses piled on top of each other. After dragging them back to the central clearing, she leaned up against a tree, exhausted by the physical and emotional effort. Then she caught sight of Hanna carrying a little girl. She wanted to call out that the child was too heavy, that she shouldn't be carrying her, but the words caught in her throat when she saw the tears streaming down both their cheeks. For what seemed the thousandth time, Helena prayed for the spirit of her daughter, that the events erupting around them would not crush her will to live. It was a prayer Helena had never prayed for anyone else, but instinctively she felt Hanna's weakness and was most afraid of her simply giving up.

Finally, the day darkened. Hanna found her mother as they both returned to the cave for the last time. Only then did she realize she had eaten nothing since the broth her mother had given her in the morning. She felt a hollow rumbling inside, and her back ached. Had she really spent all day on this surreal search? Hanna had thought she would become hardened to the sight of sore and suffering women as the day wore on, but she had not. At the cave, Hanna looked around and saw a girl around her own age hugging a blanket to herself and crying. It was all Hanna could do to keep from taking the pain on herself, yet she made no move to comfort the girl. Instead, she tried to remember her mother's warning, but as with the comfort, could not summon it.

Hanna slept fitfully that night. Despite her exhaustion, the baby would not hold still, and each time Hanna woke up she felt the tension in her knotted muscles. She heard others in the deep darkness also stirring and knew she would not be the only one trying not to dream. The night seemed even longer than the day. When she tried to think about Tadeusz, his face was not there for her. When she finally did doze off, it was to the sound of her mother's even breathing. And she wondered if her baby was listening to the same.

In the morning Hanna woke up with another pounding headache. She sat upright, closed her eyes, and swallowed down her nausea. She could not complain when so many of the others were waking up from a night filled with anguish. Hanna straightened her back and tried to ignore how scratchy her scalp felt.

At that moment Mrs. Slovan entered the cave. It was evident some of the others had been anxiously waiting for her, since they immediately crowded around her and began asking questions.

"What is it?" Hanna asked her mother.

"I'll go see." Helena crossed over to the edge of the group and listened for a few moments before coming back. "She's just returned from the village. The soldiers seem to be gone, and I suppose it's as safe as it ever will be. She says it's time to go home."

Hanna wanted to ask when it would be time for them to go home. She did not doubt that they both ached for the same thing. But her mother would know when the time was right.

For the first two days after they returned to the village, Hanna took to her bed and slept, while Helena threw herself into helping bring some order to the lives around them. There was very little left in the village of any value. The Russians had not stayed long, but their mark would not be an easy one to erase. All the homes had been ransacked, and out of either greed or need, the soldiers had taken every single blanket, not to mention most of the food they could find. All that was left were the provisions the women had managed to hide or bring with them from the caves.

There were other differences, as well. When Hanna finally felt strong enough to dress herself and leave the house, she headed for the church, knowing she would find her mother there. As she walked down the main street, she noticed all the broken glass around her feet, and she noted that no curtains hung in any of the windows. At the church, the only difference was that the broken glass on the ground was colored.

Somehow she had expected nothing to be changed. Instead, all she found in the church were a few makeshift cots. Only one other woman besides Mrs. Slovan and her mother was there to tend the sick. The worst change of all was that the nuns were all gone. Not one had returned from the forest alive. The sisters' quiet presence had sewn the fabric of the village together. Now that they were no longer there to give, and to give an example of giving, a selfishness settled over many of the women who had managed to survive their "liberation." Those who had some form of supplies refused to share, and most had lost interest in helping the refugees who continued streaming through the village.

During the coming weeks Helena and Hanna worked in nearly impossible conditions, nursing without drugs or training, counseling, helping, begging, and rummaging through rubbish, along with the rest of the population, to look for scraps to eat. After a while they no longer bothered going to the church. No supplies were left, and one night the cots had mysteriously disappeared, leaving the corpse of one woman they had been nursing dumped onto the stone floor. Besides, the building was cold. The winds coming down from the slopes whistled in and out of the jagged openings in the church wall where statues of saints had once held their hands high in blessing of the congregation.

Hanna joined the others searching for firewood and roots or old elderberries in the woods. Helena continued to work herself ragged, caring for the people who had less than she. There were many who fit that description, for the flow of refugees passing through Kuron became increasingly pathetic.

Before liberation there had been people running ahead of the Russians, driven by fear from one place to the next and carrying with them all that was dear to them in this life. They had pulled carts piled high with furniture, tapestries, candlesticks, with a child or two always perched on top. And they had inevitably traveled west, trying to outrun the front.

Now, however, the old men and women straggling through Kuron came from all directions and were heading nowhere. They dragged their feet, wandering aimlessly down the streets, looking only for food, shivering in the chilly air that spring still refused to warm. Many were ill, trembling and feverish with the typhoid that hit the population in waves that year, oblivious of all boundaries.

For weeks on end these people who had not run fast enough, these people who no longer had anything to run from, shifted in and out of the village. The sight of so much need touched Hanna and her mother in different ways. While Hanna turned inward, retreating to bed for twelve to fourteen hours a day, Helena spent herself feverishly on the needs of those around her.

One day Hanna caught her mother actually giving

away their things. When Hanna came down the stairs she gasped, "Mother, what are you doing?"

Helena stood in front of Mrs. Slovan's house, passing out their skirts and sweaters and extra shoes and hats to anyone who cared to step up and take them. The faces of those receiving the clothing remained passive.

Helena turned around to face Hanna and simply said, "Casting our bread upon the waters of humanity, my child." In the end she gave away everything but their own winter coats and one change of clothes. Hanna could only stand by and watch.

At night when Hanna tried to get her mother to come to bed, Helena often refused. Hanna did not know what she did late at night, could not know that Helena had been so shaken by the events around the cave that she no longer fell asleep unless the night was half over and she could watch her daughter sleeping in safety.

In this way, as time went by, it was Hanna who grew strong while her mother grew weak. The weeks of exhausting work had taken their toll, and when typhoid struck, Helena knew the symptoms better than most. One night, without a word to Hanna, she moved herself onto the floor of their room.

"Mother?" Hanna's voice was thick with sleep. "Mother, what are you doing?"

"Go back to sleep," Helena told her.

"What do you mean?" Hanna protested. "You can't sleep down there."

"I must," her mother answered. "That way I can't infect you and the baby. Now don't argue with me about this, Hanna."

Hanna knew that tone and grew quiet. Then the meaning of her mother's words struck her. "Can't infect? Oh, God, no!"

"Hush, child."

Hanna crossed the room and knelt to feel her mother's forehead. It burned with fever. She swallowed the panic rising in her, something she had practiced often since leaving Tadeusz. She steadied her voice, "Looks like it's my turn to play nurse." And she forced herself to smile.

"You'll do no such thing. Now you stay away from me. I won't let anything happen to my grandchild . . ."

Hanna cut her off with an upraised hand, and Helena had no more strength to insist. In one night their roles had reversed. "You will get better, I'll make sure of that. There are others who have survived the fever and lived; we've seen them ourselves, remember? And I haven't forgotten what Sister Patrice taught me."

At the sound of the nun's name, a stillness settled over the room. Hanna took her mother's hand, but Helena only turned on her side to face the wall. "Don't," she whispered.

"I have to. You know that."

The first thing Hanna did was move her mother back into the bed. She was surprised at how Helena's body already trembled from the fever. She piled their two coats on top of her, despite the heat Helena was giving off. After that, Hanna left the room to search for some sort of food she could at least boil. No sooner had she reached the stairs when she saw Mrs. Slovan for what must have been the first time in days. As if reading her thoughts, Mrs. Slovan stood holding a tray with a steaming bowl of what smelled like nettle soup. "Your mother, very sick."

"Oh, Mrs. Slovan, how did you know?"

"I know. I see. She help so many, now we help her. You stay with her, keep her warm. Feed her this."

Hanna took the tray helplessly. Tears streamed down her face. "Where did you find them?" Not for the first time the deep compassion of this woman filled Hanna with gratitude.

By the time Hanna returned to the bedroom, she could tell by her mother's breathing that she had already worsened. Hanna tried to wake her so she could eat, but managed only to prop up her mother's head with one hand and spoon-feed her the soup. Sip by sip, Hanna saved the precious drops when they dribbled out of the side of her mother's mouth.

At first, Hanna would not let herself think about the inevitability she had seen in Mrs. Slovan's eyes. She could not accept that her mother was seriously ill. She nursed her as best she could. But eventually, when her mother's discomfort only increased, Hanna thought of her father. How would she face him without her mother?

This was not the first case of typhoid Hanna had seen. She knew just how fast and hard the disease hit. No, she pushed the thought aside, her mother would recover. That was all there was to it. She had to.

Soon, though, Hanna could see that the weeks of little food, little rest, and much worry had exacted too high of a price. All that day and deep into the night, Hanna held her mother's hand, while Helena tossed her head from one side to the other, moaning softly, occasionally calling out Hanna's name, or Johann's. Three times Mrs. Slovan brought them a heated bowl of soup. The last time she urged Hanna to drink it herself.

Only when it was very late did Hanna let go of Helena's hand. She had sat like that for hours, almost in a trance, but now she realized she was chilled to the bone. Hanna slipped under the coats to curl her body around her mother's. She could feel the baby between them, old against new.

She ran her right hand over her mother's tiny body, bones connected, erratic breathing, thin wrists. Hanna did not want to associate all that frailty with the strength she knew, the woman who had taught her so much about the wonders of heaven and earth, who had never once raised her voice, even when Hanna's stubbornness had endangered them.

Hanna fell asleep thinking that way, praying for her mother's healing, willing her body's own youth and strength into her mother's weak and feverish one. She lay so close she could smell her own breath.

Hanna dreamt of nothing. Then, a few hours later, a movement woke her. Helena had groped for Hanna's hand. Hanna sat up and took the wrinkled fingers into her own, bringing them to her cheek. "Mother, oh see, I knew it would be all right." But the coldness of the hand choked Hanna's flow of words. At least, she told herself, the fever had broken.

Helena slowly rolled onto her back, then looked up at her daughter, now kneeling on the bed beside her. "My darling," she whispered, moving her lips twice more.

"What? What is it?" Hanna asked, desperate for the color to return to her mother's face.

"I . . . I know where I'm going and oh, Hanna, it's so . . . I'll . . ."

"No, Mother," Hanna could barely say the words.

" . . . wait for you there."

"Mother!"

Helena opened her eyes wide at Hanna, then squeezed her hand and squeezed until she had no more strength to give. Hanna looked around her desperately. She felt as though a thief had just entered the room unseen, then left.

During the long moments that followed, Hanna held her breath, waiting for some sign, another movement, but her mother's face remained still. Just when she could bear it no longer, a deep sigh emerged from the very depths of her mother's body, causing Hanna to utter a small cry. But Helena had already gone. She was not breathing; her lungs had just released the air of her last breath.

Now Hanna threw herself across her mother's body. She sobbed like a child. There had already been too much loss, too much pain. Hanna could not imagine even making it through one day without her mother. How did the others who had lost loved ones ever cope? There had already been so much wasted, so many lives lost. Now there was one more.

Hanna lay like that for a long time. When she finally rose from the bed and opened the curtains, she was surprised to see that the sun was only just coming up. Had the night been so long?

She stared over the treetops and already knew what she had to do. Even though a part of her was still clinging, crying over the body of her mother, she needed to do something for herself and Helena. In the name of their family she needed to act, to move, to affirm her aliveness even in the face of the death that had reached out and robbed her.

Hanna combed her mother's hair, then her own, and wrapped Helena into her coat. Then she bent at the knees and lifted the body into her arms. Hanna could almost hear her mother's voice warning her again to watch out for the baby as she shifted the weight. No matter, her mother was frighteningly light. Why hadn't she noticed how thin her mother had become?

Trying not to make too much noise, Hanna carried the

body downstairs and outside. There she placed it in a handcart Mrs. Slovan used to carry firewood and gently tucked a spade in beside it.

When she entered the forest, it was as if no other place on earth existed. The mist and tall trees closed in around her. She heard nothing but the quiet dripping of dew on dead leaves. Hanna walked on, following the path she now knew well, climbing steadily upward toward the granite ridge where the caves were.

Again, as on the day she had emerged from the cave, Hanna was struck by the surge of energy that enabled her to pull so strongly after her long night. Then as now, it was a product of her rushing adrenaline, although now she was much healthier and stronger than she had been after the week spent bleeding in bed. Then as now, she walked with her mother, heading back to the cave that had protected them.

Later Hanna would not remember much of her struggle to pull the handcart up the slope, but she would remember what she did when she got there. Once she had reached the summit, she found a place that was not too rocky. Digging in the moist earth beside the cave did not prove as difficult as Hanna had expected. Within two hours she was ready. Placing Helena's body into the hole was harder, but the worst was throwing the first handful of dirt onto her mother's white, still face. Hanna tried to remember the words spoken at other funerals.

"From dust," she began, her voice cutting into the forest stillness. A misting rain drifted softly around her. Hanna shook her head, unable to finish. As she continued to shovel in dirt, Hanna's tears mixed with the rivulets forming in the dirt clods on the body. When she had finished, mud streaked Hanna's face where her fingers had wiped away the sweat.

Hanna stood quietly, watching the grave. Then suddenly she threw her head back and began to wail a keen, the sound coming from a place deep within her, somewhere she had never needed to find before. Then, with one final surge of strength, she swung the spade around her head and flung it away.

Hanna turned and ran from the site. Blindly, she stumbled over a root and fell forward, her outstretched arms only just breaking the fall. As she pushed herself onto all fours, Hanna felt her baby kick. She struggled to stand, but sagged back onto her knees.

Hanna wondered yet again how this baby inside her could live when so many others were dead? How could she bring her into a world like this? As Hanna clambered down the rocks toward the cave entrance, she gasped out loud, "Oh, Lord, protect this little one. Protect Tadeusz, protect my father. Help me . . ."

Weeping and weak then, she slipped, losing her grip on the slick stone and falling the few feet to the floor of the cave entrance.

For several hours she lay there, not moving, until finally, the warmth of the sun shining squarely on her face brought Hanna back to consciousness. She opened her eyes, surprised to find herself in that place, so close to where she and her mother had held their vigil.

Hanna took a deep breath, trying to steady herself. Even as she asked herself where she should go, she knew. It was finally time to return to Kraków, to go home. She could no longer wait for her mother to make the decision she had waited for since they first arrived in Kuron. It had become her own.

Hanna did not only at that moment remember her mother's death, for knowledge of that had moved with her into unconsciousness when she fell. Rather, she accepted. Hanna felt the cold hand, smelled the fresh earth, heard the dull thud of the spade after it spun out of sight, all things she had not noticed before.

She squinted into the sunshine until it forced her to shut her eyes. A breeze caught Hanna's hair. She felt a familiar presence moving, pausing in front of her, then moving on, as if a shadow of some shape had just passed by the opening of the cave.

# 15

JULY 1945

Hanna had no money, no clothes but what she wore, no hope. Daily she had to muster her will and throw it against desperation, force herself to keep walking, to find food, to find a place to sleep.

Hanna had already been on the road for a week. Within two days she had exchanged her only change of clothes for some moldy potatoes. These she ate raw. She walked in a crowd of others heading north, a ragged group, hardly bearing any resemblance to real people. She had finally joined the ranks of those she had watched coming through Kuron, and now she was just one more among the mass of humanity moving across Central Europe—people looking for people, people running away, people trying to forget. And people going home, as she was trying to do.

Hanna walked and walked, across dry and dusty fields, along crowded roads, through rural villages, and finally into the mountains. There one afternoon she passed a lake and saw berries hanging from the bushes along its shore. Jaded with exhaustion, Hanna headed for the fruit and ate as she picked. When she looked up she was amazed to discover no one had followed her here from the road.

A short distance away she saw a sheep shack. She made her way over to it, eating as she walked. Inside she found fresh hay, and as she let herself down into its dry sweetness she relaxed. Hanna groaned; it felt so good to be alone and not moving, safe and not threatened. She fell asleep almost instantly.

In the middle of the night Hanna woke up to find that three sheep had joined her. She smiled at the semicircle of wool, sat up and stroked one of the ewes at her side. A lamb, already a few months old, nuzzled its mother. Hanna rubbed the wool, then smelled her hands, heavy with the musk of lanolin. She looked up and saw the moon dancing in and out between the trees.

Hanna let herself remember another time, when her feet had almost touched the floor in a wagon riding past another lake, pointing at the same moon, "Look, Father, the moon is following us!"

"That's God's eye watching over my little girl."

Hanna had smiled at the trees running past. Those had been her woods, the woods where they had traveled on Friday nights to escape the foul air that sometimes cloaked Kraków in the summer.

There had been a bridge in a little town where the Wda River joined the Wisła. Hanna knew where it was because she had once traced the route on a map, years after they had stopped going there. Now she watched another lake and the river that ran into it and wondered why this river could not take her back to that place again. When would she ever be back there again?

As the moon climbed higher in the night sky, Hanna imagined that up this river, deep in the middle of a wilderness forest somewhere dotted with lakes, was the farm they used to visit. Hanna's memories of this place were vivid, exaggerated by time. Hanna floating in cold water with the touch of her father's palm against her back. Hanna telling her parents, "See, the moon's come down to play in the lake." A stone rippling in the water. Climbing up into the farmer's lap, riding a horse. She remembered the animal's smell, but not his color.

It was a very long time ago, she thought, a time of her very first memories. But she had always wanted to spend her honeymoon there. She had planned on it since she was old enough to dream about being a glamorous bride in a white silk dress.

Hanna sighed, but then gave a little inward smile. There had been no dress, no glamorous wedding, no dream honeymoon. Those dreams, like so many others, had been shattered by the war. And yet what had happened on that first secret night with Tadeusz had made none of it matter. She and Tadeusz had become one, would always be one.

Hanna rolled over, then sat up. She cupped her hands around her belly, large for a seven-month pregnancy. The baby lay still. She promised herself that after the war she would bring Tadeusz to her lake. Perhaps if he saw the site of her first memories, they might somehow be bound even closer. They could bring the baby and be a family there, building up memories of something other than the war.

Hanna had lost track of time as she stared out into the night woods. Trees that once could have been guardians of her childhood fantasies were now probably sheltering armies and bandits. Hanna was too tired to care. She lay down with her back to the sheep, felt the summer breeze lift the hair from her face. Then she fell asleep again.

That night was the only one out of her long trek north that she would ever be able to think back on and clearly remember. It stood out as an island of peace in the long, exhausting flow of the journey. From then on, Hanna's travels exacted a daily toll, wearing down what little was left of both her strength and stamina.

She struggled over the summits and into Poland. Sometimes she hitched rides on the backs of wagons. Most of the time, though, she just walked. But by the time she reached Katowice, Hanna felt she could go no farther. She wandered around the center of the city in a daze, finally ending up at a railway crossing. Then she just sat down by the tracks, too tired and hungry to do anything else. She knew it should feel good to be back in Poland, but she had grown too numb to feel anything at all.

Hanna sat and waited, not knowing for what. After some time she noticed the ground shaking. She looked up, squinting her eyes, and saw something black coming toward her. It took a few seconds for her exhausted brain to process the information. A train was heading her way.

Hanna watched the huge black engine crawling closer. She was in no danger from where she sat in the weeds, but a thought had just occurred to her that sent her heart racing. For a few moments she managed to push aside the cloud of fatigue hanging over her mind and think one clear thought. This train was heading east, toward Kraków, toward home. If she could somehow get on board, she would no longer have to walk. Anything was worth not walking.

Hanna looked at her feet. She could not remember when she threw away her shoes, but it must have been when the soles had worn clear through. Dirt caked her feet, infecting the open sores and blisters. Yes, she told herself, the train was the only way she would get home.

The engine approached very slowly, giving Hanna plenty of time to see the masses of people hanging on to its sides. A premonition came over Hanna that if she did not somehow manage to catch this train home, she would die where she sat, in an obscure field, and never see home or Tadeusz again.

Hanna waited until the train rolled slowly right in front of her before she stood. Weak with the burden of her pregnancy, Hanna bit her tongue to focus the pain from her feet. She could only manage one thought at a time. She must get on the train, no matter what, she must.

The train slowed even further. But where on the train could she go? All those people looking at her now, they had places, either inside the freight cars or on top. The only place where few people rode was underneath the train. Hanna squatted down to look just as the train hissed to a stop. There, right in front of her, Hanna saw a free space. Under the car to her left, a man was already hanging on to the axle.

He spoke to her now, as if reading her thoughts, "You can do it. Just hook your ankles around the axle, like I have. Don't worry; we don't go very fast, not with this crowd on board."

Hanna hesitated. Her head was pounding again, and there was the baby to think about, yet this man made it look easy. Perhaps this was the way home she had been looking for. Hanna stared at the man. "I don't have much choice, do I?"

"You had better hurry before we start moving again."

Hanna did not waste her breath answering. She crawled under the car and swung her feet up as the man had told her. She wiggled her back onto the other axle and swung her arms around it at the elbows so it could support and steady her. Just when she thought she had found a position she might be able to maintain, the train began to move.

Hanna hung on, willing her strength into her arms and

legs, refusing to see herself fall onto the rails that flashed beneath her. She stared at the greasy metal above her, sometimes hanging her head loosely backward, sometimes bringing it more upright. She stayed in this position until she could no longer feel anything in her arms. When the train finally stopped again, Hanna did not trust her muscles to let go. She knew she would never be able to crawl back under if she stood up and stretched, so she stayed where she was and noticed the man in front of her was doing the same. His eyes were closed.

Hanna clung to the underparts of the train from stop to stop, interminably. She thought she must have blacked out, but did not know how often or for how long. Even then, her body was wedged beneath the train so tightly that she did not fall off. When the train finally stopped in what was obviously a large city, Hanna shook her head and saw many feet passing by her. "Kraków? Is it Kraków?" her voice croaked, but no one answered. She looked for the man under the car in front of her. He had gone.

Hanna could not hold on any longer. She had shaken off her stupor enough to look around her, and now she knew she was in serious pain. The muscles in her calves and across her back had locked, and her head felt heavy. She sucked in her breath and tried to move, but her muscles cramped in protest.

Hanna cried out with each movement. But there was nothing else to do. She had to unwind herself from the buffers and somehow find the strength to crawl out from under the train.

Hanna clenched her eyes shut and slowly straightened her arms, lowering her body onto the track despite the pain. The gravel cutting into her back smelled like urine. Hanna looked to her side and almost screamed when she saw a rat watching her from less than an arm's length away.

"Get away! Get away!" She was frightened enough now to make her arms work.

The rat stood its ground, twitching its whiskers and watching Hanna with beady eyes. Hanna used her arms to roll onto her side, then she edged her way out from under the car. As soon as she could, Hanna sat, pushing herself up with her arms. She could still feel nothing in her legs. But at least the rat was gone, even if she could still smell the stench of sewage around her.

Hanna grappled with the side of the train, trying to find something she could pull herself up on. When she had a handhold, she swiveled around so that she faced the car and pulled with all her strength. Twice her knees buckled, but the newfound strength in her shoulders and arms did not fail her. Soon Hanna stood, panting against the rusty train door, leaning against it as the blood began to circulate in her legs again.

Then she opened her eyes and looked around. At the head of the train she saw a familiar sight, the hall of Kraków train station. The last time she had been here, Tadeusz had held her in his arms.

Hanna almost cried out loud at the thought. Had it really only been a matter of months? In that time her whole world had been turned inside out. Her mother was dead. How had she even made it back? Hanna could feel the tremendous improbability of it all starting to overwhelm her. Then the baby's kick brought her back to the present.

She shuffled her feet forward, grateful that she could move again. Hanna followed the tracks to the front of the station and stopped only once when she heard a man's voice calling out her name. She whirled and saw an old man and an old woman working their way through the crowd toward each other. Every time he cried, "Hanna!" the woman smiled.

She should have known, of course, that there would be no one to meet her. Hanna bowed her head and crossed to the main doors. She was still having difficulty with her legs; they ached with every step. She knew she needed to stop and rest, but she saw nowhere that looked safe. Besides, now that she was back in Kraków, Hanna could think of nothing but going home.

That afternoon Hanna walked slowly down the familiar streets. As she passed from one neighborhood into another, she did not see the skyline full of church towers, nor did she hear Polish being spoken with the familiar accent. None of it made any impression on Hanna. She walked in a daze, intent only on placing one foot in front of the other, not tripping, and heading in the correct direction so that no effort would be wasted. Her entire body trembled with weakness and muscle fatigue. A practical part of her, very far away, warned that she would soon collapse if she did not stop. Hanna squared her shoulders. She would not let that happen. She would get herself home.

Home. What would she find? Could home mean Tadeusz? And her father? She prayed they would be there waiting for her. Home might mean safety, perhaps even food. Home was so close now.

But on the way Hanna could not help but become increasingly aware of the many changes in Kraków. In Kraków, unlike Kuron, the Russians had left troops behind. As she neared her own street Hanna saw signs of destruction all around her, not only the familiar broken glass, but also people crouching in corners.

She rounded the last corner and stopped. She was almost afraid to approach the house. In one window she could see a shredded curtain caught in the jagged glass. Yes, she could see clearly now that the house had been broken into. She stepped up to the front gate and heard voices coming from inside. Two of her mother's tapestries lay in the front garden, evidently thrown out the window of her father's upstairs study. Hanna noticed small details like the boot marks left in the garden and trampled crocus plants that must have bloomed at least five months earlier.

Hanna stood outside, listening to what were now shouts in Russian from soldiers who sounded drunk. With each passing moment what few hopes she had managed to carry with her vanished. She thought back to what she had heard in Breslau. The Russians had been here since January. It was time enough to leave a mark in more than just the soil around the house. Slowly, very slowly, Hanna forced herself to face the fact that her father and Tadeusz were not home. They had not been home for a long time.

Hanna had been so lost in her thoughts that she jumped when a man shoved past her. It was a soldier with a red star at the middle of his cap. He grunted as he pushed her out of the way and walked through the gate. His hair was shaven close to his skull, so she could see a scar running up from one ear, and he had slanted eyes. Red sores ran all the way around his neck. As he opened the door and disappeared into the house, the gate swung closed, its rusty hinges squeaking just as it always had.

It was this sound that hurt Hanna the most, more so even than all she had just witnessed. The gate clanging shut conjured up too many memories that Hanna did not have the courage to compare with the present. She turned away and lurched down the street, weeping savagely.

All around Hanna there were signs of the vandalism

and breakage. She made her way through the streets, homeless like so many others, too tired and hurting to even wonder where she should go. She begged the Lord to take her and the baby to himself. She thought over and over, *I will never see Father or Tadeusz, and we will both die here.*

Finally, in a corner under a bridge, Hanna sank to the ground and fainted, staying that way as she faded in and out of consciousness. Once or twice she came to her senses enough to drink from the dirty river water, but it tasted so foul that she gagged and fainted again. When she finally did wake up all the way, she felt confused and heavy-headed.

Why was someone shaking her? Whose hand had not let her sleep on? Hanna opened her eyes. The face swimming in front of her was that of an old woman. And whoever it was, she knew Hanna's name.

"Look at you, poor dear. Hanna wake up, you cannot stay here. Hanna!"

Slowly, very slowly Hanna recognized the voice. Only then did the face become familiar. "*Pani* Fisiak?" she asked. This was the woman who had cleaned the house for her mother when Hanna was younger, before the war. She used to live on the other side of town. Hanna had seen her a few times during the German occupation when she had come to talk to her mother.

Mrs. Fisiak was explaining to Hanna that she did not usually walk that way, along the Wisła, but that today she had, and for no apparent reason.

"And when I saw you, I thought, can that be the Müller girl? How is it possible? She looks so much older." Mrs. Fisiak bit her upper lip. "You are older." It was more of a question than a statement, but still one Hanna did not answer.

Mrs. Fisiak bent down to help Hanna stand. "Oh, Hanna, come with me. When did you last eat?"

"I don't know," Hanna mumbled.

As Hanna stood, Mrs. Fisiak noticed she was pregnant and sucked in her breath. "Hanna . . . " Then she put her arm around Hanna and helped her climb the hill away from the river. "Come, dear, I will take you to my home. It is not much, but it is better than this place."

Hanna heard only fragments of what the older woman was saying. With each step she felt weaker and weaker, and so dizzy. Mrs. Fisiak continued, "I have a room just outside the city center." Hanna stumbled, almost pulling the woman down. "Come, Hanna, you must try and keep going. I am not so strong anymore. You will have to walk; I can only keep you from losing your balance."

A part of Hanna wondered why she could not be grateful that God had sent her help. Submissively, she did as the old woman told her. She took a deep breath, and her head cleared slightly. They were walking down a busy street, and it was already dusk, but then they stopped. Hanna heard Mrs. Fisiak swear softly. "Russians," she whispered. "I hope it is not another roundup."

Hanna raised her head to see a tall man with a blond moustache approaching them, his hand outstretched. Despite his speaking in a foreign language, Hanna understood that he wanted some sort of identification.

If Hanna had felt stronger she might have laughed. In what sort of absurd world would any of the war's victims who had managed to survive be able to prove they belonged anywhere? Hanna had discarded her German papers back in Kuron, a few months before the Russians arrived there. Helena had told her to.

Now Hanna shook her head. *"Nie mam,"* shrugging her

shoulders. She could not be the only one. Was it such a crime?

Mrs. Fisiak looked at her, alarmed. She quickly fished her papers out of a small bag around her neck and handed them over. He nodded, running his eyes back and forth along the lines of text. As he returned them he glanced at Hanna. She stood still, her eyes cast downward. It had just dawned on her that the man was speaking French.

"There is no reason for the *mademoiselle* to be afraid. Do you have reason to be afraid?" His eyes bored into her.

"*Non, monsieur,*" Hanna answered. Mrs. Fisiak stared at them both.

"Fine. Everything is in order here, then." The officer turned and moved down the street.

Mrs. Fisiak let out a deep sigh. "Whatever you said, it was a good thing. What was he talking?" When Hanna told her she whispered, "Why French?"

"I think to show us he is educated, from a titled family, perhaps. I don't know." Hanna shivered. "He assumed I was Polish." It was strange the thoughts that did come in clearly. Hanna was acutely aware that she would be safer if, now that the war had ended, she drew on her Polishness and showed no signs of coming from a German family. Hanna had just not believed she had the strength to say such things.

Mrs. Fisiak said, "Of course." The Müllers had always treated her well. She was certainly not about to betray any details about the Müller family to a Soviet soldier.

Mrs. Fisiak noticed Hanna was swaying from one side to the other. "Come," she said. The two women continued a short distance, then turned up a hill. Mrs. Fisiak already knew she would not manage to carry the girl up the stairs to her apartment.

When they entered the building, the stink from the stairs reminded Hanna of the river she had just left. Urine . . . and something else. With both hands Hanna heaved herself from one step to the next, up and up until Mrs. Fisiak finally told her they were there. She took out a ring of keys and unlocked a door.

Inside Hanna saw a room with a table and chair in one corner and a mattress on a floor in the other. It was a small room, with one window, and it looked as if it had once been used as some sort of pantry. The walls were lined with shelves, all empty.

Mrs. Fisiak led Hanna to the mattress on the floor and pointed to a candlestick beside it. "There are the matches." Then she helped Hanna lower herself onto the bed and asked, "When is the baby due?"

Hanna shook her head, "I don't know." Mrs. Fisiak stared at her for a few moments, then said, "I must go to work now. You sleep. No one will bother you here." The last thing Hanna heard before she lost consciousness again was the sound of Mrs. Fisiak's footsteps slowly making their way back down the stairs.

It was dark when Hanna woke up inside the stuffy room. She lit the candle and found a mug beside her pillow. When she brought it to her lips, to her amazement she tasted goat's milk. She was so surprised that she brought the candle closer until she could see the white stuff. She smelled the mug again, nursing it with both hands. Then she took another sip.

She did not know how it had happened, but she was safe, and taking in her first nourishing food in weeks. And yet it was not enough, not enough to make her want to live. At some point during the train ride Hanna had lost what little will to fight she still had after her mother's death. Under the bridge she had been ready to give up.

That mug of milk became the first of many. In the days that followed Mrs. Fisiak cared for Hanna, never failing to bring her the precious milk at a time when even bread was hard to come by. Mrs. Fisiak recognized the danger the girl was in. Hanna's physical weakness was not all that posed a threat to Hanna and her baby's survival; her inability to fight would be harder to combat. And there was only so much Mrs. Fisiak could do.

So despite the old woman's care, Hanna's depression deepened. Day after day she lay in bed, not even waiting for her baby anymore, just watching the flies throw themselves against the windowpane.

# 16

## August 1945

When Tadeusz finally reached the Polish border, he worked his way southwest, traveling in the wake of the Russian troop movements that had preceded him six months earlier. To Tadeusz it looked as if some mammoth monster had gone before him.

In the east of Poland, the Soviets had reduced whole villages to rubble and burned-out shells of houses. Tadeusz missed the children and geese who should have been crossing those roads. Once, he passed a great mansion tucked back in the woods, its windows left open and the gardens overgrown, abandoned by wealthy owners in what must have been a panicked flight west.

As Tadeusz neared Kraków, he allowed himself to think back to the last time he had been there, to that January night when he and Johann were arrested. So much had happened, it was hard to find hope. Yet all those months he had prayed for Hanna, that she could still somehow be alive.

Not until recently had he found out about the bombing of Dresden. He had heard about it on the road from some stranger. Tadeusz had waited until the man passed on, then sat down on the edge of a field somewhere and carefully calculated the dates in his own mind. The bombing had taken place two weeks after Hanna and her mother were due to arrive there. Had they died that night as so many others had, at the hands of British bombers?

Again and again Tadeusz had felt deep down into his heart to see if Hanna were still alive. Although he did not feel her loss, he did feel a deadening fear whenever he tried to imagine Hanna's whereabouts and what the past months might have brought her. She must be alive, and the baby must also be alive. The baby was due this month. That too he had carefully calculated. They had to be alive, both of them, he kept telling himself every step of this final journey back home.

The trust he had been forced to summon was also changing Tadeusz in other ways. During these weeks Tadeusz was struggling with his grief for Johann's death, as well as a nagging uncertainty about what he would find when he finally did return to Kraków. The grief brought back the same numbing emotions he had felt when he heard from Henryk that his mother and father had been killed. The uncertainty loomed like a bad dream he might never wake up from. Together their effect, combined with those of the long journey, wore Tadeusz down until he could focus on one thought only. And that was not even a thought as such, certainly not the hatred that had consumed him after his parents died. It was more an image: Hanna's face smiling up at him at the station when they saw each other for the last time.

Again and again Tadeusz kept her eyes and mouth before him. And as he did so, he grew in his ability to trust that Hanna would be kept safe. It was an exercise. More than anything else, he believed in his heart that Hanna lived, somewhere, somehow. He felt as if he could step over a cliff and not even notice, so focused was he on the certainty that God was even at that very moment protecting Hanna and the baby.

From this perspective then, as if through a veil, Tadeusz experienced the ending of the war. He hitched rides on carts and trains. He walked during the day and some nights, sleeping on roadsides, all the while preoccupied, sometimes hardly noticing his surroundings. And he was not the only one. All of Poland was in a state of upheaval. The thousands of homeless were searching for loved ones and searching for food.

One night Tadeusz took shelter in the woods, together with a small group consisting mostly of old men and children. That night, when it was very late and too dark to see what was happening, Tadeusz woke up to the cruel blows of somebody kicking his side. Instinctively he backed up meekly, thinking he was still in Kazakhstan. Even as he tried to protect his head, Tadeusz struggled to wake up. He heard the words being yelled at him in Polish, "Give me your money, give me what you have!"

Hands in the dark ran over his twitching body, into the breast pocket of his jacket, then down into his trousers. He moaned once and only then realized that he was free, free to fight back. In the name of all those times when he had been forced to submit, Tadeusz now threw all his strength into tackling the foot he knew must be somewhere to his left. A large body thudded against the ground as he brought the man down. Behind him Tadeusz heard a child whimpering in the dark bushes.

"I have nothing," he gasped. "Why can't you leave us alone?"

The hands struck him once in the mouth, a man's voice swore, and then Tadeusz was alone. The night became even darker. When Tadeusz woke up again, it was daylight and he was alone in the clearing. The children and their grandparents, or whoever they had been, had all vanished.

Tadeusz sat up and rubbed his sore jaw. Despite his aching muscles, he felt a rush of pleasure at the thought that there had been nothing for the thief to take. And he had realized in time that he was still the old Tadeusz, ready to take on a fight.

But even this incident did not startle Tadeusz out of the calm his focused thoughts had produced in him. He had chosen to turn his fear and uncertainty into a sureness that he could hold on to. When he finally topped the hills surrounding Kraków and looked down on the city cloaked in early morning haze, this same calm rose up in him and finally bore fruit.

He thought, *Surely God is able to bring this one miracle, His miracle, out of the chaos I have just passed through. Surely the Lord is able to bring this good out of Johann's death. I am not afraid. I will find her, somehow.*

So it was that caked in mud, bitten by fleas and lice and the summer's swarms of mosquitoes, his face covered in dirty, matted hair, his eyes a clearer blue than ever, Tadeusz began his search for Hanna.

The first thing Tadeusz noticed as he worked his way down into the valley and entered the city was that the church towers were still standing. Then he spotted other surviving landmarks that raised his hopes. And yet, despite the lack of physical destruction, despite the absence of the Germans, it was still obvious that Kraków did not yet belong to the Poles.

The dullness inflicted on him by the long journey fell away as Tadeusz began to focus on what had happened to the city. He felt the old clearness of thought, the awareness of small details, the watchfulness for unspoken messages he had first trained himself to tune into back when he had plotted the ruin of Johann, back before so much had changed.

Tadeusz shrugged off his hunger and fatigue. He needed to know what was going on now that he no longer was merely one of the mass moving through the country, now that he had finally arrived somewhere. Now that he had something to do, someone to find.

Tadeusz went straight to the Müller home, only to be met by a drunken soldier stumbling out of the gate. The signals he had been picking up from snatches of conversation he had heard elsewhere now made sense. As he had always feared, his people had just traded one occupation for another. Looking up at the Müller home, hearing the same foreign sounds coming out of the open window that he had heard so often in Kazakhstan, he realized his dream of finding Hanna here would not come true. As he looked up at the top of the wall separating the garden from the street, this realization caused Tadeusz to doubt for the first time since Johann's death.

Since it was obvious the house had been taken over by Russians, Tadeusz waited until another soldier left the house and turned down the road in his direction. Then Tadeusz stepped in front of him and pointed at the house. "The owners, have you seen the owners?" He purposely spoke in Polish.

Tadeusz did not know what he had expected for an answer, but it certainly was not the snort of laughter the short, ugly man breathed on him as he brushed past. An old anger rose up in him, demanding equal attention with the question now pounding through his mind.

How could he possibly find Hanna now? She might

even still be in Germany. She might have been in Dresden . . .

As the calm fled, Tadeusz walked back and forth, gazing up at the window from which he used to watch Hanna in the garden. The uncertainty he had kept at bay now threatened him from all sides. He stayed like that for hours, a caged panther pacing. Eventually Tadeusz's tired imagination took over and he revisited old horrors, old fears, old dreads.

Finally he heard a voice, strangely his own, reminding him of who he was. "Tadeusz, Tadeusz?" What was it he had wanted to ask himself?

Tadeusz started walking, his head turned upward, staring at the windows above him. He could not remember the last time he had eaten, and sleep felt like an old friend long ago left behind. He would not stop to rest, though, even as the streets he passed through became less familiar.

His young head rolled back, Tadeusz continued to gaze at windows. In the old buildings of the city's center, medieval gargoyles threatened to spit down upon him. These were not what he saw, however. Instead, Tadeusz saw faces, mostly frightened and old and female, watching him watch them. He would do this until the faces he saw became the very one he so cherished. He didn't know what else he could do.

Window after window, street after street he searched for her, driven by the innate knowledge she was near, was safe. The urge had no words as his prayers became more an ache. As he kept searching for her face in the windows staring past him, Tadeusz had no idea whatsoever where he wandered.

It was late in the evening, almost dark, when he found himself climbing a hill, then staring at a door with red paint peeling off the sides. He came to himself as he raised his hand to push the door, heard the scuttle of a nearby rat, and felt the heavy summer air weighing down upon him. There was no breeze. The door moved inward, and part of him did not recognize anything, even as he climbed the stairs two at a time. Then he stopped in front of yet another door, a place he had never visited before.

---

Hanna knew her baby would be born any day. Almost two weeks earlier the baby had already dropped. Lately she was heavy and hot and always hungry.

These things Hanna knew because Mrs. Fisiak told them to her. If it were not for Mrs. Fisiak's friendly comments about her health, the temperature, the baby's position, the discomfort of pregnancies in summer, Hanna would not have been any more aware of her state than she was of the changes going on in Europe at that time.

In the weeks since Mrs. Fisiak had taken Hanna into her care, Hanna had sunk only deeper into depression. In the end, the trip north from Kuron had demanded too high a price, even more so emotionally than physically. Hanna had surrendered almost gladly to the numbness brought on by her despair. She had slept. For days and nights and more days she had done almost nothing else.

Mrs. Fisiak had tried to snap her out of it with talk, but although Hanna was never impolite, she simply paid no attention. She woke up when Mrs. Fisiak arrived home from work in the mornings, and then Mrs. Fisiak would tell her something about the outside world. This is how Hanna came to hear, for example, that the loudspeakers the Russians had strung up around the city to broadcast their version of the news were more annoying than the mosquitoes that summer. She herself had never even noticed them.

Hanna had also learned from Mrs. Fisiak that during the last weeks more people had been returning to Kraków. They came from Russian camps and German camps and places in the south and east and west. She did not even know where Tadeusz might be returning from. The fact that her home was now occupied by Soviet soldiers did not necessarily mean that he and her father had been arrested, or did it?

The scenarios of worry haunted Hanna day after day as she lay sweating in her bed. After that first visit back home she could not bring herself to return again, let alone leave Mrs. Fisiak's rented room. The darkness that had descended on her when she surrendered to it had robbed her of any will to act.

At some point, when she became rested, the really difficult days had begun. Her mind wandered for hours, playing tricks on her. Her mother was dead, Tadeusz was gone forever.

Slowly Hanna returned to the idea that had first occurred to her under the bridge before Mrs. Fisiak had found her. If only God would take her and the baby, sparing them from a life without Tadeusz, in a world as terrible as this one. Gradually she came to realize that, more than anything else, she did not want to live.

At first the thought had startled her, shocked her even, but she quickly fell into the habit of returning to it like a safe haven from even more destructive thoughts. Hanna fell asleep and woke to the idea of dying. It was, in a warped way, what got her through the days. Under the spell of such a thought, she did not have to face the future. She did not even have to accept the present. Mrs. Fisiak's small efforts to save her, to comfort her, to include her in the world meant nothing when viewed through the terminal perspective Hanna had now chosen. What was there to fight for, she reasoned. What kind of world was this to bring a child into?

The selfishness of such a surrender did not occur to Hanna. After all, she had come so very far, but there was no one to share it with. She prayed constantly and often knew for certain that she was not alone in the stuffy room. But this did nothing to reduce the power of the thought holding sway over her. She wanted to die, and she was almost at the point where she no longer felt guilty about it.

Hanna now accepted the fact she would never see Tadeusz. That she would have to live without him and raise their baby alone, she would not accept.

On a day like so many of the others during the last four weeks, Hanna stood staring at the peeling paint on the ceiling, her hands reaching behind her to support her lower back. She could feel the baby's weight strain against her lower muscles. She walked back and forth across the room, unable to think of leaving, unable to think of anywhere to go. Over and over again she returned to the only window, cupping her stomach in one hand while she stared at the building across the street.

Hunger pains pounded in her head. Mrs. Fisiak had brought her the milk faithfully every day, and Hanna knew it was much more than the woman herself was eating. Somewhere inside she also knew that Mrs. Fisiak was doing something far braver than Hanna. She, at least, was working, trying to put sense into her world. And Hanna knew there were others so much worse off than she. How had it happened that she had the luxury to choose? No matter. She had chosen.

Hanna crossed the small room to where she knew Mrs. Fisiak kept a knife. She took it out of the box and ran her finger along its blade. Then Hanna returned to her mattress. For a very long time she lay on the bed, her old friend, stroking the knife, a new friend. She lay on her back, holding it above her, turning it to catch the light. She was not really thinking about anything in particular. Finally her arms dropped and she closed her eyes. As she fell asleep, Hanna's hand uncurled with the knife resting on her palm.

As Hanna slept, she became more troubled. She saw soldiers tearing a baby from her arms. She cried out loud, her own voice waking her so that she sat straight up on the mattress, her heart pounding. Then she heard the sound again, a knocking at the door. Hanna looked around desperately, already knowing there was no escape. The sweat ran down her back despite the cooler evening air.

Hanna's hand fell on the knife by her pillow. She grabbed it as she struggled to stand, easing her weight backward onto her other hand stretched behind her on the bed. Once she was standing she crossed the floor.

At the door she waited, but she heard nothing more. The knocking had stopped. Very slowly she lifted the latch, then waited a few moments before opening it. When she finally swung it open, she saw no one. Hanna held the knife behind her back and poked her head out the doorway. She looked up the hall to the right, then swiveled her head to the left and stopped breathing.

In a heap on the ground at her feet, his back to the wall and his eyes closed, head back, lay her husband.

Hanna cried out, "No, no, no!" dropped the knife and crumpled to the ground beside him. Both hands flew over his face, the beard, across his eyes. "How did you get here? Who brought you?"

Not even thinking about her newfound strength, or what it might mean that he was actually light enough for her to drag, Hanna pulled Tadeusz inside. Every action was a separate event.

Once she had closed the door, Hanna knelt down beside Tadeusz and ran her hands up and down the length of his body. When she could find no bone breaks or wounds or bleeding, she took his head in her lap and stroked his face, her tears leaving small trails in the grime around his eyes. She listened to his hoarse breathing and timed her own to match it.

Only then did it strike Hanna just how old and gaunt Tadeusz looked. Beneath the dirt around his eyes and mouth were many lines, wrinkles she was sure had not been there before. As Hanna stretched a finger out to trace them, Tadeusz opened his eyes.

Hanna's heart leapt at the sight of their color, as if someone had just opened the window and shown her a mountain meadow instead of the dull, gray city. She stared at him through the tears, absolutely unable to believe he was back in her arms, surely the only place he had ever belonged.

Tadeusz reached up and touched Hanna's cheek, his disbelief trembling in his fingertips as he saw her now for the first time. The last thing he remembered was the darkness rising up to meet him after he had climbed the stairs. And knocking.

Now together, they bent toward each other, crying and laughing, the reunion complete. "Hania. My Hania." Tadeusz whispered her Polish nickname, almost afraid it might send her back to the place where he could not find her.

Neither of them knew how their reunion had come about. Tadeusz told Hanna what little he could remember about his search since he had arrived in Kraków.

"Oh, Tadeusz, an angel of the Lord took you by the hand. Tell me more, tell me where you came from. Have you been hiding in the city all along?"

"All along?" As he echoed her words, Tadeusz was struck again by the enormity of what had just occurred. "No, my love, I haven't been in Kraków all these months." He hardly knew where to begin. "Tell me first about your mother," he asked instead.

She turned away from him, amazed at the potency of the pain his words brought on. Hanna could not bring herself to answer the question directly. Instead she told him about her journey. It took several hours to work backward in her story until she reached her mother's death. This she finally told brokenly, between sobs.

The two were silent for a very long time. Tadeusz held Hanna, rocking her back and forth as they huddled on the floor. Hanna wanted to hear Tadeusz's story, wanted to know about her father, but now she did not dare to ask. He read her thoughts, though. "There is more. Helena will not be alone."

For the first time since she had found Tadeusz outside the door, Hanna's hands left him, flying to her mouth instead. "Not Father! Oh, not them both!" Hanna began to cry again. The tears leapt out of her eyes.

Tadeusz pulled her back to him, taking in her smell, feeling the sobs shake her over and over again. Without any expression in his voice he told her about the camp, and about her father's bravery, and about that last day. He knew they both were exhausted, but he had to cleanse himself of the knowledge of Johann's death, and Hanna's eyes told him she could not rest until she heard the truth. There had already been too much uncertainty, too much waiting.

When Tadeusz finally stopped talking it was almost dawn. Hanna lay still in his arms, but her eyes remained open. He kissed them both, closing her lids, and whispered their wedding verse from Isaiah. Then he added, "So despite the waves of fear and fires of grief, the Lord has rescued us from it all." Then he closed his own eyes and they fell asleep like that, with Hanna's tears still wet on both their cheeks.

---

They woke up to the sound of Mrs. Fisiak coming home from work. Her voice preceded her as she came through the door, "I found this outside the door, child. Tell me nothing terrible has happened."

When Mrs. Fisiak saw Tadeusz sit up next to Hanna she caught her breath. Then a smile spread over her old and wrinkled face like the sunrise in summer. "Ah, Hanna, I think this time you are the one who has news for me."

She stretched out her right hand toward the man who looked like a beggar from the streets. "So you found her."

Before clasping Tadeusz's hand in her own small one, Mrs. Fisiak carefully set the knife down on the table. The movement was not lost on Tadeusz. He rose to greet her, bringing the dry hand to his lips. He smiled and thanked her for the warm welcome and for her part in looking after Hanna, but his eyes remained on the knife.

Hanna watched him carefully. She hoped Mrs. Fisiak would think she had carried it to the door to defend herself against whoever had knocked, then dropped it in surprise.

At that very instant Tadeusz shifted his gaze from the knife to Hanna's eyes, reading there what she had just been thinking. This was the explanation he had most feared, what she could not say. Now they both knew. It was that simple. He knew that the thing on the table would have done what the war and the Germans and the Russians and the disease had not done. He stared at Hanna, a treasure made even more precious by its pending loss. Ashamed, Hanna began to cry.

All of this was lost on Mrs. Fisiak, who was still going on about how they could possibly have found each other. When she saw Hanna's tears she stopped and shook her head. "The child is so tired. And of course, there is so much to say. If we are going to have a party, then I should go see what I can find for us at the market." Mrs. Fisiak slipped out the door, a smile resting on her lips.

When they were alone Tadeusz crossed to the table without a word. He picked up the knife and did the same thing as Hanna had done. He ran the blade along his fingers to test its sharpness. Satisfied, he crossed the room and put it out of sight. When he turned back to Hanna, she would not look at him.

"Oh, Tadeusz, I'm so . . ."

But he did not let her continue. "Don't. We both know it was another world yesterday."

He folded her back into his arms and Hanna felt a flood of relief wash over her. Now she really was home. Her fingers felt the muscles in his shoulders and along his back, down his spine. She felt her own tension ease. Yes, another world.

# 17

AUGUST—SEPTEMBER 1945

Hanna's labor began during the day while Mrs. Fisiak was sleeping on a pile of rugs in the corner and Tadeusz was out trying to find them some food. Hanna had been resting on the mattress when she felt the muscles around the baby tighten. She waited. About ten minutes later it happened again.

Hanna knew enough to wait and try to relax. So it was going to happen, after all. She felt relieved that the waiting was finally over, and she clung to the comfort that Tadeusz was back home, safe.

Within an hour the contractions became harsher, and were coming only five minutes apart. Hanna searched her memory for what her mother had told her about childbirth. This seemed to be happening much faster and much more painfully than what seemed right.

Another hour passed, with the contractions still coming every five minutes. Hanna was moaning out loud, trying to keep from waking Mrs. Fisiak. When one particularly sharp muscle spasm hit, however, she cried out involuntarily.

Hanna leaned back panting when she heard Mrs. Fisiak's voice ask, "Why didn't you wake me?"

"You work so hard every night. Besides, I didn't think it would go this fast."

"How fast?" Mrs. Fisiak ran her hand over Hanna's belly.

When Hanna told her, Mrs. Fisiak said nothing. Her fingers probed around the baby. "He was quite active last night?" she asked.

"Yes, how did you know? I hardly slept at all while you were gone."

Mrs. Fisiak frowned. "Now, I may be wrong, but I believe the baby has turned. He's breech now."

Neither woman said a word, and in the silence another contraction hit. Hanna was already at the point where she could only cope with it by arching her back and clenching her teeth. When it passed, she fell back onto the mattress.

"My dear, I will have to get help. You know that, don't you?"

Hanna nodded, sweat running down her neck.

"I know a woman who has helped at many births. She does not live far. I must leave you. I'm so sorry, but please try to be strong."

Hanna saw Mrs. Fisiak letting herself out the door, and the next moment lights danced across her gaze. Slowly, Hanna felt panic seep into her. She was alone. The baby was not in the right position. She was weak with hunger. And the baby wanted to be born now—that much she could feel. She knew that women had died from less.

Hanna wanted to get up off that mattress on the floor, walk out of the small, stuffy room, leave the pain of childbirth behind. She did not want this to happen.

Then Hanna remembered something Tadeusz had whispered to her that very morning when he woke her up, "Soon now you will hold our child in your arms." The thought calmed Hanna enough to keep her from screaming out loud the next time the pain ran across her middle.

This was not the way her mother had said it would be. She had said the pain could be handled. This was out of control, Hanna felt sure of it. Again and again the contractions racked her, until finally Hanna lost what little stability she had managed to summon with the memory of Tadeusz's words. As the intensity of the contractions increased, she began to call out his name, chanting it to calm her, yelling it to keep from blacking out.

"Hanna! Hanna!"

Everything was so blurred that at first Hanna did not trust her own hearing. It seemed that all she had heard during what must have been hours was her own voice and the ringing in her ears. But at some point she knew it must be true. Tadeusz was near and he was calling her name.

"Hanna, Hanna! I'm here, but you must let me in! Mrs. Fisiak, open the door! Hanna, I'm here!"

The effort it took to clear her thoughts and focus on the act of standing left Hanna shattered. Somehow she crossed the tiny room and unlatched the door. Just as Tadeusz crashed into the room, his face wild with worry, another contraction grabbed Hanna. It proved too much; she pitched forward in a faint.

"Dear God," Tadeusz said in a hoarse whisper as he caught her.

She regained consciousness minutes later when yet another contraction came on. They were sweeping over her like tidal waves, each one leaving her wracked and trembling. In between she managed to gasp to Tadeusz the news of where Mrs. Fisiak had gone, and why. His face grew whiter as she spoke.

"I don't know what to do," Tadeusz said more to himself than to Hanna. Their eyes locked, and Hanna stretched out a hand toward him.

"Be with me," she gasped. "That's enough."

Tadeusz had the horrible premonition that the next hours could be the worst in his life. *Lord God, I cannot believe You would work the miracle of bringing us back together just to take Hanna from me when this baby is born. Oh, God, let her live.* It was an all too familiar prayer, prayed now in utterly different circumstances.

Besides praying, Tadeusz had no idea what to do, but he let himself be led by Hanna's need. He sat behind her and held Hanna around the waist so that when the contractions came she could push against him. Over and over and over again her body went rigid with pain. The contractions were coming more often, and their intensity had only worsened. Tadeusz prayed some more.

After a very long time Tadeusz heard Mrs. Fisiak enter the room. He waited and counted to three, wiping the sweat from Hanna's forehead. Then he looked up again and saw a second woman pass through the doorway.

"I've brought a midwife," Mrs. Fisiak told him. Her glance took in the sight of Hanna lying limp in Tadeusz's arms, her eyes closed, panting as she waited for another wave of pain to pass through her.

Tadeusz looked at the midwife desperately. "Surely it's not supposed to be like this?"

The woman did not answer. Short and squat, with black hair and a pug nose, she could have been anywhere between fifty and sixty years of age. She did not even bother to glance up at Tadeusz, but instead spread Hanna's legs to examine her.

"Of course this is worse than normal; your baby is trying to come out backward. I have nothing here to help him except my hands, and it is going to hurt worse than what your wife has already been going through."

Tadeusz shook his head. There was no worse. Hanna's face had not changed to show whether she had heard the midwife's words or not.

"It looks like the baby has been ready to come out for some time." The woman withdrew her hand, and Tadeusz saw it was covered in blood. He gasped and swallowed. If Hanna's body had not been pinning him down, he would have leapt up and ran out of the room. Again a contraction shuddered through Hanna.

"I have nothing to soak up the blood." Mrs. Fisiak's voice shook.

"It doesn't matter. All I need is one knife in boiling water and one clean cloth for the baby. The rest we'll take care of later." She lifted up Hanna's skirt, and Tadeusz could see for the first time since he had gone to the head of the bed to hold Hanna just how much blood had been lost.

The midwife dipped her hands into the steaming pot of water Mrs. Fisiak had started warming for her as soon as she came home. Tadeusz began to pray a chant to himself: *Let her live, God, let her live.*

The midwife's hands disappeared. She looked up at Tadeusz and said, "Hold her; I'll try to turn the baby . . . no, I can't. Oh, God in heaven! All right, girl, push, push now!"

For the first time in that hour Hanna's eyes flew open. She looked wildly from side to side.

"Up here." Tadeusz knew the fear he felt was nothing compared with what he saw on Hanna's face. He steadied his voice. "Up here, Hanna."

She searched for him, had been searching for so long already. Then it happened in the space of time it took for Hanna to look up, find and focus on Tadeusz's eyes. She started to push. She threw her entire life force into pushing.

She wasted no effort in yelling, but grunted low and reached deep within herself.

She heard the midwife from far away, from the place she had brought herself to find that strength. "I have him!" She felt Tadeusz's arms around her, those arms, home again.

"She's fainted," Tadeusz said.

"And with good reason," the midwife answered. She handed the tiny, red-faced baby to Mrs. Fisiak and fished the knife out of the clean water at her side. Then she tied off the umbilical cord and with one quick stroke cut through it. The next second Tadeusz heard his son's first cry.

This caused him to suddenly look up from Hanna. "You said 'him.' It's a boy?"

Both older women beamed over the baby at Tadeusz. "It certainly is, and he looks healthy in every way, although he is small." The midwife was wrapping the baby in the one clean cloth Mrs. Fisiak had managed to find for her. Then she handed him over to Tadeusz.

Instinctively but awkwardly, and with Hanna's head still in his lap, Tadeusz took the baby into his arms. As he held the child over her Tadeusz said, "So. You're not a girl after all. But I know what we will call you. Jasiu, for my father. Your mother insisted, she was not so convinced as I was that you would be a girl. Ah, our son . . ." Tadeusz sat still, his head bowed, as the two women busied themselves with Hanna.

She did not stir as over and over again they rinsed out the scraps of old clothes Mrs. Fisiak had once again managed to find somewhere. The bleeding would not stop. Tadeusz refused to move. He cradled the baby with one arm and stroked his wife's face with the other.

Finally the midwife said, "There is nothing more I can do. She is soaked clear through with her own blood. It must stop from inside. Let her sleep and feed her. It will not be easy . . ." She looked down doubtfully on the little family on the mattress.

"I—" Tadeusz nodded. "We can never repay you. I don't know what would have happened if you hadn't been here to help."

"The worst may not be over. Take good care of her. Your little Jasiu is a fighter, but she fought even harder." With a shake of her head the midwife left the room.

After seeing her to the door, Mrs. Fisiak returned and sat down on the room's only chair. "Ah, I must go to work again, and I should go now, before the curfew starts." She sighed.

Tadeusz looked out the single window and could not believe that dusk had fallen. Surely it must be another day, or at least the middle of the night. Mrs. Fisiak looked as exhausted as he felt. She had, after all, worked a full shift at the factory, only to come home to this. Tadeusz was only too aware that her income and her kindness was what had kept them going since his arrival in Kraków. Without Mrs. Fisiak, his son might have been born in a gutter somewhere.

"I can't believe what has just happened," Tadeusz mumbled. "You must be so tired."

"I'll be all right."

They both looked down at Hanna, wondering if the same could be said for her.

---

That night Tadeusz learned to know his son's face as well as he did Hanna's. Once Mrs. Fisiak left, he placed

Jasiu at Hanna's side, even then wondering why the baby did not wake up hungry. This concern was soon overshadowed by the realization that Hanna had still not stopped bleeding.

Tadeusz knew what the loss of so much blood, combined with Hanna's already weakened state, could mean. He wanted to go out and find them all some food, but he dared not leave her. Not again. So he spent the long night rinsing the blood out of the cloths and holding Hanna's hands and staring out the single window, praying with every fiber of his body.

Finally when he looked out the window he saw light filling the gaps between the high clouds. As the first streaks of light from a red sun marked the beginning of yet another hot August day, he realized that Hanna had stopped bleeding. Tadeusz felt too tired to be relieved. Besides, she had already lost so much. Was it too late?

He had cleaned her one last time and sat back to watch the patterns trace the sky when he heard a sound he did not know. He glanced down and saw little Jasiu wide awake next to his mother, sucking one very tiny fist. His son's eyes were a deep, mysterious blue; the wispy hair on the little head was black. "Jasiu." He said the name and the boy made more sucking sounds.

And then for the thousandth time that night he glanced at Hanna and saw, to his surprise, that her eyes were also open. "Ah, my Hania, I knew it, I knew you would be here in the morning." For the first time since their reunion, Tadeusz burst into tears and fell softly at Hanna's side, gingerly reaching out to pull her close. Now it was her turn to stroke his face.

This was how Mrs. Fisiak found them when she returned a little later carrying her usual goat's milk and another bag of dried beans. Tadeusz was sleeping beside Hanna as she was trying to feed the baby.

Mrs. Fisiak stopped short at the sight and smiled, despite her shock at the contrast of Hanna's bright red lips against the pale, pale skin, as if the blood she had lost would mark her permanently. "You are feeling better?"

"The milk Jasiu is trying to find will be thanks to you," Hanna said.

Mrs. Fisiak was so surprised that Hanna could even sit up. All she said was, "Yes, yes." Then she sighed happily. "Your milk will come in any day now. I will show you what to do." Then she hurried over to put the beans into a pot of water to soak.

When Tadeusz woke up and stretched, he insisted on helping Mrs. Fisiak clean up the room and prepare a meal. Later, as they ate, he thanked Mrs. Fisiak once again for taking care of them.

"But it won't be long, I hope," he added. "Now that the baby's here, we need to live in our own home."

"Surely there is no hurry," Mrs. Fisiak said. "Your baby is barely one day old. And Hanna cannot be moved," she added in a lowered voice.

"I know that." They both glanced over at Hanna. She sat on the mattress, slowly feeding the beans into her mouth and gazing at the baby on her lap. "But she will be better soon," he added. "And remember, we already have a home in Kraków. I just need to make arrangements to get it back."

Now Hanna shot him a glance as Mrs. Fisiak insisted, "This can be your home for as long as you need it. You are welcome to stay here. And I am working."

These last words only aggravated Tadeusz's resolve. "We do have a home," he insisted.

"But is what you are planning safe?" the older woman asked.

Hanna answered from the other side of the room. "No it's not safe. Tadeusz Piekarz. You should not even try to get back Father's house. It's too great a risk. We've both seen the soldiers living there. Please, Tadeusz, listen to Mrs. Fisiak. You know we have to let the house go."

Tadeusz looked at Hanna grimly. "I can't let it go." He crossed to her, already knowing he could not explain the decision he had made during the night. In those long hours after Jasiu's birth, he had promised himself that if Hanna recovered, he would do everything in his power to care for her and Jasiu. That meant providing a home and the security she had missed all that year. He would do it no matter what, and not on the back of an old woman.

He knelt beside Hanna and murmured, "Don't you understand? That house is your father's, and now it belongs to you, not the people who murdered him."

Jasiu stirred and started to cry. Hanna reached down to bring him to her breast, but even that small effort caused her to flinch. "No, please, Tadeusz, don't do it. Let it go. I couldn't bear it if . . ." She shot a glance upward to find Mrs. Fisiak, but she had slipped out of the room without either of them noticing.

"I won't let it go." The tone in Tadeusz's voice was final. "The Russians have had me in too many corners this year that I couldn't fight my way out of. This time I'm going to follow what little recourse I can find. I won't let the house go. Your parents would want Jasiu to grow up there."

This last stopped Hanna, but then she said, "And what if they send you away again?" Now she could barely make the words heard above Jasiu's screams. He kept turning his head from side to side, refusing to calm down.

Tadeusz said, "It won't happen again." Then he turned and headed for the door.

"Tadeusz, please! Not today. I don't want the house!" But the door was already shut before Hanna had finished speaking. Once he was gone, she could do nothing but try to comfort Jasiu.

Mrs. Fisiak returned a few moments later. Tadeusz's absence and one look at Hanna's wet cheeks told her everything she needed to know. She offered to take the baby from Hanna. "Let me try and calm him while you do the same for yourself. Ach, Hanna. How did this happen?"

"Our first fight, our very first fight, and it was all so . . ."

"He's very tired, and so are you. He needed to get some fresh air, that is all. This room is too small for a big man like that. Here, look, Jasiu is quiet again. You take him, and I will check you." Mrs. Fisiak had already noticed the rinsed out rags drying around the room. "Has your bleeding stopped, then?"

When Hanna nodded, so did Mrs. Fisiak. "All right, let's all go to sleep, shall we?" She made sure Jasiu and Hanna were settled, then curled up on the pile of rugs in the opposite corner.

In the weeks to come Tadeusz made the rounds of the various communist-controlled offices of housing, asking questions and filling out forms. Hanna did not tell him again to leave well enough alone; she had no choice but to accept that he would not let the matter rest. He insisted on leaving the apartment every day to pursue the next level in the bureaucratic web the Russians had even then begun to spin as a form of daily harassment in the lives of the Polish people.

Hanna prayed for his protection every time Tadeusz left the room. Then she concentrated on regaining her strength. Two weeks after the birth she was walking again, and in another week she could even descend the stairs. Meanwhile, Jasiu ate and slept, and Mrs. Fisiak continued working nights at the factory, always careful to come and go before and after the curfew restrictions.

The day finally came, though, when Tadeusz returned to the room with a piece of paper clutched in his fist. It was late in the afternoon and Hanna was alone, feeding the baby. "Tell me what it says." She nodded toward the paper.

"It just confirms our worst fears. The State has now officially confiscated the house as property belonging to a former Nazi corroborator." He spat out the last words.

Hanna couldn't even connect the words with her father. She just hoped that now, finally, her husband would accept that the Russians could not be thrown out of the old Müller house. "Then there's no question anymore?" she asked.

Tadeusz shook his head.

At that moment Mrs. Fisiak entered the room, carefully carrying a package before her as if it contained precious jewels. Before she could tell them what it was, though, she stopped, sensing the tension in the room. She glanced at Hanna, who told her about the news.

Tadeusz paced the floor of the small room. Utterly frustrated, he said, "I must find somewhere for us to live."

Then he heard Mrs. Fisiak greet his news with the words, "Ah yes, ah yes," which surprised him. He had expected her to respond with the usual, "Of course you are welcome to stay here as long as you want."

When he looked at her curiously, she set her package down and said instead, "That may be sooner than you think."

Tadeusz and Hanna looked up, surprised. When Tadeusz stared at her, Mrs. Fisiak continued, "I ran into a friend of a niece of mine at the market. And she gave me a message someone had given her from my niece, asking if she could come back to Kraków. I would like her to live here . . ."

"Of course," Tadeusz cut in. "We understand. You have done so very much for all three of us." He nodded at the now-sleeping form of Jasiu in Hanna's arms. "We will be gone before tomorrow morning." He could not keep the bitterness of the day's events from his voice.

Mrs. Fisiak stretched out her hand to stop Tadeusz. "No, that is not what I meant. When I worked for Pani Müller, she was always very kind to me, even helping my family when I asked her. Later, after I no longer worked for her, Hanna's father actually saved the life of one of my nephews when he was arrested and got him out of the country. You did not know that. So you see, I could not do too much for her grandson. Listen now, my niece has an apartment in Gdańsk, but she does not want to stay there since her parents were killed and, well, that is also a long story . . ."

As Mrs. Fisiak paused, Tadeusz eased himself down next to Hanna and laid his hand over hers. She was silent, expectant.

"So, would you want to take the apartment in Gdańsk and protect it from looters? I think it would be large enough."

Both Hanna and Tadeusz gasped. This was far beyond what they had expected just a few moments earlier. "Are you sure?" Tadeusz sputtered.

"Of course," Mrs. Fisiak said.

"Do you want to go to Danzig?" Tadeusz joked, using the German name for the city. Hanna knew what he really meant: would she mind living in a city shared with Germans.

"I've never felt less German . . ." As Hanna hesitated, Mrs. Fisiak spoke up again.

"No, no, not Danzig. Tadeusz, haven't you told her the news yet? Listen, you can hear them talking about it outside." Mrs. Fisiak heaved open the window as the sound of a crackling monotone of the loudspeaker below rose up to meet them.

Hanna had long since stopped listening to the endless drone of propaganda that poured out of the loudspeakers day after day. Now, however, she leaned out of the window to hear better.

> "The People's Republic of Poland has been gloriously liberated. The treaty signed on April 22 with the Union of Soviet Socialist Republics was only the first step on the path of harmonious cooperation between these two great allies. The formation of the Provisional Government of National Unity at the end of June further enhanced a liberation which has now been completely achieved in this historic month of September 1945. The People's Republic of Poland has been awarded the western lands which were rightfully hers. Śląsk and Gdańsk have been taken away from the enemy and placed inside Polish borders. The deserving liberators have been rewarded with the annexation of the Ukraine and other eastern lands . . ."

Tadeusz looked at his wife. "So they have all of Poland now."

Hanna had an image of new darkness descending, but then she shook her head hard.

"No, Tadeusz. Think instead of what Mrs. Fisiak is offering us here." She squeezed his hand as hard as she could.

He raised his gaze from the street to meet hers. "A new beginning in a new part of Poland." This appealed to him as much as the idea of providing a safe haven for his young family. He looked down at the paper in his other hand. It might have shut one door, but perhaps it signaled the opening of another.

"A new beginning," he repeated, turning the idea over and over in his head as he gazed at his wife and baby son. Already, for the first time in so many months, he was thinking of possibilities.

---

Once again they stood on the platform of the Kraków train station. Mrs. Fisiak held little Jasiu while Tadeusz hugged a bundle containing Jasiu's few cloth diapers and some pieces of clothing Hanna had managed to gather together.

Hanna gave Mrs. Fisiak a hug and took the baby from her. "I will never forget how you saved my life. Both our lives." She looked down at Jasiu's small face.

"Thank you," Tadeusz added. "Again. "

Mrs. Fisiak nodded solemnly. "Be sure to rest often and ride inside the trains all the way." Everyone laughed. "You have the address and my letter? If all goes well, my niece should still be there waiting for my answer. And that will be you."

"As you were ours," Hanna said softly. *"Do widzenia."*

And then the train was pulling into the station, and Hanna and Tadeusz were walking toward it, not looking back. Both of them realized this trek north would be different from their other journeys that year more than in the fact of their togetherness. Just when it seemed everything had been lost, so much was returned to them. Now they were taking their first step in a new life together. They had finally found hope.

Just before they boarded the train, Tadeusz took his wife's face in his hands. Hanna said nothing, but just reached out an arm and pulled him close to her. She hugged her husband and her boy, praying for the three of them, praying for their future, when suddenly she remembered another man. He had watched her do this same thing in the same place less than a year ago, saving her life on the night Dresden was bombed.

Hanna looked around her at the station, almost seeing him standing there such a short eternity ago. Then she turned to step up into the car, not even noticing that she could weep no more.

# Epilogue

SEPTEMBER 1945

Jacek stands by the little gas burner, hardly noticing the trucks with loudspeakers outside in the streets of Warszawa, broadcasting the message that the Soviet occupation was now official. This is no news to him. It took him months of careful maneuvering to achieve a toehold in the new Soviet-run Polish government. Today he will officially start his work as an aide to Marshal Rokossovski. Surely it's a fitting day to be making a break with the past.

Methodically he feeds his papers into the flames without even looking at them. When he comes to the last two pages, however, he stops and reads over the terse statement one more time, ". . . killed in an automobile accident, no need for your presence at the funeral."

"No need," he repeats softly to himself. "No need. When was I ever a husband to Barbara, anyway? When was I a father to Amy? She never even saw me."

Deliberately he holds the paper to the flame, watching as the corner catches and the flames creep down to eat the words. The edges curl as he drops it onto the burner, the last evidence of his ties with another time and place.

Jacek knows now he will never leave Poland. He has become much too valuable. Too many decisions half a world away depend on information he can manage to glean as he moves his way up in the government.

"And I will move up," he mutters. "Up is the only way I can go."

The paper has finished burning now. Jacek checks to be sure the fire is out, carefully sweeps the ashes into a wastebasket, then picks up his new set of papers from the table nearby and hurries out the door.

———— ✣ ————

The men who have aimed Jacek at his target could not have been more pleased at his progress. He used blackmail and cunning which the Russians had recognized as their own tools of control, both earning their respect and ultimately achieving this new appointment.

Now that his wife is dead, they have a good excuse to break off the last ties Jacek has with his old home. After all, he has not been back for seven years. And there is no need for him to know about the girl.

———— ✣ ————

The truck with the loudspeakers is just passing by as Jacek emerges on the street, boldly proclaiming the news that at long last, Poland has been completely liberated.

# Bibliography

Baranczak, Stanislaw. *Breathing Under Water and Other European Essays.* Cambridge: Harvard University Press, 1990.

Cieślak, Edmund and Czeław Biernat. *History of Gdańsk.* Gdańsk: Wydawnictwo Morskie Gdańsk, 1988.

Czapski, Józef. *Na nieludzkiej ziemi* (On atrocious ground). Excerpted in Klukowski, Bogdan. *My deportowani: Wspomnienia Polaków z więzień, tagrów i zsytek w ZSRR* (We the deported: recollections by Poles from prisons, camps, and other forms of exile within the USSR). Warsaw: Wydawnictwa 'Alfa,' 1989.

Davies, Norman. *God's Playground: A History of Poland.* Vol. 2, *1795 to the Present.* Oxford: Clarendon Press, 1986.

Dybowski, Janusz. *Gdańsk since 1920: Archival and Contemporary Films.* Sopot: Unitronic, 1992.

Dziewanowski, M. K. *Poland in the Twentieth Century.* New York: Columbia University Press, 1977.

Grass, Günter. *The Tin Drum.* New York: Vintage Books, 1964.

Konecki, Tadeusz and Ireneusz Ruszkiewicz, *Marszałek dwóch narodów* (The marshal of two nations). Warsaw: Wydawnictwo Ministerstwa Obrony Narodowej, 1976.

Miłosz, Czeslaw. *The Captive Mind.* New York: Vintage International, 1981.

———. *Postwar Polish Poetry*. Berkeley: University of California Press, 1983.

———. *The Seizure of Power*. London: Faber and Faber, 1982.

Ostrowski, Jan K. *Cracow*. Warsaw: International Cultural Centre, 1992.

Ranelagh, John, *CIA—A History*. London: BBC Books, 1992.

Roczmierowski, Antoni. *Krzyżackie widmo* (Teutonic specter). Kraków: Wydawnictwo Literackie, 1974.

Wroński, Tadeusz. *Kronika okupowanego Krakowa* (Chronicle of occupied Kraków). Kraków: Wydawnictwo Literackie, 1973.

Zwarra, Brunon. *Wspomnienia gdańskiego bówki* (Recollections of a Gdańsk "bówka"). Gdańsk: Wydawnictwo Morskie, 1984–86.